PIRATES

OF THE

NARROW SEAS 2

Men of Honor

SECOND EDITION

M. KEI

KEIBOOKS
PERRYVILLE, MARYLAND, USA
2011

KEIBOOKS
P O Box 516
Perryville, MD, USA
Email: Keibooks@gmail.com

PIRATES OF THE NARROW SEAS

BOOK ONE : THE SALLEE ROVERS
BOOK TWO : MEN OF HONOR
BOOK THREE : IRON MEN
BOOK FOUR : HEART OF OAK

The ebook versions of the series are published by Bristlecone Pine Press, Portland, Maine

POETRY BY M. KEI

Slow Motion : The Log of a Chesapeake Bay Skipjack (2nd edition)

Heron Sea : Short Poems of the Chesapeake Bay

Take Five : Best Contemporary Tanka, Volume Three (editor)

Take Five : Best Contemporary Tanka, Volume Two (editor)

Take Five : Best Contemporary Tanka (editor)

Fire Pearls : Short Masterpieces of the Human Heart (editor)

Atlas Poetica : A Journal of Poetry of Place in Modern English Tanka

TABLE OF CONTENTS

Chapter 1 : Hookah Dreams

Captain Peter Thorton, or more correctly since his confirmation in the Muslim religion the day before, Peter Rais Thorton, Sallee rover and newly sworn citizen of the Sallee Republic, woke with pain in a very sensitive portion of his anatomy. He lay blinking and disoriented. Something was wrong, very wrong. His head was muddled and his mouth was dry. The ship wasn't moving. There was no gentle rise and fall as it bobbed at anchor, no sound of water slapping against the rudder. The tapestries were not drawn round his cot. A tall rectangle of pale dimness told him it was dawn, but it wasn't his window. Or his bed. Or . . .

He bolted upright as he discovered someone lying in bed with him. The movement jostled the aching portion of his anatomy and made it throb. He realized he was naked. What had happened?

Checking his lap, he saw the neat white bandage wrapped around the tip of his virile member. Memory came flooding back. At least the portion that had occurred before Captain Tangle had passed around the hookah did. After that he had only a hazy memory of singing, and Shakil attempting to hold him up . . . He eyed the slender form clad in a white nightshirt next to him. Yes, it was Shakil bin Nakih, his commanding officer's brother-in-law. Had they had sex? He couldn't remember. Certainly he could not have performed the manly portion of such an encounter, thanks to his brand new circumcision. He tested his bum cautiously, but it seemed normal. How could he know if he had been sodded when he was so intoxicated with hashish he couldn't even remember how he had wound up in bed with Shakil? Now that he knew what hashish was he would never touch the stuff again.

The cool dawn air chilled him and brought with it the sound of birds (too loud for a man with the start of a drug-induced hangover) and the smell of newly mown hay fields. He lay down and pulled the covers up to his chin and tried to remember.

He and Lt. Maynard had sworn their oaths of citizenship before the vizier of the Sallee Republic. The vizier, a tall thin man with a pointy beard going grey and the broad flat nose of a man with some African ancestry, apparently saw nothing strange about a pair of Englishmen in turbans and purple uniforms. Then again, half the Sallee rovers were renegades—usually from the Mediterranean countries, but Spaniards, Germans, Swedes, French, Irish, Danes, Hungarians, Italians,

Dalmatians, Greeks—even strangers from the Indian Ocean and beyond had taken the turban and turned corsair. It was a lucrative business that attracted adventurers from every horizon of the globe.

Thorton and Maynard had received their passports. Thorton kept his passport and officer's commission close together. They proved he was an officer of a legitimate (albeit very small) navy, should he be captured. If the Spanish were inclined to be merciful, he would not be hanged but merely chained to the oar of a galley to live out the rest of his days. In fact, the *Arrow*, the galiot of which he was now captain, was formerly the Spanish coastguard *Santa Teresa de Ávila*. His commander, Isam Rais al-Tangueli, had captured her after Thorton had rescued him from the *San Bartolomeo*. Well, that was a long story and did not bear repeating. Everyone in Zokhara knew the tale by now.

Thorton had worn his new uniform which consisted of buff pantaloons, a white shirt, white turban, tall black boots, and a long purple coat cut in the Turkish fashion. Gold buttons closed it to the waist and bars of gold lace crossed the chest. His insignia, two crossed scimitars, had been expertly embroidered on the standing collar and patch pockets by Jamila bint Nakih, Shakil's sister. She also happened to be the wife of Isam Rais, whom the English called "Captain Tangle."

Tangle was more or less a commodore in the English way of reckoning. Not to mention, Thorton's former lover. The Englishman blushed red at that. He had gone from celibate and junior (very junior) British lieutenant to celebrated Sallee rover in a matter of weeks. The circumcision, required of all Muslim men, was usually administered when a boy was old enough to understand what it meant to submit to Allah. At twenty-nine Thorton was a little old but his faith was no less sincere. He was a genuine convert. There was no turning back now. His very body was marked with his new religion.

How nervous he had been! Yet he didn't dare say a word. Not when he had seen the scars on Tangle's back from being whipped and abused while chained naked aboard a Spanish galley for two years. Tangle had undergone his own circumcision when he was twelve. The next day he seen his father die with his intestines sprawled across his quarterdeck. Maynard, the other convert, was only fifteen and on crutches because his stump was still too tender to be fitted with a peg. A Spanish cannonball had blown it off during the glorious action in which Tangle had captured three out of four Spanish galleys. To fret about a trivial operation like circumcision in the presence of such men would have branded Thorton a sniveler. He had kept quiet and sweated under his stock and wished it were over.

Maynard went under the knife first. Thorton had stared at the boy's face and seen him blink, but his smile never faltered. The deed was swiftly done. Maynard sat up and did up his pantaloons announcing, "I have decided to take the name in religion of Aruj." If the older men thought there was hubris in naming himself after the founder of Turkish power in North Africa, they didn't show it. Instead they grinned and slapped his back and congratulated him. Aruj Silverarm had lost his arm while fighting the infidels, perhaps they saw a parallel between the young officer who had lost a leg fighting the Spanish. Either way there was no doubting Maynard's courage.

Thorton had gone under the knife next. Never a talkative man, he kept silent through the procedure. He had laid stiffly on the divan but had flinched in spite of himself. He was embarrassed by that but no one said anything. Tangle helped him up and put an arm around his shoulders. When asked what name he would take, he just shook his head and said, "'Peter Thorton' is good enough for me."

After that there had been food and the hookah pipe. Shakil, being a pious man, would not allow wine; the Qu'ran forbade it. He was scrupulous about his faith. The Qu'ran said nothing about the American herb, tobacco, so it went around instead. Tangle, with a mischievous grin had said, "This will enliven the party!" and added something to the mixture. Thorton was not a smoker, but he was polite, so he had inhaled deeply as they watched him. Everyone partook except Shakil and the little boys. Once the corsairs had begun to sing everything grew fuzzy. Smoking had separated his senses from his body so that he no longer felt the pain of having his member scalped, but beyond that he was lost.

Still, one thing was clear: he was in bed with Shakil. It was something he had desired for weeks. His heart thudded in his chest and he rolled over to slip his arm around the other man's waist. He kissed the sleeping man's shoulder blade through the cloth and felt the amorous warmth in his blood even though the affronted organ declined to rise to the occasion. He was still a little intoxicated from the hashish or he never would have been so bold, but even though his mouth was dry as cotton and a headache was starting, he kissed Shakil's shoulder more passionately."

Shakil woke and yawned. He made a little noise, then woke enough to whisper, "Peter?"

"I love you," Thorton replied.

Shakil yawned again. "You're slewed and spoony." They spoke Spanish as their common language.

"No, really. I do. I swear it! I will show you." He kissed his nape and pressed himself against his back.

Shakil squirmed away and swatted him. "Go to sleep, Peter. 'Tis not even dawn and I have to get up at six."

He hadn't actually said 'no,' so Thorton persisted in trying to kiss him.

"Sailors! A randy lot of rogues," Shakil grumbled. "Isam has been teaching you bad habits."

Thorton shook his head. "I'm not like that. I swear it. I love you and only you."

Shakil sighed again. "I like you Peter, but I'm not that easy. Besides, Isam is carrying a torch for you."

Thorton flushed. "That's over. 'Tis been over for more than a month."

"A whole month! Such a long time," Shakil replied with audible sarcasm. "I'll wait. You have to prove you mean it, Peter."

"You brought me to your bed! Don't you want me?"

"You were witless from the hashish. He shouldn't have done that. He knows you aren't used to it. I put you to bed where you'd be safe. He would never pursue you into my room."

Thorton had a new worry. Had he and Tangle done something? He searched his brain frantically to try to remember. The amorous corsair was both charming and persistent. Thorton had all he could do to resist the man when he was sober; intoxicated he would have folded like tissue.

"Did I do something I shouldn't have?" he asked anxiously.

Shakil was silent a long while, then he shook his head and patted Thorton's arm. "No, not yet. It was Isam. He was flirting with you. I removed you before you did something I'd regret."

Thorton wilted completely. "I'm sorry, Shakil. I didn't mean to. I didn't know what I was doing. I hate being drunk and I didn't know it was hashish! I didn't even know what hashish is! I will never ever touch it again! I swear it."

Shakil wrapped an arm consolingly around him. "I know, Peter. I know. I like and admire Isam, but he is a rascal. You have no idea how hard it is to be his accountant. He's a gallant man, but he has a streak of avarice, and on top of that, he's vain and arrogant. He thinks he is entitled to what he wants."

Thorton snorted. "He's arrogant all right. Not even a Spanish galley could knock that out of him."

Shakil was quiet again. Then he said softly, "He is not as formidable as he appears. He would never admit weakness before any man, but Jamila tells me he has nightmares. He wakes up fighting, thinking he is falling into Spanish hands again. Don't tell him you know that. 'Twould wound his pride."

It was Thorton's turn to be silent. Finally he said, "I know that side of him, too. When we were first in the *San Bartolomeo* he asked me to tend his wounds. He was very sick. He didn't want his steward to see him like that for fear it would undermine his authority. Those were desperate days. I think he made the men obey through sheer force of will."

Shakil said softly, "While he was gone, I was happy because I was no longer in his shadow. I am a quiet man. I cannot compete with the legendary corsair. I did what had to be done. I slipped into Sebta disguised as a Jewish merchant and made secret contacts to try to ransom him. They wouldn't release him, though. Not him. Of all the corsairs in the world, never him. They fear and despise him that much. I snuck across the Pinch to Spain and managed to buy back the *Sea Leopard* using intermediaries. We couldn't afford it; I had to offer shares to investors. Which is how Kasim wound up owning a share."

Thorton's eyes were wide as he listened to this tale. The gentle and bookish Shakil bin Nakih, Thorton's tutor in Arabic and Islam, skulking through the back alleys of a hostile port, wheeling and dealing with corrupt Spanish officials and mendacious merchants?

His voice trembled as he said, "Shakil, we are going to retake Sebta for the Sallee Republic. What you know will be immensely valuable. Will you help?"

Shakil lay on his back and stared up at the ceiling. Dawn was whitening the air outside the window. The house was still, the birds sang, and the smell of the fields that had been in his mother's family for three generations drifted through the window. It was bucolic, comfortable, and far from the rumbles of war. It was safe.

"Yes."

CHAPTER 2 : PLANS

Thorton and Shakil sat at the table in the great cabin of the *Arrow*. Charts of the Strait of Gibraltar with the African and Spanish coasts were spread before them. The two young men were washed and shaved, dressed in clean clothes, and had broken their fast. Now they were drinking coffee made in the Turkish way: boiled thrice to a fine froth, black, and sweetened with honey. The boatswain's call shrilled on the deck outside and the sound carried even to the captain's cabin.

"That'll be Isam," Thorton said matter-of-factly.

Shakil was mystified. "How do you know?" He was dressed in a loose white cotton tunic with a blue vest over it, a turban, and loose pantaloons, all in white.

Thorton smiled. "Each rank has its own call. There aren't many men of Isam's rank in Zokhara, and only one of them has the right to come aboard without requesting permission first." He listened to the clatter of feet as the marines lined up to greet the corsair commodore. "Courtesy requires that I attend him."

He rose and pulled his jacket on. Today he had opted for a short purple jacket in the Zouave style, loose cotton pantaloons in white, and sturdy European shoes. He still wore a stock, cravat and European linen shirt. He rose and ducked his head so that he didn't mash his turban against the deckhead above. The deckhead was low enough that he could not stand up straight. He stepped out into the morning's warmth.

Tangle came aboard with the rest of the *Arrow's* hungover officers. His eyes were blood-shot, but he looked fine otherwise. His black beard was neatly trimmed with a streak of white down the middle, and he wore his long purple coat with the crossed scimitars and star of his rank on the collar. Maynard—Aruj—looked worse for wear. His tanned face was peaked and he had the greenish look of a man whose stomach objects heartily to bobbing along in a rowboat. Aruj was never ever seasick; the hashish must be to blame. Miscellaneous officers in various states of bleariness followed their commander over the side and onto the deck.

Thorton saluted smartly. "Welcome aboard, *kapitan pasha*. May I offer you coffee in my cabin?"

"Orange juice if you have it," Tangle croaked. His usually melodious baritone had been made raspy by smoking. He saw Shakil, jumped to a conclusion, and gave Thorton a jealous look.

Shakil addressed his brother-in-law politely, "Peace be upon you, Isam."

"And also upon you," Tangle replied gruffly.

Thorton received the salutes of the rest of his returning officers. He gave them each a stern looking over that made them quail. Turning to the marine lieutenant he said, "Today is an excellent day for the band to rehearse. Have your men practice strenuously, Lieutenant Yazid."

The officers groaned and gave him beseeching looks. He returned their looks coolly. "You knew you had duty today. 'Tis your own fault for debauching yourselves last night."

Not one of them dared to point out that Peter Rais Thorton had been singing along with them, making up nonsense because he had no idea of the actual words. They could not understand how he appeared devoid of crapulence. It impressed them — he seemed superhuman.

Thorton turned back to the marine lieutenant. "Lieutenant. My officers who are not on duty may join you for the drill. See that they understand it thoroughly."

The marine lieutenant was a man who had stayed to guard the ship while the majority of her commissioned and warrant officers were enjoying the festivities ashore. He grinned back at Thorton. "My pleasure, sir." Turning on his heel, he called, "Clarinets! Drums! Cymbals!" The band consisted of only five men, but they made an infernal racket. The miserable officers held their heads and went to their posts.

In the cabin the music was somewhat muffled. Tangle, who would never admit weakness in public, clapped hands over his ears. "What have you done, Peter?"

Thorton took his seat at the head of the table. Shakil took the seat on his left. Tangle already had the seat on his right. It had taken work to break the corsair of his habit of sitting at the head of the table in Thorton's cabin, but he had learnt it. Thorton understood exactly what Shakil meant when he talked about living in the famous corsair's shadow. He was determined to yield nothing to the man unless he absolutely had to. He would be his own man and succeed or fail on his own merits.

"Serves them right. If I make them miserable here in port where it is safe to do so, then perhaps they will refrain from intoxicating substances and keep their minds on their duty when it matters."

Tangle uncovered his ears. "A man needs a little merriment, Peter. Even you."

Shakil said softly, "You never took your merriment in such a manner before, Isam. You know it will ruin you if you let it."

Tangle's eyes flashed. "I do as I please. It won't hurt me to enjoy myself once in a while!"

Thorton set his jaw. "You are four hours late! What kind of example is that? My officers followed you instead of me! Kaashifa has missed his watch entirely, but I cannot punish him because he was attending *you.*" Thorton slapped his hand against the table. "You are undermining discipline on this vessel!"

Tangle glared back at him and his beard bristled as his jaw worked. He rose to his feet and towered over the seated Thorton. "I am your superior officer and you will show me the respect due my rank!" His looming was not quite as imposing as it would have been in other circumstances because he was a tall man and had to crouch under the deckhead.

Thorton was not intimidated. He tilted his head back and snapped, "Then act like my superior! I'm sorry you suffered for two years in a Spanish galley, Isam, but you must not let that diminish you."

Shakil gaped at Thorton. He was amazed and astounded that anyone would dare to beard the leopard in his den.

Tangle glared back at Thorton. "I do not diminish myself!"

"Don't you? Before the Spanish would you have been four hours late to a meeting with your captain?" Thorton himself had been an hour late, but there was no need to mention that.

"No," the corsair admitted.

"Then why are you late now?" Thorton demanded.

Tangle frowned and looked puzzled. His jaw worked and he glared at Thorton, but not nearly as ferociously. He sat down in his chair again. "I am sorry for being late, rais." Shakil nearly fell out of his chair in shock. "Do not gape at me, Shakil. I am man enough to admit when I am wrong."

It was true. Thorton had seen it before. He trusted it. He never would have dared to upbraid his commanding officer if he didn't. Men who could not admit their mistakes did not take kindly to being chastised for them.

"Apology accepted." He turned to the chart of Sebta and tapped it. "Shakil tells me that this beach is shallow. Fishboats and other small craft beach here. I think we could put one of our own boats on the beach at night and land a spy." Sebta was located on a peninsula. The outermost tip was Mount Hacho, one of the Pillars of Hercules. The north side held a deep harbor defended by Fort Hacho and a mole with the town clustered around it. A low ridge separated the southern beach from the town.

"A spy?" Tangle asked.

Thorton looked at Shakil and they both took a deep breath. "Shakil has been there before. He has contacts inside the city."

Tangle dropped his jaw and stared speechlessly at his brother-in-law. "You?"

Shakil said mildly, "I went there when you were captured to find out what had happened. It is the nearest Spanish territory. The Duke of Coimbra is a prisoner there. Some whisper that he is the rightful King of Portugal."

"Carlos III is the King of both Portugal and Spain. It is a Dual Kingdom," Tangle replied.

Shakil shrugged. "It was supposed to be, but over the decades, Spain has absorbed more and more of the Portuguese prerogatives. The Portuguese aristocrats in Madrid grow up speaking Castilian. Those who are not favorites of the king resent their power and influence."

"Do you think he will revolt?"

"I plan to ask him."

Tangle stared at him. Slowly he said, "You'll need the Dey's permission." Shakil nodded. "The Spanish will burn you at the stake if they catch you." Shakil nodded again.

Thorton's heart turned over, but he kept quiet.

Tangle rubbed his beard and turned his gaze to Thorton. "Is this what the two of you have been up to this morning?"

Thorton nodded. "It is. He has been telling me all that he knows about Sebta. I want to leave as soon as we can to scout it."

"I have not been home very long, Peter. I missed my wife and children. I know it needs to be done, but I don't want to leave my family so soon."

"Stay. We can do this without you. 'Tis only a scouting mission."

"You'll need to take some prizes to make it pay, or we'll never get the soldiers we need."

"Scout first, cruise after. I thought I might poke my head into Gibraltar and see what the English are up to as well."

Tangle smiled crookedly. "I was right to make a captain of you, even if you are a hard-headed Englishman. Very well. The plan has my blessing. How are we going to bring it off?"

They put their heads together. They hardly noticed the rattle of the snare drum and the piping of the clarinet that sounded in the background.

CHAPTER 3 : BELOVED

Spain's misfortunes had brought out every man who had ever hungered for wealth, revenge, or fame. Anything that could float—and some things that couldn't—were equipped as corsairs. The dockyards were bustling as vessels were fitted as cruisers, other cruisers came back in need of repair, and the naval patrols returned to resupply. Prizes came in frequently. Work on the *Arrow* was constantly interrupted as bribes were paid by other vessels to get preferred treatment in the dockyards. Thorton was furious about the bribes and refused to pay them.

There were a great many other vessels. They did not bother with the formality of posting bond and obtaining a letter of marque authorizing them to raid the enemy; they knew there were plenty of merchants in Zokhara (many of them agents for European merchants) who were pleased to receive stolen goods. Holding a letter of marque also meant the corsair had to use the Prize Courts and give up a tenth of the profits to the government in exchange. It was faster, easier, and more profitable to turn pirate.

The pirates gave the Sallee rovers a bad name: with no bond, no letter of marque and no accountability, they did as they pleased. They correctly surmised that as long as they attacked the enemies of the Sallee Republic no one would do anything to stop them. If along the way they snapped up a vessel or two or three that wasn't Spanish—ah well, mistakes happen.

It was August before the *Arrow* set sail. The swells on Detwan Bay were small, no more than three feet, but Shakil was feeling queasy all the same. He lay next to Thorton in the large cot, both of them casually dressed in pantaloons and shirts because of the heat—even the sun's setting did little to lower the temperature. Shakil, being Tangle's accountant, was explaining the financial details of who owed what to whom in a pleasant tenor voice. Thorton pretended to listen out of respect for the man he wanted as his lover, but it was difficult. His eyes closed anyhow.

Shakil noticed. "Are you asleep?" He received no answer. He leaned over and kissed Thorton's brow (which would have pleased Thorton exceedingly had known it). When he didn't react, Shakil knew the truth.

"You *are* asleep."

He had been a little nervous about climbing into the cot with the English captain, but a ship was not a hotel. Giving Shakil his own cabin would have required dislodging an officer, who would have then taken over the cabin of a lower-ranking officer, who would have rousted out his junior, who in turn would have ousted one of the midshipmen, who would have been obliged to find a place to sleep somewhere in the vessel, which would have been nearly impossible. She had her full complement of crew and marines, plus nearly two hundred soldiers of fortune eager to seize and man any prizes they took. In short, sleeping space was worth fighting for and there had been quarrels already. Thorton had promised him that the sleeping arrangements were strictly practical and that no one would think ill of it. With marines sandwiched with marines, sailors crammed with sailors, and mercenaries bickering for their bit of deck space, it was quite plausible.

As the evening light faded the accountant studied the young captain. In his eyes the blond man was very handsome, and the long hair that English sailors habitually wore seemed romantic and exotic to him. He was used to short-haired Muslim men. Thorton's grey-blue eyes were closed now and long lashes lay on his well-tanned cheeks. Feeling quite lascivious, Shakil dared to unbutton two of the sleeping man's shirt buttons. The slice of chest revealed was lightly tanned. Even though Shakil had been to sea before, he had not learned that a man's sleep is sacrosanct. He wiggled down in the cot so that he could kiss Thorton's breastbone. He waited expectantly to see what reaction it brought.

Thorton was asleep, but in addition to the sailor's ability to sleep anywhere at any time, he also had the sailor's sixth sense about when something had changed. His eyes blinked open.

Shakil smiled at him. "*Habibi,*" he said in Arabic.

Thorton knew that word: beloved. Men used it as a term of endearment to each other—to friends as well as lovers. It was the first time that Shakil had used it to him. He smiled. It always made him nervous when Tangle had addressed him so, but he welcomed it from Shakil's lips.

Shakil bent and kissed Thorton's chest again, and Thorton's breath caught in his throat. He lay very still. When Shakil raised his head, Thorton let out a soft groan. He didn't dare move. His eyes were liquid with desire. Shakil was flushed with his own daring, but feeling he had gone too far, scolded him faintly. "You fell asleep while I was talking."

"Your voice is like a lullaby. I like listening to you. Will you sing to me?"

Shakil blushed again. It had been safe to flirt with Thorton when the man was asleep and unaware, but now that he was awake Shakil was nervous. "I only know children's songs."

"Sing me one."

Shakil propped on his elbow and sang a song that his nieces and nephews liked, a song about a cat who went to sea in a bathtub. It was Arabic and Thorton didn't understand more than six words, but he loved the sound of his darling's voice. He lay on his back and smiled at the slender Moor. Shakil grew more confident and smiled as he sang. When the song was over he rested his hand lightly on Thorton's chest and felt the strong heart beating beneath the breastbone. Thorton held his breath as Shakil's eyes darkened and roamed over his body.

"You're very handsome," Shakil whispered.

No man is ever displeased to be told he is handsome, but the compliment was particularly effective with Thorton since he rarely received compliments. His heart thudded in his chest and he thought the other man could surely feel it. Shakil's hand slid across his chest to caress his shoulder and squeeze his biceps. The blond man's breath came quicker but he didn't move.

"I haven't had many lovers," Shakil confessed. "I'm nervous. You must be very experienced."

Thorton shook his head. "Only one for me."

"Isam?"

Thorton blushed and nodded.

"He still loves you."

Thorton blushed again. "I don't think so. He's just randy."

Shakil shook his head. "He moons over you. I know him. He's a sport when it comes to sex, but serious about you. He's jealous of me. He told me so himself."

"He's married!"

Shakil's hand roamed over his chest and unbuttoned more buttons. Then his hand slipped inside the opening. Thorton gasped as he felt the shock of Shakil's palm against his skin.

"He's not bound by other men's rules. You should know that by now. As his accountant it is all I can do to make him abide by the law. He stretches the limits on everything. If he wasn't married, he'd be a pirate for sure."

His fingers found Thorton's nipple and the blond man arched. Shakil's hand withdrew. He watched in fascination as Thorton struggled to maintain his composure.

"I can't believe you would prefer me over him. I'm not at all like him. He's tall and handsome and virile and dashing and brave and famous."

"And intemperate, vain, arrogant, and lewd!"

Shakil laughed at that. "He is, isn't he? I was petrified when I first met him, petrified and infatuated. He knew it. He flirted shamelessly with me just to make me blush. He knows how good-looking he is."

"I suppose he's good-looking in a roguish sort of way," Thorton grudgingly admitted. "But you're handsome in a very fresh and innocent way. You're trustworthy. I like you very much. You aren't like him at all." He reached up to cup Shakil's face and stroke his hair. His short hair was alluring to Thorton who was used to shaggy sailors. He traced the other man's ears and ran his fingers along his jaw where it was starting to roughen with evening shadow.

Shakil brightened. "You really prefer me?"

"I do," Thorton replied firmly.

Shakil was delighted and some of his reservation evaporated. He slid his hands over Thorton's body more freely, exploring the masculine curves and the warm firmness of his flesh. He unbuttoned the linen shirt to the waist and slipped his lips over Thorton's nipple. Thorton wrapped his arms around him and bucked. He wanted the slim Moor badly, but he liked letting him take the lead, too. Shakil was not immune to the allure of flesh, and the way that Thorton let him do as he pleased without trying to take command excited him. He threw a leg over the blond captain and kissed both sides of his chest and groped him more eagerly. Yet he was still a little reticent and kept his fondling above the waist. Thorton writhed under the seduction. He wanted so much more! When Shakil's hand slid over his flat stomach, he took hold of the hand and guided it lower.

"I want you," he whispered.

Shakil was nervous again, but his hand cupped Thorton's anatomy on its own. "The circumcision is fully healed?"

"It is." Thorton blushed a little at the mention of it. Weeks of repairing the *Arrow* and getting her ready for sea had sped by.

"I want you, too," Shakil confessed.

They pressed together, groin to groin, chest to chest, mouth to mouth. They rubbed against each other as they hugged and kissed. Other lovers had pressed Shakil too hard and too fast, but Thorton did not press him at all. It was incumbent upon him to take the lead. Finally they slept.

CHAPTER 4 : THE DUKE OF PORTUGAL

Shakil approached Sebta late in the afternoon. The road was dusty with farmers leaving the city in a weary stream as they headed home from market. A pedlar on a camel passed him by, as well as several carts pulled by nags. The pedlar was loaded but the carts were empty. A few men and women on foot trudged along the road. Muslim women wore veils and long sleeves of coarse hemp cloth while Christian women wore bonnets and aprons stained with their work. The men who traveled with them were as thin and worn as the women. They spared Shakil and his blackamoor only a brief glance.

Shakil walked up to the gate where a pair of guards in red coats with blue reverses were as dusty and tired as the rest. More loitered nearby and the wall above was topped with lethargic sentries. His heart beat faster beneath its weedy coat. He had his hand in his pocket ready to produce his papers.

The guards gave him a desultory look. "Name and business?"

"Siso da Silva," he replied. "I'm a clerk for Isaac Baca of Zokhara. I've been sent by my master to collect a debt." He held out the letter that identified him.

The guard didn't take it or look at it. His hawkish blue eyes narrowed and Shakil trembled. He stood his ground, the proffered paper hanging heavily between them.

"That name sounds Jewish."

"It is," Shakil replied. He waited. This was his disguise, one that would account for him being circumcised if he was ever seen disrobed, one that enabled him, an enemy, to gain entrance to the city by pretending to be one of its second class citizens.

"Damn thieves, all of them," the guard said.

His companion, a heavyset man with black curls, shrugged but said nothing.

"Get on with you," the guard snapped at him.

Shakil tucked his letter into his pocket and bowed. "Thank you, *señor*," he said.

"Don't *señor* me, dog, I'm Portuguese!"

"I beg your pardon. Please forgive a stranger."

The guard grabbed him by the lapels. His breath smelt of wine and garlic. Shakil held his breath. The guard saw the fear in his eyes and smiled evilly. "There is a world of difference between an upright, manly Portuguese and a slimy, spineless, bootlicking Spaniard, do you hear me?"

Shakil nodded.

The other guard said, "Hey, I'm Spanish! Watch your tongue!"

The guard let go of Shakil and turned on his companion. "Your mother is a French whore who laid with a Spanish pimp."

The second guard did not take that kindly. He punched the first guard right in the mouth. Shakil and his servant pressed themselves against the tan stone walls. More guards came running to try to separate them. A sergeant bawled at the combatants, "Break it up you two, or I'll have you both flogged!"

Shakil did not wait to see how things turned out. With his servant at his heels, he slipped into the city.

He got a room at the Red Cap Inn. The maids wore red caps that only partially covered their hair, but they were honest maids and not whores. The inn titillated but did not debauch, so a man could enjoy the wickedness of seeing a well-turned ankle, but if he tried to get up to any mischief, the innkeeper's sons, both substantial men in body if not brain, would toss him into the street. It also happened to be owned by a Jew. Shakil got a room and asked for the man to attend him.

Aknil de Abrantes was a large imposing man with small eyes, a big belly, curly dark brown hair, a curly salt and pepper beard, and a brown jacket and breeches. He smiled as he saw Shakil and bowed to him. "Master Siso. So nice of you to lodge with us again. I heard you had success in your previous business. What brings you back to us today?"

"I'm here on behalf of Isaac Baca of Zokhara to collect a debt from one Abraham Sarfati."

Aknil nodded. "I know him. I can arrange the introduction if you need it."

"Thank you. I'll want a bath tonight as well." Behind him the blackamoor was unpacking his things and laying them on the bed. Lowering his voice, he said, "And other business. Quiet business."

Aknil's eyes narrowed and he nodded. He said, "What sort of business?"

Shakil studied him a long time. He began indirectly. "You know I am a Muslim."

Aknil nodded.

"You know who my kinsman is."

Another nod.

"He's a commodore in the Sallee navy now." Aknil was listening very intently. Shakil stared at the man long and hard and wished he could read minds. "You know the difference between Catholic and Muslim rule."

"I know it well. There was another persecution last year. Taxes, fines, confiscations of property, forced labor, arrests, beatings. No rape or murder this time, though."

"Jews, Christians and Muslims are all People of the Book. That wouldn't happen under Muslim rule."

Aknil nodded. His expression turned thoughtful. "Let us have some cider and talk about parchment and sealing wax. Will your servant fetch us cider?"

"Akil, go to the kitchen and get it." The tall slender eunuch bowed and left the room.

Aknil seated himself at the table. "Your kinsman was not the only man condemned to the galleys. My niece's husband was aboard the *San Antonio*. We're glad to have him back. Tell me what you want and I will do it." The *Antonio* was one of the Spanish galleys that Tangle had captured and whose slaves he had freed.

Shakil heaved a sigh of relief. "Information. As much as you can give me. A safe haven. Introductions to anyone who might help."

"Help with what?"

Again a long silence. "I would like to meet the Duke of Coimbra."

Aknil sucked in a deep breath. "Here I thought you were only spying to help the corsairs attack Sebta. What are you going to do if you meet him?"

Shakil smiled but didn't answer.

Aknil raised a be-ringed hand. "All right, all right. Some things I don't need to know." He shook his head. "I don't know how we get you to see him. The Spanish screen all his appointments. But there might be a way . . . How trustworthy is your servant?"

"I trust him with my life."

"He's not unattractive. Have you considered using him as your agent? You could send him as a gift to the Duke."

"He's not a slave. Why would his looks matter?"

"The Spanish don't let the duke have women. Women bear heirs. They let him have pretty boys instead. A man has needs, after all." He shrugged.

Shakil sat very still. "I could not ask Akil to do that."

Aknil shrugged and spread his hands. "I don't know how we get past the Spanish otherwise. Perhaps my friends will have methods."

Shakil's mouth was very dry and he licked his lips. "I've been told I'm pretty," he said. "If it is the only way, I'll do it."

Aknil looked at him critically. "You're comely enough," he admitted. "Well then. If you've come on this mission you must have the necessary nerve. I'll see what I can do."

"I have money, if that helps."

Aknil shook his head. "My friends will help because we want to help. We hate the Spanish."

Aknil was as good as his word. Two days later he supplied Shakil with the necessary clothes. The Moor was a modest man. To wear mustard-colored stockings, tight-fitting brown breeches and a short waistcoat of russet embarrassed him. The jacket was short and brown. It was cut very close and molded to his form, except for the shoulders which had been lightly padded to make them seem broader. He preferred the loose-fitting clothing of his native country. That he was being dressed to emphasize the delectable roundness of his small rump and the trimness of his narrow waist made it even more disconcerting. The colors were selected to compliment his eyes and hair, which were hazel and light auburn respectively.

Aknil's wife applied a powder to whiten his face, then used kohl to draw a line around his eyes. The makeup was not obvious but it was effective. When Shakil looked at himself in the mirror he saw a pretty boy who looked ten years younger than his actual thirty-one. He was exactly the sort of primped and soft creature that made him purse his lips in disapproval when he saw them on the streets.

Aknil escorted him to the office of Master Toboada, the banker, and left him in the antechamber. Alone. As for Toboada, Shakil would never meet him. The banker would disavow any knowledge; as far as he was concerned Siso da Silva was a complete stranger and minor functionary on his master's business. Toboada had provided them with one critical piece of information: the Duke of Coimbra had an appointment with the banker—and the banker was going to be late for it—as late as they wanted him to be. He, too, was a Jew.

A bit of brandy was on the credenza, the blue velvet chairs were small and elegant, the paneling darkest mahogany. The candles were all in crystal sconces, but they weren't needed. The window was open and a fresh breeze blew in. It carried the smell of the sea, jasmine, and dust. Shakil stood by the window and stared out. He could see buildings and over their tops, masts in the harbor. He wondered where the *Arrow* was. If this business took too long he was going to miss his rendezvous. All that he knew about Sebta, the maps and information in code that he had prepared over the last three days, had been entrusted to the servant. Akil would not fail him. Thorton would not fail him. It was only himself that might fail. He trembled at the thought.

Finally, at a quarter after two, a servant threw open the door. The duke entered, accompanied by his servant and a guard. Whether it was his own guard to protect him from the footpads in the street, or a Spanish guard to prevent him from causing Spain any trouble Shakil didn't know. The Moor turned his head and stared in surprise: the duke was the most unattractive man he had ever laid eyes on.

Henrique, Duke of Coimbra, was tall but round-shouldered and slightly hunch-backed. His nose was bulbous and hawkish together at once. His watery blue eyes were set too close together and had a tendency to cross when he wasn't squinting. His mouth was extremely wide, his lips thin. His hair was nearly gone, but that was concealed by the wig he wore. Falls of blond curls reached his shoulders. His adam's apple protruded and his skin was so pale it looked blue. It was dappled with large freckles and the freckles continued on the back of his hands. He was thin and gangly and his toes turned in enough to give his legs an awkward line. All of this was dressed in a lemon yellow suit with great cascades of white linen around the throat and wrists. His waistcoat was black and white diamonds in a Harlequin pattern. He wore diamond earrings at a time when earrings were not the fashion for men. More diamonds sparkled on his fingers and the buckles of his shoes. Looking him up and down Shakil was desperate to find something attractive about the man and settled for calling his calves 'well-turned.' But not out loud. When he looked up and met the man's eyes, the pale blue orbs were staring at him with great interest.

"Hola, who's this?" the duke asked in lisping Spanish. He walked towards Shakil with a mincing gait that was either a gross affectation or evidence of some defect of the hip. His walking stick tapped on the parquet floor, then sank silently into the thick rug that occupied the majority of the room.

"Siso da Silva, my lord," Shakil replied. He had drilled his story into his head so thoroughly that even when astonished it came out with the naturalness of truth.

The duke leaned on his gold-headed walking stick, reached out with a long-fingered hand, and caught Shakil under the chin. "What a pretty name for a pretty boy. How old are you, Siso?"

Shakil was pretty sure the macaroni did not want to hear his true age, so he said, "Twenty-one."

"Come, step away from the window. Let me see you!"

Shakil walked dumbly into the center of the room. He turned to watch the duke anxiously over his shoulder. The duke was appraising him quite frankly as he walked around the smaller man. Catching

Shakil's eye, he asked, "Do you like sherbet? I have some at my house."

"I do, sir." Sherbet was a costly luxury. Snow had to be brought from the mountains and kept packed in sawdust so it wouldn't melt until it was mixed with fruit juice to make a delicious cold dessert.

"Excellent! You will join me then." It was an order, not an invitation.

Shakil asked, "But who are you, sir? Please, I mean no disrespect, but I'm a stranger here. My master sent me on business."

The duke was astounded. "You don't know me?"

Shakil shook his head. "I'm sorry, but I have never seen you before. I am from Zokhara."

Something flickered deep in the vacuous blue eyes. When Shakil looked into them, he saw something that the duke did not want anyone to see. He kept a baffled look on his own face. It wasn't hard. He had never encountered a creature like the duke before.

With a dramatic gesture the duke announced, "I am Henrique, Duke of Coimbra."

Shakil bowed deeply and said, "I'm pleased to make your acquaintance, Your Grace. But I'm nobody you need notice. Really."

The guard and servant were watching with looks somewhere between amusement and boredom. The duke shooed them. "Go away and don't bother me. Tell Master Toboada I have been unexpectedly delayed." He offered an elbow to Shakil. Up close his expensive perfume was noticeable. "Walk with me. We'll have a lovely stroll through the park and go up to my house for sherbet."

CHAPTER 5 : PARKING

The duke waved off attempts to get his coach. A bevy of guards and servants followed in his wake while another ran ahead to clear his path. He walked right down the middle of the street. Other travelers, including coaches, had to get out of his way. There was some cursing but his guards drew their swords and ran toward the miscreants, so they shut up and fled. Shakil walked arm and arm with this strange apparition and heard the comments: "'Tis the Mad Duke, out for a stroll."

The duke heard them, too, but waved his walking stick with a flourish and smiled and bowed. "I am delighted to make your acquaintance. I am Henrique, Duke of Portugal. You have my permission to tread in my shadow," he informed his hecklers.

The arm hooked into Shakil's elbow tightened for support when he waved the walking stick. Shakil realized there really was something wrong with his leg; his cocked gait was an affectation to disguise the limp. The mad duke would rather be thought a coxcomb than a cripple.

They reached the park and strolled through it. The duke lifted his hat to ladies on parade and bowed to them. To an especially plain and plump woman he said, "Ah, 'tis the Queen of Sheba surrounded by the ladies of her court. Good morrow to you, Your Majesty."

The woman curtsied to him and tittered behind her fan. "You do me too much honor," she replied. She batted her eyes at him over the edge of her fan. Mad or not, the man was a duke and rich, too.

Henrique tightened his grip on Shakil's elbow and said with hearty good cheer, "On the contrary, madam, you don't do me honor enough!"

They left her puzzling over what he meant. The duke pulled Shakil onto a side path away from the ladies in dresses like blooms amid the foliage. The cool shade covered them and the scent of greenery and late-blooming flowers was pleasant. The duke's aimless rambling somehow avoided the populous paths and the rest of the visitors disappeared.

When they were quite alone (except for the guards and servants), the duke stopped and smiled down at him. "What a quiet little bird you are. Don't you sing?"

Shakil stared up at him with wide eyes. What on earth could he say to such a peculiar peer? "I can sing a little, my lord. I sing to my nephews and nieces."

The well-practiced smile and shallow eye wavered a little as he studied Shakil. Finally he said, "Sing to me." He threw himself on the green sward like a stack of blocks toppling.

Shakil knelt on the grass beside him. He racked his brain for a song and came up with the only Hebrew one he knew, one that he had learned while in Sebta seeking Tangle's release many months ago. His voice was a light tenor that didn't carry far. The song was a sad one about lovers parted by cruel fate. The duke leaned upon his elbow and stared into Shakil's eyes. He listened in rapt silence. When it was done Shakil looked at him anxiously to see his reaction. The duke murmured something to himself in Portuguese. Then he leaned forward, took Shakil's chin in his hand, and kissed him on the mouth.

Shakil was startled and shied away. In the privacy of the Red Cap Inn he had been grimly determined to do what must be done, but he had not thought it would be anything like this.

"Don't turn away from me." The duke's lisping Spanish was firm.

Shakil turned to look at him with something like dread. "I'm sorry, Your Grace."

"Don't play coy. I know a doxy when I see one, even if he is a boy." He kept his voice low so that their conversation would not be overhead by his escorts.

Spots of color appeared on Shakil's cheeks. "I'm not a doxy, sir."

The duke flicked his finger hard against Shakil's cheek. It hurt. He showed the tip of his finger to him. "Powder," he said. "Don't tell me you're not a pretty little bird set to snare the Duke of Portugal. I may be a madman, but I am not stupid." His face was even uglier when he snarled.

Shakil swallowed hard. "I was sent, sir. But I didn't choose the manner of my sending."

"Who sent you?"

Shakil kept silent. He was shaking. He looked around the park and especially at the guards and servants. They had wandered a bit and were engrossed in their own idle conversations.

The duke glanced slyly over his shoulders, then back at Shakil. He grabbed a handful of Shakil's lace and dragged him close. He put his face right into Shakil's and said, "You were sent to me as an offering. I could take you right here on the grass and not one of them would lift a hand to help you, so don't toy with me."

Shakil trembled, but something about the duke's demeanor was strangely familiar. When he realized what it was, he calmed. "You remind me of my brother-in-law," he said matter-of-factly.

It was not the response the duke was expecting. He let go of Shakil's lace and the smaller man dropped back on the grass. He adjusted his clothes. He watched the duke through his lashes as the duke watched him.

The duke blinked first. "Who is your brother-in-law?"

Shakil spoke in a very low voice. "Isam Rais al-Tangueli."

The duke was very still, but the pupils of his eyes widened. *"Capitán Tanguel, o corsário,"* he breathed. He sat up abruptly and stretched his left leg out before him. Once again the vapid expression returned as he massaged his left hip. "Come over here and massage me. My leg hurts," he said querulously. He gave Shakil an imperious look.

Shakil cautiously put his hands on the yellow velvet. "Here, my lord?" he asked.

"A little closer to the front."

Shakil moved his hand forward.

"A little more."

Shakil froze and the duke broke out in a peal of coarse laughter. He chucked him beneath the chin. "Not afraid of a snake, are you? Mind you, 'tis a very big snake."

Shakil withdrew his hands. He was nettled by the strangeness of the duke's behavior, but again there was something familiar about it. His brother-in-law used to torment him so.

"I've seen bigger," he replied. "And tamed them, too." His fingers dug into the man's flank and found the tight muscles and unnatural knots.

The duke jerked and let out a sudden groan. "Good God, man, you're going to rip my leg off!" The mincing manner had completely evaporated.

Shakil let up. "Should I stop?"

"I'll slap you if you do."

Shakil dug in again. The duke's leg twitched and jerked. He groaned and dropped back on the grass. "Mercy!" he gasped. Shakil let go. After he caught his breath, the duke said, "Again!"

Shakil dug in again. The man thrashed on the ground and Shakil got kneed for his pains, but he persisted. "Were you hurt, sir?"

"I jumped out of a burning house when I was young. I broke my hip and ankle. They said I'd never walk again." His voice was a pleasant baritone with a noticeable Portuguese accent when stripped of his foppish pose.

Shakil kept twisting and pulling, rubbing and pressing. The duke's hat was lost and his wig was eschew. He coughed violently and spit phlegm.

Shakil stopped in alarm. "You're not well, my lord!"

The duke sat up and glared at him. "'Tis the weather, nothing more."

The weather was hot, a little humid, and fair, with white cotton clouds drifting through the sky.

"I don't believe you, my lord."

The watery blue eyes narrowed. "I don't believe you, either." He picked himself off the ground and complained in a falsetto voice, "Look, you've gotten grass stains on my clothes!"

Shakil got up and eyed him cautiously. "'Twasn't I that made you sit on the grass, Your Grace."

"Impudence!" The duke's hand flew and Shakil ducked. The flying hand knocked the cocked hat from his head. "I'm going to spank you for your misbehavior. I'm going to pull your britches down and leave your arse red, I am!"

Shakil laughed and retrieved his hat. "I call your bluff, sir."

"Bluff!" The duke was scandalized. He turned to his attendants. "Did you hear that? He says I'm bluffing! Me! Of all people! I've spanked plenty of boys!" he blustered.

They laughed and grinned at him. The duke grabbed Shakil by the arm, leaned on his cane, and dragged him further off the beaten path. They disappeared behind some bushes. The guards stayed where they were. One of the guards called after them, "Show 'im how they do it in Portugal!" More laughter, mocking and crude.

The duke and the spy were alone. Shakil looked up into the homely face of the ridiculous popinjay and asked a simple question. "Who is the rightful King of Portugal, my lord?"

The weak chin suddenly set in a pugnacious line as the duke ground his teeth in fury. "I am. And will be as soon as I escape this gilded cage."

"The *Arrow* will be waiting for me at sunset in the village of Arzoga. Are you coming?"

Hope flared in the duke's eyes. He turned to look over his shoulders, but the guards could not be seen. He kept his voice low. "Who sent you? Hold still and howl." He wrapped an arm around Shakil's waist and swatted his rump hard.

Shakil yelped in surprise. He did not need to fake it. He gulped and whispered, "The Dey of Zokhara. Will you ally with the Sallee Republic?"

Another swat and another cry. "Mercy, my lord!" Shakil gasped.

The duke rubbed his sore butt to soothe it and pressed his face very close to Shakil's neck. "I will. Anything to escape Spain. They would have killed me if they thought I was any sort of man at all."

A guard came and peeked around the shrubbery but seeing them in an embrace withdrew.

"Can you run, my lord?"

"I can do anything that takes me away from here."

They ran.

It was impossible to hide a six foot tall man in a yellow suit, but Shakil's clothes were much too small so they couldn't trade. The duke was a man of great fortitude and few inhibitions. He stripped down to his smalls and ditched the wig, scrubbed the powder from his face using his waistcoat, stripped the diamonds from his ears and fingers, and left the shoes with their diamond studded buckles. He left the cane, too, and with Shakil beside him, loped in ragged, lurching strides through the streets in his underwear. So accustomed were the people of Sebta to the overdressed, made-up, effeminate figure of the Duke of Coimbra that they did not recognize the balding, limping greyhound in his small clothes.

When soldiers on patrol stopped them, Shakil explained, "My friend was robbed in the park. They took his clothes and everything! It was a pack of eight men. They were wearing . . ." He gave them a description of the duke's servants. The soldiers ran past them toward the park.

Shakil knew his way around Sebta; he had a head for mathematics and that included geometry. He lead them through alleys, stole a cloak from an open door, and brought the runaway duke through the kitchen door of the Red Cap Inn and up the backstairs to his room. He shouted for Aknil.

Aknil entered the room and seeing a flushed and sweating Shakil, asked, " What happened? Were you successful?"

The cloaked figure turned to face him. The duke dropped the hood onto his shoulders. "He was. The King of Portugal is grateful for your service."

Aknil staggered as if he had been hit. "Your Majesty!"

The fop had vanished. The king limped forward with a certain dignity and said, "I need clothes. Turn this ring into money. Keep half for yourself. What is your name?" He handed the man one of his rings.

"Aknil, sir."

"Kneel and swear homage to the rightful ruler of Sebta."

Aknil knelt, and weeping, took the duke's hand, blessed him, and kissed it.

Henrique, would-be king of an independent Portugal, laid his hand on the man's head and shoulders. "Rise, Sir Aknil."

"God save the King," innkeeper replied.

"I am not insensible to the good operations of God, but for the moment, I will settle for clothes and transportation. Siso—who I am sure is not truly named Siso—has a ship waiting for us."

"I am Shakil bin Nakih, my lord. I am a man of no particular importance, but my sister married Captain Tangle. He owns the ship that will pick us up."

"I look forward to meeting him. If anyone can rescue me from this Spanish prison, 'tis he."

Shakil cleared his throat. "He's in Zokhara, sir. Peter Rais Thorton is our captain."

"Who?"

"A trustworthy man. We must bustle, Your Grace."

Henrique looked perplexed. He had never heard of Peter Thorton. "Very well. I trust I'll meet the famous corsair soon enough."

CHAPTER 6 : THE HAG OF GIBRALTAR

The *Arrow* haunted the environs of Sebta for three days. She scooned along, dodged Spanish *guardacostas* and accomplished little of obvious use, much to the ire of the soldiers of fortune aboard her. Thorton reminded them repeatedly that they had known in advance that he must spend time on his duty before they could cruise. This did not placate them at all and they demanded to be allowed to take a fishing smack at least, but Thorton denied them. He took soundings as much as he could, spied on Mount Hacho with its imposing fortress, and considered whether the watchtower on top of the mountain could be toppled. He gave it as an exercise to Foster and Aruj to work out whether their guns could be elevated sufficiently to reach. The men-at-arms were not interested in a profitless activity like burning the watchtower. Fight their way up the seven hills of Hacho and get shot for no reward? The mood aboard the galiot was foul and Thorton unpopular.

Late on the third afternoon life suddenly became exciting. Thorton was standing on the poop deck staring at the great tan bulk of Hacho when a spot of color caught his attention. He pulled the glass from his pocket and took a look. The Spanish semaphore was raising a signal. As he read the message all color drained from his face. He snapped out his orders. "Beat to quarters. Make all sail."

Lt. Aruj asked, "Captain?"

Thorton had been four years as a pressed man in the Spanish navy. More than that, he had memorized a captured Spanish signal book. "The Spanish are sending a squadron after us! They are ordered to sink or capture us."

Aruj shot him a look. "Why would they do that? Unless—" He broke off.

"Unless Shakil Effendi has been captured." Thorton's heart was heavy. Why else would the Spanish take a sudden interest in him? They would take no chance that the spy had already communicated vital information to the galiot; they would take or sink her before she could escape to Zokhara with her intelligence. "We must run for Gibraltar."

The wind was out of the west and he needed to run a little west of north to make Algeciras Bay. The galiot could run fairly close to the wind and that course would take him where he wanted to be. He gave orders and the bow came around. He kept the glass to his eye and watched the *guardacostas* coming out in force. They were frigate-rigged xebecs with low, lean, fast hulls, square sails on the fore and mainmasts and a lateen sail on the mizzen. Creamy mustaches of white foam arched up as their bows sliced through the water. They were fast. His heart sank. He was two miles off Sebta. Would it be enough of a head start?

"Heave the log, Mister Arrellano." The midshipman fetched it and counted off the seconds. "Eight knots, sir."

At that rate it would take them a little over an hour to reach the safety of Gibraltar. How he would like to meet an English frigate this afternoon! He calculated it would take the *guardacostas* about the same amount of time to cover the greater distance from Sebta to Gibraltar at twelve knots. Tangle had boasted his xebec could make fourteen. He would be caught just outside the haven of Gibraltar if the Spanish could run like that.

"We must lighten the load now. Throw all the food and water overboard but two casks each."

"Sir?" Aruj asked.

"If we make Gibraltar, we won't need it. We can resupply there. If we don't make Gibraltar, we won't need it."

"Aye aye, sir. Wafor!" Aruj went to confer with the black boatswain.

"Master Marino," Thorton addressed the sailing master. "Secure our papers. Weight them with cannonballs. Mr. Arrellano, if we are taken, you'll drop them overboard so the Spanish don't get them."

"Aye aye, sir," they answered.

"Tighten the sheets. We must run as close to the wind as we possibly can. 'Tis our only hope."

If they could run even one point closer to the wind than the Spaniards they would be almost two miles apart when the Spanish overhauled them—and out of range of the Spanish guns. To catch up to them the Spanish would have to tack back and forth across their wake, and the tacking would cost them valuable minutes. Even so, if the *guardacostas* were good, they could catch him. He prayed to Allah to make them fools.

The men-at-arms were put to work using their brute strength to haul the victuals out of the hold and toss them over the side. They sweated and swore, but as xebec after xebec came out from behind the mole, they worked feverishly. They knew what their fate would be if the Spanish caught them.

Thorton held his glass to his eye. "Six," he moaned. "Six!" They fanned out in a line abreast and began their run. They were definitely after the *Arrow*.

The sun was sinking into the west. Thorton prayed for it to sink faster and provide him with the cover of night to make his escape or for the clouds to pile up more thickly, but by his calculations they'd reach Algeciras Bay in time for the evening prayer, and that was not dark enough to hide anything.

"Shakil," he whispered in despair. Was he even alive? Or were the Spanish torturing him to give up his secrets before they burned him at the stake? He rubbed his sleeve across his eyes and blinked back tears. It was his fault. Shakil was no corsair. He was a part-time farmer and bookkeeper, a man whose hobbies were reading and calligraphy, a pious man who read the Qu'ran regularly, a gentle man who was teaching his little nieces and nephews to read and count. Thorton had been selfish. He did not want to be alone, so he had persuaded Shakil to come with him on a dangerous mission.

Achmed bin Mamoud came up to the poop and stared south. They were supposed to drop him in Gibraltar to arrange joint action with the British; he was still the envoy to England. Achmed put his hand on Thorton's shoulder and gave him a sympathetic look. "The fortunes of war." No one had to explain to him what it meant to have a squadron of Spanish xebec-frigates hauling wind as fast as they could in their wake.

"For myself I have no fear. I have escaped the Spanish twice before. My luck will run out eventually. 'Tis Shakil—" He choked.

"Allah watches over you, Peter Rais, and also over Shakil Effendi."

More splashes. A cask bobbed past the quarter and disappeared in their wake.

"It doesn't make any sense. One spy is not worth six *guardacostas*, yet there they are." Thorton despaired. Until now he had dealt only with the dregs of the Spanish navy, the remnants left to guard the western coasts while the best commanders and ships went east to fight the French. Now was not a good time to meet competent Spaniards and well-equipped vessels.

"Perhaps it has nothing to do with him and he is safe. Maybe they think it is Isam Rais out here. They have probably recognized the *Arrow*. They have a grudge against him," Achmed suggested.

"That is entirely possible." Thinking it made Thorton feel a little better. But if was true, he was abandoning Shakil to save his own skin. He looked into the waist crowded with nearly four hundred men and knew that he could not risk so many lives to save one.

Achmed continued watching him. "Are you going to lace on the bonnets?" His tone was polite, as if he were asking Thorton to pass him the salt at dinner.

Thorton gave him a startled look. "Lateen sails have bonnets?"

"Indeed they do."

Thorton whirled round. "Clap on the bonnets!" He cursed himself. He was a novice captain and even more a novice to the lateen rig. Tangle had never used the bonnets when he was master of the *Arrow*, but he had never needed to, either.

The sailmaker and his mates hauled the rectangular pieces of cloth on deck. Thorton would not let the sails be lowered. They had to stand on deck and lace the cloth to the bottom of the lateen sails. It was an awkward and uneven way to do the work. Every spare man threaded thongs through the grommets to lash the two together. More men held up the weight of the canvas to keep it in place. The bonnets were not smooth when they were done, but they extended the size of the sails.

Thorton barked, "Toss the log."

"Ten knots less a quarter, sir," Midshipman Arrellano reported.

"Achmed. What else can I do?"

"Throw your powder, shot, and guns over."

"That I will not do."

"You will be smashed. A galiot is no match for a frigate. Six will turn her to kindling."

"Tangle once told me that a galley could, if conditions were right, take a frigate."

Achmed snorted. "If she has consorts, no wind, and a stupid enemy, anything is possible."

"Do you think he was exaggerating?"

Achmed hesitated. "If anyone could beat a frigate with a galiot, 'twould be Isam Rais. But I wouldn't like the odds."

Thorton stared at the Spanish xebecs in his glass. "By Allah, they're fast!"

"Yes. They learned that from us." Achmed sounded rueful. "Thank Allah the wind is on their beam. If it were a little south it would be perfect for them. You'd see them really fly then."

The wind became fitful and shifted to the north, then back to the northwest. No ship can sail into the eye of the wind; Thorton was forced to alter his course to run more north. He would pass east of Gibraltar if he continued. He had to constantly tend the trim of the sails to respond to the gusty conditions. His crew was well-drilled and he kept his course as westerly as he could, but he did not think it was enough. He would have to tack suddenly and dart into Algeciras Bay at the last minute. The Spanish could guess what he would do. His only help was that the wind was contrary for them as well. At the end it might well come down to who could tack fastest.

Then the masthead lookout yelled, "A sail! Fine on the larboard bow!"

Thorton hurried over to the other side. A knot of fear coiled in his stomach. If it was a Spanish ship coming out of Algeciras he was doomed. He clapped the glass to his eye and saw a fishing smack with a single lateen sail. He heaved a sigh and rubbed his chest. He gave Achmed a rueful look. "I was worried for a moment."

Achmed smiled. "You're doing fine, rais."

Thorton gave him a grateful look. Achmed was a retired corsair of considerable skill himself. "Any advice you can give will be greatly appreciated."

Achmed shook his head. "We have lightened ship and are running as fast as we can. All we can do is pray devilment to the enemy."

The fishing smack bobbed on the water. She made no effort to get out of the way of the racing galiot. On the contrary, her course meandered a little east, right in their way.

Thorton remarked, "Do you think she's some mad Spaniard, trying to slow us down by getting in our way? Don't they know I'm happy run them over and never slow down?"

Achmed shrugged. "You don't know who it is. Privateers will go to sea in anything."

"At that size she couldn't hold more than fifteen men if they were packed like sardines. She's no threat to us."

"Probably not. But if she sets herself alight, 'twill be a different story."

Thorton's blood ran cold. "Fireboat."

"I'd do it, if I had a dinghy to take me off and thought it important enough. Anything being chased by six xebecs is important enough."

The wind weakened and sometimes the great lateen sails with their bonnets hung limp. Thorton cursed in English and Arabic and Spanish. Then he set his mind to working. The wind was failing for the Spanish, too. The race slowed to a crawl as the evening calm settled on the strait. The highlands to the north and south channeled the wind so there was still some breeze; it was a rare day for the wind to die completely in the throat of Gibraltar. As much as it racked his nerves, Thorton decided it was a good thing. The galiot was lighter than the xebecs (not that they were heavy, no, not by any European measure) so she moved better in the light airs. Still, her sails were not as large as the xebecs, and when all else was equal, more canvas meant more speed. But things were ever equal. The eastern sky was darkening and the first star could be seen. Tendrils of mist rose from the waters. Dusk was creeping across the surface of the sea. With a little luck they could lose the Spanish in the dark.

He swung the glass and looked again. There was the fishboat dead on the bow not more than a hundred yards away. People on the boat began to wave their arms and shout. He could not make out the words but the men were waving their hats.

"Good God!" Surprise made him exclaim in English. "There are women in that boat!"

Achmed took a deep breath. "Refugees, fleeing Spain. They come across the Pinch in whatever will float. There is an endless stream of them, each with some new horror to relate. That is why we fight, Peter Rais. Because Spain is not content to rule; she must destroy. Europe, Africa, America, Asia—where she goes, she spreads ruin. She is Shaitan's empire on Earth."

Thorton squeezed his eyes shut. He didn't have time to stop and rescue refugees. Yet if he didn't, they'd get picked up by vengeful Spaniards. He looked back at where the *guardacostas* were still pursuing him about a mile and a half distant. Their courses had fanned out further. None of them was on exactly the same course as the *Arrow*. Hope flared. Their square sails would not let them sail as close to the wind as his lateen sails. Two of the frigates had abandoned the chase and were tacking across the wind, trying to reach Algeciras before him. They would ambush him in the mouth of the bay if they could.

The distance between the galiot and fishboat closed to fifty yards. The people on the fishboat were hugging each other and cheering. The wind veered and flitted and the great lateen sails luffed like thunder. Thorton swore in English. Nothing suited a man like his native tongue when it came to swearing. He bellowed his orders in English, then gathered his wits and repeated them in Spanish. Kaashifa translated them to Arabic. The sails grew taut, but he was another point away from north.

"Heave the log."

"Four and a half knots, sir."

Achmed said nothing. He watched Thorton. In spite of the danger he was curious to see what kind of man the renegade Englishman was.

Thorton glanced back towards the xebecs. His eyes narrowed. "I think they might have slipped a little."

Achmed shielded his eyes with his hands. He studied them for a while and said, "I think you might be right, but not by much."

The fishboat was right under their bow. It was so close the hull hid her from view and Thorton could only see the mast sticking up with her limp sail. "Grapple. Get them aboard, then—" He paused. "Send her aft and set her alight. Let the Spanish have something to play with."

Wood scraped wood and grapples bit. The women were sent up first. They tied up their long skirts and scrambled up nimbly, but there was an old hag in the party that had to be helped up. The men came aboard last. All of them hurried as much as they could, including the pair of fishermen that had handled the vessel. Lt. Aruj limped forward to meet them and Thorton was surprised to see that the old woman was taller than the boy, even with her hunched back. Aruj lead them aft. Thorton glanced over the side to make certain his orders were being followed, then descended to the main deck to meet his guests. He had seen the trouble the beldame had had getting up the ladder and would not make her climb the steps to the quarterdeck. Besides, he was jealous of his quarterdeck. He did not like strangers on it.

Thorton was never more startled in his life than when a young woman clad in a pink taffeta dress and bonnet threw her arms around his neck and kissed him on both cheeks.

"Madame!" he exclaimed. "There is no need! We are not yet safe!" He pushed her away, then stopped in sudden shock.

Shakil was grinning at him from within the confines of the bonnet.

Thorton's jaw dropped. "Wha-at? Shakil? What on earth—what are you doing? What's this?"

"'Tis a disguise!" he exclaimed exuberantly, then untied the bonnet strings and pulled the frilly thing from his head to show his short auburn hair. His hazel eyes were sparkling with excitement. He grabbed Thorton's hand, and with the bonnet dangling from the other, dragged him to the group. He stopped in front of the hag. "Your Grace, I have the pleasure to present Peter Rais Thorton, captain of the *Arrow*. Captain, this is Henrique, Duke of Coimbra and rightful King of Portugal."

The hag had kept her head down, but now she raised it and smiled. The mad duke lifted his hands and removed the bonnet to reveal his wispy strawberry blond hair that was going prematurely bald. Thin strands were disheveled across his bald pate and a monkish tonsure went around his head above his large ears. His pale blue eyes were slightly crossed, his nose was hooked, his mouth too large, his chin was weak, and he was wearing face powder and rouge.

He smiled warmly at Thorton. "Never was I more delighted to make a man's acquaintance than with the possible exception of Shakil Effendi."

Thorton's jaw dropped and hung open. He had never seen a duke up close, let alone met one. His eyes raked up and down the dowdy white and yellow dress, the shawl and apron. He looked around at the figures in dresses and asked, "Are you all men?"

Shakil laughed and the women tittered. Aknil stepped forward and said, "My wife and daughters."

Henrique said, "Allow me to present Sir Aknil. I have knighted him for his help in making my escape. His family has come with us because I would not be so insensitive as to leave them behind to suffer the wrath of Spain." His face turned grim beneath its paint.

Thorton bowed deeply. "Welcome aboard, Your Grace. I will have a cabin made ready."

Achmed had followed him and bowed deeply, pressing a hand against his forehead to keep his turban from falling off his head. "Peace be upon you, Your Grace. I am Achmed bin Mamoud, envoy to England. May I offer you my cabin?" He had displaced the first lieutenant.

"Why, thank you. I am happy to accept." The duke offered his hand. Achmed took it and kissed it. It was the custom for European men to kiss the hands of those much higher in rank than themselves.

"Mister Nazim!" Thorton called his third lieutenant and gave instructions. "We must keep the identity of our distinguished guest from the crew and men-at-arms. Madame," he used the term with some irony, "I regret to say that you will be safer in your dress than breeches if the Spanish catch us. I hope to Allah they will not detect you."

Duke Henrique was no sailor. "Will they catch us?"

"They might. It might get hot before very long."

Henrique put the bonnet back on his head and tied the strings under his chin. He sank in on himself and pulled the shawl up to his chin and said in a querulous old woman's voice, "'Tis fine for young men to gallivant about in the evening chill, but I have rheumatism!"

Thorton smiled. "Madame, the stage has missed a thespian!"

CHAPTER 7 : FEELING THE PINCH

The wind had continued to decline until they were barely ghosting along in the gloaming. It died completely with the galiot less than a mile from the mouth of Algeciras Bay. Five miles wide, it was filled with dusk and slowly rising mist. The Spanish squadron still pursued. Thorton had a new fear: what if the fortress of Algeciras sent them a welcoming party? He ordered all lights doused. Looking south he could see the light of the burning fishboat. The *guardacostas* had their oars out and were rowing. They kept well clear of the minor obstacle. "Out oars," Thorton commanded.

Shakil arrived on the poop deck. He was properly dressed in buff pantaloons and a purple coat with the plain collar of a warrant officer No gold lace for him; the brass buttons were the only ornament to a severely plain grape-colored coat. A white turban wrapped his head. A pair of knives were thrust into his sash.

Thorton looked at them and raised his brow in question. He shrugged, "Isam Rais taught me how to fight. There are footpads in the street and I must carry large sums of money at times. I take a guard with me, but 'tis better to defend myself if necessary."

"Can you shoot?"

"If necessary. The noise bothers me."

What a mollycoddle thing to say. Thorton simply looked at him. What did he expect? The Moor was gentle and mild and that was why Thorton loved him. The knives were incongruous enough.

"Stay here and I'll do my best to protect you. The marines will protect us." He did not say that with six xebecs in pursuit the probability of anybody protecting anything was nil.

Shakil smiled warmly at him. "I rescued the King of Portugal! Can you believe it?" He laughed in boyish delight.

Thorton couldn't help smiling at him. "You did! However did you do it?"

Shakil launched into his story, but Thorton gave it only half an ear.

The galiot's oars swept across the sea. The mercenaries and sailors put their backs into it and pulled. These were no ordinary oars, but long sweeps that required four men each to fling their weight upon them to make them move. He looked back at where the Spanish *guardacostas* had fallen further behind. Exulting he exclaimed, "We're going to make Gibraltar!"

Shakil gave him a puzzled look. "Was there any doubt?"

Thorton grabbed him and whirled him around. "We're going to make Gibraltar!"

The good news quickly spread and there was a ragged cheer. The rowing slackened. Thorton charged to the rail and roared down at them, "Row, damn ye! We're not there yet!"

So they put their backs into it again. The xebecs raised Spanish signals and Thorton put his glass to his eye, but he could not make them out in the gathering darkness. Hopefully the Spanish lookouts ashore could not make them out, either. The Rock of Gibraltar loomed as a dark mass to the starboard. The space between the headlands was darker than the sea and more misty. The sun was behind the hills above Algeciras and the bay was a bowl of night. There was the gauntlet of the fortress to run, but in the dark they just might make it. The lateen sails were brailed tight to their masts.

As the *Arrow* slid into the welcoming darkness, the orange horizon disappeared. The Spanish *guardacostas* were still out there. He could see their lights in the gloom, but they were not gaining. As the *Arrow* penetrated deeper into the bay, four of them disappeared from view, blocked by the headlands on either side. The *Arrow* was now trapped in the bay. If she wanted to escape, she would have to run out past the Spaniards. For a moment of panic Thorton worried that Gibraltar might have fallen, but he swept his glass over the town and saw the Union Jack still flying. The lights of the town glowed brightly at the foot of the mighty Rock. Equally bright, larger, and more impressive were the lights of the Spanish town of Algeciras on the western side of the bay.

"Creep along the eastern shore and stay as far as possible from the Spanish side of the bay," he ordered his sailing master.

The *Arrow* turned her bow towards the lights of Gibraltar. Something dark flitted across the distant lamplight. Something large and multi-limbed. With horror he realized it was a frigate. But what sort? English or Spanish? She had no lights.

"Silence," he whispered. "Muffle those sweeps. No talking, no sound at all. We must creep past her."

The whispered words were passed. The *Arrow* was dark. With her sails down there wasn't much of her to be seen gliding along the still surface. Thorton trembled. "Please let it be English," he prayed. His head swiveled over his shoulder. The *guardacostas* remained outside. Did they know which it was? Did they give up the pursuit thinking him safe in the embrace of the British, or were they cats waiting at the mouse hole for their consort to flush him? Sweat trickled down his neck.

Duke Henrique enjoyed the Turkish luxury of Achmed's cabin, but it was still a wooden box barely eight feet square. How could he sit silently in the dark, not knowing what fate was overtaking him? He came out on deck by himself. He kept his old woman's disguise and hobbled along the gunwale. He wasn't sure about shipboard protocol and stayed in the waist, looking up at Captain Thorton and Shakil Effendi. Achmed the envoy was up there and the officers, too.

Everything and everyone was very quiet, and the quietness of the men as they strained at the oars was peculiar. He hobbled up to the black boatswain and whispered petulantly, "What's the matter? Why aren't we celebrating our escape?"

"Hush, old woman," Wafor hissed. "That's why." He pointed at the dark shadow of the frigate on the water. No lanterns glowed on her bow or masts. No light escaped from her binnacle.

"What is it?" Henrique asked in a whisper.

"We don't know. Spanish or English. Friend or foe."

"Aren't we too close?"

"We are. Unfortunately we must pass her to reach Gibraltar. Now get below and keep quiet."

Henrique had played the role of the spoiled pawn so long that he almost lost his temper with the man, but upon reflection, an old woman would not act that way, so he sniffed, tucked his chin into his shawl, and shuffled away. Yet the charade chafed him. He, who had been a prisoner so long, found himself a prisoner still. How he longed to throw off this disguise and take a man's place on the silent poop deck with the other men! He mounted two steps before a marine intercepted him.

"Hey, old biddy, get down!" The marine remonstrated forcefully but quietly with him.

"Can't an old woman peek—"

"Damn it, no! Get below, wench!"

Henrique retreated under the break of the poop but he didn't go below. He hunkered there, stoop-shouldered and tottering, as his role required.

"God, that's the ugliest old woman I've ever seen!" one of the sailors exclaimed.

Laughter answered him.

"Not so loud, she'll hear you!" someone remonstrated.

The whispers were coarse, but not quiet enough. Thorton flew halfway down the steps and hissed, "Corporal! Take the names of those men!"

The marine marched over and got their names. They shut up.

Thorton retreated to the poop deck and whispered further orders. Men ran on tiptoe to their battle stations in the forecastle and loaded the guns as quietly as they could. The same happened on the poop deck. The swivels along the gunwales were likewise manned.

Suddenly a voice rang out on the frigate. It carried well across the still waters. *"Barco a la vista!"*

Men grew restless at the sound of Spanish.

"Keep quiet! Keep rowing!" Thorton hissed. Again his whispered orders were passed. The men settled down.

Lights broke out on the Spanish frigate. A clear voice hailed them, *"¿Cuál barco?"*

Thorton had an excellent command of Spanish and called back, *"Santa Teresa!* We're running from corsairs!"

They passed in front of the frigate's bow at a distance of a hundred yards. The word 'corsairs' excited the Spanish. Praise Allah it had been too dark for the shore to read the signals from the Spanish squadron. Praise Allah that the guards of Algeciras were not nearly as concerned about one runaway galiot as the guards of Sebta. They didn't know what precious cargo Thorton carried.

Noise and lights stirred aboard the frigate. She hauled her anchor and put out her sweeps. She had a dozen of them and she used them to stroke towards the mouth of the bay to investigate. As the frigate pulled away from them, Thorton had a good view of the stern. The windows of the great cabin were lit up and he saw figures limned against the glass. He put the spyglass to his eye and studied them. He could not make them out, but he could tell that they were looking at the *Arrow*. Suddenly the figures bolted from the cabin. The frigate swung ponderously back towards them. A warning shot fired from her bow.

The charade was over. They had been discovered. Thorton bellowed, "Row, damn you! Row like all the fires in hell were breathing down your necks!"

The men bent their backs with a superhuman effort and the galiot gained speed. That was when Thorton saw the second frigate in the distance. She spit fire in their direction.

"No no no no no," he moaned. She was a mile away and didn't have the range. Her shots fell short. Even so, he must cross her path to reach Gibraltar. "North," he cried. There was no need for silence now.

The galiot's course changed. He glanced over his shoulder. The first frigate was sweeping hard, but her dozen oars manned by two men each were no match for the *Arrow's* fifty oars with four men each. The *Arrow* glided away but was still in range. The frigate slowly swung her broadside around.

"Helm a-lee! Left wheel! Fire as she bears!" His bellowed orders could be heard the length of the ship.

He would not give his vulnerable stern to the enemy. A single shot to the rudder at close range and the *Arrow* would be a sitting duck. He dared not tarry, either, or the second frigate would come up on him. He had to swat her nose as hard as he could, then run as far and fast as the narrow confines of Algeciras Bay would let him. His haven had become his trap.

The *Arrow* spun in place. Her larboard sweeps backed, her starboard sweeps pulled, spinning her around to bring her bow guns into action. With such a maneuver she could turn completely around within her own length. The range was less than a hundred yards. "Aim well, Archie," Thorton prayed.

The two massive thirty-two pounders roared and sent out tongues of flame eight feet long. A resounding double crack echoed across the water. The four smaller guns spoke a second after the big guns. Thorton clapped his spyglass to his eye and scanned the frigate desperately.

"Well done, Maynard!" In his excitement he called the lieutenant by his English name. "My compliments to Lt. Aruj, and tell him do it again as fast as he can."

Midshipman Kaashifa was the messenger on duty. He ran.

One of the shots smacked into the frigate's bow next to the gammon knee. The bowsprit was not blown away, but it canted up at an unnatural angle. The forestay lost its tension, which let the foremast lean backwards. The cries of the wounded carried across the water. The *Arrow* cheered.

"Back oars!" The *Arrow* rowed in reverse almost as well as she rowed forward. Her stern tapered in a sleek fish-like shape. She was not pink-sterned, but narrow enough. Narrower than the frigate. Thorton looked for the other frigate and saw the splash of white as the sweeps dipped and swung. She was slowly rowing up on the them.

Thorton swept his glass over the enemy deck. He could only fight one ship at a time. To be doubled was to be doomed. Suddenly his glass swept back and he looked again. There. That man. His arm in a sling. Maybe . . . Thorton slammed his glass shut and shoved it in his pocket.

"Bring me the tack, I'm going up!" He ran down to the deck, seized the woolding at the bottom of the lateen antenna, and shinnied up. Halfway up he raised his glass.

The deck of the Spaniard was a bustle of activity—but not nearly as much activity as there ought to be. He saw the man with his arm in a sling, or maybe another wounded man. There were some other white blurs that were bandages wrapped around skulls and other body parts.

He howled, "She's undermanned and wounded! Charge! Prepare to board! Double grape in all the guns! Stand by swivels!"

That put heart into all of them. In a state of high excitement the men stroked the sweeps and raced toward the enemy. Aboard the frigate there was panic. In the darkness they were not entirely sure what they were up against. Two sails, lateen, and aggressive—a corsair brig, perhaps? In which case, they would receive a sharp broadside and be overwhelmed by boarders. They had barely enough men to work one set of guns.

The bow guns spoke again. The distance was only fifty yards. Aruj was aiming for her foremast and he got it. It was not a direct blow, but it weakened the poorly supported timber. It toppled like a tree being felled. Tangled in lines and sails, it fouled and hung up. Half of it trailed over the bow while half was caught on deck.

"Bow to bow!" Thorton roared. He did not want the frigate's broadsides to have a shot at him. Her broadsides would shatter the galiot. The rowers sweated and pulled, and the galiot shot across the calm waters. When the two bows crashed together the grappling hooks were thrown. Marines in the rigging peppered the enemy as they attempted to cut loose the debris. The swivels barked and sent their loads of grape across the defenders trying to cut away the grapples. Marines in the frigate's tops responded in kind. Balls whined and splattered against the poop deck. Thorton and his officers were under fire.

"Shakil, go below! Make sure the old woman is safe!"

Shakil ran as fast as his legs would carry him. He was glad to be out of the maelstrom of combat but was frightened for Thorton. He prayed to Allah as he ran. He found the excited duke in the coach. Henrique wanted to stay and watch the battle, but Shakil dragged him down the companionway to the deck below.

"You'll be safer below the waterline, Your Grace!"

The men-at-arms abandoned their oars and snatched up their scimitars. They charged across the boarding bridge formed by the galiot's sturdy prow. Shrieking their battle cries, they fought their way onto the frigate.

Thorton glanced back and saw the other frigate coming up. "Cut grapples!" The mercenaries would have to fend for themselves. Either they would take her, or they wouldn't. Thorton dared not wait.

The prow of the *Arrow* fouled in the frigate's debris. She stalled as the few men left to work her sweeps tried to back oars and couldn't. "Cut that wreckage loose!" Thorton shouted.

Aruj was in command of the forecastle. He hopped on his wooden leg and exhorted his men. Axes hacked and the frigate's foremast fell the rest of the way. Part of it flopped over the *Arrow's* prow and part landed in the sea. They shoved and hacked and it all went over the side.

"Hard to starboard! Out sweeps!" Thorton's own sailors had to man the oars. There weren't as many of them as mercenaries, but most of them were experienced rowers hardened by their previous captivity aboard a Spanish galley. They knew how to row and they had the backs for it. The *Arrow* turned with majestic slowness, but gained way as she went.

"Bring her guns to bear! Fire when ready!"

In the minutes of battle the second frigate had halved the distance. She swung slowly and presented her starboard broadside. Shot whined and splashed. Splinters flew. She had the range. All hell broke loose then: the first frigate fired her broadside at point blank range. The *Arrow* was caught between two fires. The larboard quarter was pocked with multiple holes and Thorton lost his footing as the *Arrow* shuddered beneath him. He flopped on the deck and somebody shouted, "The captain's down!"

Thorton leaped instantly to his feet. "Belay that prattling, you weak-minded whoresons!" he roared.

Should the men think their captain was dead they'd lose heart and he needed everything they had: heart, balls, sinews, spine, spleen, stomach, guts. Hell, he wanted their very toenails. Any sliver of effort might be the difference between victory and defeat. They cheered when they heard him cursing them; it was proof their captain was still alive.

Thorton got his bearings, decided he'd just have to hope the mercenaries silenced those guns soon, and turned his attention to the other frigate. "Charge!" he roared.

The crew threw their weight on the oars. She gathered speed. It took five minutes to cross the distance to the other frigate—enough time enough for her to load and run out a second broadside. The *Arrow* took it on the nose. Aruj had lost his leg in just such a barrage a few months back. Thorton didn't stop. When the frigate saw the galiot charging her, she fled. She knew what kind of forces corsairs carried: hundreds of bloodthirsty warriors hungry for the chance of worldly wealth if they lived and Paradise if they died. She was just as undermanned and wounded as her consort. Thorton didn't know that, but he saw her nerve fail.

"Chase her down! We'll take her!"

The frigate fled down the glassy waters of Algeciras Bay with the galiot in hot pursuit.

When Shakil heard them cry that the captain was down, he went pale and cold. When he heard Thorton roaring and very much alive he sprang to his feet and ran out on deck. He clawed his way up the shattered steps to the poop deck. Thorton was at the quarterdeck rail, leaning forward, hands gripping the top, shouting, "Take her, you misbegotten sons of bitches! TAKE HER!"

Shakil paused as he came onto the poop deck. Looking aft he saw the stern lantern of the frigate glowing brightly. Something red and gold fluttered down and pooled on the quarterdeck. A moment later the purple flag of Sallee rose up. Beneath it was the captured flag of Spain. "She struck! They took her!" he cried in jubilation.

Thorton's head snapped around. A mighty roar came from the throats of the victors. They manned the sweeps and charged in pursuit of the fleeing frigate. Thorton smiled grimly. Aruj was not slack; the *Arrow's* bow guns fired again and splashes fell around the stern of the fleeing frigate. One of them struck home and the sound of shattering glass came across the waters. The *Arrow* ran after her, and Thorton grinned as they gained. The lights of Gibraltar grew brighter and nearer on the right bow. Shakil laid his hand on Thorton's sleeve.

"*Habibi*. We fight to deliver Duke Henrique to the safety of Gibraltar."

Thorton hardly knew him. His eyes were alight with battle fever. He blinked. He stared at Shakil, then looked to the shore. The English battleships were awake and their flagship had run up signals.

"We'll take her. You'll see. She won't fight."

The galiot overhauled the running frigate a few minutes later. Aruj held his fire until he was positive of his shot, then the thirty-two pounders roared. They smashed in the stern of the frigate. Shattered glass and wood scattered in the wine dark sea. The frigate's sternchasers barked. A ball went skimming down the galiot's deck and shattered the companion hatch, caromed off it, and knocked around inside the coach for a bit.

"Ram her! Prepare boarders!" Thorton shouted.

The prow of the galiot was a sturdy spur. As recently as a hundred years before they had been used for ramming, until mariners realized that they served as an excellent location for belaying a sail. Ramming was no longer an orthodox tactic, but the galiot an old-fashioned vessel and the frigate was weak in the stern.

The ramming was not as hard as Thorton had hoped. The frigate tried to turn and let him have the blast from her larboard guns. Some of the shots hit his quarter. His cabin and the chartroom were going to be a mess after this. Some of the sweeps were lost as the men who worked them were wounded. Both vessels lurched as the prow caught in the shattered frame of the frigate's stern. The sound of grinding timbers and breaking glass filled the night as the last of her windows came apart.

Aruj fired his swivels as defenders rushed into the captain's cabin. They fell back, but knowing that he had to reload, took advantage of the opportunity to leap over the dead and charge into the room.

Aruj was ready for them. "Fire number three."

The medium-sized gun in the bow thundered. With the gun practically aboard the frigate he couldn't miss. The ball blew through the bodies like tissue paper and smashed through the bulkhead. The wounded screamed. Frantic men jumped back and scrambled to escape the cabin.

Meanwhile, the Spanish on the frigate's quarterdeck were attempting to depress the stern guns enough to defend. Sallee marines threw grappling hooks and swarmed up the carved and ornamented stern. The *Arrow's* sharpshooters in the rigging picked off defenders, but still some of the brown-coated marines fell. Somebody tossed a grenade up there. There was a blast, then a lull. Brown coats swarmed over the frigate's tafferel. More boarders poured over the *Arrow's* prow and into the captain's cabin. The defenders gathered outside the captain's cabin to get them as they came through the door one by one.

Aruj shouted, "*Arrow*, down!"

The boarders dropped. He fired the fourth gun. Due to the angle of the prow he had to traverse the gun. He aimed it not at the door, but the space next to it. The shot blasted through the bulkhead and scattered the men gathered outside the door. The bulkhead might have held against swordsmen—but not a twelve pound shot fired at point blank range. The shot was so close that a Sallee man howled as he was burned by the muzzle blast. His fellows left him writhing on the deck as they fought their way through the door and shattered bulkhead.

Thorton looked over his shoulder as the captured frigate overhauled them. He shouted orders across to them, "Give her a broadside! Take her by the bow!"

The captured frigate passed slowly and presented her starboard with all guns run out. The second frigate saw the purple flag of the Sallee Republic glowing in the light of the stern lantern and knew they were doomed. The guns thundered. The flag of Spain came down.

They secured the second frigate, locking her crew in the hold below while a prize crew manned her above. The triumphant *Arrow* ushered her prizes towards Gibraltar. They hove to near the frigate at the end of the English line. Thorton was close enough he could read the frigate's signals, "Sallee ship, send boat."

"Foster, you have the conn. I'm going over. I won't be long. Remain alert to fend off a Spanish counterattack."

"Aye aye, sir."

"My compliments to the crew. Excellent work tonight."

"Thank you, sir."

Thorton went over the side into his gig. The little boat shot across the placid waters.

"What ship?" the English boatswain's mate hailed them.

"*Arrow*," came the reply, so they knew a captain was coming. In a very real sense, the captain *was* the ship, and so he was known by the ship's name.

Thorton heard the pipes calling the sideboys to line up for a captain and clambered over the gunwale in high spirits. He paused as Lt. Perry stepped forward and said, "Welcome home, Mr. Thorton. Arrest him."

CHAPTER 8 : THORTON'S ARREST

Thorton was escorted onto the quarterdeck of the frigate by Perry and a pair of marines. He dreaded coming face to face with Captain Bishop, but it was not Bishop who received him. The new captain was a man as tall as Thorton but thinner and older. He was forty at least, judging by the deep lines that ran from the corners of his nose to his down-turned mouth. His coat was serviceable, plain, and well-mended dark blue serge. His cocked hat had seen better days but was still presentable. He had a piercing blue stare. Thorton stopped in front of him.

Slowly recognition dawned. "Ebenezer Horner!" Thorton had never met him, but he'd seen him, read about him, and knew exactly what he owed the man. "Where is Captain Bishop?"

"Convalescing in England. He had a heart attack in France. I am his substitute. If he recovers the ship will be his again. If not . . ." He let the words trail off. "So you are the notorious Peter Thorton."

Thorton straightened his back and said, "Peter Rais Thorton, captain of the Sallee galiot *Arrow*, sir."

"Galiot?" Horner's bushy eyebrows shot up into his hat. He turned and looked at the dark form of the galiot hove to two cables away. Her great stern lanthorn was lit and the purple flag of Sallee glowed in its light. "You attacked two Spanish frigates with a *galiot?*"

"Aye, sir. Captured them, too." Thorton could not help sounding smug about it.

"What on earth possessed you to throw a galiot against a pair of frigates?"

"Necessity, sir. There are six xebecs outside the mouth of Algeciras. They were chasing us."

Horner stared at him. "You are either mad or a firebrand."

Thorton's mouth crooked a little. "Said the kettle to the pot. You drove into a squadron of French frigates to rescue the *Dauntless*. I know, sir, because I was on the *Dauntless*." He squared his shoulders. "We are captains, sir. We do what circumstances require."

Horner sighed heavily. "We do indeed. It pains me to say it, but the circumstances require me to arrest you and turn you over for court martial. You know the charges."

"No, sir. I don't."

"Articles One, Two, Fifteen, Twenty-Eight, Thirty-Two and Thirty-Five. I imagine they can think of others if they exert themselves."

Thorton staggered. The *Articles of War* spelled out exactly what was expected of His Britannic Majesty's navy and the penalties for violating those expectations. One established the Church of England in the fleet. Two covered blasphemy and other scandalous conduct. Fifteen was the prohibition on desertion. Twenty-Eight prohibited the detestable and unnatural sin of sodomy and buggery. Thirty-Two covered conduct unbecoming an officer. Thirty-Five covered anything not explicitly spelled out in the others. Fifteen and Twenty-Eight carried the death penalty.

"Will you give me your parole, or do I need to clap you in irons?" Horner asked him levelly. Again that merciless stare.

Thorton found his voice. "You have my parole, sir." It was a faint tenor that Horner and Perry had to strain to hear. He unbuckled his sword belt.

"Very well. Mr. Perry tells me you are a man of honor according to your lights. You will serve as the fourth lieutenant of the *Ajax* until the court martial decides otherwise. I shall find something useful to do with you."

"I know the Spanish signal book by heart, sir." Thorton's voice sounded hollow even to him.

"Excellent. Have you been a signalman before?"

"Aye, sir. I was the signalman on the *Dauntless.*"

Horner fell silent for a long moment as he studied Thorton. "You were promoted for your part in that action, weren't you?"

Thorton nodded, surprised and immensely gratified that the great Horner knew it. "Aye, sir."

Horner spoke again. "I'm afraid you'll have to bunk with the midshipmen. The *Ajax* isn't rated for four lieutenants."

"Aye aye, sir. May I send for my dunnage?"

"You may."

"And my servant, too?"

"Yes, we'll read him in. We can always use more hands."

"Sir! He is a Sallee sailor. You cannot press a member of a friendly navy!"

Horner ruminated a bit. "Very well. See that he either makes himself useful or stays out of the way. I'm not running a hotel for frivolous gentlemen."

"Aye aye, sir."

"You're out of uniform, Lieutenant. Get dressed and report to me in my cabin."

Thorton looked down at the long purple coat. The crossed scimitars of his Sallee rank seemed a hollow mockery. He'd just thrashed two Spanish frigates with a galiot, and here he was, under arrest and busted back to signalman. He sighed deeply. "Aye aye, sir." There was nothing else to be said. Not in English.

A boat was sent to the *Arrow*. The news of Thorton's arrest and detention by the English caused considerable consternation, but his steward and the sea chest arrived promptly. The foresighted Ra'uf brought with him provisions for his master's table, including couscous, oranges, coffee, cinnamon, and other items likely to be in short supply aboard a *ferenghi*[1] vessel.

The Spanish fortress did not know who was aboard the *Arrow* and did not press the matter. The fleet in Algeciras was composed of the casualties from the war in the Mediterranean. The badly trounced vessels had been sent in for repairs while their crews had been stripped of able men to replace casualties in other vessels still in the line of battle. The wounded were left in Algeciras.

Seventeen Spanish vessels were in the bay. Two were in dry dock, two drawn up on the beach, and the rest anchored in a line just in case the much smaller British force decided to get frisky. British vessels damaged in the fray had been left behind for repairs and to defend Gibraltar. Eventually the Spaniards would finish repairs. Gibraltar was bracing for an attack.

The single lantern in the gunroom shed a warm radiance. The doors were closed and there were no windows. The tiller swept overhead, requiring the occupants to be alert and duck whenever course was changed. With a sigh Thorton opened his sea chest and took out his English coat. It was the second hand coat Perry had given him a lifetime ago. He had a good cocked hat which was a gift from Achmed (who had worn it as part of his disguise while spying in London). He had his old blue breeches, a good white waistcoat and linen shirts, new stocks and cravats, silk stockings, new brown shoes. His hair was bound into a pigtail. He doubled it up into a club. He brushed the coat and got dressed. The lieutenant's braid on his collar made him sigh. In Sallee he had been a captain, found a lover, converted to a religion he believed in, and was free to speak his mind. He had done so very boldly to some important people. He dared not speak a word aboard the *Ajax* or in any British port. Anything he said could be used against him. They thought him a deserter, a turncoat, a renegade, and a sodomite. He hung his head.

---

[1] *ferenghi* Turkish (lit. 'French') European or Western.

With wooden steps he climbed to the berth deck and from there to the weather deck. He encountered Perry loitering in the coach.

Perry erupted when he saw Thorton. "Is that my old coat? The one I gave you?"

Thorton nodded.

Perry pounced on him and dragged it from his shoulders. "I didn't give it to you so you could disgrace it!" he shouted.

Thorton let Perry pull the coat off his body. Shame colored his cheeks and he said nothing. This is how it would be day after day until the court martial. Sailors loitering nearby sneered at him. One of them made a show of spitting over the side. Thorton adjusted his stock. It felt like the noose was already around his neck.

The marine at the captain's door let him knock. How very familiar everything was, how dreadfully familiar. He was glad it wasn't Bishop in the stateroom, but Horner was even worse. Ebenezer Horner was one of England's truly great captains. Why couldn't he have been the captain of the *Ajax* in the first place? None of this would have happened if Horner had been captain from the start. Thorton cursed himself for a fool. He should have leaped for the *Ajax* that morning Tangle had drawn along side. If he had stayed with the *Ajax*, he could have had Horner for his captain. What a stroke of luck! He had missed it through his own folly.

"Enter," came the command from inside.

He opened the door, ducked under the lintel, and stepped inside. He shut the door and stood stiffly at attention with his hat over his heart. Horner was standing by the stern windows. One was raised up to let in the damp night air. The room was stuffy even so. He turned around to examine the lieutenant.

"You are out of uniform, mister."

"I don't have a coat, sir."

He'd thrown out his own shabby old coat last time he packed his sea chest. He hadn't thought he'd need it. Why he'd kept the coat Perry gave him he couldn't say, unless it was nostalgia for the man who used to be his friend. He fixed his gaze on the beam above Horner's head. Horner's hat was off and the hair on top of his head was getting thin. Horner, hero that he was, had had little prize money for his efforts. He was a dogged hound who did what his master told him even when it didn't profit him. He believed in duty. Such a man would have no mercy or patience for Thorton's foolishness. A lesser captain might have understood and forgiven.

"Why not?" His tone suggested that he did not expect Thorton's answer to be satisfactory.

Thorton colored again. He cleared his throat. "My coat was worn out, so Mr. Perry gave me his old coat last spring. Just now he saw me wearing it and took it back."

Horner clasped his hands behind his back. He grunted. "Purchase a length of blue wool from the pursuer in the morning and have a new coat made."

"Aye aye, sir."

Horner continued staring at him. Thorton continued staring at the beam over the captain's head. Neither of them said anything. For most of his life Thorton had been a taciturn man. The habit returned readily. Horner was not given to prattle. The silence lengthened.

Finally Horner spoke. "You have a lot of explaining to do, mister." It wasn't a question, so Thorton remained silent. "Well?"

"I'm sorry, sir. What is the question?"

Horner spread his hands. "What do you have to say in response to the charges?"

"I am guilty of violating Article One, sir. I am a Muslim."

"And the others?"

"I am not guilty of violating Fifteen and Twenty-Eight. The others I am unsure of since I don't know the details, sir."

"What is your defense for Fifteen?"

Thorton had to compose himself to speak naturally. "I was carried off against my will by the Sallee rover, Isam Rais Tangueli. After I converted to Islam, Acting Captain Perry requested my resignation and I gave it to him. I did not leave the service voluntarily, sir. I made every effort to return to duty until Captain Perry told me I couldn't."

Horner's eyes narrowed. "Do you have it in writing?"

"I have his receipt and a copy of my letter of resignation, sir."

"Let me see them."

"They're in my sea chest."

"Fetch them."

Thorton went down to the gunroom. The hazing had already begun. His Sallee coat was drenched in bilge water and lying over his chest. It stank. The back was ripped as if someone had stabbed him in the back. Thorton stood and stared at it. He blinked back tears. He looked around, but nobody was near. Who had done it? Perry? Somebody else? He would never know. He had not thought Perry so spiteful, but given that Article Twenty-Eight was laid against him, Perry must have talked. Thorton moved the wet coat aside and hunted up his papers. The contents of the chest were disturbed and his Arabic sextant was missing. Coming upstairs again, he passed the word for Ra'uf. The man appeared promptly and Thorton sent him to the gunroom to mend and clean his coat.

With heavy steps the wayward officer returned to the captain's cabin. The interview took up where it had left off. Thorton didn't mention the hazing. Englishmen did far worse to each other on some ships and for less reason. Horner settled at the desk and read Thorton's papers in silence. Finally he looked up.

"Lt. Perry overstepped his authority by acting as captain in the absence of Mssrs. Bishop and Forsythe. He has already been disciplined for it. However, you erred by not waiting for an answer from the Admiralty. You are absent without leave."

Thorton gave him a stunned look. "But I am a Muslim, sir. A man cannot serve as an officer if he is not in good standing with the Church of England."

Horner sat heavily in a chair. "Very true. However it is for the Admiralty to decide and for you to wait."

"But sir—"

"Sit, Thorton. Tell me everything."

Thorton had no intention of telling the man 'everything,' but he sat on the locker under the window. He stared dumbly at the man and wondered where to begin. He never got the chance. A commotion at the side of the frigate interrupted. Horner pinched the bridge of his nose like a man beset by fools. After he composed himself he said, "Pray continue," but somebody was knocking at the door.

"Enter!"

Perry burst in. "Your pardon, sir, but there's an old woman in a boat that says she's the King of Portugal and wants to talk to you. Mr. Achmed and another rover are with her!"

Thorton smiled. "That'll be Henrique, Duke of Coimbra. Whatever he has to say to you is more important than anything I might say."

Horner stared at him. "You're jesting with me."

Thorton shook his head. "That's why we were being chased by six Spanish xebecs, sir."

"You could have mentioned this sooner, Thorton."

"I apologize. I was selfish to waste time worrying about being hanged."

Horner's eyes narrowed again. "Impertinence does not become you, mister. The charges are serious." His voice sounded a warning.

Thorton slumped a little. "Aye aye, sir."

Horner rose. To Perry he said, "I'm coming."

Thorton decided to follow him on deck. Six months ago he would not have dared to move from where he was put. Horner was right. He was impertinent. Something about being a captain in his own right had given him independent ideas.

Henrique, encumbered by skirts and bonnet, managed the climb up the battens and flopped over the gunwale. He landed in a heap on the deck, picked himself up, and cursed in Portuguese. He struck a pose, limp wrist extended haughtily. His other hand was on his hip, "Henrique, Duke of Coimbra, and rightful King of Portugal at your service, sirrah. Whom have I the dubious pleasure of addressing?" He spoke a lisping Castilian Spanish.

Shakil came over the gunwale next and put himself beside the mad duke. His eyes lit when he saw Thorton with his neck still unstretched. He was properly dressed in his Sallee uniform. Next Achmed came over the side with a little more dignity than the younger men. He was soberly dressed in a dark green short jacket, brown-striped pantaloons, and turban. His scimitar hung at his hip.

Horner looked the bizarre figure of the duke up and down, looked at the two rovers who seemed to be taking him seriously, and replied, "Ebenezer Horner, captain of His Britannic Majesty's frigate *Ajax*. What evidence do you have to prove your identity?" He spoke Spanish fluently but with a marked English accent.

Shakil replied, "I'm Shakil bin Nakih, brother-in-law of Captain Tangle. I snatched him from under the noses of his Spanish guards. He was wearing a lemon velvet suit. If you ask your agent in Sebta, they can verify his identity." He spoke Spanish well enough.

Achmed extended a heavy cream colored envelope. "My passport and credentials. I'm Achmed bin Mamoud, envoy from the Sallee Republic to England. I can vouch for His Grace's identity."

Horner took them, but before he could look at them, Henrique opened the bosom of his dress and hauled out a leather thong with a signet ring on it. He held it up. "This is signet of Coimbra."

Horner inspected it, then Henrique removed it from the thong and put it on his hand.

"I'm afraid I'm not well-versed in Portuguese heraldry, so I can't evaluate your evidence," Horner said. "I suggest you pay a call on the commodore. You might want to change before you do so."

Duke Henrique was not a man to be balked. His eyes flashed and he said, "I would, but you've arrested my captain. I want him back."

Horner was bland. "You'll need to discuss it with Commodore Whittingdon."

"Captain Thorton rescued me!"

"Mr. Thorton is a commissioned officer of the British navy. He didn't have permission to rescue you."

Henrique's eyes narrowed as he attempted to determine if Horner was jesting with him. Horner's dour face was devoid of humor. Henrique continued, "If you humiliate Portugal's savior, I shall be very put out. 'Twill bode ill for a treaty between your country and mine."

Horner did not care for the guest at all. "We don't plan to humiliate him. We plan to hang him. Now if you will excuse me, Commodore Whittingdon is waiting. I won't delay you. Lt. Wright! Convey His Grace to the *Pegasus*."

Achmed said, "The Sallee Republic takes a dim view of the arrest of our subject and officer, Peter Rais Thorton. If the matter is not resolved to our satisfaction, it will further strain relations between our countries."

Horner shrugged. "I have orders from the Admiralty. The commodore is my superior. You must appeal to him."

"I am going directly to the commodore!" Henrique stomped his foot and made his skirt flounce.

Lt. Wright, the new third lieutenant and Thorton's replacement, said, "Your boat, Your Grace." He did his best to keep a straight face.

Horner turned his back on the Portuguese and strode into the coach. He called over his shoulder, "Mr. Thorton!"

Thorton followed him. He could not believe they would really court martial the man who had delivered the heir to the throne of Portugal to them. All the same Horner's rigid back had him worried.

CHAPTER 9 : AN OLD SECRET

Horner dropped his three-cornered hat on the table. Without it he could just barely stand up straight under the deckhead. He stood at the stern and stared out into the darkness with his hands clasped behind his back. He was silent for a long time. Thorton stood with his hat in the crook of his arm and the damp slowly seeping into him. It was August, but the first chill of autumn was giving its warning. He wished he had a coat. Finally Horner turned around.

"Mr. Perry says you had an improper relationship with Captain Tangueli." He could pronounce the name correctly, unlike most Englishmen.

"We did not violate Article Twenty-Eight, sir."

Horner continued staring at him with his bushy eyebrows and piercing blue eyes. Thorton remained steadfast under his gaze.

"But you admit there was a relationship?"

Thorton relaxed a little. "He is my commanding officer in the Sallee navy, and a good friend. I respect him highly. He is the greatest captain I have ever had the privilege of serving under."

Horner contemplated this. Only after a little silence fell did it occur to Thorton that Horner might feel insulted. He gave the man a worried look. Bishop and Tangle were both vain men. Had it been either of them Thorton would have been in trouble. Horner did not react to the remark.

"Are you . . . 'in love' with him?" It was a distasteful subject and Horner was dancing around it as delicately as he could.

Thorton sucked in a deep breath. Making up his mind, he replied quietly, "No, sir. I am in love with Shakil bin Nakih, who rescued the Duke of Coimbra. My affectation for Isam Rais is what a man gives to someone he honors and admires."

Horner's eyes were hooded. He continued clasping his hands behind his back as he studied Thorton. "Is your relationship carnal?"

Color appeared on Thorton's cheeks. "We have kissed and hugged. Nothing more."

"Can you swear to me by whatever you hold holy that you have never at any time violated Article Twenty-Eight?" Horner's iron voice nailed him to the floor.

Thorton paled. "No sir." His hand crushed the brim of his hat as it tightened. His stomach tied itself into a square knot and he felt ill. He was trapped in the manacle of Horner's gaze.

"If not Tangueli or Shakil, then who? Was it Lt. Perry?"

The younger man swallowed hard. He was unable to lie or refuse to answer. He could not allow Perry's reputation be damaged by such a suspicion. He shook his head and whispered, "No, sir. Not Roger. He is not that sort of man. He is a ladies man."

Horner stared at him with that implacable stare. "Who?"

Thorton did not want to tell the story, but there was no way out of it. "When I was first pressed aboard the *Marigold* . . . the boatswain's mate . . . pestered me for favors." Thorton's voice faltered. All the horrible details that he had tried to blot out of his mind came rushing back. He swayed on his feet.

Horner had not expected such a story. He thought he was rooting out corruption aboard the *Ajax*. "How old were you?" His voice was surprisingly gentle.

"Nineteen, sir."

Horner did not want to ask but his duty drove him. "What happened?"

Thorton was dizzy. "He got his friends to help, and they caught me below decks. They threw me over a barrel—" He struggled for composure. "And took turns with me." He could not bring himself to say exactly what they had done, but Horner knew well enough. Thorton's voice trembled. "So you see, sir, I understand perfectly well why Article Twenty-Eight exists, and I support it entirely."

"Sit down before you fall down, Thorton." Horner pulled the chair from behind the desk and put it behind his knees.

Thorton plunked his butt down hardly aware of what he did. He was staring into the darkness of the past. Horner walked around the desk and opened the credenza. He brought brandy, set a glass by Thorton's elbow, and poured. He poured one for himself as well and sat down on the locker facing the younger man. "Drink."

Thorton blinked blankly at him, then took the glass and drank, then coughed.

When Thorton could breathe again, Horner asked, "Did you report it to your superior officer?"

Thorton shook his head.

"Why not?" Horner thought he knew, but he went through the formalities."

"Lt. White found me. They'd called all hands on deck and I didn't go. He came looking for me. I—I couldn't get up. He found me like that. He told me not to tell anyone, to get dressed and hurry up on deck. I was whipped for being late." That pained him. It hadn't been his fault, but he had been punished all the same. He drank more brandy.

Horner's face was grave as he refilled the brandy. "What did Lt. White do about it?"

"I don't think he did anything, sir."

"Nothing?"

"Not to my knowledge, sir," Thorton replied apologetically.

Horner's face tightened and Thorton saw that he was angry. The reluctant lieutenant drank more brandy. "I'm sorry, sir." He was acutely miserable. "I never told anyone. I tried hard to be a good sailor and follow the rules. I never tried to cause any trouble. Maybe I'm not cut out for the navy."

The captain's formidable reserve broke enough to say, "Any man that can whip a pair of frigates with nothing more than a galiot is the kind of officer England needs."

Thorton hung his head. "It doesn't matter, does it? I am a man who loves his own sex. I can't help it. I tried not to. I didn't want to."

It was Horner's turn to drink brandy and struggle for words. "You pose a difficult question, Mr. Thorton."

Thorton rubbed a hand over his face. "They're going to hang me, aren't they?"

Horner didn't answer.

Thorton reached inside for the fortitude to bear this. How many times had he reached down deep into his soul and wondered if he had what it took. Each time he grabbed onto something, something he couldn't even name, and held it tight. He endured whatever he had to endure. Battle held no fear for him; if he died it meant an end to struggle and peace at last. Yet he did not want to hang. The thought of his body dangling in midair, branded with shame, while the fleet watched . . . that was more than he could bear. But bear it he must. Everything must be born.

"It depends on whose testimony they believe. Perry insinuates that you and Tangueli were intimate." Horner knocked back the rest of his brandy and poured another. "'Twould be a waste to hang you."

It was a peculiar sort of compliment but Thorton was grateful for it. "Thank you, sir." He was worried though. Perry had talked. He drank again and resigned himself to his fate. What else could he do? He never thought to hurl himself through Horner's open window and swim for it. Instead, once he accepted the reality of his hanging, he started thinking about what needed to be done before he was dead. "May I send orders to my ship, sir? They will need direction."

"Yes. Use my desk." Horner rose and set paper, quill, and ink well on the desk.

Thorton moved the chair around behind the desk and took up a quill. He thought a long time what he would write, then penned a letter to Shakil in simple Arabic. Then he penned his orders to his crew. He thought they might try to rescue him; he forbid it. He forbid Foster, Aruj, or any other Englishman to set foot ashore or on any English ship for fear they would be arrested. If rescuing the Duke of Coimbra could not protect him, there would be no mercy for them at all. They were ordinary men who had gone over willingly. They had truly deserted. He ordered them to make a run for Zokhara and take the Duke of Coimbra with them. That was more important than whatever happened to one wayward English lieutenant. Thorton watched the ink drying and tried to comfort himself with the thought that at least he had lived long enough to do something that mattered. If Henrique escaped, Portugal could gain her independence.

Horner asked, "Mr. Thorton. What was Lieutenant White's Christian name?"

Thorton turned white beneath his tan. "I'd rather not say, sir."

Horner nailed him with that iron gaze again. "I asked you a question, mister."

Thorton licked his lips and gave Horner a beseeching look. Horner was a highly competitive and aggressive captain—he had the hunter's instinct to know when his prey was mortally wounded. "Answer, Lieutenant." His voice was cold.

"Zeus. Lieutenant Zeus White." The words came out in a rush. Thorton held his breath and gave Horner a worried look.

There were many men named 'White' in the navy, but only one 'Zeus.' Son of an Oxford professor of Greek, his father was the younger brother of the Earl of Waverly. The Earl just happened to be First Lord of the Admiralty. Zeus White was ascending the ladder of command at a rapid pace as a result.

"Rear-Admiral Zeus White?" Horner was thunderstruck.

Thorton nodded shamefacedly. "Please, sir, I didn't want to say."

Horner poured himself more brandy. "I disapprove of officers who fail to take corrective action for outrageous breaches aboard their vessels. I admit I had thought I might look into the matter, but there is nothing I can do about a rear-admiral."

Thorton gaped at him. "Why?" he asked in confusion.

Horner misunderstood him. "I am told I have excited a certain amount of attention at times, but that is hardly sufficient standing from which to wag my finger at an admiral."

Thorton blinked in confusion. "No, I meant, why do you care? Nobody else ever did."

Horner's eyes darkened and he ran his finger around the rim of his glass. He was silent a long time before he answered. "Naval service is onerous enough without inflicting injustices and indignities upon one another. Men have mutinied for less."

Thorton was completely bewildered, but he said, "Aye, sir." He was silent for a time. Finally he said, "You remind me of Captain Tangle a little."

That pulled Horner out of his brown study. "Do I? I cannot imagine any possible resemblance between myself and a notorious Sallee rover."

Thorton struggled to put his finger on just what it was. Finally he said, "You are both big enough to think about the men under you. Tangle's men would follow him into the mouth of Hell itself, if that's where he lead."

"I have been to Hell, Mr. Thorton, but none of these men have. I pray they never do."

The interview was over.

The sound of hammering resounded off and on through the night. The galiot and her prizes were making repairs. Her boats went ashore and fetched water and landed the worst of the Spanish casualties. Their lanterns bobbed and the sound of weary Arabic oaths came to them periodically. The stillness of the water magnified everything. Thorton had intended to stand at the rail and watch over his ship all night long if necessary, but he was powerfully tired and his legs felt like they might give out. His stomach growled. He had missed supper; he had been busy fighting a pair of frigates at the time he usually took his evening meal and said his prayers. It had been at least twelve hours since he had eaten. He was tired, downhearted, hungry, and alone. He went below.

Thorton found Ra'uf camped upon his sea chest to protect it from further indignities. The coat was washed and mended and hanging from the beams to dry. With a sigh, he knocked on the door of the midshipmen's cabin.

Maynard's replacement opened it and scowled at him. "What?" he asked in a surly voice. He was a red-headed boy with short hair and a rumpled nightshirt.

"Captain Horner requires me to bunk with the midshipmen since there is no space in the wardroom."

"We don't share our quarters with turncoats, you sod." Add another suspect to list for the desecration of the Sallee uniform.

"What's your name, boy?" Thorton's voice held the whipcrack of authority.

He hesitated, but finally gave it. "Niall Jones, sir."

"Is Chambers in there, teague?" Thorton asked, giving back the insult.

"He's on duty. He doesn't want you in here either. And don't call me 'teague'!"

Jones couldn't be more than thirteen. He was putting up an act of bravado.

"Choose your companions wisely. You won't learn anything that will do you any good from Nelson Chambers."

Jones slammed the door and set the hook. Thorton could break it down easily enough, but what was the point? He didn't want to bunk with them either. He thought about going to the captain, but no captain likes a tattletale. He'd sent Thorton to the gunroom as a punishment. He sighed.

He spoke Spanish to his servant. "I'll make a bed of my sea chest, Ra'uf."

"Aye aye, sir." The Arab got out the sheet and blanket and made a bed for his captain on top of it.

"Get me a hammock tomorrow. I'll hang it in here." Thorton slipped out of his clothes and into the makeshift bed. The waters of Algeciras Bay were calm, otherwise the rocking of the ship would have pitched him off his makeshift bed as soon as he slept. Ra'uf curled up in a blanket on the deck beside him. Like a loyal hound he slept by his master to keep him from harm.

Thorton couldn't sleep. "Ra'uf?"

"Rais?"

"I'm hungry. Do we have any stores?"

"Yes, rais." So the man padded away and returned with an orange and some cheese. Thorton ate enough to quell the hunger pangs and curled up on the chest again. "Wake me before everyone else so that I can pray before they wake up."

"Aye aye, sir."

They settled down again. Thorton still couldn't sleep. "Ra'uf?"

"Rais?"

"They're going to hang me."

"Seems unfair, sir."

"It does, doesn't it? But England was never kind to me."

"You rescued the Duke of Coimbra. That should count for something."

"Shakil rescued him. I just gave him a ride to Gibraltar. The credit goes to Shakil."

"Shakil Effendi did a marvelous thing."

Thorton couldn't sleep. "I love him, Ra'uf."

"I know, sir."

"Do you think it wrong?"

"Love is never wrong, rais."

Thorton sighed. "I miss Sallee. I have hardly been there, but it feels like home."

"You'll see it again, Allah willing."

"Thank you, Ra'uf." The sea chest was hard, but Thorton was exhausted. He slept.

Chapter 10 : The New Midshipmen

Thorton had only slept a couple of hours when he was awakened by Chambers punching his shoulder. He pried open his eyes and stared up into the lantern light. Chambers gave him another hard thump.

"What?" Thorton asked groggily. "What time is it?"

"Captain wants you on deck, traitor." Make that suspect number three for the desecration of the Sallee uniform.

Ra'uf sat up and growled at the boy in Arabic. Ra'uf was not especially tall, but he was a sharp-faced man and needed a shave. He had slept in his drawers and shirt. He looked a ruffian.

Chambers backed up as Ra'uf rose. He swung the lantern angrily. "You stay back, mongrel! 'Tis a crime to strike an officer!"

Thorton sat up. "He doesn't speak English. It will behoove you to remember that I am still your superior officer. You will mend your tone."

He had never had any particular feelings one way or another for Chambers when he had been Bishop's favorite; now he disliked him intensely. The boy had a round face and bad attitude. He was a poor influence on Jones who was young enough to be easily influenced.

Chambers spit on his blanket. Ra'uf tensed and Chambers backed up hastily, but Ra'uf did not spring. The Arab looked to Thorton for guidance. Thorton was shocked and offended by the gesture, but he understood why Chambers did it. He felt the brand of his disgrace keenly.

"Did you dunk my coat, Mr. Chambers?" His tone was severe. Standing there in his nightshirt he did not looking very imposing, but the matter needed to be dealt with immediately.

"Me? I don't know what you're talking about." Chambers glanced involuntarily at the damp coat hanging from the beams.

Thorton gave the boy his best stare. "Then you are a coward and a liar. If a man does something, he should be man enough to say he did it and bear the consequences. If he isn't man enough to own up to it, then he ought not do it."

"You don't know I did it!"

Thorton snorted. "But I do."

"You can't accuse me! Nobody would believe a renegade over a true Englishman!"

"You are insubordinate, mister. Get out."

Chambers fled. Unfortunately he took the lantern with him. Thorton had to fumble in the dark to get dressed. "Ra'uf, guard my chest. That boy will get up to mischief."

"Aye aye, sir."

Thorton went on deck. The night was cool and he had no coat. He was wearing the same clothes he'd worn earlier. He glanced at the stars and saw that it was after midnight. The breeze was faint. He climbed to the quarterdeck where the glow of the binnacle illuminated the helmsman's face. Horner was on deck with a pair of officers. White falling collars showed them to be midshipmen. The tall one carried a satchel over his shoulder. So. Dispatches. Their backs were to him. He stepped up beside them and saluted.

"Lieutenant Peter Thorton reporting for duty, sir." Horner knew who he was; he said it more for the strangers' benefit.

Horner was in his nightshirt with his dressing gown over it. Slippers were on his feet. He returned Thorton's salute. "Mr. Thorton. I have the pleasure of presenting Mr. Midshipman Henry Cummings and Mr. Midshipman Sheldon Norton. They are carrying valuable dispatches for Admiral Walters."

Thorton turned to greet the new officers, but the words died in his mouth. Duke Henrique smiled at him and in bad English said, "I'm happy to meet you."

Shakil knew no English at all and could only smile and nod.

Horner was speaking. "I don't think I need to impress upon you the importance of these officers reaching Admiral Walters with their intelligence. However, they are new to British service, so I count upon you to see to their training. You are a supernumerary lieutenant, so you will have the time to tend them. You will not stand watches but will devote yourself to their education and protection."

"Aye aye, sir," Thorton replied in astonishment.

"Given the need to protect them and their dispatches, I am going to give them the first lieutenant's cabin. I'm sorry to inconvenience the wardroom, but it must be done. Whatever arrangements the officers wish to make for their berths is agreeable to me."

"Aye aye, sir." Thorton couldn't do anything except agree.

Henrique could understand only a fraction of what Horner said. "What's he saying?" he asked in Spanish.

Horner sighed. "Do your best to make seamen and officers of them, Mr. Thorton."

"I will, sir."

"Roust up Mr. Forsythe and send him to my cabin." Switching to Spanish he said, "Mr. Cummings, Mr. Norton, I'm sure you are fatigued. Mr. Thorton will show you to your berth. Mr. Thorton, once they are settled, you will accompany me to the flagship. It will take me a few minutes to get dressed. Meet me on deck in ten minutes. Mr. Perry, you have the deck."

Thorton was delighted by the news. The suppressed exuberance of the two counterfeit midshipmen cheered him. They'd been to see Whittingdon; everything would be set straight when he saw the commodore.

"Shall I get my Sallee coat, sir?" Thorton was positively perky and ready to dash below.

Horner fixed him with a hard stare. "When I give an order I expect it to be obeyed, Mr. Thorton. You are insubordinate to think you can countermand my standing orders."

Thorton wilted. "Aye aye, sir."

"Dismissed."

The junior officers turned away.

The first lieutenant's cabin was a trifle larger than the other cabins in the wardroom, but what really distinguished it was the stern window at the back and the roundhouse at the side. The first lieutenant, like the captain, had a private privy. There was a bed, but Forsythe's steward collected his mattress and pillow. Henrique was left with a wooden bunk. Fortunately, Commodore Whittingdon had provided him with a sea chest and other dunnage. Ra'uf became Henrique's servant, as well as Thorton's and Shakil's. He made up the bed for the duke and dragged Thorton's sea chest into the room. Henrique's sea chest was stowed under the bunk and Shakil's valises piled on top. With three Sallee men and a Portuguese duke in the room, it was overcrowded, but that did not stop Thorton from finally giving into his feelings.

He hugged Shakil tight and whispered, "I'm so glad to see you! I thought—" He broke off. He had thought he'd be hanged without seeing him again. Now that Shakil was here, he was glad, but afraid too, because he did not want Shakil to see him dance the hempen jig. He was sure the commodore would set things to right, but had no confidence that he would. Commodores on station had considerable discretion, but disobedience to a direct Admiralty order would take a great deal of justification.

Shakil hugged him back. "I'm glad you're safe."

Henrique smiled indulgently at them. "Ah, gentlemen. You make me jealous! I am cheated twice of the opportunity for charming company!"

Thorton blushed. Shakil gave him a sheepish look. "I had to tell him about you. He was flirting with me."

Thorton's jaw dropped.

Henrique flipped his wrist at him. "Is that so odd? You're both handsome men. Of course I flirt."

Thorton was flabbergasted. "Article Twenty-Eight of the *Articles of War* forbids the crime of sodomy and buggery with man or beast and punishes it with death. You can't say such things here, midshipman."

Henrique arched his eyebrows. "Can't I?" he murmured with a tone of rebellion. "I don't see any female company on board, so what are we supposed to do? Live like monks? I refuse."

"'Tis only until we find Admiral Walters. Please, Mr. Cummings. While in uniform you must obey the *Articles*."

"Feh. I'll do as I please."

Thorton's face fell. How was he to turn this spoiled and peculiar lordling into a close enough semblance of a British officer that he would go undetected if captured? "We must come up with some sort of story to explain you."

"I am Lord Whittingdon's nephew. I have my warrant." He pulled it from his breast pocket.

Thorton examined it. It was a very fine fraud, indistinguishable from the real thing. He even had a jocular letter from Whittingdon addressed to "My Dear Nephew Henry" and dated several months before.

Henrique remarked, "I must say that Whittingdon is an artful liar. I almost believe him myself."

Thorton returned the paper to him. "I can't stay. Horner and I are going to the flagship as soon as he's dressed."

Shakil grabbed his cheeks and kissed him swiftly on the mouth. Thorton's heart summersaulted and he grinned in delight. The world was full of perils both naval and personal, but that one kiss obliterated his gloom. He whistled cheerfully as he went on deck and MacDonald the boatswain had to hiss, "Sir!"

Thorton checked himself. Men were sleeping. He had been thoughtless. He looked over the side towards the *Arrow*. She and her prizes were still lit up, and there was still the sound of hammering and sawing. They were fishing a jury mast on one of the frigates. He wished he was there. He was the captain and they were his prizes. He was staring at them still when Horner came on deck. The captain paused and watched him. The look of yearning was plain on Thorton's face. Horner sympathized with that look; what captain wouldn't want to be attending to his ship when she was wounded? He schooled himself to do his duty.

"Mr. Thorton! We are not at the theatre."

Thorton jumped and spun around. He flushed and saluted. "No, sir! I mean, aye aye, sir!"

The two went down into the gig. Horner sat in the stern while Thorton sat in the bow. He did not want to look at Horner or the men in their dark blue jackets as they rowed, so he turned around and stared ahead into the darkness. They passed a fourth rate and a third rate battleship before they came upon the flagship. She was an old third rate with a high poop over her quarterdeck and half-deck. She would be unhandy with so much above the waterline, but her cabins would be commodious. He looked across at the town of Algeciras. The Spanish ships were anchored in a line outside and did not seem changed. Not that he could be certain in the dark, but he saw their lights. Were they having midnight meetings as well?

Horner was silent in the stern. He had nothing to do but to watch Peter Thorton. Many thoughts were going through his mind: about the *Ajax*, past and present, about the current situation, about the Duke of Coimbra and what it would mean (indeed, whether it would mean anything at all), about Lieutenant-cum-Admiral Zeus White and much more. Mostly he chafed at the inaction of being trapped inside the Spanish blockade and the reticence of Whittingdon to give the Spaniards a fight. Now something would happen. The ruse about the midshipmen with dispatches was clearly the prelude to something bigger. While Horner had sufficient rank for a fourth-rate battleship, there were no such postings available to a man lacking political connections. He was not entirely discontent; as much as he would have liked a ship with the head room of the *Pegasus*, he liked the speed and agility of the *Ajax* more.

The cockswain of the gig attempted to chat with the captain and the men overtly eavesdropped, but much to their dismay, Horner proved to be a monosyllable. The cockswain tried with Thorton then, but had even less luck. Any other man would have been happy to share the tale of his victory over two frigates with an eager audience, but when asked if it was true, Thorton merely nodded. He went back to gazing at the night. The cockswain was disappointed. Here he was, rowing around in the middle of the night when he ought to be sleeping, carrying the firebrand Thorton and the hero Horner in his boat and he couldn't get one word out of either of them. Defeated, the cockswain lapsed into silence. He was cross with his crew when they came up on the flagship. "Hey there! Look alive! Grab that chain!"

Horner went up first. The correct number of sideboys in white gloves were there to present arms. The rattle of the snare was sharp, the boatswain's whistle properly timed. The *Pegasus'* first lieutenant saluted him smartly as he came in through the entry port. All the uniforms were very handsome. Whittingdon was a man with money and he had spent it to turn his men out well.

Thorton waited and listened, delaying until all the honors due a British captain had been satisfied. With fifteen feet of wall-sided ship above him he couldn't actually see what was happening there. When he judged that they must have stepped aside, he clambered through the entry port (how grand the ship that had an entry port!) and was rather surprised to see the four marines present their arms and hear the snare rattle and boatswain pipe him a captain's rank. Caught in the lantern light without a coat, he looked like a deer about to flee. He coughed. Did they not know he had been arrested? Looking chagrined he hastily caught up to Horner and saluted the ship's lieutenant.

"Welcome aboard the *Pegasus*, gentlemen." The lieutenant saluted sharply. Thorton totally missed the lieutenant's name, but he would remember the great amount of gold lace and fine cravat. Horner stood silent and grim. He was wearing his best coat, but it was not nearly as handsome a specimen as the flag lieutenant's.

Thorton found his voice. "Thank you." If he was a captain, he should not call the flagship's lieutenant 'sir.' If he was a junior lieutenant on a frigate, then 'sir' was obligatory. He resolved to say as little as possible until he knew where he stood.

"Capital action, taking two Spanish frigates! Is it true you have a galiot?" The lieutenant smiled at him.

"Yes."

The lieutenant waited, but nothing more was forthcoming from either Horner or Thorton. He had expected jubilation, arrogance, pious gratitude to God—something other than this gloomy silence. "My felicitations, sir," he proffered, thereby solving the question of who was to call whom 'sir.'

"Thank you, Lieutenant," Thorton replied.

"Captain Whittingdon is waiting for you. This way, if you please, sirs."

CHAPTER 11 : THE COMMODORE'S TABLE

Light and heat. Silver and lace. Space. Luxury. These were Thorton's first impressions of the great cabin of the *Pegasus*. It was as spacious as the great cabin and wardroom combined aboard the *Ajax*. The supper table could have seated twelve with its leaves in. A crystal chandelier hung over it. Wall sconces provided more light with fine white beeswax tapers. The footmen were marines in their scarlet coats and pristine white cross-belts. The urn-backed chairs were mahogany and intricately carved. A sideboard groaned with dishes. The splendor made it a little difficult to pick out the commodore himself.

Whittingdon was a short stout man with a florid face. He wore a white powdered wig with curls neatly at the side of his face. His stock was high and his ruffles voluminous. His uniform coat was navy blue velvet laden with gold braid to obscure the skirt nearly up to the hips, brilliant white satin reverses, glittering gold (real bullion, not yellow cloth) braid, cuffs folded well back from his elbows and the buttonholes cut into the scalloped pattern known as *marinère*, an embroidered white-on-white waistcoat, white linen shirt with the finest lace cuffs, blue velvet breeches that had never known a blemish or patch, fine white silk stockings, high-heeled black shoes with gold buckles (real gold, by the mellow way it gleamed), rings on his hands, and a gold watch chain. Thorton was dazzled. It was his first time meeting an English commodore in person. Captain Tangle was a commodore, too, but he was not a glittering creature like this lord. This magnificent personage would never be found singing around a hookah with a pack of mongrel corsairs. At that moment Thorton missed Tangle very much.

Commodore Whittingdon pushed past Horner to grip Thorton's hands and smile warmly at him. "Thorton! Damme, but you're a young fellow! Two frigates! Two!" he crowed. "You have my complete and utter congratulations—magnificent feat. Quite astonishing. Really, there are no words for it."

"You overwhelm me, my lord," Thorton replied with complete honesty.

"Where is your coat? Was it a casualty of action? 'Tis chilly tonight. Here, let me lend you mine." The velvet coat was whipped off and swiftly draped around Thorton's shoulders like a cloak. Thorton's mouth hung open in astonishment.

Finally the man deigned to notice Horner. "Horny, good to see you this evening! I should have known Mr. Thorton was one of your protégés. Come sit down. We'll have a bite of supper."

"I never met Mr. Thorton until this evening," Horner replied.

"Never?"

Horner nodded the affirmative. Thorton shook his head to indicate that they hadn't met.

It was Whittingdon's turn to be astonished. "What, never?"

"No, sir," Horner replied. "Not ever."

"Yet the two of you are so alike you could be father and son." It was an observation that startled them and they looked at each in surprise. Neither of them could see any resemblance. "Come, have a seat. We have much to talk about."

Horner moved first. Thorton could almost hear his joints creaking as he unbent enough to pull out a chair for the commodore. Thorton remained where he was with the commodore's coat draped over his shoulders. The commodore seated, Horner let a marine pull a chair out for him. He took a seat at Whittingdon's left hand. The commodore smiled and patted the chair to his right as the marine pulled it out. Thorton was highly embarrassed to discover the seat of honor given to him. He did not want to take it, but he was tired and his legs trembled. He carefully removed the commodore's coat and handed it to the marine before he sat.

He was asked what he wanted to eat and he must have answered something because food appeared on a plate before him. He ate without tasting. He listened without speaking. He realized that he was being asked a question. He chewed slowly with a mouth suddenly dry, but Whittingdon waited as long as it took. Thorton drank a little red wine to wet his mouth. Desperate not to make a fool of himself, he did not want to admit that he had missed the question entirely. "Perhaps Captain Horner could answer better than I."

Whittingdon blinked and Thorton knew it was a bad answer. He was petrified. He wished he'd paid better attention when Perry had tried to teach him social graces.

"I'm sorry, sir. I'm not used to talking to a fine gentleman like you. I was a pressed man."

"Pressed, by Jove! You came up from the weather deck?!"

"Aye, sir."

Whittingdon turned to Horner, who acquainted him with as much as he knew of Thorton's history, right up to his arrest. He kindly omitted the specific charges. His biography of the wayward lieutenant was a mercifully brief and dry recitation of facts. His voice and expression gave no clue to as to his opinion on the subject.

"You didn't think to bring the arrest order with you, did you?"

"I did." Horner reached into his breast pocket and pulled them out. He passed them to Whittingdon.

Whittingdon put a pair of bifocals on his nose and reviewed them. He sighed heavily, then took the glasses off and waved them in the air. "This is a bad business. Very awkward. Most inconvenient to court martial a hero. Highly embarrassing."

Thorton sat in silence with his face turning red. He knew what the charges were. He was glad he'd removed the man's coat. He could imagine a scornful commodore ordering one of the marine footmen to snatch it from his shoulders. He had been right not to trust this show of geniality. He kept his head down and stared at the china plate.

Whittingdon was a political animal. "Bishop must have important friends. I can't imagine why this nonsense would be coming up if he didn't. That he even got a command smacks of interest. God knows you're more qualified than he, Horny."

It had never ever crossed Thorton's mind that the motivation for the charges might be revenge, pure and simple. He had honestly thought his own conduct was the cause. It relieved him at the same time it frightened him. Maybe he hadn't done such a horrible thing after all, but then, if the charges were political, how was he to get a fair trial? He might be convicted for being disliked rather than for having done wrong. He was very sorry indeed that he had not learned how to ingratiate himself with his betters. He had never thought a lack of social skills could have such dire consequences.

"Damme, we haven't got enough captains to court martial him here. You're his commanding officer, you're recused. That leaves us one short. We'll have to send him to Admiral Walters. I'd write a letter of recommendation, but Jonathan Walters is no friend of mine. Anything I might write would only set him against you." He tapped the order. "This business with Articles One and Twenty-Eight is bad. Walters is a religious man."

A trickle of icy dread worked its way down Thorton's spine.

"Does the court martial have to be immediate? The *Wasp* might come in," Horner asked.

"She might. If she hasn't been blown to pieces by the Spanish. She's late. For that matter, we can't keep Henrique here. Once the Spanish sort themselves out they'll come for him. Those two special 'dispatches' have to reach Walters and quickly. I want you to go tonight." He turned to Thorton. "Will your vessels be going out? If so, may the *Ajax* accompany them? A break out in force will have much better chance of success."

Horner saw the desperate light in Thorton's gaze and did not trust him to resist that much temptation. He turned to Whittingdon. "Is it your intention for Mr. Thorton to resume his post aboard the Sallee cruiser, sir? I cannot think the Admiralty would be amenable to such an assignment."

Whittingdon puffed his lips and said, "Feh. What do I care what they think?"

"I lack your intimate knowledge of the workings of the Admiralty, sir."

"You have more friends than you know, Ebenezer. Really, you do. However, I suppose you are right to worry how this will affect your career. 'Tis on Bishop's head, really. The *Ajax* is his ship and it happened on his watch. Still, 'tis fixed in everyone's mind that you're captain of the *Ajax*. That it is only a temporary assignment doesn't mean much to the mob or the politicians. How very awkward." He picked up Horner's orders and fanned himself with them. He drank more wine and thought about it. Horner watched Thorton. Thorton stared at his plate and said nothing.

Whittingdon turned to him and said, "Well, young man. What were your orders or your plans when you came tearing up Algeciras Bay? Why are you here, throwing yourself into the ever loving arms of His Majesty's justice?"

"I was to scout Sebta, land Achmed at Gibraltar, and return to Zokhara with the intelligence. I was to pick up our spy at sunset, but the Spanish came out with six xebecs. I suppose Shakil Effendi and Duke Henrique told you the story."

"They did, but I want to hear it from you."

"There is nothing more to tell. We ran for Gibraltar, stumbled onto the frigates, and had to fight."

Whittingdon gazed at him expectantly. Thorton said nothing more. He sat in silence and waited dumbly for whatever would happen next.

Whittingdon spoke. "I'm sure we can beat down these charges. The first one will be the most damning in Walter's eyes. I can have my chaplain administer communion to you and that will be that."

"I am a Muslim, sir. I cannot accept Christian communion. I am guilty of violating Article One."

Whittingdon gave him a skeptical look. "They forced you. Everyone knows what hideous treatment the corsairs mete out to their prisoners. I cannot blame you, but we will soon set you to rights."

"No, sir. I never did understand the mystery of the Trinity. How can there be such a thing as a 'three-personed God' when the First Commandment clearly states, 'Thou shalt have no other God before me'? There is only one God worthy of worship, and Muhammad is his prophet."

Whittingdon sat back and gave Horner a reproachful look as if it were somehow his fault.

Horner replied, "I have conversed with Mr. Thorton and find him adamant in his Mohammedan faith."

Whittingdon turned a level gaze on Thorton. "The rest of this business could be swept away as youthful error and enthusiasm, but the Church of England is an immutable principle. There is good reason why it is Article Number One."

"So I will hang."

"Save yourself, Mr. Thorton! 'Tis all upon you. Come, see the folly of your course and correct yourself before it is too late!"

Thorton looked around at the fine cabin and thought how, if he had had more fortitude, someday he might have risen so high in the British service. Then he looked at the grim grey Horner and knew it was all a dream. If Ebenezer Horner could not reach the rank of commodore, the rank of wealth and ease, how could Peter Thorton? Sallee had offered him opportunity. Compared to the grandeur of England his Sallee rank was a tawdry honor, the uniform gaudy, and the officers all rogues, but he missed it.

Thorton shook his head. "For a few brief weeks, I stood and fell on my own merits. For that I love my new country. I will not abandon it."

Whittingdon threw down his spectacles. He gave Horner an exasperated look. "Knock some sense into him between here and Minorca. Run the blockade, find Walters, deliver the dispatches. Do whatever you have to. I shall write you broad orders."

"Aye aye, sir," Horner replied.

It was odd to Thorton to see a captain obliged to give unquestioning obedience to his superiors as a lieutenant to his captain. A captain was not a god aboard a ship, but he might as well be, given the power he had over his men. But even captains were pawns to the lords of the sea who moved them—and sacrificed them—whither they would.

CHAPTER 12 : SALLEE SILVER

Midshipman Henry Cummings was late to breakfast. A landsman and an aristocrat, he was accustomed to rise as late as eight or nine of the clock. Rising at four in the morning was an unwelcome novelty and he complained bitterly about it. Thorton had jerked the covers off of him and snarled, "Don't make me get the tawse, mister!" but he had not roused. Thorton had had far less sleep in a less commodious bed. He was not inclined to sympathy. He went to breakfast without him.

Hunger forced the ersatz midshipman to rise at last. The wardroom was cramped with three new men at the table in a vessel that was not rated for them. Henrique was obliged to squeeze in between Thorton and the pursuer. The pursuer was traditionally the least popular man on the ship and for good reason. He bought the ship's stores but shorted them to the men to turn a profit. It was one of the many hallowed traditions of the British navy. Thorton was at the end of the table with the pursuer on his left, showing that he was slightly less popular than that despised figure. Shakil sat across from them. Normally mere midshipmen would have been housed below in the gunroom, but these midshipmen were special.

Ra'uf waited on his gentlemen. He wore his turban, along with purple pantaloons and a loose shirt of blue and white check, but he went barefoot. The other officers were served by marines who were pleased to act as mess servants in exchange for getting the leftovers (especially the wine) and a few other favors. Henrique ate heartily; at least he was not precious about his meals. Shakil ate modestly, either from good manners or because he found the British food strange and disagreeable. He made no remark about it. In his midshipman's uniform he looked ten years younger and so was taken for a young man of two-and-twenty.

Thorton, who had exerted himself mightily the day before and eaten little at the commodore's table, was ravenous. He regretted his temperance of the night before and further regretted the lack of social graces that had made him so unequal to events. Had he comported himself better he could have come off as a hero and perhaps dodged the whole nasty business of the court martial. He was sure the duke had turned his interview with the commodore to his own advantage.

"How long until we reach Minorca?" Shakil asked Thorton in Spanish.

"At this rate, a week or slightly more." Thorton glanced at Henrique to include him in the Spanish conversation. He noticed 'Midshipman Cummings' was not carrying his satchel. Thorton lowered his voiced and asked, "Where are the dispatches?"

Henrique shrugged. "I don't know. In the cabin, I suppose."

Shakil glanced at the midshipman-duke, then asked Thorton, "Shall I get them?"

Thorton fixed a stern eye on Henrique. "The dispatches are your responsibility. You and Mr. Norton must take turns guarding them."

Henrique spooned his cold and lumpy oatmeal with haughty indifference. "They aren't going anywhere."

"When an order is given in a British ship, it is obeyed, midshipman," Thorton said sternly.

Henrique didn't even try to focus when he rolled his crossed eyes at the lieutenant. "'Tis only temporary. I pray you remember that."

Shakil rose. "I'll take my turn watching them." He disappeared through the louvered door to the first lieutenant's cabin. Henrique continued eating oatmeal, then helped himself to an orange that Ra'uf brought him. He peeled it with a small silver fruit knife that was probably the only fruit knife in the entire ship. Thorton remained silent as he scraped his bowl for the last of his oatmeal, but he was not left in peace.

Perry rose and stood in the space Shakil had vacated. "Thorton. I'm the caterer of the mess since you left. You need to explain to them about how the mess works so they can pay their subscriptions."

"I will."

It seemed Perry had something else on his mind, but he did not get to broach it. Shakil returned with the satchel strap over his shoulder. He paused next to Thorton when he saw Perry standing in his spot. "What is it?" he asked in low Spanish.

Thorton explained, "The king provides a certain amount of victuals, but the officers pool their funds to purchase more and better food."

Shakil was an accountant; he grasped what was wanted immediately. "How much?" he asked in English. He was starting to pick up the language.

"Twenty pounds," Perry replied. It was a modest mess. Other wardrooms subscribed as much as forty pounds, or half a lieutenant's yearly pay. They had better food and wine, too.

Shakil translated the sum from pounds sterling into Sallee sequins. He then prorated the amount to get the weekly rate and calculated the cost of three men. He did all the figures in his head as quick as a man might say 'The Duke of Coimbra' and told Thorton, "Three sequins ought to cover it."

Thorton translated his answer to Perry. Perry replied, "A sequin's not worth as much as a pound. I'll need a pound a week for each of you to cover your food and wine."

That was double what the other officers paid. Not to mention, Thorton had already paid his subscription last spring. Thorton snorted. "Shakil and I don't drink wine. Why should we pay for what we don't use?"

Perry glared at him. "You always were cheap, Peter."

Thorton was not in a good mood to begin with. Once Perry had been his best friend. Now he wasn't. He was a spiteful man, Thorton was discovering. Maybe the desecration of the Sallee uniform had been his handiwork. His temper flared. "Bring me my purse, Shakil."

Shakil did not know what the two had said to each other, but he knew they were arguing about money. He slipped back into the cabin and returned with the small leather bag that Thorton kept his coins in. Thorton poured the contents on the table. Some twelve or fifteen coins, mostly silver, gleamed in the lamplight. Half the coins were Spanish reales and half were Sallee sequins. Some copper and electrum coins of various nations mixed with them. Thorton pushed it across to him.

"Take it all and don't bother us with your chiseling anymore."

Perry started scooping it up. "I'll take it. I spent far more when I was supporting you when you were an out-of-work midshipman."

His words stung and Thorton replied tartly, "You never did anyone a favor you didn't expect to be paid double for."

Perry's hands were full of Thorton's money. He flung it in his face. Thorton threw up his arm to ward against the blow and coins flew everywhere. He leaped to his feet. Henrique also jumped to his feet.

Blakesley the sailing master cried out, "Gentlemen! No quarreling in the mess! Take it ashore if you must!"

Perry and Thorton glared across the table at each other. A long tense silence developed. Perry broke it first. "No need. The hangman will deal with him when we reach Minorca." He seated himself without retrieving the coins.

Thorton straightened up. "To think I ever called you friend."

Perry looked coolly back at him. "'Twas you who disgraced yourself. I tried to warn you, but you wouldn't listen."

Henrique slammed his fist on the table so that the dishes jumped. "Call him out, Thorton!" he begged in Spanish. "I will be your second."

Thorton took a deep breath. "I hope everyone here knows how well you keep a confidence, Roger. I hope they trust you exactly as much as you deserve." He whirled away from the table and swiftly mounted the ladder to the main deck.

The indefatigable Horner was on the quarterdeck already. Not having had any breakfast drama to delay him, he had arrived at his post before his officers. Thorton saluted him and said, "Good morning, sir."

"Good morning, Mr. Thorton." Horner was dressed in an old uniform that had seen better days. A torn sleeve was neatly stitched so that the mending barely showed, but the rub points had gained a shiny texture that no amount of brushing would remove. His waistcoat was very long as had been the fashion ten years ago when it was first made. Thorton was glad his own poverty would not be a topic of disdain for the new captain. Bishop's insistence on dress uniforms except for foul weather had been a trial to men with shallow pockets.

Thorton searched the horizon all around. To the south were the three silhouettes of the Sallee rover and her prizes. Where once lateen vessels had been a mystery to him he instantly recognized the distant triangular sails as belonging to a galiot. With her were a pair of frigates, one with an unnaturally short foremast. That was the one where they had fished a new jury mast.

"Do we have company this morning?" he asked.

"Not a jot. The rovers broke off when we were clear of the Spanish. I have another duty for you. Bring my potted plants on deck today and see that they're well watered. I had them stowed when we cleared for action last night."

"Plants, sir?"

"I was reading Doctor Lind's paper on the effectiveness of oranges, lemons, and limes in the prevention of scurvy. Growing citrus fruit on board a ship is well nigh impossible, but it seems to me that some other orange-fleshed fruit might prove beneficial, so I have a tub of cantaloupes in progress. Doctor Gibbs gave me some zucchini seeds while I was in Gibraltar, so I have planted them as well. Have you ever had scurvy, Mr. Thorton?"

"Not bad, sir."

"I lost my front teeth to it years ago. These are dentures." He tapped his front teeth. "Bad thing, losing your teeth, Thorton."

"Aye aye, sir. I'll get your plants, Captain."

So the weary Thorton, the least rested man among the crew, went below. He could not help feeling a trifle aggrieved to be made a gardener instead of being lionized as the victor over a pair of frigates. He eventually found the pots with the help of Horner's steward. They lugged them up three flights to the quarterdeck. The cantaloupe was very lush with two nearly ripe fruits and several smaller ones on it. The zucchini were merely a few short green vines.

Midshipmen Cummings and Norton came on deck. They stood in the waist and looked all around. Having a corsair captain for a brother-in-law, Shakil had absorbed more nautical knowledge than he realized and instinctively headed up to the quarterdeck. Henrique followed him. They found Thorton watering potted plants in his waistcoat. He still had no coat. Neither Henrique's nor Shakil's coat would fit him. One was much too large and the other much too small. Fortunately he didn't really need one. The August day was swiftly warming.

Thorton looked up from what he was doing and said, "Good morning, lads. I might as well start your English lessons. This is the 'quarterdeck.' That down there is the 'waist.' That raised structure in front is the 'forecastle.' When facing forward, 'larboard' is to the left and 'starboard' is to the right. Those lateral lines that support the mast are the 'shrouds.' The longitudinal lines that support the masts are the 'stays.' The 'ratlines' make a ladder of the shrouds. Follow me."

He lead them up to the tops. Shakil was nervous and climbed slowly. Henrique, in spite of his lamed and twisted leg, clambered up rather quickly. He wasn't bothered at all by the height and was delighted by the novel exercise. Thorton crawled over the edge by way of the futtock shrouds while Shakil crawled through the lubber hole. Henrique came up through the lubber hole after him. Shakil clung to the mast and his eyes grew wide as he looked down and around. The sea was vast and the ship only a small wooden plank floating in it. Clouds were piling up but were a long way from rain. Henrique was quite interested and looked all around. The seas were mild, but at that height the mast swayed through a great spiraling circle twenty feet in diameter. Shakil was white.

"To go down, we take the easy way. We slide down the stay. Like this." Thorton sat on the edge of the top, wrapped his legs around the stay, and whooshed down the long slanting line.

Henrique peered over the edge and watched Thorton all the way. "That looks like great sport!" he exclaimed. Shakil refused to look.

Thorton came scrambling up the shrouds and crawled over the edge to join them. "Who wants to go next?" he asked, a little breathless from his climb.

"I will!" Henrique sat on the edge. He had some trouble getting the lame leg to wrap around the stay, but locked his ankles firmly and went zooming down.

Thorton hung over the side and shouted, "Not so fast!"

Henrique reached the bottom and catapulted to the deck like a falling marionette.

"Are you all right?" Thorton called anxiously. As if he didn't have worries enough, now he had to worry about the pretender to the throne of Portugal breaking his neck.

Henrique righted himself, hopped up, and crowed, "Wonderful!" He ran for the ratlines with his strange lurching gait and scrambled up.

"Your turn, Shakil," Thorton coaxed him.

"Must I?"

Thorton looked around hastily, then pecked him on the cheek. "You must. 'Tis only frightening the first time," he assured him. "No one will believe you're a sailor if you're afraid of it."

"We don't do this on Sallee ships," Shakil told him.

"I know. Lateeners don't have stays."

The smaller man trembled as he put his legs over, grabbed onto the stay, and clung there. He clung so tightly he didn't slide at all.

Thorton encouraged him. "Loosen up a little."

Shakil loosened, slid six inches, and frantically clamped on again.

"That's right. You can go as fast or as slow as you like."

Shakil slid a foot. Bit by bit he slowly worked his way down the stay until he was able to drop onto his feet on the deck.

"My turn!" Henrique said gleefully. He swung over and shot down the stay like a thunderbolt falling from heaven. He thumped onto his feet and didn't fall this time.

Thorton skimmed down the stay and landed with a smile. "Let's all go again," he suggested.

With a look of grim determination Shakil climbed up. He went through the lubber hole while Thorton climbed over the edge using the futtock shrouds.

"Why do you do that?" Henrique asked him as he followed Shakil through the hole.

"'Tis what sailors do," Thorton replied.

"Why do they do it?" Henrique asked.

"I don't know. To show that they are seamen, I suppose. Landsmen are afraid to try it."

"So if I do it, everyone will think I am a sailor?"

"'Tis a good start," Thorton agreed.

So Henrique did it. He squirmed and twisted, groped and grabbed, until he finally crawled over the edge. He sat in the top and panted. "My leg didn't like that at all."

"You don't have to do it. You can use the lubber hole."

Henrique scowled at him. "I *will* do it."

The duke slid down the backstay again, but this time his lame leg gave out and he lost his grip and fell. He dropped fifteen feet and crashed to the deck in a heap.

Shakil watched in horror. "He's hurt!" Quick as a flash he slid over the edge, wrapped around the line, and shot down to the deck in a controlled slide. He dropped lightly onto his feet next to the prostrate duke. MacDonald the boatswain and several sailors ran up to inspect the fallen duke.

"Och, ye ill-feckit thrawn laddie," MacDonald said, lapsing into Scots.

"Is he dead?" somebody asked.

Shakil knelt and put a hand to his throat. He felt the pulse, then patted the duke's face and said, *"Vuestra merced, dígame!"*

Thorton landed on the deck next to them and bent to check him. Henrique's eyelashes fluttered and he groaned. He tried to sit up but Shakil hushed him. Thorton straightened the twisted leg and he groaned again.

Dr. Ferncastle, the surgeon, arrived and felt his leg. "Not broken. He probably sprained it. I'll give him some liniment and wrap him up." He inspected the supine officer's other limbs and his skull. "A minor mishap. A few contusions. He'll be fine in a few days."

They helped the temporary midshipman onto his feet and down the ladder to his cabin. He was put to bed with his ankle bound in bandages and propped on a pillow. Vinegar plaster was applied to his head. Shakil and Thorton hovered by him until he growled, "Stop watching over me like a bunch of Spanish guards!" They left him alone then.

CHAPTER 13 : A RESCUE ATTEMPT

Leaving the recumbent duke Thorton came on deck to discover all eyes looking south. Seeing what they saw, he hurried to present himself to Horner on the quarterdeck. The captain was studying the Sallee squadron as it swept closer. They had piled on all sail and the froth at their bows said they were breaking six knots. The breeze was light and the seas were low easy swells. The fog was gone and the sun was getting hot.

Horner lowered his spyglass and gave Thorton an opaque look. "It seems we have company after all, Mr. Thorton. Can you explain this?"

"I ordered them into Zokhara with their prizes and intelligence, sir." Thorton was unhappy as any captain must be when his orders were so flagrantly disobeyed.

Horner gave him a long level look. Thorton met it squarely. Horner slammed the glass shut with bony hands. He turned to look again. "Clear for action. Mr. Thorton, remain on deck. Your post is signalman."

Horner's steward came to retrieve the tubs of potted plants, then went below to secure the captain's quarters. Deadlights replaced the glass windows to prevent boarding by the stern. The captain's papers had to be weighted with shot so that they could be dropped overboard if circumstances required it.

The galiot was in the center of her consorts. They flanked her and formed a semi-circle with the frigates leading like the horns of a crescent moon. It was an ancient tactic not seen since the days of galleys. Any vessel that fell into the trap would be raked by the frigates' broadsides and the bow guns of the galiot in a withering three-way crossfire. Modern warships fought in line ahead formation; it was a function of their different gunnery that they must pace one another in parallel lines to slug it out broadside to broadside. The galiot's small guns barked: one, two, three, pause, four.

Thorton said, "'Tis the Sallee private signal, sir. They want to talk to you."

Horner put the glass into his pocket. "I imagine I already know the thrust of their conversation," he said drily.

The galiot sent up signals. It was short and simple as messages communicated with flags must be. "Send Thorton."

Elsewhere the boom of the guns had brought Henrique hopping out of his bunk to hobble up to the quarterdeck. Thanks to his fall he was lame in both legs now, but that didn't stop him. Shakil knew the signal and made his own decision. When he came on deck he was wearing his purple Sallee uniform. Britons stared at the turban in shock, then the marines whose duty it was to guard important things (such as the quarterdeck) leaped to bar his way. The lieutenant of marines came up swiftly to report.

Horner was too busy to receive him. He gave Thorton instructions. "Make a signal. 'Keep off.'"

Bitterly Thorton opened the signal chest and took out the signals he needed. The bits of color rose up the halyards and opened in the air.

Although the range was very long, the galiot answered with a single shot from one of her thirty-two pounders. They saw the puff of gunsmoke and heard the deep-throated roar of the gun. The shot skimmed cross the water ahead of the frigate's bows. They were at long range for the rovers, but the warning was clear. Horner clasped his hands behind his back.

"Mr. Thorton. Will they press the action?"

"I have no idea. But Lieutenant Aruj is a capital marksman with the big guns."

"So I see. That warning shot was nicely placed. Beat to quarters. Load and run out the guns. Double shot, please."

The orders were given in the same conversational tone as the rest of his short remarks, but his officers heard him. They leaped into action. The snare drum rattled and the pipes twittered. Instantly all was controlled chaos as the men ran to their posts and began doing what they must do. Forsythe took his place on deck next to Horner. Perry and Wright went below to command their respective broadsides. Chambers had the bowchasers and Jones the sternchasers. Thirteen-year old Jones was white in the face as he hurried to do what he had been drilled in so many times.

Horner saw the boy officer's frightened look and spoke cheerfully to him. "Steady, lad. Here's your chance to show what you've studied! I know you won't disappoint me!"

Jones stood up straighter. "Aye aye, sir! I'll do my best!"

"I'm sure you will. Carry on."

Shakil was finally permitted on deck. Horner met him with a stern and frigid face. He addressed him in Spanish. "Mr. Shakil! What is the meaning of this!"

Shakil replied in the same language, "I don't know. I am not privy to their plans, Captain."

Horner's steely gaze pinned him to the quarterdeck. Shakil's long acquaintance with his brother-in-law (the most notorious corsair of the age) had taught him how to withstand a withering gaze and mercurial temper. He stared the captain down.

Horner was more used to his own officers who must necessarily stand in dread of their captain. "Do you swear on whatever you hold holy that this is none of your doing?"

"I do, sir." Shakil spoke with a quiet dignity. "Peter Rais forbid any rescue attempt. As much as I long to fly to safety with him, I cannot."

"Hm, hm," was Horner's answer. "I require your parole that you will remain a spectator and not attempt to aid the Sallee cause."

Shakil said quietly, "I cannot do that, sir. I must obey my superiors. However, I will agree to do nothing that they do not direct me to do. I will also serve in the cockpit. I have done it before."

Horner stared at him. "Very well. I accept your terms. You may go below. Take Mr. Cummings with you."

"I don't want to go below," Henrique broke in although nobody had addressed him. He wasn't carrying his satchel with the dispatches either.

Horner turned on Henrique. "Mr. Midshipman Cummings, you are out of order!"

Henrique took a step back as the captain roared at him. "But—"

Thorton grabbed the duke's sleeve. "Begging your pardon, sir. I'll deal with this." Switching to Spanish he hissed at Shakil, "Help me get him below. For God's sake, see that he minds the dispatches!"

Henrique dug his heels in and wouldn't budge.

"A sail!'

That diverted everyone from the obstinate midshipman.

"Where away?" Horner called.

"Due west!"

Horner pulled out his spyglass and stood looking over the taffrail.

Thorton snapped at Henrique in Spanish, "Get below. It may get hot up here. You must guard your life, Your Grace!" Shakil tugged his other arm and the duke finally descended with a grumble.

Over head the sails flapped a little. Horner snapped at the helm, "Keep her full and by!"

"I'm sorry, sir, the wind's shifting," the quartermaster replied.

The frigate had been running a little south of east. That had brought the western breeze over her starboard quarter and filled every stitch of canvas she had. Studding sails and topgallants, everything, even the bonnet on the lateen driver had been set. The wave crests were starting to break and here and there were whitecaps. The ensign, which had fluttered only faintly before, began to show its colors more clearly.

"Bring us two points south," Horner commanded.

"Two points south, aye."

The rigging began to hum like the strings of a harp in a breeze magnified twenty-fold. The frigate heeled a little but scudded along with a lively bobbing motion as she charged up and down the waves. With her fine and narrow hull she sliced through the water and accelerated well. A creamy white bow wave arched up and bits of spray sometimes broke over her deck. She had the bit in her teeth and was running with it—straight towards the Sallee rovers. The rovers, seeing her charge them could not help but think her hostile.

For a moment Thorton stared at Horner in dismay. Did he really mean to engage three enemies at once? He might discount the galiot, but to be doubled by the frigates was an appalling thing. Did Thorton's lucky victory the night before make him overconfident? Was he—God forbid—competing with him? Thorton gave the other vessels a sickly stare. The galiot's big guns would rake him before he could bring his broadsides to bear. The galiot was nimble. If she kept her distance, the two frigates could pin the *Ajax* while the galiot crushed her from a distance.

"Deck!" came the lookout again. "Two sails due west!"

The strangers were not visible from the deck. There were many things they could be, but 'friends' were not among the options. Horner pursed his lips. "Thorton. You've a good glass. Up to the top with you and tell me what you see."

Thorton scrambled up the ratlines until he reached the lookout. He looked west and saw the two white pyramids of canvas the lookout saw, but maybe more. Were those other white spots breaking waves or vessels so far down on the horizon that the waves were covering and uncovering them? He pulled out his glass and stared west.

"My God." Thorton was white beneath his tan and had to take a deep breath to steady himself. He must be absolutely positive what he saw. "Deck ho! Five sail due west! Hull down!"

Horner's head snapped around. He peered up at Thorton. Another captain would have asked, 'Are you sure?' but Horner knew that Thorton would not have said it if he were not certain. He assessed the Sallee vessels. The vessels held their formation, then a crash of shot erupted from the frigate to the west. A ball plunked into the water short of the *Ajax*. Horner ignored it.

"What kind, Mr. Thorton?"

They were smudges of white. What else could Thorton say about
them?"

"I don't know, sir! Five abreast!"

That made up Horner's mind. "Come down, Mr. Thorton!" Thorton
flew down the stay. When he reached the quarterdeck Horner said,
"Make a signal, 'Five enemy sail west, course due east.' My guess is
that the Spanish are sweeping the narrow seas for us."

Thorton swiftly got the flags and attached them to the halyard.
They rose up and broke open. The freshening breeze displayed them
well.

There was a slight delay, then the galiot sent a new signal, "Send
Shakil."

Horner snorted at the preposterousness of the request. No boat
would be forthcoming. "Prepare to wear ship. Our new course will be
east northeast when we come around."

The *Ajax* had very good headway on her. She swung around when
the helm went hard over and never even hesitated. She thundered onto
her new course and then some as the helm oversteered.

"Steer small, man!" Horner snapped. The two men wrestled her
wheel and she snaked again before they got her on the heading the
captain wanted. How she could run! Bishop had never really put her
through her paces.

Thorton sighed in relief as they showed their heels to the Sallee
rovers. Horner had been bluffing. Looking back, he saw the Sallee
rovers change their courses to pursue them. The point was favorable for
the two frigates and reasonably good for the galiot, but after a quarter
of an hour it was apparent that the galiot could not keep up. The *Ajax*
was clipping along, moderately heeled over, every sail on her drawing
full and taut. It was perfect sailing weather. Half an hour later it was
clear that the prize frigates were also falling behind.

"Mr. Thorton to the top." Horner spoke matter-of-factly. For a
moment Thorton did not realize he was addressed. He hopped to it.

"Deck ho! Five sail west. Hull up now! Frigates!" Thorton sang
out. The strangers had changed their course to run north of east. Their
course and the *Ajax's* course formed two sides of a triangle. The apex
of the triangle was where their paths would cross. At this rate the *Ajax*
would cross well ahead of them.

Thorton slid back down to the deck and returned to his place on the
quarterdeck. Eight bells rang. Every eye was the quarterdeck. Would
the captain send the hands to supper? Horner studied the sea, the Sallee
rovers falling behind, the western horizon where the strange frigates

were not yet visible, and said, "Secure the guns. Don't unload. Send the hands to supper."

The guns were snugged down with their deadly loads still in place. The ship returned to its usual routine, but the men were buzzing with excitement. It was the custom of the British navy to feed the hands before they went to battle. They thought men worked better on a full stomach. Thorton went to the cockpit and passed the word that no action was imminent. Henrique was very pleased to come up. Watching the surgeon and his mate lay out their saws and bonecutters had worked wonderfully to instill in him the notion that he should learn to make himself useful. Men who were fit for nothing else were sent to help in the cockpit. No one in that day and age thought nursing to be a noble profession—it was a horrific, dirty, nauseating, and foul duty that that few men performed voluntarily.

Supper in the wardroom was animated. The discussion ranged over the intentions of the Sallee rovers, the speed of the *Ajax*, and how very handily she had answered her helm. Speculation was rife regarding the strange vessels and the general thought was that they must be Spanish. That in turn directed attention Henrique's way. Now that Perry knew who Shakil was, he had a very good idea who Mr. Midshipman Henry Cummings was. Fortunately, nobody else seemed to have grasped it.

CHAPTER 14 : THE SHADOW OF THE HANGMAN

After supper the captain and officers went on deck. The strange frigates were hull up now and spread in a long line across the Alborán Sea. South of them the Sallee rovers had turned around and were heading to Africa. They did not care to tangle with a superior force. The afternoon heat was starting to cool and the sails sent long shadows over the seas.

Horner studied the wind and the sea and the sails. The frigate ran along close-hauled and he said, "Hm. Wind's veering a little north."

The quartermaster replied, "Aye, sir. We won't be able to hold this heading if it continues."

"Give me another point east."

The helm turned a little and the heel eased slightly and her speed improved. Horner smiled in satisfaction. "That is exactly how I want her kept."

As the sliver of moon rose in the east and the lurid sun sank in the west. The air was luminous and the clouds streaked the sky with purple and gold. The sea laid out a crimson path from the sun to the *Ajax* and the strange frigates ran along it.

Thorton frowned. The frigates were gaining. The other officers had gathered at the rail and were studying them, too. Shakil pulled the tail of the turban over his face to protect it from the sun. He also watched the ships. Henrique, being cross-eyed, saw nothing. He could see that the men around him were very intent on something and whispered, "What is it?"

So Thorton explained to him, ending with, "They may catch us at dawn tomorrow, if this keeps up."

Down in the waist the common sailors were drawing the same conclusion. Tension returned. Close by the larboard quarter a swordfish leaped from the sea. The sailors began arguing over whether that was a good omen or a bad one.

Horner spoke at last. "The enemy shall not spoil a lovely evening. Gentlemen, I propose dancing."

Thorton stared at him like he was mad. The other officers cheered up and nodded. They infinitely preferred dancing over whist which was Horner's other frequent choice of evening entertainment. Perry, who had not been in the best of moods since Thorton returned, brightened noticeably. He was very fond of dancing. Forsythe liked to dance as well. Wright didn't, but he was the officer of the watch and couldn't participate anyhow.

The fiddler was sent for and the officers trooped into the waist. The idlers sat on the forecastle with their legs dangling or perched in the rigging to watch the officers cavort. Horner called for a Virginia reel, and the fiddler, a white-eyed blind man named Sam, began a lively tune. The officers sorted themselves into two lines facing each other. Naturally Horner was head of the men's line. The midshipmen (except for the lame Midshipman Cummings) were cast as ladies, but fortunately there wasn't much difference between the men's and women's parts. Barnes, the lieutenant of marines in his red coat, and Ferncastle, the surgeon, joined the men's line as well. That put Thorton over to the ladies' line, but they were still short a lady. Shakil, who had planned to merely watch, was dragged in to make up the requisite number.

Thorton found himself as the head lady thanks to his rank. He danced at an angle to meet the foot gentleman, who turned out to be the surgeon. They bowed, then danced back to their places. Horner as the head man and Shakil as the foot lady danced towards each other. Shakil caught on quickly that all he had to do was imitate what had just been done. Thorton and Ferncastle advanced towards each other again, put their hands up at shoulder height to lightly touch, turned a circle, then returned to their places. Horner and Shakil did the same. Next Thorton and Ferncastle advanced and grabbed each other's hands and swung around. Ferncastle was rather boisterous and sent Thorton whirling. The ship was heeling as she rolled down a wave, so Thorton overshot his place and crashed into the watching sailors. They caught him and laughed and threw him back. The captain set Thorton firmly on his feet. The junior lieutenant was dizzy and braced his legs to remain upright.

Next came the do-si-do. Thorton and Ferncastle accomplished it without mishap even though it involved passing each other backwards. Shakil did not understand the movement at all and collided with Horner. More laughter. Thorton had to jump to catch up to Horner so they could sashay down the line and back again. In spite of themselves, they were all having a good time. It was impossible to dance and feel bad at the same time.

Horner smiled and his blue eyes were bright. His years sloughed off of him. The captain and the renegade linked arms and reeled around until they were facing the opposites lines. Thorton hooked arms with Forsythe on the gentleman's side while Horner linked arms with Chambers. They reeled and parted and grabbed the third on each side. Thorton found himself face to face with Perry. There was a moment's hesitation, then Perry firmly hooked his arm and swung him around right neatly. His face was neutral. Perry was gentleman enough to dance politely even when he would rather not. The turn was quickly done and Thorton and Horner were grabbing the fourths. Then he was linked up with Ferncastle again who gave him a good spin. He caught a glimpse of Shakil's flushed face as Horner reeled him around and a spike of jealousy stabbed him.

They parted and Thorton and Horner grabbed hands again to sashay up the middle to their place at the head of the line. Horner turned neatly around the end of the men's line and Thorton turned down the ladies' line. The men followed Horner and the 'women' followed Thorton. He hopped over a coil of rope, but Jones tripped over it and crashed into Chambers.

"Wot dance is this?" one of the sailors asked.

"Skittles," another replied. They had a good laugh at the officers' expense.

Meeting at the foot of the line, Thorton and Horner touched hands and walked to the head of the line again with all the couples following until they were back in their original places. The other couples raised their arms and formed a bridge. Horner and Thorton ducked and sashayed under the bridge to the end of the line. They parted and raised their hands to join the bridge. Perry and Chambers were the new head couple.

Some of the sailors got up and formed a set of their own. Several of them knew the dance—the Virginia reel was one of the dances that could be danced by high or low without regard to class (although not together). The sailors exaggerated their manners and their 'ladies' curtsied and simpered. The head lady was a boatswain's mate of considerable girth with a great hairy beard. He primped and minced and made the sailors laugh. Thorton caught a glimpse of him and laughed, too. The sailors romped through the chasses with heavy-footed stomping that made the deck thunder. More sailors clapped along. One of them recognized the song and began to sing in a lusty bellow. Somebody picked up a belaying pin and began to beat it on the match tub in time to the music. Not to be outdone another sailor pulled out a jaw harp and began twanging along.

Thorton whirled through the evening as the vermilion sun sank into the long sea. Stars came out and the five white sails on the western horizon became briefly clearer before dusk settled. He danced and smiled, laughed and spun, and thought it was the happiest evening in his life. For a quarter of an hour he had no worry or care and everything was as beautiful. When the fiddler finally ceased, he was panting for breath. When the sailors offered a hornpipe, he was glad to step back. He found Shakil at his side.

The Moor smiled at him and his hazel eyes sparkled. "That was fun!"

Thorton wanted nothing more than to kiss him, but he couldn't. The pain clenched around his heart and his smile faltered. "Let's sit down."

They took seats on the leeward steps of the quarterdeck. Shakil sat on the second step from the bottom and Thorton on the step above him. Because of the narrowness of the stairs his leg pressed against Shakil's arm. Shakil leaned against him and gave him a smile. Thorton sat up very straight. That they sat together excited no attention. Sailors leaned against each other and put their arms around each other's shoulders all the time. Sitting like that nobody could see him when he twined his fingers in the hair at the nape of Shakil's neck. Shakil shivered and gave Thorton a yearning look.

Across the deck Horner was standing with his hands clasped behind his back. Although he seemed to be watching the hornpipe, in reality he was watching the sky, the sea, the sails, the distant ships, and the men. He was especially watching Thorton and Shakil, but that could not be determined from his pose or expression.

With the disappearance of the sun, the wind died. The sea settled. The waves rolled on, but their crests were no longer breaking. The end of the dog watch sounded. Horner turned on his heel and went up to the quarterdeck. Forsythe was a little preoccupied, but recollected it was his watch and hurried up after him. From the quarterdeck came the command, "Fiddler stand down."

With a collective sigh, the sailors slowly put away whatever they had made merry with. The watch below turned in while the watch above took their places.

Henrique limped over to where Thorton and Shakil were lingering on the steps. He was making use of his cane to get around. "That was a marvelous new dance. I enjoyed it greatly. What is it called?"

"The Virginia reel," Thorton replied.

"Will we dance again?"

"I suppose the *Ajax* shall, but we are only going as far as Admiral Walters. He is somewhere near Minorca."

"You must teach me all the fashionable dances."

"That was merely a country dance. Everyone knows it," Thorton replied. With Henrique blocking anyone's sight, he dared to squeeze Shakil's upper arm. Shakil swiftly bent his neck and brushed the lightest of kisses against his hand. Thorton turned a little pink, but his blush could not be seen in the dusk.

Henrique watched them, then said, "I am going to stay up a while. You two don't have to wait for me."

Thorton's heart thudded and he nodded. "All right then."

He and Shakil rose. They went casually to the companionway and descended. Lanterns were lit in some of the cabins. Bars of yellow light shone through the louvers. The sound of sea chests opening and closing came through the bulkheads, followed by the creak of bunks. Lights were blown out. Thorton and Shakil slipped into the first lieutenant's cabin they shared with the duke and shut the door. Swiftly Thorton's arms went around his lover and he kissed him hard there in the darkness. Shakil's arms were tight around him. They pressed each other body to body in silence. They heard Perry and Wright talking to each other in the next cabin. Finally the other lieutenants were silent.

Thorton wanted to lie naked in Shakil's arms but he didn't dare. Instead they changed into nightshirts and cuddled together on the pallet on the floor—the bunk was reserved for the pretender to the Portuguese throne. They kissed and hugged, but they were prime young men and longed for more. Thorton held Shakil tightly and whispered, "I want to make love to you. They're going to hang me anyhow. I want to feel everything good before I die!"

Shakil's arms tightened around him. "You're not going to die," he said fiercely. "I won't let them kill you!"

"I don't want you to see me hang."

"Sh! Don't say such things!"

Thorton buried his face in Shakil's neck. He trembled. Battle did not frighten him, but the thought of his body dangling in air, twisting and kicking while his lover watched—that he could not stand. The shame of it, to be exposed and destroyed as a deterrent to other men of similar feeling, condemned to death for the love he felt.

"I'm afraid," he whispered.

"I will save you!"

Thorton should have laughed at that. How could Shakil save him? He didn't even have a ship. If the did save him, where would they go? He didn't laugh. Instead he snuggled into Shakil's arms and let himself believe the fantasy. Shakil would keep him safe. Finally he slept. Shakil stared into the darkness and worried.

CHAPTER 15 : THE CLIFFS OF ALBORÁN

Cold water in the face woke Thorton. He blinked up at the dim square of the stern window, realized it was raining, yawned and got up. The ship was well heeled and he had to brace his legs to accommodate the rolling motion as she bucked. He looked out, saw darkness, rain, and whitecaps. The sea was rougher than when he went to bed. He hastily unhooked the window and swung it down and into place just in time as a pooping wave slapped the counter. He fastened the window, shivered in the chill, and checked himself. He was a little wet, but he decided the dampness was bearable and crawled back under the covers. It was warm there next to Shakil and he startled to curl up with him, but suddenly went stiff. He jolted awake, turned his head, and stared at the dark window.

Shakil yawned and asked, "What is it?" sleepily.

"The ship's lanthorn is out."

Ordinarily the stern lantern would have been sending a golden glow over the quarterdeck and spilling its radiance into the sea aft the transom. Instantly awake, Thorton grabbed his clothes. He knew exactly where they were. Shakil fumbled for his clothes in the dark. He didn't remember where he'd left them and collided with Thorton. They knocked heads and said, "Ow!" and "Sorry!" to each other.

"What's wrong?" Shakil whispered. "Why isn't the light on?"

"I don't know," Thorton replied. "Maybe the wind blew it out. Maybe we're running dark. Maybe the enemy has snuck on board."

The prospect of Spaniards sneaking up the stern shocked Shakil into wakefulness. In the bunk above them Henrique snored obliviously. Dressed for the weather in an oilskin and southwester, glass in one pocket and pistol in the other, Thorton made his way cautiously into the wardroom. The deadlights were all shut and the glasses stowed. It was Ra'uf's job to set the deadlights in his master's cabin as well, but he hadn't done so. Maybe he didn't know, maybe his lack of English had prevented him from understanding, maybe he had been waylaid—imagination supplied plenty of reasons.

Thorton hissed to Shakil, who was still putting on his turban, "Wake Henrique. Tell him to put the deadlight in!"

Shakil shook the duke. The duke snorted and groaned. Shakil kept shaking him while Thorton tiptoed through the wardroom and up the companionway to the deck. He found sailors huddled in the coach as the cold wind blew. With no moon or star or land he had no way of telling where the wind was coming from, only that it blew over the larboard quarter. He looked out into the darkness of the deck. No lanterns were lit. Running dark? It made sense. Horner would want to disappear in the night and rain to escape the Spanish.

Faint lightning flashed in the northwest and showed him the ship as a ghost of white: she still had every stitch of canvas set. Satisfied that the men were at their posts and they had not secretly been taken by the Spanish, he hurried to the windward stair. A gust blew him and he nearly slid off the steps, but grabbed the rail and held on. That was why sailors always used the windward ladder. If he had fallen, he would have fallen onto the deck. Had he used the leeward stairs, he would have fallen into the sea. On a night like this he doubted anyone would notice he was missing.

All around him the rigging sang a high-pitched siren song. The canvas thundered overhead as the wind veered, then returned to its original point. He came up on deck and found Horner and Perry there. It was Perry's watch and he was drenched through in spite of his foul-weather gear. Horner was only damp, showing he hadn't been on deck long.

Thorton saluted. "Evening, Captain," he raised his voice to be heard above the creaking of the timbers and the song of the wind.

Horner returned it and said, "Good evening, Mr. Thorton. Did you sleep well?"

"I did, sir. You?"

"Excellent. A lively sea makes a good cradle. I'll have the stu—" A sudden crack interrupted his words. It wasn't particularly loud, but it had a wooden sound. Horner's head instantly swiveled and he stepped between the guns and looked up into the rigging. "What was that?"

The answer was carried from voice to voice. "Larboard fore top stuns'l carried away! She's fouled in the fore topmast stay!"

Horner replied, "Clear the debris and douse the studding sails, Mr. Perry."

"Aye aye, sir. Clear debris and douse stuns'ls!" Perry bawled.

The men who had huddled in the shelter of the coach came out and went into the rigging. They had to do it mostly by feel as dark as it was. A tiny hooded light illuminated the binnacle, but that was all. Horner had drilled them mercilessly, but it was not an easy set of conditions in which to work.

Shakil came on deck. He told Thorton quietly, "We got the deadlight in and I stowed our bedding. 'Tis getting damp in there."

Thorton nodded. "With this lively a sea the seams will work. Pass the word for Ra'uf. Get a couple of billets from the firewood and lift the sea chests and your valises a few inches off the floor. Get Mr. Cummings to help. He might as well learn these things."

Henrique hobbled up as Shakil was going down. He was quite alarmed and wouldn't go down with Shakil. He accosted Thorton. His face was a white blur in the night but Thorton could hear the anxiety in his voice. "Is it a bad storm?"

Thorton laughed at that. "'Tis not a storm. 'Tis not even a gale."

"Our room is leaking!"

"'Twill get wetter. Go help Shakil put some billets under our things. We might get four or five inches sloshing around in there before 'tis over."

"But—"

Thorton patted his shoulder. "'Tis nothing. Really." A flash of lightning and crack of thunder drowned him out. After the rumble died away, he repeated himself. "'Tis a lively night, nothing more."

"Will it go on all night like this?"

"I expect so."

"God's wounds! How is a man supposed to sleep?"

"In his bunk, Mr. Cummings. You ought to be dry enough. Go, help Mr. Shakil, get us a couple of hammocks, then back to bed."

Henrique went below, shaking his head in amazement.

Horner stood his quarterdeck with his head cocked. "Do you hear anything, Mr. Perry?"

Perry and Thorton listened. The helmsmen listened, too. Nobody heard anything except the growl of distant thunder, the wind, the sea, and the ship.

Perry shook his head. "No, sir. What is it?"

Horner continued listening, then got out his glass. He couldn't see a thing. Black night was black night, no matter how it was magnified. More lightning flashed. "Breakers is what I think I hear."

Thorton strained his ears.

"Breakers?" Perry asked. "In the middle of the Sea of Alborán?"

"The Isle of Alborán," Thorton replied. He had been the captain of a Sallee rover. He knew his charts. "A tiny speck of an island with no water, low and flat, nearly invisible in the best conditions. There are reefs around it and no lighthouse."

Perry listened more diligently. Lightning flickered and thunder rumbled. The wind quickened.

"You have good eyes and a good glass. Go up, Mr. Thorton."

Thorton headed up the windward shrouds to the top. The rain slicked the tarred ratlines and the wind pressed him against the shrouds. He caught his breath, didn't look down, and climbed. The wild gyrations of the ship sometimes made his climb easier and sometimes more dangerous. He clung tightly and waited until her motion tilted the mast to his benefit. He climbed hastily, clung, climbed, and clung again, matching his movements to the vessel. He had nearly reached the top when suddenly the ratline beneath his foot gave way.

Shakil was watching him and cried out, "Peter!" All heads turned at the fear in his voice to see Thorton clinging to the shrouds.

Thorton had been holding tight with both hands while raising his right foot. His right shin scraped the ratline below and his knee fetched up against it. His left leg was through and dangling. The shoe plummeted to the deck below. He clung tightly as the ship gyrated and swayed him backwards. He kicked his foot back, found another ratline, and snaked his stocking-clad toes under it. Thus locked in, he rode out the twist. His heart was hammering in his chest and he squeezed his eyes shut and breathed deeply to steady himself.

Slowly he righted himself and no one thought him unseamanly when he chose to go through the lubber hole to gain the top. The lookout there greeted him heartily.

"Holla, Lieutenant." In the dark he couldn't tell which lieutenant it was. "You all right, sir?"

"Fine, but I lost a shoe," Thorton replied.

The man was barefoot. He replied cheerfully, "That's all right then."

"What do you see?" Thorton asked. "Any breakers?"

"Lord, sir! How you jest! I can't even see the Dagos."

Lightning forked overhead and thunder crashed close at hand. Thorton was none too pleased to be up a tall tree with lightning around, but there was no help for it. He strained his eyes but saw nothing. He waited for the next lighting flash.

What was that white glow down low? An almost phosphorescent gleam, instantly gone. He trained his glass on the spot. When the lightning came again, he saw it again. He lowered the glass and shouted.

"Breakers fine on the starboard bow! About a mile distant!" The quarterdeck couldn't hear him, but the men in the rigging around him took up the cry and passed it to the quarterdeck. Suddenly the sense of urgency doubled. Men who had moved cautiously to get the studding sails in moved rapidly now. The old hands were not much worried by the blow, but they were powerful worried by the rocks.

"Douse t'gallants," came the command. The men who had already got the studding sails in climbed up to douse the topgallants. In front of Thorton men were laboring with boat hooks to drag the debris of the blown studding sail out of the stays before them, but the wind kept wrapping it around the lines.

Thorton raised his glass and studied. With the help of the lightning he thought he could see a mass of darkness and against it the white teeth of waves breaking. Then he swung his glass around the horizon. Lightning revealed a sail.

"Deck ho! Sail on the larboard beam!"

Thorton knew Horner was in a pickle. He must pass around Alborán, but with the wind blowing out of the northwest, to pass west of it would place it on his lee. A mile was not enough sea room. If he did, he would continue his course to Minorca and find himself in close company with the strange frigate. If he passed along the south side, he would be heading south, further away from the British Mediterranean fleet, and perhaps lose sight of the Spaniard. The other option was to set anchors and hope they held—but that would make them a sitting target for the Spanish.

Word was passed for the carpenter and his mates. It was their duty to cast the lead. Horner made his decision swiftly; the ship turned her head south. If he could make it into the island's lee it would hide him from the Spanish and give him some protection from the weather. The ship groaned as she wore around to her new heading and the whistling pitch of the rigging climbed higher. She was clawing off close-hauled. Square-rigged, she could only point so high into the wind.

Thorton trained his glass around and gave his reports. They were drifting nearer the island which was now distinguishable as a low mass when the lightning flashed. The breakers were audible over the wind. The pumps clanked into action. It was not a very big island, but there were reefs around her and that worried him.

A second frigate appeared briefly in the storm. "Deck ho!" Thorton sang out. "A sail fine on the starboard bow!"

He turned his glass on the first and saw her clawing her way north of Alborán. She had the room, she would clear it. He shouted that down as well.

A mighty scrape sounded along the bottom of the frigate. She shuddered in all her fibers and Thorton turned sick inside. She hung up just a moment, then was lifted clear of the rock. She bounded along, running free before the wind.

"Man overboard!"

One of the carpenter's mates had fallen into the sea while taking his soundings. Men ran to the side, but it was too late. The frigate was streaming past and there was no way she could stop and return. Thorton saw them launching a boat and shot down to the deck. He charged up to Horner and asked, "May I take the boat, sir?"

Horner glanced at him once, then at the breakers. "Go."

Thorton whirled away and joined the men in the boat. As they put their oars out and stroked away from the frigate's side, Shakil clung to the rail and watched him go. Thorton looked up at the quarterdeck, saw the blur of his turban, and waved. They came out of the lee of the frigate and the full force of the wind and waves caught them. A wave over a fathom high lifted the boat and they whooshed down the side, only to rise again. White foam broke around them as they crested the next wave. They carried a lantern in the boat but it availed them little. Mostly it allowed them to be seen by the man they were trying to rescue and by the frigate when it was time to pick them up.

Shakil turned on Horner, "'Tis dangerous! They'll be swamped in that little boat!"

Horner's Spanish was imperturbable. "Possibly. But if I thought it likely, I wouldn't have sent them out."

"There are reefs! They could be smashed!"

Knowing what Horner knew, he understood Shakil's anxiety. "Thorton has a stout heart. He'll be fine."

"But what if he's not?"

"Then he'll die a hero and avoid the embarrassment of a court martial," Horner replied crisply.

Shakil's eyes flashed. "Monster! You have no feelings!" He turned away from the captain and went to the taffrail to watch the point of light bobbing in the heaving seas.

CHAPTER 16 : A ROCKY DAWN

The boat pulled strongly. The would-be rescuers rode the waves, rocked, took a bow full of water, were soaked and blinded by the driving rain, then nearly broached when the men on the starboard side all caught a crab.

"Pull!" Thorton shouted. They righted themselves swiftly. Thorton swung the lantern in the bow and the golden rays illuminated a faint circle at the head of the boat. He could see nothing beyond it, but he could hear the roaring of the waves as they dashed against the cliffs. He tried to think. The *Ajax* had been running close-hauled to the southwest, the man must have been swept towards the cliffs (if he hadn't sunk already), if he kept the wind on his left cheek he would be on the right course—he thought he saw something.

"A point starboard!" he called. He had to shout to be heard over the noise. Lightning flashed and a few seconds later thunder growled. "There!"

The man disappeared as the boat dropped into the trough. They pulled harder and Thorton held the lantern high. They rose on another wave but there was no sign of him. Again the trough and Thorton despaired; were they too late? Once again they rose.

"I see him! Hang on man, we're coming!" Thorton waved his lantern up and down then side to side several times, signaling the *Ajax* that they had found their man.

On board, Shakil did not understand the English when the boatswain reported to the captain, but he saw Horner's face grow grim. From that he deduced 'stove in' must be bad. He knew very well what a 'sail' was, including raising and lowering them, but 'fothering' was outside his ken He hoped it would fix things, but judging by the expression on Horner's face, it was a slender hope. He wished very much that his brother-in-law Isam Rais al-Tangueli was here. He was certain that the indomitable corsair could fix it when ordinary men failed. Although he was obliged to take Thorton's word that Horner was a fine captain, he had a poor opinion of the British in general and Horner in particular. No one who arrested his beloved and intended to turn him over to be hanged could rate very highly in Shakil's estimation. He devoted himself to watching the pinpoint of light that was Thorton's lantern. He could not see the boat or any man in the darkness, but he could see a golden star of light.

"He's waving the lantern!" he called in Spanish. Surely that must be a good sign.

Horner glanced over the taffrail. "I'm afraid he will have to fend for himself, Mr. Shakil. The *Ajax* is in no condition to assist."

Shakil's blood ran cold at that report. "Why don't you run her on the beach? It can't be far."

Horner opened his mouth to retort, then closed it. Horner had never beached anything larger than a cutter or barge in his life. There wasn't a warship in the British fleet that was suitable for beaching. But the *Ajax* had been a French corvette before she had been an English frigate, and her hull was shallow with a moderate deadrise. He pulled out his glass and studied the island in the lightning flashes. He recollected his charts very well; the island had two beaches, both on the south side. He glanced at his sails, considered the wind and waves, and made his decision. "Stand by to beach her, Mr. Perry."

"Stand by to beach, aye," the lieutenant replied.

Perry had never beached anything but small boats, either, but he had at least seen the galleys pulled up on the beach at Eel Buff. That was more than either Wright or Forsythe could claim. He racked his brain to think what must be done.

The word was passed through the length of the vessel. They were in luck because MacDonald, being a boatswain, had paid a great deal of attention to the beaching of the galleys in Tangle's squadron when he had been aboard. The *Ajax* was deeper than any of those but he thought it could be done, especially since the choice appeared to be sinking. Speaking English perfectly well and being the boatswain, he knew that the bottom was stove in and she was filling fast. The pumps were working as hard as they could, but the water was gaining rapidly. He'd want her to come to rest on her starboard bottom to let them get at the break. They could rig tackles and drag her high enough to work. Assuming the Spanish let them.

Meanwhile Thorton had his man. Unfortunately, his man had no belt or even breeches. He was wearing only his shirt. Thorton grabbed his collar. The swimmer got an arm over the larboard gunwale, but as the men grabbed, or attempted to grab onto him, the boat tipped.

"Balance the weight or we're all going in!" Thorton barked.

Some of the mean leaned over the starboard while others grabbed and tried to get hold of the skinny, slippery nearly naked man. They hauled him aboard and shipped a great deal of water as they did so.

"Bail!" Thorton ordered. Buckets went to work. "Who is it?" Now that the man was in the feeble circle of lantern light, he still couldn't tell. He was face down over a thwart.

"Jack Wilson, carpenter's mate, sir."

"What on earth are you doing in the water, man?"

Wilson looked up and coughed. "Drowning, sir," he said apologetically.

Thorton took off his oilskin and wrapped it around the man. "Where are your clothes?"

"I took off my jacket to keep it from pulling me down, sir. The waves ripped the rest of them right off me."

"The important thing is that you're safe." Thorton looked around for the frigate but couldn't see her. He signaled with his lantern again but saw no answering signal. His chest grew tight with fear. How bad was she hurt? He did not think Horner would have put a boat over he didn't intend to pick up.

"All right, men. Let's row into the island's lee and wait to get picked up."

"Aye aye, sir."

With the island to shelter them they could still hear the wind roaring and feel a little of it, too, but the seas were calmer. Thorton signaled with his lantern again. This time a light answered: up and down, side to side.

"There she is!" he sang out with good cheer.

The men heartened. They put blistered hands to oars and rowed with a right good will.

The worst of the weather was blowing past west of them, but it offered one last flash of lightning. It revealed the *Ajax* aground at the foot of the cliffs before them. She was canted over and waves slapped her stern. Men moved in her rigging to furl the useless sails.

The bottom of the boat grated on pebbles, then Thorton and the men hopped out to drag it high on the pebbly beach. There was sand and rock underfoot, driftwood, and shells. A few wasted weeds grew. Thorton still had only one shoe as he trudged through the wet sand to the bow of the *Ajax*.

"Ahoy the ship!" he called. The bow watchman was clinging to the headrails above him.

"Ahoy the shore," he answered. "We're bilged!"

Thorton scrambled up over the bow with the help of the head rails and a boost from his men. The deck was askew but no worse than during a storm. A pale glimmer appeared in the east and the men and masts were shadows limned against a somewhat lighter shade of dark. His stomach rumbled and told him that it was time to break his fast, but he doubted breakfast would be served anytime soon. He made his way up to the quarterdeck by crawling up the slippery steps and clinging to the rail.

Perry had the quarterdeck. He was bracing a foot against a gun carriage and bending his other knee to keep himself upright. He was huddled in his oilskin with his chin sunk in his collar. He straightened when he saw a dark figure crawl onto the deck and salute.

"Lt. Peter Thorton reporting, sir. We retrieved the man overboard. Jack Wilson, carpenter's mate. He's alive and unhurt."

"Very good, Lieutenant," Perry replied. "We are bilged."

"So I heard. What would you like me to do, sir?"

Perry sighed. He rubbed a hand across his face and scratched the stubble of his beard. "Horner's in the hold with Forsythe and the boatswain and the carpenter. I expect we'll have orders presently."

"How about a spot of tea?"

Perry brightened. "Aye, tea would be well." Then he dimmed. "No fire in the galley, the stove's not safe."

"I'll make it ashore, sir."

"Very well. Carry on."

"Aye aye, sir."

Shakil scrambled up the canted deck by pulling himself along the quarterdeck rail. "Peter! You're safe!" He braced his feet and kissed Thorton on each cheek in the Continental fashion.

Henrique, still lame in both legs, had a devil of a time slithering, lurching, and crawling across the deck, but with the binnacle to brace him, clapped Thorton on the shoulder. "Damme, I thought we were done for!"

"Not yet. But if the Spanish find us like this, we might well be," Thorton replied. They all frowned at that. "Have you got the dispatches safe?"

"I do," Shakil replied. He hefted the satchel that hung from his shoulder.

"Good. You'd better figure out how to destroy them in case the Spanish catch us here. You can't just drop them overboard now."

Shakil nodded. "I will."

Meanwhile Thorton crawled down the steps, passed the word for Ra'uf, and the two of them clambered through the tilted hull to the wardroom stores. They were on the lowest deck in the stern—and the stern was in the water and the water was in the stern. They had to plunge into water up to their chests. Thorton held the lantern up high to keep it from swamping. Most of the officers' supplies were ruined, but they found a tin of tea, a kettle, a teapot and most of the cups. They added in some things from Thorton's private store. Then they got over the side and joined the fire that the men on shore had made out of driftwood. Thorton was frozen from the cold water and very glad to huddle by it.

The rain was now a drizzle, but hard against the face of the cliff they were dry except when a gust blew rain at them. Ra'uf poured water from his waterskin into the tea kettle and boiled it. Thorton let Wilson have a cup, but told the men, "The second kettle is for you, lads. I'm taking this to the officers."

Ra'uf made up a tray very nicely with the china teapot and cups, pewter teaspoons, a bowl of sugar with a lid and tongs, and napkins. Thorton put his sou-wester over it to keep it from the drizzle. Getting the tray aboard required careful maneuvering, but the men were glad to make the effort. They were feeling helpless and were glad to be given some small task within their powers to accomplish.

Gaining the quarterdeck Ra'uf held the tray level even though his legs were bent to accommodate the canted deck. Steam rose from the spout of the china pot. The clouds were clearing in the east and the pink aurora lit them from beneath, providing enough light to make out faces and even the rose pattern on the china.

Horner stared in astonishment. Water dripped from the brim of his hat and his shoulders were hunched against the cold. He was an exceptionally thin man, and appeared even more cadaverous in the grey light. He could not speak at first.

His officers (including Shakil and Henrique) gathered in a semi-circle and waited politely. Etiquette required that the captain be served first, but the ritual, performed at this time, spoke volumes about their regard for him.

"Thank you, gentlemen," he said with genuine emotion.

Thorton poured for him. "One lump or two, sir?" he asked as politely as any majordomo.

"Two, please." Plunk, plunk. Sugar dropped from pewter tongs into the tea. Thorton stirred it with a pewter spoon, then handed the cup and saucer to him.

"Thank you, Mr. Thorton."

Horner lifted the cup to his lips and drank. Without thinking he nearly drained it in a single draught. He recollected himself and lowered the cup. "Capital tea, Mr. Thorton. I am indebted to the wardroom." He had recognized their china.

"No trouble at all, Captain."

The rays of the sun broke over the horizon and turned the sodden sails to gold. It was a dismal scene with the masts aslant and the sound of hammering coming from the hold, but the scent of tea rising from a rose-bedecked teapot fill them all with good cheer.

"Won't you join me, gentlemen? I think we have time for a spot of tea before we get to work."

They chorused their assent and Thorton got busy pouring out tea. Even Chambers and Jones received cups. Thorton served himself last. The teapot was empty, but Thorton pretended to drink so they would not know he had been shorted. All his sugar was eaten up as well, but he made no complaint.

Horner had been sagging very low (not that he would admit it to anyone), but the tea restored him. His shoulders squared as he issued orders.

"Mr. Chambers, you are to take the cutter with Mr. Cummings and his dispatches. You will provide it with victuals and water for one week and a suitable crew of men. You will hide in a sea cave and stay there no matter what. When the coast is clear, you may come out. If we are dead, you are to find Admiral Walters or any safe port. It is essential that Mr. Cummings and his dispatches reach safety, even if you must lay down your lives to do it. I authorize you to take any and all actions to accomplish that goal."

Chambers was wide-eyed at the responsibility. He stood up straighter and said, "Aye aye, Captain."

"I have secret orders for you as well. Walk with me, Mr. Chambers, Mr. Cummings."

The three stepped aside. Nobody could hear what he said, but when Chambers' jaw dropped and he stared at Henrique, Thorton knew that he had told the midshipman the secret. To Chambers fell the duty to guard and deliver the person of His Grace, Henrique, Duke of Coimbra, rightful king of Portugal, safely into British hands.

Horner returned and issued more orders. Thorton was to get the guns ashore and Perry would emplace them. Forsythe was to empty the hold so the carpenter and his mates could get at the broken planks and repair them. Mr. Wright was to supervise the crew throwing up dirt to form embankments to provide cover to the guns. Mr. Jones was to take a boat and go on patrol. He was to fire a pistol shot in warning if he found the Spanish.

To accomplish what they needed would take three days. Horner knew they wouldn't have it; the Spanish ships would be hunting for them. Since they had been last seen near the island, naturally they would look there. There was no point in saying so. All he could do was what he could do.

CHAPTER 17 : THE BLUFFS

All the hatches were open. Thorton worked from the forward hatch while Forsythe worked through the aft hatch. Getting the bottom fixed was the priority, so Forsythe had the use of the capstan to haul tuns of water and victuals and other supplies out of the hold. Thorton's crew reeved up the arm tackle to use for a winch. They wrapped the guns in nets, then swayed them up and over the side. They landed on the wet sand. More tackle was reeved to the rocks for mechanical advantage as they dragged the three thousand pound behemoths up the bluff. There wasn't a single tree on Alborán, not even a shrub. The predominant form of vegetation was a sort of daisy that was no use to them at all. Getting the guns up over the brow of the bluff was pure sweat. Thorton had the ship's boys gather driftwood which the men trimmed into rollers. That helped a little. The ship's boys ran to pick up the rollers and carry them to the front of the gun in an endless loop. What with the false starts, setting up the tackle, and the confusion of a novel task, it took them an hour to get the first gun to the top of the cliff.

Thorton stripped down to his jersey and drawers to save his uniform. He tied his blue and white checked kerchief over his head—a memento of his service aboard the galleys with Captain Tangle. He missed his turban. He could have dragged its tail across his face to save it from sunburn as Shakil was doing. Shakil was part of the crew hauling the guns up the hill. Slender though he was, his body had been hardened by farm work in the dark days when Tangle had been a prisoner and his family deprived of his support. The work settled into a steady rhythm: get a gun up, send up its carriage after, get another gun. In between another gang hauled sledges loaded with shot and powder. A gun was no good without ammunition.

Thorton arrived atop the bluff with the third gun. His men wrestled it over, then let the hands building the redoubt take charge of it. Horner sent a barrel of beer to the top of the cliff. The refreshment cheered the men considerably. A boy handed them each a biscuit and a piece of cheese. The men had had no breakfast and were ravenous. Thorton made a mental note to rotate his crews so that the men in the ship would get a turn at the beer and breakfast. Neither Thorton nor Shakil was a drinking man, but beer was what there was, so beer was what they drank.

The first of the Spanish frigates showed up in the middle of the morning. She busied herself taking soundings and sent them no message nor demand. In the broad light of day and with her no more than half a mile away, the strong prow and overhanging lazyboard aft the transom could be seen. She was a frigate-rigged xebec. That boded ill—she could work in close to the shore over the reefs. When she made her turn against the wind, the magnificently carved and gilded stern flashed in the morning light and showed her galley ancestry. She carried the broad pennant of a commodore.

Horner stood with his glass to his eye and studied the enemy flagship. Thorton and Shakil sat on the ground amid the daisies and watched him as they ate their bread and cheese. It seemed a little unreal. Thorton was so used to being at sea in one vessel or another that the land seemed to move beneath him. He finally revived enough to become curious, and tramped over to Horner to take a look.

Thorton swept his gaze full circle along the horizon and saw another xebec-frigate to the north of the island and another on the southwestern horizon. He watched them a while and guessed the first would arrive around noon. Horner was lost in his own thoughts, but Thorton knew he had seen them.

The lieutenant trudged back to his men. "All right, boys. Let's go sweat some more."

They groaned a complaint, but Thorton said very reasonably, "The *Ajax* can't fight, sail, or defend herself. We've got to get the guns into the redoubts before the Spaniards decide to get frisky."

The men looked across the cerulean sea to where the xebec-frigate made a fine picture. She was a beautiful sight—even if she did mean to do them harm. Thorton didn't tell them about the other vessels. It would only frighten them. They trudged down the hill, spit on their hands, and went back to work. The beer helped.

By noon the second Spaniard came up. She sent a boat over to the flagship. Meanwhile the xebec-frigate on the north side of the island was coasting east to round the small islet off Alborán's tip. Thorton had succeeded in getting six guns up the hill and was struggling with the seventh. His men were tired, but he exhorted them, so they kept straining at the lines. After the Spaniards finished their conference, the flagship flew a white flag and launched a boat. She skimmed along under a single lateen sail: the Spaniards were coming to parley.

Thorton walked down the beach to meet them. He sent a runner to Forsythe who was deep inside the hull where hammers were sounding. He got a message back quickly enough.

"Mr. Forysthe don't speak no Spanish, sir, so 'e leaves the Dagos to you. 'E's workin' on the bottom. 'E says they should have 'er patched some time this evening."

"Thank you."

The man ran back to his post.

The Spanish boat ran aground on the pebble beach. The Spanish sailors splashed into the water and pulled her up so their *teniente* could jump over the bow and land on the beach without getting his shoes wet. The Spaniard was splendidly dressed in a blue coat with scarlet facings and gold lace. His hat had gold braid around the brim and white ostrich feathers floated gently in the breeze. His white silk stockings were very fine. He looked Thorton up and down and in heavily accented English asked, "Where is your officer?"

Thorton replied in pure Castilian Spanish, "I'm Lieutenant Peter Thorton. Captain Horner is at dinner." He had no idea what the captain was doing, but he wanted the dandy in front of him to feel unimportant.

The man looked down his nose at Thorton even though Thorton was the taller man. He had a thin face, light brown hair, and hazel eyes. "Please inform your captain that Lieutenant Lucian Morales y Floridablanca of His Most Catholic Majesty's xabeque-fragata *San Anthurius* desires a word with him."

Thorton shrugged. "All right. I'm going up the hill anyhow." He turned his back on the man and walked away. He neither hurried nor dawdled. He thought if he kept the man waiting long enough they could get the seventh gun into the redoubt. The more guns on the cliff, the better. The *Ajax* would be smashed to smithereens when the enemy opened fire. The more of her guns he could rescue before that happened the sharper their resistance would be. Not that it would make much difference with two xebecs versus the grounded and vulnerable vessel. Thorton felt sorry for Horner. Such a beautiful career, now cut short. The navy would never forgive him for being hopelessly outnumbered and outgunned.

Horner waited at the top of the hill. "Well?" he asked as Thorton arrived. The gun struggled up the hill a little behind him.

"Lt. Lucian Morales of the *San Anthurius* begs leave to speak with you. I told him you were at dinner and he'd have to wait. I wanted to bring the gun up while I could, sir."

Horner's stomach rumbled. "Capital idea, Thorton. Kindly invite Lt. Morales to join me for dinner. If you put your breeches on, you may join us."

"Aye aye, sir."

Thorton turned and strolled down the hill while Horner called his steward. The man tore down the hill at a run, swerved around Thorton, and clambered aboard. Thorton's men trotted down the hill and passed him. By the time he reached the foot they were hauling the gun carriage up the beach.

Thorton reached Morales and gave a little bow. "Captain Horner sends his welcome and invites you to dine with him." He spoke infuriatingly good Spanish in spite of being dressed in nothing but his small clothes.

Morales was livid. He snapped back, "I will speak to Captain Horner now!"

"*Claro que sí, teniente.* But you'll be more comfortable doing it over dinner."

"Take me to him!"

"I will." Thorton retrieved his uniform from the rock where it was waiting. He pulled on his breeches and waistcoat. Morales was seething by the time he pulled on the unlined coat Ra'uf had made for him, pulled the kerchief down around his neck in place of a stock, and donned his hat. "Follow me."

He walked slowly up the hill, buttoning his waistcoat as he went. The captain's steward ran past them with a pair of baskets. The man beat them to the top of the hill. When they arrived, he was laying out a linen tablecloth on the ground and setting out wine and cold meat.

Horner frowned at Thorton. "You are out of uniform, Lieutenant."

Thorton looked down and was chagrined to see his knee buttons still unfastened. "I'm sorry, sir. Lt. Morales was impatient to meet you."

"That is no excuse for a slovenly appearance, especially in front of the Spanish! You will correct the fault immediately."

Thorton reddened and bent over to fasten his buttons as quickly as he could. "Aye aye, sir."

Horner glared at him until satisfied that the lieutenant was putting his uniform to rights as quickly as possible. That done, he turned and gave a grim smile to his guest. "Welcome, Lt. Morales. I am delighted you could join me for dinner. I'm afraid I can only offer you a *pique-nique* as the French call it, but the view is excellent." He addressed the man in Spanish.

Morales was about to burst from the delay. "Stalling won't do you any good! The *San Anthurius* and *Santa Clara* outnumber you. Your vessel is helpless on the beach! We demand your surrender!"

Horner was unruffled by the Spaniard's outburst. "That being the case, it can only rebound to your commodore's credit to handle the matter like a gentleman, no?"

Just then Shakil hurried up. He pulled the tail of his turban away from his face and let it hang down by his shoulder. "You called, Captain?" he asked. He also spoke Spanish.

He gave Shakil a smile with no real warmth in it. "This is Lt. Lucian Morales. We were about to sit down to dinner. I hope you will join us. Lieutenant, this is Mr. Shakil bin Nakih of the Sallee Republic. We are transporting him to Minorca."

Shakil and the Spaniard bowed very slightly to one another. Horner seated himself on a corner of the tablecloth.

Shakil sat down cross-legged on another corner. Morales couldn't very well talk to them when they were down there, so he knelt uncomfortably on his knees.

"This is not matter that requires a conference! We hold the upper hand. You must surrender. There is no reason to die. We are prepared to offer humane terms."

Horner gave an almost Gallic shrug. "We know what you really want. Smashing the *Ajax* won't do you any good."

The lieutenant narrowed his eyes. "What do you think we really want?"

Shakil was curious, too. He watched Horner pouring wine and handing it around.

"Mr. Shakil has been to Sebta recently," Horner replied.

Lt. Morales frowned and peered at Shakil, who nodded. "Why do you think that matters?" the Spaniard asked suspiciously.

Shakil replied with a grin, "Because you are missing a duke."

The lieutenant's expression grew even more sour. "I'm listening."

Horner shrugged. "You want to know where he is. You want to retrieve him."

"You are prepared to offer this information for the saving of your ship?"

Horner gave him a smile as he sliced the cold roast beef. "Not at all. I plan to sell our lives dearly to prevent that. You may smash the *Ajax,* but then you shall have to storm the shore, and the cliffs provide an excellent defense. The sea will run red with Spanish blood."

"You are playing games with me," the Spanish lieutenant said darkly.

Horner plopped a cold side of potatoes on his plate. "If you destroy us, you can't find the duke. From your point of view it makes more sense to let us go and follow us."

"Why would you allow that?"

"I won't allow it. But on the sea, anything can happen."

"Why would I believe you could lead me to the Duke of Coimbra?"

"Because Mr. Shakil is going to meet him."

The lieutenant narrowed his eyes at Shakil. "You know where he is?"

Shakil nodded happily. "I'm not telling, either."

Morales was beside himself. "You lie!" He might very well explode from the intensity of his feelings.

Usually Shakil would be offended at being called a liar, but instead he fingered his diamond earrings. "Recognize these? Duke Henrique gave them to me for helping him escape."

Morales was not as stupid as they were hoping. "He's here! He's somewhere on this island!"

Horner didn't want him to figure it out, but it didn't really matter. He shrugged. "If you want him, you have to fetch him. We have the advantage of the high ground. Accordingly, the fact that you have two frigates is immaterial."

Morales never touched the slab of cold beef Horner served onto his plate. He stared coldly at Horner. "If you want us to come and take him, we will."

Horner was complacent. "You can try."

"There is no water on this island! You will be dead of thirst within days."

Shakil spoke. "There is water. My brother-in-law dug a well when he was here."

Morales eyes popped out of his head. "What?"

Shakil nodded again. "Isam Rais Tangueli. We're rendezvousing with the Sallee fleet here." Morales goggled at him some more. "You don't think we ran onto Alborán by accident, do you? Time is on our side."

All vessels carried a finite amount of ammunition. In the case of a xebec, the amount was smaller than other vessels. Being intended for speed, they were narrower and shallower and didn't have the same cargo capacity. They could, if fully laden, gorge themselves for a six month voyage, but the Spaniards were coastguards. They were lightly equipped since they cruised a fortnight at most before returning to their base. They were not equipped to make a protracted siege. Especially if they might fall prey to a much larger force.

"How many Sallee rovers?"

Shakil shrugged. "I don't know. But he is the third highest ranking sea officer. The Sallee Republic is well aware of the importance of Duke Henrique and has pledged to support the independence of Portugal. I expect to see them out in force."

Morales' eyes were wide and they saw a trace of fear. The Sallee rovers meeting up with Henrique and launching a major offensive? This was something his superiors needed to know. "I have to report to my captain."

Horner waved his fork at him. "You haven't eaten a bite."

Morales jumped to his feet. "I must go."

"Please, if you do not accept my hospitality, I shall be offended. It is a point of honor," replied Horner.

"'Tis good roast beef," Shakil added.

"I don't give a damn about English honor."

Horner used his napkin to delicately clean his fingers. "Really, Lieutenant, you embarrass yourself. I hope you are not this excitable in battle."

The Spanish lieutenant glared at him, then turned and stalked down the hill in a huff.

When he was gone, Horner asked, "Is there a well?"

"There must have been when al-Borany lived here, but that was two hundred years ago," Shakil replied complacently.

"And the Sallee navy?"

"Isam Rais is ranked right behind Murad Rais and Admiral Saadiq. They are going to besiege Sebta as soon as they get the intelligence I carry."

Horner finally looked at him. "Do you expect to meet them here?"

"Only in my dreams."

"You have the makings of a good whist player, Mr. Shakil. You finessed him well."

"I equivocated, but I think Allah will forgive me." His eyes darted to Thorton. "I know Isam will come when he hears the news. If they put to sea immediately and the winds favor them, they could be here in three days. I think five to seven days more likely, though. Do you think we can hold out that long?"

Horner pinched the bridge of his nose. "If we must, we must. Mr. Thorton, I'll trouble you for a tun of water before they blow the *Ajax* to bits."

"Aye aye, sir."

Down below the Spanish lieutenant launched his boat and shoved off. His sailors immediately began bailing. Thorton took out his glass and watched their consternation. Meanwhile Ra'uf jogged up the hill.

The man was soaking wet. Thorton lowered his glass and walked to meet him.

Ra'uf grinned at him. "I found something you might want, Effendi." He put a boat plug in Thorton's hand.

Thorton couldn't help laughing. "How did you get this?"

Ra'uf looked pleased but abashed. "I used to be a pearl diver."

The Spaniards stuffed a shirt in the hole, bailed, and rowed back to the flagship. Thorton walked back to the picnic, tossing the plug in his hand as he went. He bowed and offered it to the captain.

Horner took it, looked at it, looked at the grinning lieutenant, looked at Ra'uf's wet clothes, and raised his bushy eyebrows. "A unique souvenir from the Isle of Alborán. I assume this was your doing, Ra'uf?"

Ra'uf touched his forehead, grinned shyly, and backed away. Thorton could not keep a straight face as he replied, "The Spanish lost it and Ra'uf found it. I thought you might want to return it to them."

"If they want it, they can ask for it. I am not of a mind to do Lt. Morales any favors." Horner resumed his seat upon the linen and waved his knife. "Come, sit. Eat. You haven't touched your plate."

"Ra'uf, tell them to get a tun of water up the hill next." Thorton dropped to the ground and fell on the food with a good will. He was suddenly ravenous.

Horner continued talking in between bites of cold beef and potatoes. "Mr. Thorton, it is your duty to bring up as much powder and shot as you can. You must keep the cliff batteries supplied. I don't need to advise you that it will be difficult and dangerous."

"Aye aye, sir." Thorton wiped his mouth on a napkin.

"Leave your men here to eat and drink. Go to Forsythe, tell him to leave off mending the hull. Take as many of his men as you need to do the work. Send Forsythe to me. After the men up here have dined, I'll send them down to you, and you can send the men down there up to get their meal."

"Aye aye, sir," Thorton said with a mouth full of beef.

"Don't talk with your mouth full, Mr. Thorton."

Thorton washed it down with wine. "Sorry, sir." He picked up a loaf of soft white bread. It was only a little stale from the two weeks it had been on board the ship. He broke it in half and picked the weevils out. "Do you mind if I take this with me?"

"Not at all."

Thorton broke the half open and put meat and cheese inside it. He tied it up in his linen handkerchief and stuffed it in a pocket. He did the same with the other half, bound it in his blue and white kerchief, and pocketed it as well.

Shakil watched and listened. When Thorton rose so did he. "Peter." He could tell from the direction of Thorton's steps where he was going.

Thorton paused. "Mr. Shakil?"

Shakil swallowed hard. *"¿Está tu puesto?"* He nodded at the disabled frigate.

"Sí, lo mismo."

Shakil's jaw worked and his eyes filled with emotion. "You're going to die."

"Very likely."

"I love you."

"I love you, too."

Horner pretended he neither heard nor understood their soft Spanish conversation. He took a flask from his pocket and knocked back a deep drink. Every man had his own way of fortifying himself against the inevitable.

"Allah will watch over you."

"And you. Give my love to the family."

"I will."

Thorton started away, then turned back. "Shakil. Don't let them bury me in blue. I want to wear my Sallee coat."

Shakil nodded and tears started in his eyes. "I will. You are a Sallee man and a Muslim, *habibi.*"

"Good bye, *habibi.*"

"Good bye, beloved."

With that Thorton turned and made his way down to the ship.

CHAPTER 18 : GYRONNY, ARGENT AND SABLE

The *Santa Clara* piled on all canvas and scudded away. The flagship *San Anthurius* was left alone. She tacked away as well and at first the men heartened thinking that the two xebec-frigates were leaving, but the flagship came around and began her run. With the wind out of the northwest she skimmed along parallel to the shore. Her guns ran out and she tried a ranging shot. It smacked into the cliff face below and away from the eastern battery. The other guns were set up in a battery to the west of the path. By splitting the batteries Perry had made it harder for the Spanish to take them both out.

The gun hauling crew was trying to get the eighth gun up. They ducked and covered but the shot was far enough away that the rain of rock and sand didn't touch them. The pockmark in the face of the cliff was enough to put fire to their arses and they redoubled their efforts. A moment later the Spanish broadside crashed out. Balls flew high and passed over the eastern battery. They smashed into the grassy hillock behind it and plowed long grooves in the sod. Someone screamed—the bounding shot had crested the hill and dropped among the men eating dinner on the other side.

Horner ordered, "Ranging shot, if you please, Mr. Carson." The gunner grunted a reply, aimed the shot himself, and fired. It arched high over the *San Anthurius*.

"Again."

Carson adjusted for the height advantage the cliff offered. The next shot was still a little high, but it tore through the *Anthurius'* rigging.

"Excellent, Mr. Carson. Hull them, please." A xebec-frigate was still a xebec. Dismasting her was pointless. She would simply put out her sweeps and row. "Fire as she bears."

The guns of the western battery thundered out. Their shots fell into the sea ahead of the xebec-frigate. Towers of water splashed her bow but caused her no hurt.

Down in the *Ajax's* hull Thorton and Forsythe were having a discussion. "I don't want to go up, Peter. We can fix her. A few hours more. That's all we need. They aren't firing on us—they think we're dead on the beach. Our guns are useless so there is no reason for them to waste their shot on us."

"You may be able to patch her, but how will you float her, Albert? She'll need to be towed off, and if they see us towing her, they'll smash the boats."

"I don't know. But if I don't patch her she won't float. The tide might raise her."

"There's not more than three feet of tide in the Mediterranean and it won't come until nightfall!"

"I don't know what else to do, Peter! What can I do up there? You and Perry are much better working the guns than I am. This is something I know how to do. Please let me do it."

"You are the first lieutenant, sir. You can order me if you wish."

Forsythe's fundamental flaw as an officer was that he did not know how to make decisions or give orders. He was a hardworking man when given work he understood and the tools to do it, but he did not have the creative mind necessary to think through all the possibilities, weigh them in an instant, come to a decision, and act on it. In short, he was not a leader.

"Very well. I order you, Lt. Thorton."

"Aye aye, sir. I'll send word to Horner." He remembered his pockets and dug in. He handed the white handkerchief-wrapped food to Forsythe. "Eat something. You'll need it."

"Thank you, Peter." Forsythe gave him a grateful smile.

Thorton saluted and Forsythe returned it. "God go with you, sir."

"And you, Peter." The first lieutenant slogged back into the hold.

Thorton did not think would see him again. He turned slowly away. He stood watching the men laboring to get shot and powder out of the hold. They had stripped down to their drawers. Sweat glistened on their hairy backs and their feet were black from tramping in the flecks of gunpowder that inevitably sifted from the barrels. He wondered how long before they were red shreds on the deck.

The *San Anthurius'* second broadside roared over head and Thorton snapped back to work. He had not checked his watch. How long had it taken them to reload? He pulled his watch out and timed the Spaniard's next broadside: a little over four minutes. The batteries on the bluff replied in three. So, an exchange of four for three. In a quarter hour the British would fire thirty-two shots compared to sixty-six from the Spaniard.

"We are faster with the guns, lads, so that's good news," he said with forced bonhomie.

They were unschooled sailors. They gave a cheer and grinned.

"Move your asses, you limp-boned monkeys! We've got to get the powder up!" His hand dipped into his pocket and out came the tawse. He stung them liberally. "Work, damn you!"

They laughed and went to work with a will. One of them began to sing a bawdy tune.

Shot whistled over Thorton's head and buried itself in the cliff face. A small landslide poured down and onto the beach. Thorton was not unduly disturbed—they were still firing on the batteries above. He could be hit by a stray shot, but they were not actually shooting at him. Still, his men must run the gauntlet of Spanish shot to bring their sledge up over the top. He paused beside a buried ball and dug in the sand until he could gauge its size. "Nine pound shot. That helps."

He did the math as he trotted to catch up to his men. Thirty-two shots at twelve pounds each was—round off to make it easier—three hundred and sixty—add the two that were dropped—three hundred eighty-four pounds from the batteries on the bluffs.

"Come on lads! We've got a minute while she reloads! Get it up!"

One of the men muttered, "I could get it up all right if I had a lass to help!" They all laughed.

Thorton ran down the hill and borrowed some men from Forsythe's gang to make another sledge. It was little more than a shallow box, but they could haul more powder and shot with the sledges than trying to carry them by hand. With two sledges they might be able to keep up with the rate at which the batteries were expending their shot and powder.

He turned his head and saw the enemy reaching the end of her run. Now she must tack back and forth across the wind to bring her starboard guns to bear. She could tack close or far. Near and she would be among the reefs she had sounded earlier. If she knew her way, she could pound the battery at close range. He held his breath as she turned on the other tack. She chose the outside course. Shot peppered the beach and bluff. The batteries roared above, but Thorton was too busy to note if their shot did any good.

"Move, you sons of bitches! Up while she reloads!"

He went up the hill again. His shins and ankles hurt from all the running up and down he had done today.

The world exploded.

Thorton was thrown from the path. He tumbled over and over as he rolled down the bluff to land in a heap at the bottom. He lay insensible to anything but the ringing in his ears and the fiery pain in the left side of his face and neck. How long he lay there he didn't know. It seemed only an instant, but it must have been longer because someone poured cold water over his head.

"Mr. Thorton! Mr. Thorton!" He had no idea who was calling him.

He couldn't move or speak. He blinked but everything was dark. He dragged his hand towards his face but couldn't find it. He tasted sand. They rolled him onto his back and somebody brushed sand off his face. Bright. It was painfully bright. He blinked up. A circle of faces he didn't recognize was staring down at him.

"Stretcher!" somebody bawled.

"Belay that," he croaked. Was he hurt? His head was ringing. God, how it rang and rang. His chest heaved as he tried to breathe. His neck and left shoulder ached; the blast had caught him in the side. They helped him sit up. "What happened?"

"They had a shot left, sir. They hit us. The powder blew. Tolliver's dead."

Thorton had just spoken to him. He rubbed a dirty hand across his face.

"Lord, sir. You look a fright! Your ear is all black. Are you burned, sir?" Whoever it was brushed his arm and shoulder.

Thorton didn't know. "Am I? I can't feel anything. I feel like a marionette with broken strings."

"Get him to the hospital, lads," said another voice.

"No. Help me up. I have work to do," he countermanded him.

"Begging your pardon, sir, but we can't get the powder up with them shooting at us!"

"But we must get the powder up all the same. We'll have to time it. When she makes her turn she cannot fire—we'll dash to the top with it. We may need to lighten the sledges to make it."

They heaved him to his feet. A sailor at his side pulled his arm over his shoulders to steady him. Thorton looked around, but he couldn't see. "Where is she?"

Her broadside roared and they were covered with chips of stone and dust. "Southeast, sir."

"Now, lads. Now! She'll can't fire until she turns and runs up again!"

They ran. One sailor supported Thorton and took him down the beach to shelter under the bow. The second sledge disappeared over the top of the cliff with many hands helping to haul. The *Anthurius* came around again. Since no crew was carrying powder up the slope, she turned her attention to the batteries again. Thorton's head was slowly clearing. He rubbed his eyes, but that just put grime from his sleeve into his face.

The sailor said, "Here, sir. Let me help." The man got out his own kerchief and cleaned Thorton's face. He spit on the kerchief and wiped some of the sand and soot out of Thorton's eyes.

"Thank you, man." He leaned against the bow like a drunk man. He could see the trail was now shattered with deep gouges in it. "Tolliver! Take some men and shovels and fill those holes."

"Tolliver's still dead, sir. D'ya want Bixby instead?" somebody replied in a respectful tone.

"Bixby!" Thorton bellowed. "Fill those holes! Put the boys on it!"

Bixby hesitated, then said, "Aye aye, sir." They had no shovels but the men who had been digging the redoubts up top did. He grabbed several of the ship's boys and sent the children to fetch them. They laid low during the next broadside, then ran down the cliff with the shovels and started filling the holes.

Thorton remembered that he had been trying to calculate the relative weights of metal possessed by the two sides. He forced himself to finish it to prove that he could. He needed to know his brain was working.

"Sixty-six Spanish balls at nine pounds each is a little less than ten pounds each, would be six hundred sixty. Less a tenth—" The English batteries roared and drowned out the sound of his thoughts. "Less a tenth . . a tenth . . . sixty-six . . . Where was I? Six hundred sixty less sixty-six . . . Yes, mister?" He couldn't remember the man's name.

"The new sledge is ready, sir."

"Loaded?"

"Working on it."

"Shelter under the bow until she fires her next broadside. Whatever you've got on the sledge then, run with it."

"Aye aye, sir."

"Sixty-six . . . Six hundred something . . . No . . . Five hundred ninety-four. Remember that, man." The world was tipping and swishing in unpredictable ways. He clung to the bow for support.

"Aye aye, sir. Five hundred ninety-four. Begging your pardon, but what does it mean?"

Thorton couldn't see straight. "How much metal the Spaniard throws in three broadsides."

The sailor wasn't sure what to think of Thorton mumbling mathematics at such a moment. "How much are we throwing, sir?"

"I've forgotten. I knew it, before I got knocked down. Let me work it out again . . . eight guns . . . What is your name, man?"

"DuBois, sir."

"French?"

"No, sir. I'm from Kent."

The Spanish broadside roared over head. A scream from up top announced the blow had struck. "What has happened, Mr. Kent?" He was swaying on his feet in spite of having the bow to hold him up.

"DuBois, sir. Looks like one of the guns has been dismounted."

"Damn. I'll have to refigure. Let me see, seven times four is twenty-eight . . ." Thorton's knees buckled and he slumped to the ground.

This time when he woke and insisted he didn't want a stretcher they ignored him. They ran him up the hill as the Spaniard made her turn. The powder, shot, and wounded lieutenant came over the brow of the bluff all at once. Horner saw him go by and set his jaw grimly. He went over to check on Thorton.

"Captain! I can get up, sir. I can." The wounded lieutenant struggled to roll out of the stretcher.

"Lie still, Mr. Thorton." Horner put a hand on his chest to hold him down.

"Captain! She's coming!" Perry shouted.

Horner ran back to the redoubt and the stretcher men ran for the top of the hill. Behind them the roar of the Spanish broadside was followed by the whistling of balls and the dull thud and shake as they smashed into the earth around the batteries.

A pistol shot sounded in the distance. "What is it?" Thorton asked feverishly.

"'Tis Mr. Jones in the launch, sir. He's warning us another Spaniard is coming up. We've got two of them to deal with them now." His stretcher bearer spoke consolingly. He was only a loblolly boy. Worrying about the number of the enemy was a job for officers.

"Powder! Get it in here!" Horner bellowed.

The sledge was the last of the powder and shot at the top of the cliff. They could load and fire faster than Thorton's men could keep them supplied. "I have to get up," he said, but they wouldn't let him.

They carried Thorton into the shelter behind the hill and laid him on the ground next to the previous casualty. Shakil was working in the hospital. He had stripped off his purple coat and wore a leather apron over his white shirt with his sleeves rolled up. "No! Allah forfend, Peter!" He ran to the stretcher.

"I'm not hurt," Thorton told him.

"You're a mess! Here, lie here on the soft grass." He helped drag Thorton off the stretcher and laid him out.

A second broadside roared close at hand and a wild cheer erupted from the English. "What is it? What has happened?" Thorton asked. He struggled to sit up.

"I don't know," Shakil replied.

"Let me see! Help me up!"

So Shakil helped Thorton to the brow of the hill. They laid on their bellies and peeked over the top.

"What flag is that?" Thorton asked. "My eyes are bleary, I can't make it out. Black and white?"

The cheering continued and hats were tossed in the air. Shakil shouted with joy, "Gyronny, argent and sable!"

The language of heraldry meant nothing at all to Thorton.

"What?" He stared down where the newly arrived xebec-frigate was flying a flag that looked like a black and white pinwheel to the untutored eye. She had caught the *San Anthurius* by surprise and smashed her stern. The flagship's rudder wouldn't answer and the *Anthurius* had to put her oars out to steer. The strange ship yawed and brought her other broadside to bear and smashed her stern again. With a mighty roar that shook the entire island, the powder magazine blew.

The flagship disappeared in a cloud of dust and smoke. The wall of sound flattened the waves for a cable's length around her, and then she was a rain of debris. Bits of her even flew onto the beach. Her masts toppled like trees in a storm. They could not hear men screaming; her death was instantaneous. One moment she had been there in all her glory; in the next, she was gone.

"My God," said Thorton.

The other ship launched boats, but there were no survivors.

"Gyronny, argent and sable. The colors of Coimbra. She has declared for Henrique! Give thanks to Allah, we are saved!" Shakil hugged him.

CHAPTER 19 : THE ORDER OF THE DAISY

The officers of the Portuguese and British navies supped on Alborán under a quarter moon. The *Ajax* was afloat; after her repairs the two Portuguese vessels had towed her off. Two, yes, because another of the Spanish squadron had come up, and after parley, declared for Henrique. The duke had come out of his hiding place and was hosting a royal banquet to honor the officers who fought so gallantly on his behalf. He gave the xebec-frigates new names: *Royal Guardian* for the vessel that had rescued them all, and *Loyalty* her consort. The last of the Spanish squadron had nosed up late that afternoon but had been run off by the Portuguese rebels.

The batteries were still on the bluffs, likewise the hospital and mess hall. Mess tables and benches and linens were brought out of the ship and the various vessels contributed victuals and cooks to make the banquet. The exhausted men were given a double shot of rum with their rations. Once fed, they strung their hammocks below deck and slept like logs even as the officers made merry.

Thorton attended the banquet. He was concussed and couldn't see straight. He had to be kept awake all night for fear he would never wake if he slept. Shakil was by his side to shake him and hiss at him. The Moor kept the wine away and plied him with hot frothy Turkish coffee instead. Thorton's ear was blackened by the blast and he had lost his hair on that side. The doctor wanted to apply lard to it, but Thorton refused and asked for cinnamon. He had been impressed by the remedy when Captain Tangle had used it on his own wounds. It seemed a life time ago, but it was only a few months. As a consequence, his neck and left ear was cinnamon powder brown on top of powder burn black. He looked hideous, but nobody begrudged him his place at the table.

Horner was all in one piece, but Perry had his arm in a sling and a slash of red across his face held together by stitches. He'd caught shrapnel when a gun exploded. His face wasn't so handsome now. Forsythe was all right, apart from having mashed his thumb with a hammer while working in the hold. Wright was dead. Chambers, Jones and the other midshipmen were in fine fettle and drinking too much with the abandon of young men far from parental supervision. The sailing master had come safe through the barrage, but the pursuer had been hit in the buttocks by a piece of stone that flew up when a ball struck nearby. No small arms had been involved and the marines had come through with only minor injuries. The batteries had taken many casualties, as had the crew hauling powder and shot. The butcher's bill was nine dead, thirty-seven wounded. That could not quench the high spirits of the men around the table.

Captain Souza, the Portuguese captain, was speaking Spanish for the benefit of those English who could understand it. "When I heard that Henrique had escaped, I was determined to do him some service. I bided my time, and lo, I was lucky enough to arrive in the nick of time! I am not the only one. There are other Portuguese men and officers who will follow you, Your Grace. They resent the way the Spanish dominate everything. The officers of the fort and battleships, all Spaniards. The Portuguese get minor posts, like coastguards and supply ships. We, who are the posterity of King Henrique the Navigator! We look to King Henrique the Liberator to restore our fortunes, our honor, and our independence!"

"Here, here!" a chorus answered him. The men raised their cups Henrique smiled graciously and bowed a little.

All the English officers knew that King Henrique the Navigator had opened the way around the Cape of Good Hope and made Portugal a wealthy rival to Spain—until marriage united the two crowns. The union had not benefited Portugal.

Horner raised his glass in toast, but otherwise kept quiet and drank moderately. He sat to Henrique's left hand and Captain Souza to the right. The tables were set in a horseshoe with the duke at the apex. Thorton was well regarded and sat at the head table next to Horner. Shakil, the immediate agent of the duke's rescue, was with him. He helped to hold Thorton up and find his food when it seemed to wander across the plate. Thorton continued swaying gently as if he were still at sea instead of on solid land. He had no idea what he was eating. His sense of taste and smell were destroyed by the blast.

A great deal of wine went around. Dessert was a giant pudding with two masses in the middle representing Alborán and the islet of Nubes off the southeastern tip. Cheese had been carved into the shape of boats with sails made from slices of bread. Raisins represented the guns of the shore batteries. The combined tastes were not agreeable. The cooks had labored with what was at hand to provide a suitable commemoration for the event. Hungry men were pleased to eat it.

The Spanish had sunk a second time under the spoons of the Portuguese when some of the ship's boys came up. They had decked themselves with daisy garlands and carried more garlands over their arms. They were quite shy, but Reverend Pennybrigg, the *Ajax*'s chaplain, was behind them and whispered encouragement.

"Your Grace, we beg leave to present a small ode in celebration of your victory." Pennybrigg had composed the lines himself.

One of the Portuguese officers translated for him. Henrique smiled and said graciously, "We are pleased to hear it."

The head boy, a freckled tyke no more than twelve, bowed deeply and recited in his piping boy soprano,

"We wish you the greatest felicitations
and hope that you will hear our solicitation
on this victorious day of glory
as we recite our noble story."

The doggerel went on for a while, but Henrique was happy to listen to it. All the men were immensely charmed—especially those who couldn't understand English. When it ended, the boy offered a daisy garland to the duke.

Henrique bent low so the boy could put it over his bewigged head. He rose with the daisies around his neck. "Our Lord Jesus was not more honored than I to receive this gift. I am pleased to establish a new order of Portuguese chivalry, the Order of the Daisy, to be awarded to gentlemen who distinguish themselves in our naval service."

He took another garland from the boy's hands and said, "The first recipient of this honor is Shakil bin Nakih, who rescued me from my gaolers in Sebta."

Shakil was quite surprised, but Thorton elbowed him and he got up. He bowed so deeply he had to put his hand to his forehead to keep his turban from falling off. Henrique looped the garland around his neck. "Rise, Sir Shakil."

The duke gave his hand to the Moor, who bent and kissed it. Shakil stammered something in Arabic, then composed himself enough to speak Spanish. "You do me more honor than I deserve. I am just a bookkeeper, Your Grace."

"You are a brave and clever fellow and without you I wouldn't be here." He took Shakil by the shoulders and kissed him on both cheeks.

The officers clapped and the men cheered. Someone called out, "A toast! Long live His Majesty! Confusion to his enemies!" The toast was in Portuguese but it sounded stirring enough to the English. They were happy to drink to it.

Next Thorton was called. He tottered up to the duke on his own two feet, bowed deeply and fell down. Horner and Shakil helped him onto his knees. His legs wouldn't hold him, but that was all right.

"For eluding six Spanish xebecs, defeating two Spanish frigates, and teaching me how to slide down a backstay, Peter Rais Thorton." He put the garland around his neck. "Rise, Sir Peter."

Horner and Shakil hauled him up and put him in his chair again. Again the assembled officers cheered and applauded and drank a toast. Horner and Shakil let go of him to stand up and raise their cups. Without their support Thorton fell forward into his plate. Shakil dragged him upright and applied a kerchief to clean his face.

"Ow!" Thorton complained. He was starting to feel his hurts.

Next the garland was awarded to Captain Souza. He fell on his knees and kissed his liege's hand fervently. He, too, was knighted and raised up and received kisses on his cheeks. The Portuguese cheered especially hard for him.

Horner came in for the award, then Perry, Forsythe, Wright (posthumously), and the midshipmen. The officers of the *Royal Guardian* and the *Loyalty* received it. By the time all the toasts were drunk, everyone was soused except Thorton and Shakil. With the shape he was in Thorton might as well have been drunk. Shakil was the only one among them able to maintain an upright position without external support. Even Horner had developed a pronounced list to the starboard. Henrique had a prodigious capacity for drink, but he was lame in one leg and the other ankle was sprained, so he had to be carried down to the beach. He went aboard the *Royal Guardian*, singing off key Portuguese all the way.

Horner, Thorton, and the other officers had to be hauled aboard the *Ajax* one after the other in the boatswain's chair. Shakil and Ra'uf put Thorton in the bed vacated by Henrique. By all rights it belonged to Forsythe, but he was too drunk to remember. He went to bed in the bunk he and Perry had shared. Perry found himself in Wright's berth. Snores were soon resounding through the wardroom. Their stewards got them out of their coats and waistcoats, took their shoes away to polish, and put blankets over them. The daisy garlands were saved and hung on hooks next to their coats. Shakil changed into his nightshirt and crawled in next to Thorton and shook him.

"You can't sleep, Peter. Wake up."

Thorton groaned and turned. "Must I?"

"You must."

Shakil helped him to prop against the wall. Shakil called Ra'uf for more coffee. They took turns sleeping and keeping Peter company. By dawn his pupils were the same size and Shakil let him sleep at last. Not even the resounding crash of a gun falling onto the deck woke him.

CHAPTER 20 : THE LEOPARD'S PAW

The guns were put back into the *Ajax*. The *Royal Guardian* guarded them while they were so engaged but did not assist them with their labor. They liked to visit and watch though. Once the *Ajax* was armed and loaded they set sail to carry Henrique to his supporters. Horner sent him a departing present in the form of a tub planted with daisies from the island. It was Jones' duty to lead a pair of men to dig the daisies, plant the tub, and deliver it to the *Royal Guardian*. No one thought it strange that thirteen-year-old Jones should be telling men old enough to be his father or grandfather what to do. It was the British way. His white collar made him the lowliest of officers, but it was death for any of them to strike or desert him. In such minor ways a boy learned leadership.

Thorton's head and ear and shoulder ached. He was permitted to convalesce in the first lieutenant's cabin. With the departure of Henrique he ought to have surrendered it to Forsythe, but Forsythe did not ask for it back. Thorton missed all the funerals, but he heard the rattle of the drums and the sad piping of the fifes, then the splash as the bodies went over the side. He sat propped up in bed while Shakil sat next to him reading aloud from the Qu'ran. His tenor voice was pleasant and the Arabic was a pleasing lilt that no longer sounded alien.

Horner was on his rounds visiting the invalids. He paused to listen as the strange sounds came through the door. He could not understand the Arabic but he understood the devotion he heard in Shakil's voice.

The Moor translated into Spanish. "Remember the name of your Lord and devote yourself only to Him. The Lord of the East and West, there is no God but He, therefore take Him as a protector . . . He knows some among you are sick, or travelers, or at war, therefore, read as much as is easy to you, keep up the prayer, give charity, and offer good things to Allah. Whatever good you send to others, you will find it with Allah; that is the greatest and best reward—"

Horner rapped sharply on the doorframe. His face was set in its usual severe lines when Shakil opened the door.

"Good afternoon. I'd like to pay a call on Mr. Thorton." He spoke Spanish.

"Of course, sir." Shakil admitted him to the room.

Thorton sat to attention as the captain entered.

"As you were, Lieutenant. I understand the surgeon has ordered light duty starting tomorrow. I'm pleased to see you doing better."

Thorton nodded gingerly. He wondered if he was in trouble for listening to the Qu'ran. "Thank you, sir," he said politely.

Horner was a British captain; he had a duty to enforce Article One. But how could he deny a wounded man the comfort of his holy book in the confines of his own sickbed? His voice was raspy when he spoke.

"I wanted to let you know I shall place your name in the third lieutenant's position since we buried Lt. Wright yestereve."

"I'm sorry about Mr. Wright, sir."

"The fortunes of war, gentlemen."

Shakil nodded and murmured, "Peace be upon him."

"We sail at dawn tomorrow. I'll expect you on the quarterdeck then. You can further Mr. Jones' education in signal work."

"Aye aye, sir."

"Until tomorrow then."

Thorton dressed and presented himself on the quarterdeck at the crack of dawn. It was still dark. Mist hovered over a silent sea. The ship swung gently at her anchor. Perry's watch was coming to an end.

"Anything interesting?" Thorton asked him.

"Overcast, what little breeze has died. Nothing of note."

Thorton nodded carefully. The burns on his neck and face hurt horribly and his left eye was blurred. "I relieve you, sir."

"Aye aye, Lieutenant. Damn, I need breakfast."

Perry started for the steps, then paused to let Shakil come up. The Moor had a prayer rug with him and laid it out on the quarterdeck as he did every morning. He was diligent about his prayers.

"Deck ho! Ship due south!" the lookout called.

The *Ajax* was at anchor with her bow northwest and stern southeast. Thorton looked over the larboard rail and peered into the grayness. Was there something darker than the sea out there? There was. Something that was accompanied by small white flashes. For a moment he did not know what it was, then realized it was the florescence of foam swept by oars.

"Mr. Perry, would you be kind enough to inform Captain Horner there is a row galley off the larboard quarter?"

"Aye aye, Lieutenant." Fatigue forgotten, Perry flew down the steps.

Horner came up unshaven. He was buttoning his waistcoat with his steward running along behind him with his coat and hat in hand. Reaching the quarterdeck, he let his steward help him into his coat as he barked, "Report, Lieutenant."

Thorton replied. "Masthead spotted an unidentified ship due south, sir. There are some white flashes I think is oar spume."

Horner pulled out his glass and studied the southern sea. His steward, a short stout man with a florid face, stood by with the captain's cocked hat in his hands.

"Deck ho, another ship! Two points east the first!"

The sky lightened and the squadron appeared out the silver mist. Five oared vessels approached them. They formed a crescent that encircled the *Ajax*, trapping her against the Isle of Alborán. The center vessel was a two-masted lateener with her sails furled. She was flanked by two lateeners on each side. A broad swallow tail pennant hung from the masthead of the central vessel. A commodore, then. A faint ululating cry drifted across the distance. Thorton cocked his head and listened. He thought he knew it, but at this distance he wasn't certain.

Shakil knew it by heart. He immediately commenced bowing and turning. His clear tenor voice rose in time with the strange sounds drifting across the water. He could recognize the Muslim prayer with only the slightest clue.

Horner turned to look at Shakil, then at Thorton. Thorton explained, "Whenever two or more Muslim men are together in one place, they pray as a congregation. He can hear them, so he's joining them."

"I see," said Horner. He put his spyglass in his pocket as he contemplated the encirclement. "Do you know these vessels, Mr. Thorton?"

"The flagship is the galiot *Arrow*, sir. She is flanked to the east by the xebec *Sea Leopard*." It was too far to read the names, but he knew his own ship like he knew his own face.

"Who is the commanding officer?"

"I don't know, sir. The *Sea Leopard* was in the hands of Kasim Rais, but I know that Isam Rais was making every effort to recover her. The Spanish made a prize of her when they captured him. They cut down her antennas, which is why her antennas are so short."

"Short?" Horner asked in surprise. He put the glass to his eye again. "They appear long to me. They are certainly longer than our yards."

"A xebec carries a tremendous press of sail compared to her hull, sir. I have seen them in Zokhara and elsewhere. The *Sea Leopard* is —" Thorton almost said something critical. "Not to the Sallee standard."

"Captain Kasim, you say, hm?" Horner mused. "What do you know of him?"

"He doesn't have the rank or status to command a squadron unless something terrible has happened in the Sallee Republic. My guess is that Isam Rais Tangueli in command. You know him as 'Captain Tangle.' He owns the *Arrow*."

Horner's long face grew longer as his lips pursed together. "He has quite the reputation."

"He earned it, sir."

"Did he?" Horner flicked an inscrutable look at him.

The other officers were coming up from below and gathering in knots along the rail to watch. Except for the recently pressed men who were necessarily ignorant, everyone aboard knew what such an encirclement meant. The two vessels at the ends of the arc were in the shoals of Alborán so they must be galleys. Their big bow guns—thirty-two pounds if they were an ounce—pointed at the *Ajax*. Four vessels meant a weight of two hundred and eighty-eight pounds of metal could be hurled, not counting the smaller guns that ranged alongside them. Eight twelve pounders added ninety-six pounds, and eight nine pounders, seventy-two pounds. All told, four hundred and fifty-six pounds versus the Ajax's three hundred and forty-eight, not counting the *Sea Leopard* who was armed as well as the *Ajax*, plus the *Arrow* and the other escort. The *Ajax* had nothing over a twelve-pounder. They were outgunned by a margin of three to one.

"Mr. Jones, you are late," Horner said crisply. The young midshipman cringed. He had tried to slip silently into his position without being noticed. "Mr. Thorton, why are the hands idling in the waist? Set them about their chores."

Thorton strode to the rail and bellowed down, "MacDonald! Get those men to work! Do you think this is a Punch and Judy show? You have chores to do!"

"Aye aye, sir!" The boatswain's pipe twittered and he shouted his own orders. Slowly the men sorted themselves into work gangs and began the holystoning of the deck. The galley fire began to send up the scent of woodsmoke to be followed a little later by the smell of oatmeal.

"Mr. Jones. Make a signal. '*Ajax* to flag, respectfully request commodore join *Ajax* for breakfast.'"

Jones struggled with the signal book and flags as Thorton supervised him. Flags ran up the halyard and broke open. There was not much breeze and they hung limply.

Shakil finished the first set of prayers, paused a moment, then continued into the second. The sound of the prayers being chanted on each vessel came more clearly across the water as the range slowly closed.

Jones waited a while, then received a response. "Sallee flag to *Ajax*, 'Do not understand.'"

"Thorton. Is there anyone among the Sallee men that can read an English signal?"

Thorton gulped. "That would be me, sir." He gave Horner an apologetic look. Aruj had done a stint as a British signal midshipman, but he did not know the entire signal book by heart as Thorton did. Besides, he was very likely to be at his post in the *Arrow's* bow, personally pointing those big guns at the English frigate. Thorton was not so certain of the skill of the gunners on the other vessels, but he was positive he did not want to be on the receiving end of the young lieutenant's gunnery. The boy was good.

Horner gave him a level look. "Make whatever signals you think are likely to convey my message to the Sallee vessels, if you please, Mr. Thorton." His voice was crisper than usual.

Thorton said, "Aye aye, sir."

He saluted for good measure and stepped over to the signal chest. He quickly sorted through them, translated the message into Spanish, and spelled it all out. That required multiple hoists, but it was the only way to be certain of being understood. Aruj and Foster would understand commonly used signals like No. 21 (Engage the enemy) without having them spelled out word for word, but "the commodore is invited to breakfast" was not a standard signal in any country. The first hoist rose, then there was a long pause, followed by an acknowledgement. The second hoist rose, was likewise carefully examined, and acknowledged. Piece by piece the message went up. Finally it was all done.

Thorton reported. "Signal acknowledged, sir. Awaiting reply."

Shakil was into his third set of prayers. Thorton gave him a long look. Horner continued waiting. Thorton schooled himself into immobility, but as the third set drew near its end, sweat began to trickle down his back and it wasn't due to the rising Mediterranean sun. Finally he said, "Captain Horner."

"Yes?"

"Muslims pray five times a day."

"So I have heard." Horner waited patiently. Thorton was not a man who spoke unless he had something to say.

Thorton cleared his throat. "Five times a day. If a man has reason to think he might not be able to perform the prayers at the scheduled time, he can perform them in advance."

Horner gave Shakil a sharp look, but the Moor ignored him. He was busy kneeling and chanting. "Go on."

"They have done dawn and morning and are nearly finished with early afternoon. 'Tis Captain Tangle's habit to observe dawn and morning together each day himself, but he only orders a full set of five if he thinks he is going into battle."

The third set came to a close. Thorton watched Shakil. Shakil waited quietly, head cocked to listen for the cues from the other vessels. The chant was faint but steady. He began the movements of the fourth prayer.

"Late afternoon prayer, sir." Thorton's face was white under his tan.

"Any response to our signal?"

"Not yet, sir. They won't interrupt the *Kapitan Pasha* at his prayers for a mere social call. Begging your pardon, sir."

"Make a signal—" Horner had to pause to think. He could not order a commodore of a foreign navy to respond to him. "Never mind. How long until the prayers are done?"

"Twenty to thirty minutes, sir."

"Very good. Send the hands to breakfast, then douse the galley fires. Pass the word for my steward. I'll have my sword and breakfast brought on deck, please."

The work of holystoning the deck was only half done. The hands surged to put away their things and run below to get their breakfast. They knew action was imminent. Excitement was high.

Down in the wardroom the officers bolted their breakfasts. Perry, who was tired after his watch, drank plenty of tea to wake himself up. Stewards brought up trays to the men on the quarterdeck. Thorton ate his oatmeal without tasting it. Ra'uf put an orange and a biscuit in a napkin in one of his master's pockets for later. A small flask of water with a trace of rum was put in next to it. Thorton's loaded pistol went into the other pocket. The renegade lieutenant buckled his sword around his waist. He was undistinguished as a swordsman but a competent marksman. That he might have to shoot men he had commanded made him sick. He would know the names of the men he killed. The enemy was not faceless anymore.

CHAPTER 21 : THE HOSTAGE

"Mr. Thorton." Horner's voice was firm. He continued to stare at the Sallee encirclement with his hands clasped behind his back. It was his habitual pose. He looked as he looked every morning. He had even shaved. He gave no sign of excitement. The only thing different was the sword strapped to his side.

Thorton stepped over to the captain. "Sir?"

"Tell me about Commodore Tangueli. How much of a hotspur is he?"

Thorton looked out at the crescent of rowed warships. At three furlongs they were within range for all their guns to work to good effect. They held the distance with a few dips of their oars to resist leeway. The sun was rising in a glorious pink and yellow dawn, but there was no breeze. Without wind the *Ajax* was a sitting duck. An armed duck, but a sitting duck all the same. Thorton thought rather sadly of all the hard work they had done repairing her. She seemed in imminent danger of being blown to pieces again.

"He never bluffs, sir."

Horner's mouth pursed smaller and the lines alongside his nose grew deeper as his face grew longer. "I see. Hoist the anchor. Out sweeps. Hold position. You may send the hands to their stations quietly."

"Shall I clear for action, sir?"

"Do so. I want all guns loaded but keep them inboard. I wish to present a friendly face as long as possible."

"Aye aye, sir."

Thorton passed the orders in low voices. The deck became a beehive of activity as men worked the capstan to raise the anchor and others ran to their guns. They had to kick aside kits and stow the tables and other items that constituted the usual arrangements for breakfast. This lead to a great deal of cursing, stubbed toes, and annoyance, but they soon had the larboard guns loaded. The ports stayed closed. The guns on the deck beside Horner were loaded. Barefoot powder boys ran from the magazine to the gun deck carrying cartridges. Balls were placed in the shot garlands. The first broadside was laid very carefully —the first broadside, loaded and aimed in the fullness of time, was the most valuable. Afterwards speed was everything and accuracy necessarily suffered. But hurt the enemy on the first shot—there might not be a need for a second shot. Although with five warships encircling them, there would very likely be a need for not only a second, but a third, a fourth, a tenth, and plenty more.

Shakil finished the evening prayer. He was white as he rolled his rug up quietly. He tucked it under his arm and descended the steps. He went to the cockpit. He would not shoot at his brothers in religion; neither would he take their shot. He would assist the wounded.

Signals rose on the *Arrow*. In the increasing light there could be no doubt about her identity. She yawed slightly to give the officers on her quarterdeck a better view of the *Ajax*.

"Sallee flagship to *Ajax*, 'Commodore and daughter accept invitation,'" Thorton announced.

Horner sucked in a breath and let it go. Otherwise he betrayed no change. His hands remained clasped behind his back. "Acknowledge."

"Aye aye, sir." Thorton let the white-faced Jones run it up.

"Mr. Thorton, you are invited to breakfast in my cabin. So are lieutenants Perry and Forsythe, and midshipmen Chambers and Jones. Mr. Blakesley, you will have the watch while we entertain our guests. Maintain our position with the sweeps. Notify me if anything changes."

"Aye aye, sir," the sailing master replied.

Thorton followed Horner off the quarterdeck. "Sir, will you invite Mr. Shakil? He is the commodore's brother-in-law and may prove a useful check."

Horner paused to look at him. "I beg your pardon?"

"Captain Tangle is a forceful personality. Mr. Shakil is more moderate. If a child is present . . ."

"Child?"

"Miss Tahirah Tangueli is nine. Her sister, Miss Naomi, is five. It must be the elder Miss Tangueli."

Horner's face registered shock. "He brought a child with him?"

Thorton gestured helplessly. "I don't know why, sir."

Horner recovered himself. "Very well. Inform Mr. Forsythe I will see him in my cabin immediately."

"Aye aye, sir."

The *Arrow's* boat went over the side. A purple blotch that must be Tangle's uniform went down the side, followed by a small lavender blotch that must be his daughter. Two white blotches followed, probably servants.

Thorton remained on deck to receive the guests while other officers bustled to the captain's cabin. The men stood down from the guns, but the three thousand pound behemoths were kept chained and ready. Above them on the weather deck the men resumed holystoning the deck and so appeared to be engaged in their usual morning routine. MacDonald signaled six fingers and the correct number of marines lined up. He piped a call rarely heard aboard frigates: a commodore was coming aboard. The drums and fifes sounded the welcome. Tangle climbed over the gunwale with a warm smile. He turned to give his daughter a hand but she ignored it.

Miss Tahirah clambered over the gunwale with the skill of an accomplished tomboy who has conquered all the trees in her neighborhood. She was dressed in a lavender tunic with gold lace on the chest in imitation of her father's uniform. A blue and white checked cloth covered her hair. Her tunic reached to just above the knees. Her legs were incased in loose-fitting pantaloons of matching lavender. Her shoes were lavender leather with leopards stitched on the toes. She was suddenly shy at the sight of so many strange men and pressed to her father's side. The marines with their scarlet coats and arms presented were especially frightening to her. Tangle bent his head and spoke softly to her. She looked up, balked a little, then took his arm. He walked her down the aisle as if he were the father of a bride.

Thorton saluted him. *"Salaam, Kapitan Pasha.* Peace be up on you. Welcome aboard, Miss Tahirah. 'Tis wonderful to see you again."

Miss Tahirah had been coached by her father in some basic English. She held out her hand to him and bent her knees in a curtsy. "I'm happy to meet you, Peter Rais," she pronounced carefully in her little girl voice.

He took her hand and bowed over it. "I hope you had a safe and interesting voyage."

"We did. Very interesting indeed. We dined with Duke Henrique last night. He told us where to find you," Tangle replied in a melodious baritone.

Thorton was wondering just what they talked about, but he couldn't ask. Instead he said, "Miss Tahirah, Commodore, if you will follow me, I'll escort you to breakfast with the captain."

Just then the nanny and eunuch came over the gunwale. Neither of them spoke a word of English, so Thorton left them in the care of MacDonald, who didn't speak a word of Arabic. They waited in the coach in case they were wanted.

Thorton rapped on the captain's door and received a barked "Enter!" so he opened the door, ushered the commodore and girl inside, and followed them. They made their way into the great cabin. Tangle had to stoop beneath the beams. Horner and the other officers looked well in their blue coats as the rising sun streaked through the open windows and made their gold lace glow. With her larboard facing south, the sun shone directly into the cabin.

"Commodore Tangueli and Miss Tangueli. Welcome. I'm Ebenezer Horner, captain of His Britannic Majesty's frigate *Ajax*. May I present my officers?"

He named their names and Miss Tahirah said, "How do you do?" and held out her hand.

The captain took her hand gravely and gave a little bow. "Enchanted, miss."

Then they were all seated at the table. Horner was at one end and Tangle at the other. Tahirah sat next to her father with Jones beside her, then Shakil, then Thorton. Thorton was seated next to Horner and as far away from Tangle as possible. On the other side Forsythe was next to Tangle, then Chambers, with Perry next to Horner. The midshipmen were pleased to dine at the captain's expense—midshipmen were growing boys and always hungry but had few resources of their own. Free food almost made up for the torture of polite conversation.

Breakfast was oatmeal with brown sugar. Although Horner's planters were casualties of action, two of the cantaloupes had survived and were served up as wedges. A bowl of oranges and apples was placed on the table. Horner, who knew the state of his stores, wondered where the oranges had come from, but assumed the steward had used the usual prerogatives of his office to barter for them. Would he find himself short on eggs or artichokes as a result? Ah well, it made a presentable breakfast. His steward had even been at pains to knock the weevils out of the biscuits before serving them. He didn't want to frighten a child with bugs. He was certain a girl child would scream or faint if there were bugs on the table. That proved he was not acquainted with Miss Tahirah. The eldest Tangueli daughter had been known to bring bugs to the table herself. Cider replaced the beer that was the usual breakfast beverage. Horner was one of the few men in naval service who did not care for beer. His china was serviceable blue and white faience in imitation of Chinese porcelains. His tablecloth was linen with a tiny bit of lace around the edge. The steward had selected the best pieces of silver (the ones where the plate was not yet wearing off) for the serving dishes.

Horner began. "How was your voyage, Commodore?"

"Very well, Captain. Fair winds and mild weather all the way." Tangle had spent a great deal of time during his voyage improving his English with the aid of Lts. Foster and Aruj.

If the English officers were surprised to discover a savage corsair knew how to use a knife and spoon they didn't show it. On the other hand, Miss Tahirah had apparently never been taught that the highest ranking officer establishes the conversational topic. She had studied so that she could say, "I saw dolphins leaping by the bow."

Forsythe had little sisters and was still young enough to count as somebody's 'big brother' so he knew how to talk to her. "How many?"

"Six!" she replied in triumph, but thereafter her English failed.

Perry, who could usually be counted on to supply charming conversation, was mostly quiet. He kept watching Tangle warily. Then his eyes would dart to Thorton. Eventually it dawned on Thorton that Perry was trying to catch him exchanging secret signals with Tangle. There weren't any secret signals. As far as the renegade Englishman knew the breakfast was exactly what it appeared to be: a social call at sea. Life on board ship was a monotonous routine. Men hungry for entertainment and news dined with each other whenever the chance presented itself. That thirty guns were pointed at the *Ajax* while they did so was a fact of no relevance.

Towards the end Tangle took one of the oranges from the basket and started peeling it. Thorton wondered if he realized it came from his own orange grove but said nothing. Everyone was relaxed. Except Tangle. Thorton knew him. The casual ease with which he conducted himself was an excellent cover for an alert mind and active physique. The Sallee commodore smiled at Horner when he finally broached the topic that had brought him over.

"When do you think the *Ajax* will reach Port Mahon?"

"With fair weather, a week." Horner was not a man given to excessive verbiage.

Tangle nodded. "I always enjoy commanding vessels that are not at the mercy of the wind. 'Tis much easier to keep a schedule."

It was an oblique reference to the current situation and the advantage his rovers enjoyed. Had there been any wind at all, the *Ajax* could have bowled through the Sallee line. If she succeeded in fending off boarding attempts, she could have escaped by running before the wind. But there was no wind. With only a dozen pairs of sweeps the *Ajax* could not escape row galleys. Neither could she stand against boarders—the Sallee rovers had close two thousand men aboard their five hulls. They would close and take her.

Horner replied, "Still, I feel a puff of wind even now. 'Twill not be long before we can set sail for Minorca." His smile looked unnatural on his long face. "Perhaps you would care to join us for the trip."

Tangle gave him an amused look, as if he thought Horner joked with him. "No, thank you. But since you suggest it, I will be happy to transfer your passengers to my vessel. We do not wish to trouble you."

Horner continued smiling his unnatural smile. "'Tis no trouble at all. I assure you, we can make you very comfortable."

Forsythe was white and his hand was inside his coat. Nobody was paying him any attention, but Thorton noticed. Perry's right arm was in a sling, but he was coiled to spring. Chambers' eyes were darting back and forth as he watched the unfolding events. Jones' childish face was completely innocent. Nobody had told him about the trap Horner had laid. Thorton felt a knot of fearful disbelief. Horner wouldn't dare . . . would he?

Tangle stared hard at Horner. "I thank you for your hospitality, but we will return to the *Arrow*. Mr. Thorton included."

Thorton stared at the tablecloth.

Horner shook his head. "You know I can't allow that. Mr. Thorton is a commissioned lieutenant of His Britannic Majesty's navy. He goes to Port Mahon to face court martial."

Tangle continued to peel a long twist of rind from the orange in his hands. "I don't need to point out the obvious. We outnumber and outgun you. I'm sure you will see merit in my proposal."

"I do indeed. But it is irrelevant. If necessary I will order your arrest. I'm sure that if it comes to the attention of Admiral Walters that you attempted to forcibly interfere with His Majesty's justice, it will have a deleterious effect on Thorton's trial."

Tangle dropped the orange on his plate and sat back in his chair with a thump. He stared at Horner with an unreadable expression while he wiped his hands on his napkin. Tahirah tugged on her Uncle Shakil's sleeve and demanded to know what they were saying. He hushed her.

Tangle switched to Spanish and addressed Thorton. "Peter. What did he say?" His etiquette training had not included the language of imprisonment. Thorton spoke softly to translate the remarks.

"You dare arrest the commodore of an allied navy?" He had trouble pronouncing 'arrest'—it was new to his English vocabulary.

Horner switched to Spanish. "I sincerely hope that it does not become necessary. I would rather have you as my guest than as my prisoner. However, if it is necessary to clap you in irons, I will."

Tangle spoke to Shakil and Thorton, "Who does he think he is?"

Thorton answered, "Captain Horner is well-known for his determination in carrying out his duty, sir."

Tangle's face was bitter. "Very well. I concede your points. Are we all to be kept here, or may Shakil take my daughter to the *Arrow*?"

"Mr. Shakil and your daughter are free to go at any time. I will order up his dunnage."

Tangle rose slowly from his seat and spread his arms and called Tahirah to him. He held her tightly against his chest, kissed her brow, and whispered to her in Arabic. Shakil rose and stood nearby. His face was white and his eyes were worried. He touched his niece's shoulder comfortingly.

Horner continued in his implacable voice. "Mr. Jones, pass the word for Mr. Shakil's servant to bring his dunnage on deck."

"Aye aye, sir!" Jones jumped up so fast he knocked over his chair. It lay on the floor as he darted out of the stateroom.

Tangle lifted his daughter's chin and smiled at her. He continued speaking softly to her, but she pouted. Although Horner could not understand Arabic, he understood her protest well enough. He rose from his seat and so did the other officers. They waited awkwardly. Forsythe's hand dropped away from his coat. Shortly they heard the thumping of valises brought up on deck—Shakil was a landlubber with luggage rather than a sea chest. At a knock on the door, he put his arm around his niece to draw her away.

Tangle kissed his brother-in-law on both cheeks, "Take care of my daughter," he said in Arabic. He watched them go. The door shut.

Tangle had been to sea for thirty-five years. He knew how to handle himself in reverses as well as successes. Stooping under the deckhead, he came around the sunny side of the table while removing his baldric to surrender his scimitar.

Horner spoke in English and Spanish. "You are our guest, Commodore. I don't need that."

Tangle shook his head. "I am your prisoner and protest my treatment." He handed the scimitar to Forsythe who took it automatically.

The Turk was an athletic man with a long lean body. His dive was a perfect crescent aimed straight for the center of the open window. It was a beautiful thing to see—until Horner slammed bodily into him and the two went crashing against the locker and onto the floor. Forsythe dropped the scimitar and jerked out his pistol. He pointed it at the corsair. He was the wrong man for the job, but Perry had a wounded arm and could only leap to shut the windows.

Forsythe's face was white and his eyes were wild. His hands shook. He cocked the gun and held the trembling barrel pointed at Tangle's belly. "Avast!" he shouted in a voice that cracked at the end.

Tangle heaved Horner off of him and started up, but froze when he saw Forsythe's face. The Turk was on one knee, but held up both hands in surrender. He was afraid that if he did anything to startle the man, he would squeeze the trigger in a paroxysm of nerves.

Horner picked himself up and dusted himself off. He was careful to stay out of Forsythe's line of fire. He spoke placidly in Spanish, as if he had not just kidnapped a man and thwarted his escape attempt, "I require your parole that you will behave yourself as a proper guest and not get up to mischief as long as you are aboard. Mr. Thorton tells me you are an honorable man according to your lights."

Tangle's voice was full of rancor. "Well played, Captain. I never expected such perfidy from an Englishman."

"You have only yourself to blame. If you had not trapped me against this rock, I would not have sprung on you. Your parole, sir. Parole, or the irons."

Tangle knew he had been bested. "Very well. I give you my parole." He lowered his hands.

Horner stared at him long and hard. "I regret the necessity of pointing out that your conduct reflects on Thorton. I expect that weighs more heavily with you than the possibility of having a charge of piracy laid against you for threatening an armed assault on an allied vessel. As long as you behave as a guest, you will be treated as a guest. Thorton, translate into Spanish so there is no misunderstanding."

Thorton had made no move during Tangle's escape attempt. He could only watch mutely as the little drama played out for his sake. He rose and came forward and spoke softly in Spanish.

Tangle stared at Horner all the while. When the translation was done, the rover replied. "I keep my word. But mark this: I will never forgive you for putting me on my knees." With that he rose.

CHAPTER 22 : THE OLD FLAME

Tangle was given the first lieutenant's cabin. It was the largest of the officers' cabins, with a seat of ease for the private use of the occupant, and a stern window that swung up on hinges. In short, it was the most commodious space on the ship outside the captain's suite. Forsythe took the second lieutenant's cabin and Perry the third. That left Thorton without a cabin. He faced Perry in the wardroom.

"Perry, I don't want to bunk with the midshipmen again. Can't we arrange the three of us in the lieutenant's cabins?"

Perry's face was hard. "I don't see why. Forsythe is the first lieutenant. He shouldn't have to share. I won't share. Not with you."

Thorton gave him a frustrated look.

Perry shrugged. "Ask the pursuer. Maybe he'll share."

The warrant officers' berths were along the larboard side of the wardroom while the commissioned officers' berths were along the starboard side. To cross over to the larboard was to surrender his dignity as a commissioned officer. It was to admit that he was nobody the commissioned officers need respect.

"Excuse me. 'Tis my watch below and I need sleep." Perry gave him a cold smile and walked past him into his cabin. It was the same cabin that had been Thorton's when they left England in the spring. The one he had given up to Achmed when the envoy was on board. The one that should be his but never could be. The louvered door rattled in its frame as Perry slammed it.

Thorton was silent at dinner. He passed the salt when asked and ate his pork without comment. Tangle did not emerge from his cabin. The black eunuch slipped quietly through the wardroom to bring him his food. Ra'uf waited on Thorton. He and the commodore's servant had made couscous to accompany the British dinner. Thorton liked the pearl-like pasta and ate it with his salt pork. He also had cider to drink. He did not care for wine in this heat even though it was watered down. He ate slowly.

After dinner everybody left. Nobody wanted to stay in the stifling heat of the wardroom any longer than necessary. The stewards cleared away the remains of the meal by eating and drinking the leftovers, then washed the table. Thorton was left sitting at the bare board. Ra'uf sat cross-legged on Thorton's sea chest. It had been hauled out of the first berth to make room for the rover.

Slowly he rose and approached the Sallee commodore's door. To Ra'uf he said, "Warn me if anyone comes." He rapped.

"Enter!" Tangle barked in his Turkish accented English.

Thorton opened the door and stepped in. He stopped dead in his tracks. Tangle was naked, or nearly so. He wore only a small white garment about his privy parts. Thorton stared at it in astonishment. It was little more than a pouch for the genitals. Abruptly his face colored as he realized where he was staring. He dragged his eyes up to Tangle's amused face. The rover was lying on the bunk, propped on his elbow, reading a book. His sleek musculature was revealed in every detail: the powerful shoulders and strong flanks, the chiseled abdominal muscles. Short black hair swirled across his chest and gathered into a 'treasure trail' that lead to the white triangle. His arms and legs were hairy, too. A large scar ran from his clavicle to his right armpit. Small scars marked his body in other places.

"Come in, Peter. I'm glad to see you," he said in Arabic.

Thorton shut the door as if in a dream. His tongue ran around suddenly dry lips. He remembered the times he had pressed against that body. Back then Tangle had been much thinner due to the privations of the galley. Now he had recovered his health and flesh. He was a magnificent animal. Although a white streak ran through his short black beard, he had the body of a man in his prime. Even lounging on the bunk he exhibited a feline grace that was natural to him. His smile was growing as he saw how his body entranced the blond lieutenant.

"You're looking well, Isam." Thorton attempted polite small talk, but his tongue was thick in his mouth.

"Thank you, Peter. Home cooking has restored me."

Tangle had snatched Thorton out of this very ship a few months ago. It seemed a lifetime had passed. Now the wayward lieutenant was on his way to be court-martialed for desertion even though he had been carried off through no fault of his own. This man had been his kidnapper, his lover, his mentor, his superior officer, and even his friend. He admired him, was exasperated by him, drawn to him, worried by him. He stepped up to the bunk and hardly knew what he did. It was unbearably hot in the little room even with the window open. Tangle saw the expression in his face and his own pulse quickened. Thorton pulled at his stock.

"I told you a stock would suffocate you in this heat," the Turk said with a touch of humor. The crow's feet at the corners of his eyes crinkled.

Thorton bent and kissed his mouth. Tangle turned his face up and let him. Thorton kissed him harder as the heat in his body built so that he thought he would faint or explode. He was frightened and this man had come to save him. Tangle's arm went around him and Thorton climbed on the bed and straddled him. They wrapped in each other's arms and kissed wildly. Thorton pressed his aching groin against the other man's and felt the answering passion. He moaned and rocked as the lust surged through him. Lust and terror.

"I don't want to hang!" he gasped. He stared into Tangle's eyes.

"You won't," Tangle growled. "If I have to break my word to Horner, I will. I'm going to rescue you, Peter."

Thorton kissed him desperately. Their bodies ground together. A week to get to Port Mahon—he couldn't stand the tension. "If they're going to hang me for a sodomite, I might as well be one," he whispered. He tore at his collar and unbuckled the stock.

Tangle gripped his upper arms tightly. "Peter . . ." His voice broke. "Peter, no. I have no qualms about lying to the court martial to save your life, but I know you. You are an honest man. You must be able to tell them the truth when you say that we have never committed buggery."

"I don't care anymore! Everyone thinks it anyhow!"

"I want you, Peter. By Allah, you are the stubbornest man I ever attempted to seduce! But now is not the time."

Thorton's face crumpled and that made his injures hurt. He put his hand to the bandages. "Why did you carry me off? What sort of mad djinn are you? You have ruined me!"

Tangle stroked his blonde hair. "Because I fell in love with you. I would have loved anyone who set me free, but I might have hated him, too. But you, you came aboard the Spanish galley and I saw you arguing with the captain. I knew you were risking your own life to save ours. How could I not love a man who was brave and decent to his fellow men? Then you turned out to be exceptionally handsome," he twined fingers in Thorton's long blond hair, "And the most stiff-necked, gallant, and brave fellow I'd met in a long time. I saw the way you looked at me and knew you were a man like me, so I kissed you."

"You were delirious."

Tangle laughed. "Of course I was. So would you in my place."

They were speaking in soft Spanish. Thorton trembled. He felt the carnal pleasure of another man's naked body between his legs and squeezed them tight. He was still fully dressed and suffocating in his clothes. He longed to be naked and free, skin to skin with another man who knew him and wanted him as he was.

He groaned. "I admire you as a captain. I have learned a great deal from you. You promoted me, even though you shouldn't have."

"You captured two frigates with a galiot which proves I was right!"

"You confuse me. I want a lover . . ." He slid his hand over that fine male flesh and groaned. "But this is only lust. I know it, but I want you all the same."

His conscience pricked him. He had never crawled on top of Shakil and groped him with mad desire. Shakil was a gentlemen and deserved to be treated with respect. Tangle was not a gentleman; he was a barbarian chief who lived by raiding the civilized world. He made Thorton's blood run hot.

"I want you, too!" Tangle kissed him again. The kiss was hot and hard and Thorton melted into it. His lips parted and Tangle groaned as his tongue explored. Both of them felt the further stiffening of their pricks in response to that kiss.

"You make it very hard to think when you kiss me like that," the Turk breathed. His dark face was flushed.

"You kissed me first."

"You crawled on top of me."

"You looked at me."

Tangle laughed at that. "You were ravishing me with your eyes!"

"You were naked and handsome." Thorton blushed.

"Do you think so? Once before you told me that I was old, dark, skinny, and married." The corsair's baritone was amused.

"I was trying to persuade myself not to look at you."

"I knew it!"

"Stop. Shakil is my lover. I shouldn't be here."

Tangle's beard bristled as he set his jaw. "I'm a better match for you, Peter. You and I are cut from the same cloth. I love Shakil like a brother, but he is not passionate like you and I. He's sweet and makes a good friend, but you will never be content with him."

Thorton pushed up. "I will!"

Tangle shook his head. "You'll see.'

Thorton climbed off the Turk. "You ask too much of me."

"I offer you much."

Thorton wilted. "All I really want is a safe place to sleep."

That took Tangle aback. "What do you mean?"

Thorton didn't look at him. He was miserable. It was damned awkward to have an erection and feel melancholy at the same the time. "They call me 'turncoat.' They don't bother to lower their voices when they do it. You've got the first lieutenant's cabin, and that has bumped Forsythe to Perry's cabin and Perry's to the third lieutenant's cabin. I'm the junior lieutenant. I haven't got a cabin at all now. I . . . I just wanted to ask . . . if I could sleep in here. On the floor. I don't want you to think that I, uh, wanted to sleep 'with' you." He was turning red.

Tangle listened with his lips pressed together. He was not a stoic man—Thorton saw the sparks of displeasure in his brown eyes. "They don't appreciate you. I do. Of course you can stay here. You can have the bunk and I will sleep on the floor because the bunk is too damned short for me. I can't sleep folded up like that."

Thorton was grateful to have a place to stay, but worried. "You must keep your hands off me. Please?" Only a minute before he had been the forward one. He could not trust himself to behave, but strangely, he trusted the Turk. The man had an iron will.

Tangle considered the request. "Until the court martial, yes. I agree. I will not do anything that will endanger you. Still, if they know you're here, they'll think the worst."

"They'll do worse if they can get at me. They dragged my Sallee coat through the bilge and stabbed it in the back the first day I was here. They put salt in my sugar and left a dead rat in my sea chest and stole my Arab sextant and all kinds of things."

Tangle sat up abruptly and his eyes flashed. "Desecration of the uniform! Horner will pay for that!"

Thorton shook his head. "'Twill be worse if I go to Horner. Nobody likes a tattletale. If my things are in here they'll be safe because they won't dare invade a commodore's berth. You're Horner's guest."

Tangle made a face. He didn't like letting the miscreants get away with such things, but he wasn't the captain of the *Ajax*, either. "I don't think much of your precious Captain Horner with things like this going on."

"He doesn't know."

"He should know. If it was my ship, I would know. I wouldn't stand for it."

"I know. 'Tis one of the things I like about you. You have your faults, but you are never small-minded or petty."

Tangle climbed off the bed and pulled on his pantaloons. "Come, let's get your chest." He padded out half-naked like a common sailor. Thorton paused to put his clothes to rights and made certain his waistcoat was pulled well down to cover his unruly portion. He was glad to have a long waistcoat in spite of the heat.

Chapter 23 : Sirocco

The wind whipped up whitecaps and the *Ajax* heeled and rolled. Spume from the whitecaps was sucked up by the air until the atmosphere was like soup. Massive bronze clouds blotted out the sun and brought a premature twilight as the western sun disappeared. Still it didn't rain. The *Arrow* was to the east of them with signals flying. Her consorts followed her in a line. They carried more sail than Horner thought wise, but they were keeping up with the frigate by doing so.

"Mr. Thorton. What signal?" Horner asked.

"Daughter to Daddy, 'I love you. Good night.'"

"Messenger! Inform Commodore Tangueli he has a message."

Tangle came on deck with a face like a thundercloud. He did not appreciate being at Horner's beck and call. He gave a brusk nod in response to Horner's greeting then turned to read the signal. His hands clenched so hard on the rail that his brown knuckles turned white.

"May I reply, Captain?"

"Of course, Commodore."

Tangle gave his message to Thorton in Arabic and the lieutenant started sorting through the flags.

Horner asked, "What message is that?"

Tangle gave him a bitter look and translated, "Daddy to daughter, 'I love you, jewel of my heart. Sleep well.'"

Horner looked at Thorton who nodded in confirmation. "Carry on."

The sultry heat was horrid—the worst most of the Englishmen had ever experienced. Thorton had been through it in the West Indies, but that had been a long time ago. Horner retained his full uniform even in the sweltering heat, but the common sailors were stripped to the waist and some even to their drawers. Thorton struggled on for a while, then finally put his sweaty and crumpled stock in his pocket. He unbuttoned the top three buttons of his shirt so that it was open to the waistcoat. Tangle was a passenger with no obligation to suffer through the heat fully dressed. He wore a white tunic with cap sleeves that showed off his powerful arms, loose white linen pantaloons, a blue checked cloth to protect his head and neck, gold hoops in his ears, and sandals.

"Will this heat never end?" moaned Forsythe.

Tangle understood the question and asked Thorton for help answering in English. "If the wind shifts northeast the weather will moderate, but if it keeps blowing from the qibla, it may take several days. Qibli winds are strong winds. Fortunately, hurricanes usually only happen in the spring or fall." Tangle looked south again. "They are having sandstorms ashore. I hope the farm is all right."

"Farm?" asked Forsythe.

"My wife Jamila and her brother Shakil own a farm. We live there with our children."

"Oh," Forsythe replied. He would have never connected the notorious corsair with something as homey as a farm, wife, and children. He asked politely, "How many children, sir?"

"Six, by Allah! Three are triplets." He needed recourse to Thorton for the word 'triplets.'

"Triplets!" Forsythe replied in astonishment. "That is remarkable, sir."

"They are all strong, healthy, and intelligent." Tangle beamed with paternal pride. By luck Forsythe had found a topic that would improve the hostage's mood.

Horner turned to listen to the discussion. "A goodly family. I hope your wife is well."

Tangle turned pensive. "It was hard to leave when I was already gone too long." He clasped his hands behind his back, spread his feet to brace to the rolling, and gazed south.

Horner cleared his throat and turned to a more nautical topic. "Can you enlighten us further regarding the qibli winds, Commodore?"

Tangle couldn't tell a British captain what to do, but he could educate him and thereby guide his actions. "The Christians call them 'sirocco.' They can blow hard enough to wreck you on the coast of Spain. They are oppressive winds. Dogs go mad and men commit murder when they blow."

That caught Horner's attention. He had not worried about Spain on the lee more than fifty miles away. The *Ajax* was shallower than most British frigates and made correspondingly more leeway; the news disturbed him. "What is the chance of the wind veering south?"

"Excellent. It usually does. Especially a brown wind like that." He pointed to the dirty clouds. "That is the Sahara desert. The wind carries the dust and sand all the way to Europe. It can raise a gale."

The Sahara desert flying towards them was unnerving to the British officers. They stared uneasily at the turbid sky.

"Will it back north?" Horner asked.

"Not here in the Sea of Alborán. When you make the turn to run up the coast of Spain, the mistral might reach you, but it usually stays in the Gulf of Lions or the Gulf of Genoa."

"The mistral?" Horner was not ashamed to tap the corsair's knowledge of the sea and weather he must contend with.

The discussion continued in a mixture of Spanish and English with a little Arabic thrown in for good measure. Thorton was the only other officer that could follow this strange dialect; the English officers soon gave up eavesdropping. The two captains digressed into a fascinating (to them) conversation about weather and their speculations regarding the origins of wind and the law of storms. They went below and Horner showed Tangle his barometer. It was a handsome mahogany and brass staff that read pressure and humidity. Horner was quite proud of it—not many captains had barometers. The glass was reading low for pressure and over one hundred for temperature. Tangle instantly set his heart on obtaining one for himself. With a subject of mutual interest, it was only natural that Horner invited Tangle to sup with him and that he accepted. Although neither would admit it, they were enjoying each other's company.

Forsythe relieved Thorton on deck and the junior lieutenant went below. As he came down the companionway into the wardroom, he saw Chambers outside Tangle's cabin. The boy was bending down and setting a pair of boots upright. Tangle's boots.

"Ahoy there! What are you doing?" he asked sharply.

Chambers straightened with a guilty look. His brown hair was damp with sweat and he was wearing just his drawers and jersey. "Just brought the Turk's boots back from getting polished, sir," he replied blandly.

Thorton stepped forward. "What mischief are you up to?"

Chambers backed away around the end of the wardroom table as Thorton came along the starboard side. Thorton picked up a boot and caught a whiff of something. Chambers fled.

Thorton roared, "Avast there, Chambers!" but the boy was up the companionway like a shot. "Stand down, midshipman!" Thorton bellowed and leaped after him.

Thorton raced on deck, but Chambers was already in the shrouds and flying up. The angry lieutenant charged after him and was swinging into the rigging when Horner came striding out of the coach with Tangle in his wake.

"Mr. Thorton! What's all this commotion?"

Thorton hung in the rigging a few feet above the deck. He willed himself to make a proper answer. "Mr. Chambers did not stand when ordered, sir."

"Come down, Mr. Thorton. Chambers! On deck!"

Chambers had not stopped and was crawling into the top. He looked over the edge when Horner called to him. The captain shielded his eyes as he looked up into the brassy sky.

"Do not make me repeat myself, mister!"

Reluctantly Chambers started the descent. He didn't hurry.

"Smartly, lad. Smartly!" Horner called. He had strong lungs and could raise his voice to a volume heard the length of the ship without seeming to shout.

Tangle stood next to Horner with his hands clasped behind his back. He was a placid observer of shipboard discipline because he was unaware that it had anything to do with him. Chambers slid down the backstay and eventually stepped up next to Thorton to present himself. Horner nailed him to the deck with a steely blue eye.

"What's this about you disobeying an order from Lt. Thorton?"

"I was just playing with him, sir," Chambers said.

Horner unleashed the full power of a captain's disapproving glare on the youth. His voice was extremely crisp as he snapped, "You do not *play* with your superior officers, Mr. Chambers! You obey them!"

Chambers cringed as if the sirocco had blown right in his face. "Aye aye, sir. I didn't mean nothing by it."

Thorton was having a hard time containing himself. He stared at the beam of the quarterdeck's break that he could see over the captain's shoulder.

Horner continued fixing his gaze upon Chambers. "You will complete whatever task Mr. Thorton had for you, then you will go to the masthead until the end of the second dog watch. You will miss your supper, but it is your own fault."

"Aye aye, sir," the midshipman replied.

"Carry on, Mr. Thorton."

"Aye aye, sir," the lieutenant replied.

Horner went back to his cabin and Tangle went below.

Thorton glared at Chambers. "You will fetch the commodore's boots and clean them immediately! You'd better run before the commodore finds them. If they aren't clean enough to drink from, I'll thrash you myself!" His hand went to his pocket and he hauled out his tawse and stung the boy in the arm with it. "Move!"

Chambers shot down the companionway. Thorton followed more sedately. Tangle had retired to his cabin to wash and dress for dinner without stopping to pick up the boots. Chambers grabbed them, dodged around Thorton, and disappeared somewhere down the gundeck.

The minutes ticked by. Tangle emerged fully dressed in his purple coat with gold lace, buff pantaloons, and white turban. He was clean, neat, and smelled better than the English. Once Thorton had thought the man excessively fastidious with his daily bathing, but having been reacquainted with the aroma of men who for whom bathing was an imposition, he discovered he preferred it.

"Where are my boots?"

Thorton gave him an apologetic look. "I'm sorry, sir. I regret to inform you the boots are not ready yet. The boy is working on them."

Tangle gave Thorton a keen look. "Would the boy be Chambers?"

Thorton nodded.

Tangle's eyes glittered dangerously and his mouth pressed into a thin line. "Tell me?"

So Thorton had to tell him. Tangle almost laughed. In a choking voice he said, "No, you couldn't let him get away with that. I'm glad I didn't put the boots on. But I think young Chambers has gotten off very lightly. I shall draw Horner's attention to it."

Thorton's face fell. "I wish you wouldn't," he muttered.

Tangle patted his shoulder. "Trust me. I've been a captain for a very long time. I have suffered—and committed—worse pranks." He went up the companionway in his stocking feet and presented himself to the great cabin. A miserable Thorton went in search of Chambers.

Horner admitted Tangle to his stateroom. "Good afternoon, Commodore." He had adopted formal dress by wearing his coat with white facings and his best waistcoat and cravat. Having kidnapped the Sallee commodore under a pretense of hospitality he was determined to comport himself graciously—no small challenge as he was gifted with neither wealth nor sociability.

"*Salaam.* Peace be upon you and all within this vessel," Tangle replied.

"Thank you. Please make yourself comfortable." Horner gestured to the locker under the stern windows. Some captains had velvet cushions on their locker tops but Horner's cabin was spartan. The seat was bare wood. "May I offer you something to drink? Tea or cider?"

"I'll have whatever you're having." Tangle sat on the locker and crossed one ankle negligently over the opposite knee.

Horner stared at the stocking-clad foot. He could not help but think there was a hidden significance in the gesture. He wondered if the man was insulting him in his maddening Muslim way. "Is it customary to go stocking-footed to supper in your country, Commodore?"

"Not at all. Chambers hasn't finished cleaning my boots yet. Thorton has gone after him."

Suspicion grew in Horner. "Why did they need cleaning?"

"Because they were full of chicken shit," Tangle replied. He kept a straight face.

For a short moment the enormity—and humor—of a commodore's boots fouled with bird dung hung between them. Horner spoke in a strangled voice, "I trust Mr. Thorton is rectifying the situation and that you will not be troubled by any further pranks during your stay."

Tangle's dark eyes glittered with a mercurial change of mood. His voice was cool. "Since coming aboard I have discovered the level of respect England has for the Sallee Republic. I can only assume the habits of the men and officers reflect the views of the captain."

Horner stiffened. "If you have a specific complaint, I will hear it, but I will not tolerate aspersions cast upon the integrity of my crew."

"I refer to the matter of the Sallee coat," Tangle replied.

Horner's brow beetled. "I'm afraid you have me at a disadvantage. Will you be so good as to explain?"

"Mr. Chambers might be able to enlighten both of us."

Horner opened the door and bellowed for Chambers and Thorton. The midshipman was white when he entered the cabin with the freshly cleaned boots in his hands. Thorton stood to attention as Chambers stammered his apology and offered the boots to Horner.

"What's this about the Sallee coat?" Horner asked severely.

Chambers squawked, "'Twas Mr. Perry who put me up to it, sir!"

"Out with it!" Horner barked.

The words came out in a rush. "When Mr. Thorton came aboard, we were talking about the turncoat, sir. Mr. Perry said we ought to show him how we feel about that sort of thing, so I got his purple coat and dunked it in the bilge. Then Mr. Perry stabbed it with his dirk, sir."

Tangle's black eyes would have bored holes through the boy had it been physically possible, but he folded his arms over his chest and waited to see what Horner would do.

Horner stared at the boy bitterly. He wondered how many other hazing incidents Thorton had suffered. Tangle was right, this reflected upon the captain. All this was going on and he knew nothing about it. His lips pursed into a tight little moue of displeasure. "And?" There was always more to this sort of thing.

Chambers mumbled, "I took his sextant, sir."

"Anything else?"

Chambers squirmed. "Some other pranks, sir."

Horner transferred his gaze to Thorton. "What else?"

Thorton replied, "If you please, sir. I want my sextant back. That's all."

Horner said, "Call Mr. Perry."

Thorton went to the door, opened it, and passed the word. An uncombed, sleep-tousled Perry arrived in his coat and shoes but without his waistcoat or stockings. He had turned out of bed and grabbed the minimum necessary to be decent.

"Lt. Roger Perry reporting, sir." The people present in the room gave him an excellent idea why he had been summoned.

"Mr. Chambers has just acquainted me with the matter of the Sallee coat, Mr. Perry. What have you to say?"

Perry shot Chambers a look. Perry, Thorton, and Chambers were lined up in order of rank and each of them stood stiffly at attention. "'Tis a matter for the wardroom, sir."

Tangle flew off the locker where he had been sitting and came forward. "Not any more," he snarled.

"Thank you, Commodore. I will settle the matter to your satisfaction, I assure you," Horner turned back to Perry. "Answer my question, Mr. Perry."

Perry's jaw worked. "Mr. Chambers soaked Mr. Thorton's Sallee coat in the bilge, sir." He said in exactly the tone he might use to report that the hawse was stowed.

"And?" Horner prompted.

Perry's jaw worked again. "I stabbed it in the back with my knife. Because that's how I feel about a man who turns his back on his friends and goes over to the enemy."

"The Sallee Republic is not your enemy," Tangle said in a voice silky with danger.

"Mr. Thorton and I are enemies," Perry replied flatly.

Thorton ground his teeth so hard they squeaked.

Horner's face was grim. "Mr. Perry, you owe Commodore Tangueli an apology. I will not abide an insult to the Sallee uniform. The rovers are our allies."

Perry glared at the rover. "The fault is his. None of this would have happened if he hadn't carried off Peter!"

Chambers nodded, eager to shift the blame to someone else.

"None of this would have happened if the Serpent hadn't tempted Eve in the Garden of Eden!" Horner snapped back. "Your actions are your own, Mr. Perry. If you cannot take responsibility for them you should not commit them!"

Perry stiffened. "The matter is between me and Lt. Thorton. I beg leave to settle it privately."

"No," Tangle replied.

"Yes," said Thorton.

"Silence!" snapped Horner. "Sir," he added in deference to Tangle's rank.

"What your men do speaks for you." There was a great deal more Tangle wanted to say but his English failed him. He resorted to Turkish to say it. Horner didn't know Turkish, but he could guess the nature of the remarks.

Horner's mouth pursed tight again. "You are entirely correct, Commodore. I apologize for the oversight. I assure you that there will be no further defects in discipline aboard this ship. I apologize most humbly for the inconvenience you have suffered. I regret that supper has been delayed." He could not turn a guest and higher ranking officer out of the cabin to which he had been invited, so he said, "If you will pardon me for a moment."

Tangle couldn't do anything else. It was Horner's ship. He nodded curtly.

Horner stepped outside with his subordinates. The marine sentry at his door and the idlers in the coach were witnesses. "You are confined to quarters unless on duty, Mr. Perry. Mr. Thorton, invite the wardroom with the exception of Mssrs. Perry and Chambers to sup with me tonight. Inform my cook that I have additional guests for supper. Mr. Chambers, you are late for the masthead. Pass the word for Lt. Barnes. I'll have a marine posted on Commodore Tangueli's door at all times." He glared at Perry and Chambers. "You will not embarrass England any further! Is that clear?"

They all saluted and said, "Aye aye, sir."

"Dismissed." Horner returned to his cabin.

Thorton followed Perry down to the wardroom. "Roger, it wasn't me that told him about the coat."

"You're a rat and a liar, a two-faced, turncoat buggerboy and—"

"Roger!" Thorton's face was white. "What did I ever do to make you hate me?"

"You were my friend. You even said you loved me. But what did you do? You threw yourself at that damned Turk and ran off with your fine new friends. You kiss men's arses as well as their mouths, Peter Thorton. I thought you were simple but all this time you were conniving for better friends."

"I'm not like that!"

"I hope they hang you, you god damn sodomite." He slammed into his cabin.

CHAPTER 24 : A CHANGE OF WIND

Horner set a course due east. He wanted Spain as far off his lee as possible. The *Ajax* skimmed over the waves like a great swan. The wind shifted south, but it sometimes backed wildly and took the sails aback. The whole ship shuddered and her canvas flapped and roared. The helm payed off and the sound ceased as the sails drew taut again. The wind whipped the whitecaps into spindrift that was sucked up by the thirsty air. The air grew heavy with water, but it still didn't rain. The wind came again, sharper and faster, chilling the sweat on their skin and making them shiver. The men could not make up their minds whether to take their shirts off to escape the stifling heat, or to don their jackets against the cold wind. It was the most miserable piece of weather they had ever encountered. A storm at least brought a certain excitement that counteracted boredom and fatigue, but the sirocco wearied men without respite.

The Sallee squadron ghosted along through the haze to windward of them. Their great lateen sails billowed full of air as they surged over the bounding sea. They kept their position, but slowly the space opened between them. The galleys with their stubby masts and smaller sails could not keep up with the galiot and *brigantin*, who could not keep up with the xebec even though her sails had been cut down by the Spaniards. The *Sea Leopard* kept pace with the frigate even when the *Ajax* clapped on all sail; the xebec was born and bred for the Mediterranean.

Supper was a surprisingly pleasant affair. Tangle exerted his English to make himself agreeable to the company gathered around the captain's table. The tablecloth was Horner's good one with lace work. The china was blue and white and the meal was a chicken, plucked and roasted, with potatoes, carrots, celery, and onions. Barley was served with it, and a fruit compote made of apples, pears, and walnuts. Cider was served which was just starting to turn, but it wasn't strong enough to make anyone drunk. No wine was served out of deference to Tangle's Muslim sensibilities, which disappointed him as much as the Christian officers.

Horner spoke little and Tangle spoke the right amount. The Turk asked each of them about themselves and elicited tales of their previous nautical adventures. He contributed a few of his own, but not so many that he could have been said to be bragging. His baritone voice was very pleasant and his accent not too difficult to understand. He had recourse to Horner in Spanish to supply him with necessary words when his English was wanting. He paid no particular attention to Thorton which suited the younger man just fine.

At the end of supper Horner provided good Havana cigars. Half of the officers accepted. Horner said, "I hope you will not mind if I offer my officers brandy. 'Tis traditional. I can offer you more cider."

Tangle replied, "I am a Muslim, not a monk. I'll join you in a glass of brandy, if I may." He already had a cigar and was enjoying it greatly.

"Certainly, Commodore."

Horner poured and Tangle received the first glass. He drank, coughed, and his eyes watered. "Strong spirits," he said. He sipped more cautiously after that.

The other officers were all pleased to take a glass. Tangle leaned back in his chair and unbuttoned his coat. The cabin was warm in spite of the breeze eddying through the window. A companionable silence fell. They were well fed on modest but tasty food and had good brandy and cigars to top it all off. It was rare for them to enjoy such comforts. They were loathe to leave it or disturb it. Sadly, such moments were short-lived aboard ship.

Midshipman Jones was admitted. He stood to attention and said, "Mr. Blakesley sends his compliments, sir. 'Tis starting to rain. The wind is from the south and gusty."

Horner said, "Thank you, midshipman. I shall come on deck presently." He inhaled one last puff of his cigar, then stubbed it out in the pewter ashtray.

That was the signal for the rest of them to rise and take their leave. Horner went on deck while the officers went below.

Tangle lingered on deck. "Mr. Thorton. I wonder if I could have your assistance."

The blond man looked over his shoulder as he was heading to the companionway. "Of course, sir. What may I do for you?"

"I could use a hand getting to bed. A little too much brandy." Tangle couldn't hold his liquor, but all the same, a single brandy wasn't enough to loosen any man's rigging. Thorton frowned but decided it must be a subterfuge for the benefit of the others.

"Of course, sir." As he took Tangle's elbow to guide him, he discovered the man's steps were slow and careful as they went down the companionway to the gundeck. In the wardroom the marine opened the door to Tangle's cabin and held it for them, then shut it behind them. Once inside Tangle lowered himself to the bunk with a groan.

"What's the matter, Isam?"

Tangle held his head. Resorting to Spanish he said, "I don't know the English or the Spanish for a headache so terrible it makes the room spin. I thought a little brandy would help, but it made it worse. I am trying not to vomit. Help me get ready for bed, please."

"We call that a megrim headache. I had it when the powder blew."

Thorton was helping Tangle undress when the black eunuch arrived. With the window shut against the rain it was hot and stuffy in the little room, so they stripped him down to the skin. The black laid out the mattress on the rug and set the sheets and pillows for him. Tangle groaned softly as they covered him with his sheet.

"Akil, get a vinegar compress," Thorton instructed the blackamoor. The slender servant nodded quietly and slipped away. When he returned Thorton laid the vinegar-soaked brown paper on the corsair's forehead.

Tangle kept his eyes tightly shut. "The room spins less if I can't see," he explained.

"Do you often get the megrim?" Thorton asked.

"Sometimes during the sirocco. Speaking English taxed me and the brandy made it worse. I am not used to brandy or English."

"Lie still," Thorton told him. He braced himself against the wall as the ship cavorted over the waves.

Tangle pulled the paper to cover his eyes as well as his forehead. Again he groaned softly. "So hot," he murmured.

Akil brought the ewer and basin. Thorton dipped his checked kerchief into it and used it to gently stroke the corsair's sweaty body.

"That's good," the corsair murmured. "Peter, that's good."

Akil dumped the used water in the toilet of the roundhouse, then gathered up the corsair's clothes and boots to wash and brush. He did his work in the wardroom. The other officers turned out their lamps one by one as they settled in for the evening. Snores soon drifted through the louvered doors and thin bulkheads. Thorton was tired, too, so he stripped down and bathed himself, then put on his nightshirt. He knelt beside the stricken corsair, but the man was asleep. He kissed the vinegar plaster on his brow, then blew out the light.

Outside in the wardroom Perry paused to put on his tarpaulin coat. The drumming of rain on the weather deck could be heard. "Is Thorton in there?" he asked the marine guarding Tangle's door.

The man nodded, "Aye, sir."

Perry stopped at the captain's door on his way on deck. A few minutes later Horner and Forsythe descended the companionway in silence. Forsythe's tarpaulin coat was dripping with rain and runnels of water ran from his sou-wester down his back.

Akil was sitting on the floor working on the commodore's boots, but Horner held his finger to his lips for silence. A single lantern hung swaying from the beam over the black's work area. The men's shadows writhed across the far wall of the wardroom like anguished giants.

Horner held a finger to his lips and tiptoed near the door. The marine stood at attention without making a noise. Horner cocked his head to listen. He heard a low groan from inside. Perry's allegation danced across his mind, and bracing himself for what he might find, he reached for the lever.

Just then the second lieutenant's door opened and Thorton stuck his head out. "Forsythe, is that—Sir!" He snapped to attention as he saw Horner.

Thorton was in his breeches and shirt as he stood in the door of Forsythe's cabin.

"What's this, Mr. Thorton?" Horner asked in surprise. His hand was on the lever of Tangle's door.

"I'm sorry, sir. I've been waiting for a chance to speak with Mr. Forsythe."

Horner looked at Forsythe and Forsythe looked at Thorton. Horner remained poised outside of Tangle's cabin. "Carry on," said Horner.

Forsythe stepped over to Thorton. "Yes?"

Thorton cleared his throat, "Sir, I wanted to ask you where I should bunk."

Forsythe hadn't thought about it at all. "Wherever you like is fine with me."

Thorton glanced at Horner and rubbed sweaty palms against his thighs. "Begging your pardon, sir. Nobody wants to share with me. Do you want me to go down to the cockpit?" The cockpit was a horrific place, hot, dark, stifling, and full of wounded and sick men. If a man wasn't ill when he went there, he would be by the time he left.

Forsythe said, "You can share with me."

Thorton couldn't believe what he'd heard. "Sir?"

Forsythe glanced anxiously at Horner. Thorton's response made him fear he'd made a mistake. Horner kept mum and let Forsythe handle it. "Why aren't you sharing with Perry?" he asked.

"He said no. But I will if you order it, sir." Thorton's heart sank and he prayed Allah that Forsythe wouldn't put them together.

"What about the gunroom?"

"The midshipmen don't want me in their berth, either, sir." Thorton's face was getting hot as he was forced to recite the petty humiliations of his disgrace. He stared over Forsythe's shoulder.

"You could order them."

Thorton's heart sank. "Aye aye, sir. If you insist." He avoided looking at either of them.

Forsythe was bewildered. "Wouldn't you rather bunk with me?"

"You're the first lieutenant. Mr. Perry told me not to bother you."

"I don't mind. 'Tis only as far as Mahon. That's not so long."

Thorton was keenly aware of Horner listening, watching, and judging. "I'd be grateful, but I don't want to inconvenience you, sir."

Forsythe lacked the ability to make a decision without help. It was his chief flaw as an officer. He turned to Horner. "What do you think, sir?"

"I think I should not have to be arranging berths in the wardroom in the middle of the night. Make your decision and stick by it, Mr. Forsythe."

Forsythe was sweating in his wet coat. "Whatever you want to do is fine with me, Peter," he said in desperation.

Thorton had to rescue him. "Thank you for your hospitality. I am happy to accept your offer, sir."

"Well then, that's settled. Get your things. By your leave, sir." Forsythe gave a glance to Horner.

Horner gave a curt nod. "I am going to pay call on Commodore Tangueli." He turned away from the two lieutenants.

"Sir! He's not well," Thorton called out.

Horner's eyes narrowed as he gave Thorton a searching look. His knuckles rapped sharply on the doorframe.

"Enter," Tangle called petulantly.

Horner opened the door smartly. Tangle yelped as the door whacked his outflung hand. He pulled it to his chest. With the brown paper across his face he couldn't see who it was and swore in Turkish.

"I beg your pardon, Commodore," Horner said.

Tangle lifted the brown paper from his eyes to see who it was. "Horner," he groaned.

"I'm very sorry, sir," Horner said in contrite Spanish. He knelt on the rug next to the supine Turk. "What are you doing on the floor? Are you unwell? Mr. Thorton, call Dr. Ferncastle!"

"I can't fall off the floor," Tangle replied. "The room is spinning."

Thorton mouthed a silent, 'Thank you,' to the eunuch as he passed. He rapped on the door opposite.

"What is it?" a sleepy voice asked from inside.

Thorton said, "Captain Horner sends for you to attend Commodore Tangueli. He has a megrim headache."

"I'm coming," the man sighed. Rustling noises announced his rising. A moment later he stepped out in his nightshirt and dressing gown. He was a short man, a little stout, with spectacles perching on his nose. His hairline had retreated from his forehead and left a gleaming expanse of brow that was dewed with perspiration. He walked across the wardroom to visit his latest patient.

"What's going on?" Forsythe asked when Thorton entered the cabin the two of them were sharing.

Thorton spoke lowly. "Horner just popped in—I don't know why. Perry told him we were up to mischief, I suppose. But we weren't."

"What the hell is wrong with Perry? Oh, you'll need a hammock, there's a seam working."

Thorton knew that seam; it was the same seam that worked when he and Perry had been obliged to share this same cabin, back in the days when they were best friends. The hooks he'd installed to hang a hammock were still there. He was climbing into it when a burst of Turkish profanity erupted on the other side of the bulkhead. He paused to listen. After the initial expression of feeling in the language that came most naturally to him, Tangle resorted to Spanish.

"What is it now?" Forsythe asked. He was pulling on his nightshirt.

"Tangle doesn't want the surgeon to bleed him. He is invoking the names of learned Arab doctors who disapprove the practice."

"The heathen! He'll never get well if he doesn't let the doctor tend him."

Thorton adjusted his nightshirt and settled in his hammock. A little water sloshed across the floor as the ship rolled. Forsythe blew out the lantern.

"I feel sorry for you in all this, Peter. 'Twasn't your fault. I know you don't like me, but I never did you any harm." Forsythe climbed into his bunk.

"Thank you, sir. Your consideration means a lot to me. Some of them are treating me poorly."

"I don't see any point in being mean over it. The court martial will settle it. We all know you were carried off. They'll acquit you for sure."

Thorton was grateful and regretted he hadn't gotten to know the first lieutenant better. "Thank you, Albert. May I call you Albert?" he asked diffidently.

"Certainly, Peter. Whenever we're off duty."

"Of course, sir." He tried to apply the lessons in small talk that Perry had imparted long ago. "Do you still get seasick?"

"Not any more. I've gotten my sea legs. You?"

"No, I'm fine. It never gave me much trouble." He cast about in his mind for a further topic. "I'm sorry you got arrested with Bishop."

"God, what a choler he was in! He has an impressive command of French profanity, though. I learned a few new words."

Thorton couldn't help laughing at that. "Tell me? I must improve my French."

Forsythe began teaching him how to curse more fluently in French. By the time they fell asleep Thorton could tell someone to 'shake his leek,' which Forsythe assured him was a very rude thing to say to a Frenchman.

CHAPTER 25 : THE CAVES OF MALLORCA

Tangle unrolled his prayer mat on the quarterdeck and began to chant the call to prayer in a solemn baritone. The sound was ghostly in the grayness of the dawn. There was no air and the sea was glassy calm. Ra'uf and Akil scrambled up from below to join him. Thorton watched them praying and mouthed the words along with them. It was the closest he could come to sharing the prayer. Horner came onto the quarterdeck midway through. The dimness of the morning had caused him to oversleep, but the Arabic chanting drifting down through the skylight roused him. Thorton saluted him and kept mum. Horner checked the traverse boards, consulted the sky and sea, and asked a few questions about the weather and ship, which Thorton answered. Tangle's purple coat was the only color on the quarterdeck; the British uniforms were grey-blue in the dimness.

Horner had gotten used to Muslims praying on his quarterdeck; at least he gave no sign of having noticed them. He began to pace up and down the weather side as he always did. The Muslims occupied the lee side of the quarterdeck—they had learnt very quickly to stay out of his way when he paced, and that he paced his quarterdeck every morning for exercise before tackling the day's business. Thorton called his orders to MacDonald who set the hands to holystoning the decks as they did every morning. There was nothing in particular to rouse their attention as the fog lightened and the sky turned pink then yellow.

Tangle was not especially pious, but he was a sincere believer. He did his dawn prayer, felt guilty about having missed quite a few prayers while aboard the English vessel, and with the frigate becalmed, decided to keep going. He had nothing else to occupy and distract him during his extended 'visit' aboard the English vessel.

"Deck ho! A sail off the starboard beam!"

This did not elicit the excitement it would have under other circumstances—the Sallee squadron was with them every morning. Horner and Thorton took out their spyglasses and peered through the mist while Tangle kept praying.

"Deck, 'tis a lateen sloop!"

That piqued their attention—there were no single-masted vessels in the Sallee squadron. Horner spoke calmly, "Mr. Thorton, if you would be so good as to go to the masthead."

"Aye aye, sir!" Thorton replied crisply. He ran up the shrouds and climbed into the top via the futtock shrouds. He turned his glass on the distant sail.

"I think there's another one beyond it, sir," the watch told him.

Thorton swept his glass in a slow semicircle. "'Tis a fleet of small craft!" He watched them—and saw the shadows of the two- and three-masted lateeners of the Sallee squadron spreading out and sweeping through the fog after them. Suddenly a wild clatter rang out—one of the small craft was beating a wooden spoon against a tin pan to warn the others. The other small vessels did not understand at first.

"Mr. Thorton, report!" Horner bellowed.

"A fleet of small craft, sir! The rovers are sweeping after them!" Thorton grabbed the backstay and zoomed down to the deck.

Tangle twitched and jerked as he overheard the noise and reports. He stumbled in his prayers but made himself continue. For the recitation from the Qu'ran he picked a very short verse, "It is the enemy who is without issue." It was one of his favorites and hence one of the few that Thorton knew by heart. The prayer quickly came to an end and Tangle sprang up. Akil collected his prayer rug and headed below. The rover clapped his spyglass to his eye and studied the scene.

"Mallorquin sardine boats," he announced. "Very common. If they run back into Portocristo they'll warn the coastguards. The Spanish will come out."

A faint breeze stirred the limp flags. "I'll have the stunsails and staysails set, Mr. Thorton. Clap on every bit of canvas we have."

"Aye aye, sir." Thorton strode to the rail and called down. "MacDonald! All sails! Look lively lads, we can't let any of them get back to port to warn the Dons!"

Holystones were happily abandoned as the men ran to the rigging to lace on every stitch of canvas the frigate had. The fog continued thinning and the rising breeze began to shred it. They gained steerage way but could not keep up with the rowed warships. The rovers were gorging on prizes. The unarmed fishboats could not outrun them and had no weapons. They surrendered with a warning shot. Small prize crews were put on them, and the rovers charged after more victims.

Tangle put his glass to his eye and muttered, "Damn that idiot Kasim." He lowered his spyglass. "The man hasn't got the sense Allah gave a seahorse."

Without the commodore to give them directions the Sallee rovers had reverted to form: they were coursing after prizes without any thought of strategic or even tactical considerations. Tangle clenched his hands at his side.

"Land ho!" the lookout called. "Two miles to windward!"

All the officers on the quarterdeck whirled to peer through the thinning mist. With their glasses to their eyes they could make out the line of not so distant land. Fortunately they were in its lee and thus unlikely to be in any danger from the shore, but Horner's expression as he lowered his glass was dour. He had calculated the *Ajax* to be at least twenty miles to the leeward of the largest of the Balearic Islands. He had not wanted to pass so close—he did not want to meet Spanish patrols. Majorca was a Spanish stronghold with numerous coves along the coast and a good port and fleet in Palma de Mallorca. Any other captain would have thought a longitudinal error of twenty miles wasn't bad, but in the Mediterranean where islands, peninsulas, reefs, and shoals complicated navigation, it could be deadly.

The *Ajax* glided gently through the calm waters. She was making about three knots and was alone. The fishboats were to the east. They had gone out before dawn to be on the fishing grounds when the sun rose. With the dark and the fog they had not seen the British frigate and Sallee rovers coming up from the south.

"A sail! Two-masted lateener, fine on the starboard bow!"

They all turned their glasses to look. There she was, looming out of the fog, her big lateen sails and jib pulling her along at about three knots and heading directly towards them. When she saw they were a frigate she veered northwest. The gold and red of Spain flashed on her stern.

Tangle shouted in Arabic, "Get her!" Then he remembered that he was not in command of the vessel and turned to Horner and swiftly said, "Don't let her escape! She's a coastguard!"

Horner was already giving his own orders. "Clear for action."

The rattle of the snare drums rolled through the ship and the men boiled through the wooden hull. All the detritus of life aboard was stowed below and secured so that it could not impede the operation of the guns. The ship's boys ran to the powder room to collect their cartridges and bring them to their guns.

"May I signal the Sallee fleet, Captain?" Tangle asked urgently.

"What is your plan, Commodore?"

The *Sea Leopard* was far to leeward running down fishboats. The *Arrow* was on station nearest to the *Ajax*, a mile away to the southeast. "I'll signal the *Arrow* to make chase and order the rest to make certain none of them make it back to Portocristo, even if they have to sink them."

"Very good, sir. Mr. Thorton, make it so."

Thorton spelled out the Arabic orders with English letters. The *Arrow* acknowledged—she was already flying after the felucca. She passed Tangle's commands to the rest of the fleet.

The galleys were making the most of their ability to dash under oars to pick off fishboats; they were working as a team to cut off fishboats trying to dart back into Portocristo. The second galiot continued running after fishboats as they scattered to the east in a desperate bid to run away. So did the *Sea Leopard*. Tangle smote his forehead with the palm of his hand and swore in Turkish. To see only half his fleet obey was an event to bring grief to any commander.

The felucca had bigger sails than the galiot and was slowly pulling away. She turned a point in the coast and disappeared behind it.

"Keep after her," Horner instructed. Their course was bringing them gradually closer to the shore so that they would round the point tightly. "Commodore. Do you know these waters?"

"I do. The bottom drops off quickly—you can get in close. The water will be four to five fathoms right up to the shore."

"Get the lead out."

Thorton passed the word. The carpenter and his mates climbed into the channels and let their lines go. "Eight fathoms a half!"

"If you don't mind, I'd like to go forward," Tangle asked.

"By all means," Horner replied. "Mr. Blakesley, keep us on course to round that point as tight as conditions permit."

"Aye aye, sir."

Tangle and Horner hung over the gunwale and inspected the bottom sample brought up in the tallow of the lead. The tallow was cleared and renewed and sent over again.

"Six fathoms less a quarter!" the carpenter's mate called. If it made him nervous to have two captains breathing down his neck he didn't show it. He kept shouting loud enough for Thorton to hear it.

The bottom was steep and rising fast. Thorton kept his eye on the shore, watched the *Arrow* to his lee, and listened to the casts of the lead. As they approached the point, Horner returned to the quarterdeck. "Beat to quarters."

The *Ajax* swept slowly around the point of land, and found . . . nothing. The fugitive felucca had completely and utterly disappeared. There was no cove or other point to hide her. She had not run to sea. She was . . . gone. They looked around in disbelief.

"Lookout! What do you see? Where's the felucca?" Thorton called.

"Nothing, sir!"

Horner was mystified. The Englishmen scratched their heads and muttered, "She couldn't disappear into thin air."

Tangle came aft and listened to their bafflement. He scanned the waters. "Not into thin air," he said. "Into solid ground."

They gazed at him in perplexity.

"Caves," he replied. "The coast is riddled with them and none of them are mapped. There's several at Portocristo, but their openings are small." He swept his arm to indicate the coast. "Somewhere is a cave big enough to hide a ship. We have to find the entrance."

Horner stared at the land and considered his options.

"Captain Horner. The *Arrow* has a shallower draft and the agility necessary for this kind of work," Tangle said.

Horner nodded. "Aye. That she does."

"You have my parole. If you consent, I will go over to the *Arrow* and Shakil and Tahirah will come to the *Ajax*. You will stand guard in the bay while the *Arrow* noses along the coast. If we find the cave, we will go in after her. You will protect us from getting trapped by any forces that might come up while we are exploring. Fire three guns: one slow and two quick to warn us."

Horner clasped his hands behind his back. His lips pursed as he stared at the coast. "The prize will be yours."

"A fair split, each vessel doing her part."

Horner looked north. Then he turned and swept his eyes across the sea. The rising sun was burning off the fog that stood in ragged patches on the sea. The big lateen sails were still swooping after the little lateen sails. Under British law, every vessel in sight would share the prize money—but the Sallee rovers were taking the prizes to Zokhara. The *Ajax* would never see the money.

"I accept your parole, Commodore. You may use my gig."

CHAPTER 26 : CHARON'S FEE

The *Arrow* crept along the coast while the *Ajax* stood guard in the bay formed by the hook of the point. The sun grew higher and the day warmer. Shakil and Tahirah stood on the quarterdeck; they were not only hostages for Tangle's good behavior but would be safer aboard the frigate—the *Arrow* was a ferret going into a burrow after a cornered rat. Hands worked the sweeps to slowly crawl forward. The *Ajax* paralleled the *Arrow's* progress as she worked her way along the curve of the bay right under the cliffs. A pistol shot gave sign: the cave was found. Strain their eyes as they might, they could not detect it. The cliffs were rippled tan stone with lines cut in their faces by erosion. Dusty grey-green foliage topped the cliffs and spilled down the ravines.

As they watched, the *Arrow* sailed right into the solid mass. They braced themselves, but there was no awful scraping, no crash or collision. The sweeps slowly propelled the *Arrow* forward. Her prow disappeared first. Foot by foot, the fore antenna with its furled sail followed. Then her main antenna disappeared until all that was left was the lazyboard overhanging her stern, then that too was gone.

They watched in awe. Although they had seen her go, they could not pick out the division in the cliff that had swallowed her. Horner gave orders, "Helm hard over."

The *Ajax* moved ponderously until they could see the opening. The leads were calling shallow water when Horner gave the order to hold their position. The entrance was a narrow fjord, if that word could be used to describe a Mediterranean coast. It ran north into a bulge of hills, then immediately hooked west into the interior of the island. The *Arrow* was out of sight.

"Mr. Perry, Mr. Forsythe. Take the cutter and the launch and follow the *Arrow*. Quietly, if you please!"

Thorton longed to be in one of those boats, but he knew that Horner would not let him. Not when there was a good chance that Tangle would pluck him out of the water and carry him off. Horner glanced back and so did Thorton, wondering what he saw. There was nothing back there. Satisfied that his stern was not exposed, Horner continued watching the cave. With soft splashes the boats were launched and the men quietly piled into them. They rowed up the fjord and disappeared around the bend.

The earth muffled the boom of gunnery, but the double-throated roar of a pair of thirty-two pounders was unmistakeable. In almost the same instant four smaller guns spoke. Horner tilted his head as if listening to a sonata at a chamber music concert.

"Mr. Thorton, what do you make of it?"

"The *Arrow* has fired her bow guns, sir."

The softer roar of the felucca's broadside answered them. The noise had the rolling, rumbling sound of thunder caught in a cavern. Horner fidgeted. He looked over his shoulder at the clear blue sea.

"I'll have my gig. Mr. Thorton, come with me. Send for Lt. Barnes and a party of marines. Mr. Blakesley, you have the conn. Don't let the enemy take us in the rear. Withdraw sufficiently so the *Arrow* can make her escape if necessary. Cover the entrance with our broadside. I am going to reconnoitre. I expect to return before you need me."

"Aye aye, sir." Blakesley looked surprised at the captain's command, but obedience to orders was a deeply ingrained habit.

Thorton could hardly contain himself. He got his sword and pistols and climbed into the gig with Horner. All the men had an air of suppressed excitement as they rowed the small boat into the fjord. Tan walls flecked with faded grey-green foliage enclosed them. A gentle current flowed out to the sea, showing that they had discovered an underground river. They had not reached the turn when they heard the *Arrow*'s bow battery roar. The felucca answered raggedly. Both vessels would be loading as fast as possible. No matter how big the cave was, it wouldn't be big enough for maneuvering. What was happening in there was as brutal as a pair of prizefighters locked together as they pummeled each other.

They came around the bend. The opening to the cave was as high as a cathedral, narrow, and dark. The sunlight shone into the entrance and lit up the area closest to the sea, but the *Arrow* was not there. They peered into the darkness, but with eyes dazzled by the daylight they couldn't see a thing.

"Forward," said Horner.

The *Arrow*'s bow guns boomed again and the noise nearly deafened them. The felucca was deep inside somewhere, but her answering barrage echoed all around them.

The men bent their backs and the boat slid into the cavern. The marines sat tensely with their loaded muskets in their hands. Their eyes slowly adjusted as they advanced into the dimness. The sight that greeted them was one that would be blazed in their minds for the rest of their lives.

The cave was tall—not tall enough to admit the *Ajax*, but tall enough that the masts of the lateeners were in no danger of scraping the roof. The real danger was from the stalactites and stalagmites that formed massive columns. The starboard side of the cave was composed of rippled walls of white stone drapery. The visible part of the underground river was several hundred yards long and wound out of sight into the bowels of the earth. The felucca was invisible except for the orange flare of her guns. The noise echoed and reverberated after each shot. Conversation was impossible.

The *Arrow* was easing around a mighty tower of white limestone that looked like giant plates randomly stacked. The felucca had run out of room. If she ran deeper into the underground river she must expose her stern. If she tried to back in she must offer her bow to be raked while prohibiting the use of her broadsides. She carried four-pounders in her bow, but they were popguns compared to the thirty-twos aboard the *Arrow*.

The *Ajax's* boats were stroking hard across the waters. Not to be outdone, the *Arrow* launched her own boats. The felucca concentrated her fire on the approaching boarders. Thorton clenched his teeth as fountains of water erupted around the English launch, then wood shattered and men screamed. The crack of musketry added to the din. Agonized voices cried out in English.

"Pick up survivors," Horner directed. "Marines fire at will."

Barnes passed the order and his marines stood to fire over the heads of the rowing seamen. The crack of musket fire right in their ears made it impossible for the men to hear anything else.

The gig rowed into the firing range of the trapped felucca. They could see her as a shadowy figure. Her guns roared and limned her in orange. Her main antenna hung from its preventer chains. Her foremast was shot away and the fore antenna fouled her deck. Her prow was shattered. The *Arrow* had scooted over to the north side and the felucca had to traverse her guns as far as they would go. With shock Thorton realized she must be aground—she was not moving. She was at bay and fighting to the death. Musket fire whined around the gig and splinters flew as a ball plunked into one of the oars. The oar jerked in response and the sailor holding it let go and yelped. The oar was lost over the side. Thorton lunged for it and caught it up again.

"Pull, men!" Horner ordered. In a louder voice he called, "We're coming to get you, lads!" His voice was both stentorian and cheerful as he stood in the stern to get a better view. He didn't even flinch when a ball went through his hat.

They reached the first swimmers. Thorton helped hauled the men over the gunwale. "Grab on lads! Haul 'em aboard, boys! This one's wounded, easy there!" A scarlet-coated marine fired over his back and he felt a spark from the flintlock sting his neck.

The other English boat had rowed in range of the felucca's bow guns, but one of them had already been dismounted and the other was severely hampered by the fallen antenna. The *Arrow's* guns roared out again to work with deadly effect on the trapped and wounded felucca. Confined by the cavern the sound seemed to come from all around in a deafening thunder. The felucca's guns fired a ragged response.

"Where's Forsythe?" Thorton shouted at the man he hauled on board.

"Don't know!" the man gasped.

"Forsythe! Where are you? *Ajax*, to me!" Thorton bellowed. His voice helped swimmers locate the gig amid the amber flashes of gunnery.

They pulled more men out of the water until the gig was overloaded. A cannonball skimmed right past them and Horner said, "Pull along side the *Arrow*. Mr. Thorton, may we place survivors aboard?"

"Of course," Thorton replied. As they approached the vessel of which he was the putative master, he stood up and shouted in Arabic, "Prepare to receive survivors!"

Wafor, the African boatswain, looked over the side. "Peter Rais! Welcome aboard!" he answered in the same language.

For a moment Thorton hesitated. He was coming alongside. All he had to do was the grab the offered hand and crawl over the gunwale and he'd be free. No more court martial. No more worry and fear about his love life. No more petty humiliations inflicted by sly Englishmen. But he had given his word. He turned and helped a man climb up and grab the offered hand instead.

The noise of gunnery rolled and reverberated inside his skull. In the bow of the *Arrow* Maynard shouted in bad Spanish, "You must strike! We will kill you if you don't strike!"

The Spanish colors still flew and her guns still spoke. "No surrender!" the Spanish captain roared back. Cannonballs smacked into the *Arrow's* bow. With a sudden roar of exaltation the Englishmen from the surviving boat swarmed over the felucca's bow.

Horner directed the gig to pick up more swimmers and haul them to the *Arrow*. The galiot had run out of room; the water to her starboard was too shallow for her to be able to pull away from the felucca's line of fire. Orange flashes and thunder shook the limestone formations. The gunfire lit them with lurid shades of orange that made the sinuous stone shapes seem to writhe. Sometimes slabs of limestone fell where stray shots struck the Stygian grotto. Fountains of water erupted as cannonballs splashed into the underground lake. Men screamed. Wood splinters flew as the *Arrow* pounded the felucca.

Thorton shouted to be heard, "Her fire is weakening! She must strike!"

"She's sinking, Mr. Thorton." Horner pointed at her. "Look at her lading marks. She's going down."

With a sudden crack, her main mast split. The great tree hung crookedly for a moment, then the weight of the main antenna caused it to bend and slowly descend. Suddenly it collapsed entirely with a shriek of rending wood. The vessel was listing to the starboard and the additional weight on that side unbalanced her further. The felucca began a slow roll into an irretrievable capsize. Men cried out and some of them sobbed. Spanish sailors were begging for mercy, but the officers would not strike. A pistol shot rang out, then another. Spanish sailors jumped overboard. Some swam towards the small boat.

"Merced! Ayúdame!" they begged.

"Retreat. They'll swamp us if they get too close," Horner ordered. The gig was a narrow thing with no sail; it was overloaded with rescued Englishmen already. They had no room for drowning Spaniards.

The gig turned away and rowed back towards the light. Thorton watched over his shoulder as men who didn't know how to swim flailed in the waters. Those who could swim made for the *Arrow*. Looking up as they passed the galiot's stern, Thorton saw Tangle at the rail in his purple coat. The scant rays of sun made the crossed scimitars and star glow on his collar.

Outside they heard a gun fire, a pause, then two guns in rapid succession. "The enemy!" Thorton exclaimed.

Horner barked, "Return to the *Ajax!*"

"She's going!" a man cried.

They all turned and looked back into the dim interior of the cave. The felucca was sinking fast. The guns stopped. The captain's cabin was afire and the orange flames licked their way rapidly through the wooden bulwarks and decking. Orange light lit the interior of the cave like a scene from Hell. A fifty or more men were in the water. Some clung to the pillars of stalagmites. A dead fat man in Spanish lace floated nearby. Englishmen were among the swimmers. The British tars that had raided the felucca slithered over her side and into their own boat, but they had to engage in some brutal hand-to-hand combat and point blank pistolery to fend off Spaniards desperate to take the boat. Only one of the Spanish boats managed to launch.

The felucca rolled further still, then she capsized completely. Her masts and antennas went under, and she slowly slid down the underwater shelf into deeper water. For a moment orange flames lingered in her exposed quarter, then were quenched as the cabin vanished under the waves.

"*Ajax* return!" Horner bellowed.

They gave a cheer and rowed for the entrance. Thorton put his hand in his pocket and pulled out some copper coins. He tossed them over the side.

"What did you do that for, sir?" the cockswain asked him.

"Charon's fee," Thorton replied. "We left a lot of dead men for him to ferry."

"If you say so, sir." The cockswain was not an educated man.

Chapter 27 : The Battle of Portocristo

Escaping the cavern, they saw the *Sea Leopard* in the offing. She had let her sheets fly in the ancient warning of the approach of a fleet. Horner, Thorton, and the men scrambled back aboard the *Ajax*. Horner strode to his quarterdeck calling for reports. Thorton ran after him. With shock he realized Forsythe was missing and Perry was in the launch rowing frantically in their wake. Without them he was the executive officer. If anything happened to Horner, the *Ajax* was his to command.

Horner looked back, looked forward, then gave orders. "Make sail!"

"Sir!" Thorton exclaimed. "Our boat!"

"I am not going far, Mr. Thorton. The launch will catch up to us. We dare not be embayed in the face of the enemy."

"Aye aye, sir," Thorton gulped. He repeated the order. "Make sail!"

"Sound the Sallee warning."

"Aye aye, sir. Gun two, fire!" It boomed out. Thorton let a short pause ensue. "Gun three, fire! Gun four, fire!" They boomed out one after the other. The reverberation rolled across the sea and echoed against the dun-colored cliffs.

"Reload!" he shouted. Chambers and Pettigrew were on gundeck doing the work of lieutenants he suddenly realized. "Do you want me to go to the gundeck, sir? We have no other lieutenants aboard."

Horner glanced back at the launch. "Mr. Perry will be with us presently. He can go below."

The *Ajax* began to crawl out of the bay. The breeze blowing over the cliffs was slight, but there was a little. Bit by bit she began to gain headway. Thorton glanced back and saw the launch pursuing them. They were able to row faster than the *Ajax* was sailing; they would catch her but it would be a long hard row. He looked forward and anxiously scanned the stretch of sea that he could see from the mouth of the bay. He looked to the point, but it was high and blocked his view. There could be Spaniards on the other side. The *Sea Leopard* changed course, secured her sheets, and began to pull away to the southeast. With her big lateen sails and being further offshore she caught more wind. A cheer turned his head around: the *Arrow* was emerging bow first from the narrow fjord. She was rowing and made the turn into the bay neatly. Her bow guns were loaded and run out and there was a blond head and waving hand that could only belong to Archibald Maynard Aruj, boy lieutenant. Thorton was proud of them. All the training that Tangle and he had given them had made them into a very fine crew.

In the daylight the damage to her bow could be seen but the carpenter and his mates were already working to repair it. The *arrumbada* was half-wrecked—he hoped Aruj had not been hurt— while the carpenter's mate and his men were fishing a timber along side the bowsprit to brace it. The sailmaker and his mates were cutting off the tack of the foresail because the end of the antenna had been shot away. The foresail was now a settee sail. They stitched a piece of rope into the edge of the sail to strengthen it until a proper repair could be made.

The *Ajax* rounded the point and finally got a view of the sea. The scattered Sallee squadron was shepherding their prizes to the southeast. The *Sea Leopard* had been foremost when they were heading north but was now hindmost heading south. The fastest of the little fleet, she was overhauling them. The lookout sang out, "A sail! Coming out of Majorca!"

"Thorton, get up there and give me a detailed report," Horner said crisply.

"Aye aye, sir." Thorton swarmed up the shrouds and took his place in the top. He put the glass to his good eye.

"Deck! Two frigates coming out of Portocristo!" he bellowed. "Ten miles south!"

The Sallee fleet would have to run before them to escape, but the little fishboats could not outrun frigates. Running before the wind was a choice point of sail for square-riggers and not so good for lateeners. As they got out of the wind shadow of Majorca they were gaining speed— but it wouldn't be enough. As they watched, the *Sea Leopard* set her course to run interception between the prizes and the oncoming Spanish.

"He has courage, I'll give him that," Thorton said.

"Who's that, sir?" the lookout asked him.

"Captain Kasim of the *Sea Leopard*." Thorton continued studying the distant scene. Small craft were running for the shelter of the harbor, but no other warships were coming out. The main Spanish base was at Palma halfway around the island—it would take hours for the warning to reach them and the fleet come out. Thorton slid down the backstay and made his report to Horner.

"You're quite certain there are only two frigates, Thorton?"

"Yes, small ones. I don't think they're carrying more than twenty guns each. I think they're small frigate-rigged xebecs or maybe corvettes."

Horner nodded; the analysis made sense. Small warships would be used to protect the cabotage and fishing fleets. "We will support our allies the Sallee rovers in the protection of their prizes. Pick up our boat. Make a signal to the *Arrow*, '*Ajax* return.'"

"Aye aye, sir."

The signals were made and acknowledged. The *Ajax's* boat caught up to them and Perry hurried to the quarterdeck to make his report.

"I regret to inform you there are two dead and thirteen wounded in my boat. Six are missing, but I believe some of them may be aboard the *Arrow*."

"Thank you, Mr. Perry. Take your post on the gundeck and send Mr. Chambers to the foredeck."

"Aye aye, sir."

The *Arrow* came along side the *Ajax*. With so many men to be transferred it was easier to grapple. The water and wind was calm enough. Forsythe came over and hurried up to the quarterdeck to make his own report. He was soaking wet but in good spirits in spite of the casualty report. He'd lost his hat, sword, and pistol.

Horner's face lightened when he saw him. "Mr. Forsythe. I'm pleased to see you among the living."

"I'm pleased to be among the living, sir!"

"Are you wounded?" Thorton asked. He had noticed Forsythe limping.

"I got whacked in the ankle with a piece of wreckage. 'Tis not serious."

"Get it splinted and return," Horner told him.

"Aye aye, sir." Forsythe saluted and hurried down to the cockpit.

Quarterdeck to quarterdeck Tangle and Horner conferred. They were of like mind: support the *Sea Leopard*. Kasim Rais had not waited for them. He was charging after the Sallee squadron and their prizes. The consultation was a quick one—by the time the men were transferred to the *Ajax* they already had their plan. Grapples were loosed and the two vessels fended off. They set their sails and their sweeps, rowing to get off the coast enough to catch a good wind to carry them south. They struck away from the island.

Horner looked at Thorton. "Why are you still on deck, Mr. Thorton?"

Thorton saluted. "Sorry, sir!"

He ran down to the gundeck. With Forsythe and Perry back he had to resume his proper place as the junior lieutenant. His battle station was the larboard battery. "Mr. Jones, I relieve you. You're needed on the quarterdeck."

The midshipman was white in the face. Having been only a few months at sea, he was unprepared for the responsibility of managing the men and guns of the larboard battery. Thorton glanced down the line and saw the guns in good order. The men knew what they were to do, and Jones, having had some experience with the smaller guns on the quarterdeck, had told them to do it. Iron discipline supported even the weak links in the chain of command. At that moment Thorton loved the British navy.

"Aye aye, sir," Jones replied.

"And Jones. Good work." He smiled at him.

The boy brightened. "Thank you, sir." He saluted and ran to the companionway.

Thorton could not see much through the larboard gun ports. He ran over to look out the starboard ports. The *Sea Leopard* headed directly south to run between the Spanish and the squadron. With the wind on her beam she made excellent time. The *Arrow* and the *Ajax* coursed further east. With the wind on their starboard quarters they scooned along at excellent speed and the *Ajax* drew ahead of the *Arrow*. When the *Ajax* made her turn it brought her close-hauled on an angle to run ahead of the *Sea Leopard*. The *Arrow* continued running to the east. When she finally made her turn, she flew close-hauled and heeled over to race ahead. Each vessel had her best point of sail; by taking an indirect route, a vessel could sail faster and arrive at her goal more quickly.

The Spanish corvettes saw them coming and so did the rest of the Sallee fleet. The other galiot and galleys turned around and glided back to face the Spanish. Outnumbered and outgunned, the corvettes turned tail and ran back toward Portocristo.

On the quarterdeck Horner said, "Pursue, Mr. Blakesley." His voice was as congenial as if he had suggested a cup of tea.

Aboard the *Arrow* Tangle had made the same decision. The Spanish had to beat back towards the port and that was slow going, especially as they crept into the lee of the island. The frigate and the Sallee rovers raced after them. A small fort commanded the headland at the entrance to Portocristo harbor. The corvettes got safely under its guns and the *Sea Leopard* sheered off. The other Sallee rovers sheered off as well and began regrouping. Only the *Arrow* ran with the *Ajax*.

The fort opened fire. The first ranging shot was well short, but as the *Arrow* and the *Ajax* continued their pursuit they lost speed and the fort's ranging shots crept closer. The corvettes were at long range, but the *Arrow* loosed her bow guns anyhow. The shots dropped short.

"Make a signal, Mr. Thorton. 'Submit, retreat.'" Horner could not order a commodore of a foreign navy to withdraw, neither would he abandon his ally if she continued the action. He could only submit his suggestion.

"Acknowledged and affirmative, sir." The *Arrow* wore around. The *Ajax* wore too and the two vessels pulled away. The fort fired a salvo and several balls went through the rigging of the *Arrow*, but no apparent damage was done. The *Ajax* was not touched. The two vessels ran to the east. The Spanish corvettes turned around and ran after them.

The *Ajax's* sternchasers could not possibly reach the Spanish pursuers, but the roar of the gun and the puff of smoke told the Spanish that they were alert and would fight. The *Arrow* fired her sternchasers as well. She had bigger stern guns with a longer range on them than the *Ajax's* quarterdeck guns; she put a pair of shots right close to the bow of the leading corvette.

Thorton and Perry's heads nearly touched as they leaned over the gun and stared out the side. "The *Arrow* cannot outrun the corvettes. They carry a good press of sail," Thorton said.

Tangle knew it, too. He wore ship and the galiot presented her heavy bow guns to the enemy. Her sails were taken aback with a clap of thunder that was audible on the *Ajax*.

"My god, she's making sternway," said Perry.

The *Arrow* was sailing backwards with her sails pressed back against her masts. Aboard the *Arrow* sailors were frantically disentangling the sails and bracing them well around. Her retrograde movement halted. Slowly she began to gain a little headway with her sails close-hauled farther around than any square-rigged vessel could manage. Her slow motion was not enough. The corvettes split up to pass her on either side to catch her between their broadsides.

Over their heads they heard Horner's command, "Prepare to wear ship!" Slowly, sluggishly, she came around close-hauled on the starboard tack. She must beat against the west wind to come to the *Arrow's* aid. They could only watch as the corvettes sprang upon the galiot.

The *Arrow* was not helpless. Sweeps suddenly shot out of the oarlocks and dug into the water. Two hundred backs bent as the rowers threw their entire bodies on the oars in a violent dance. The small amount of headway she had let her accelerate rapidly. The galiot shot forward and the startled corvettes fired their broadsides as she raced between them. What damage she took they could not tell, but they heard the crack of wood and cries of men and knew she was wounded. As she cleared the gauntlet, she suddenly spun around. As her bow guns swung across the northern corvette's stern, she fired. Her gunnery slammed into the vessel's unprotected stern.

The southern corvette had a dilemma: if she wore around to give her other broadside to the galiot she would expose her stern to the approaching Ajax. The Ajax was not coming up fast, but she was coming up. The Ajax turned further across the wind to bring her starboard broadside to bear. Thorton leaped back to his own guns. He walked rapidly along the line of crouching men to check the elevation and transverse of the guns.

A midshipman messenger clattered down the companionway. "Fire as she bears!"

"Fire as she bears!" he bawled.

Perry's slender figure arched over a gun as he watched out the port. Suddenly he dodged out of the way. "Fire!" he shouted.

The thunderous roar of the broadside spoke. The ship heeled to the larboard in recoil. The guns shot a full ten feet across the deck before being caught up by their tackles. Gunsmoke filled the space below decks and stung Thorton's eyes, but he heard Perry exult, "A hit! A palpable hit!"

The corvette answered with her own broadside. Shot whistled and wood crashed. Men screamed. A shot went caroming across the deck and flung itself out the opposite porthole. A man lay on the deck with a shattered leg. He had been bowled down like a ninepin.

"Stretcher!" Thorton bellowed. Bare feet pattered as men came to bear away the wounded.

Perry exhorted his men, "Damn you, load! Faster!"

The Ajax tacked suddenly and hard. A heart-throbbing pause made them wonder if she was going to miss stays, but at that moment her bow guns spoke and she continued through the tack. Thorton crouched over a black gun and watched out the port. As the corvette came into view he saw her bow swinging towards them. She had decided to not worry about the galiot behind her and was concentrating her attack on the approaching frigate.

"Fire!" Thorton roared. His guns leaped and thundered. They shot back across the deck with a roar of wood and iron. He stuck his head out a port in an effort to get a view of the damage, but gunsmoke was eddying around him and made his eyes water. His blurry left eye was no help at distance viewing and he shut it to focus better.

Orders came from above. Thorton roared, "Double-shot, you pox-ridden sons of bitches! Blow the Dagos out of the water!"

Both broadsides worked frantically to reload and run out. "Fire as she bears!" Perry bellowed.

"Fire as she bears!" Thorton shouted to his men.

Thorton saw to the laying of the guns himself. On the other side Perry was doing the same. Thorton was peaceful inside. It gave him great satisfaction to do his duty amid the stench of gunpowder and the crying of the wounded. He smiled at the men around him and said congenially, "Gut her, you misbegotten whoresons!"

"Aye aye, sir!" they answered him enthusiastically.

The *Ajax* passed along side the corvette. They received her broadside and Thorton's moment of serenity was shattered. Splinters flew and men screamed. Number four gun was dismounted and broke the legs of two men as it slammed into them. They toppled and were pinned under the iron mass. Thorton picked himself off the deck.

"Sir!" someone shouted at him. They plucked at the splinters that pierced his chest and upper arm. He grimaced and gingerly opened his coat.

"Not bad." He had four or five splinters embedded in his upper arm and chest. He broke them off and cradled his right arm against his chest. Rosettes of blood spotted his white waistcoat. "Help those men. I'm fine."

He turned his attention to the rest of his guns. He could not think about the casualties. They would only distract him. He peered out the port. The corvette was running with the wind on her starboard quarter as she attempted to escape to the dubious protection of the sea. He swung his head and saw the *Sea Leopard* beating back towards them. He could not see the *Arrow* or the other corvette, but he heard the sound of their guns. The heavy thirty-two pounders were distinctive for their throaty roars. None of the other vessels carried heavy metal like that.

"Damage report!" somebody was shouting.

Thorton looked around. He counted two dismounted guns, nine wounded, and one dead. He did not include himself in the wounded. He reported to Perry, who collated the information with his own and passed it to the messenger.

A new cannonade erupted. Thorton stuck his head out the port. The *Sea Leopard* was bearing down on their corvette. The *Ajax* changed course and heeled to the starboard as she clawed north. The western breeze blew in through the larboard ports and cleared the air a little.

Thorton sucked in a great gulp of fresh air. Then he slipped in blood on the deck and fell.

"Sand that!" he ordered as he picked himself up.

"Aye aye, sir," a boy replied. He was a towheaded tike of about ten years. He ran to one of the tubs of sand that were kept for the purpose and started tossing handfuls on the blood to improve the footing.

The *Arrow* came into view through his port. The other corvette had been using her greater maneuverability and speed under sail to run around the galiot, but the galiot was using her oars to keep turning, darting and rushing, refusing to stay in one place long enough for the corvette to do decisive work. Thorton knew just how exhausted her rowers would be. Her crew was big enough they could swap fresh men to row, but human strength would soon come to an end.

"Chain shot!" came the command.

Thorton bellowed, "Chain shot, you slubberdegullions! Smartly, lads, smartly!"

The powder boys came running with cartridges. The gun captains primed and rammed, shoved the chain shot in, tamped, and ran out their guns. Thorton shouted, "Elevate, damn you!"

The guns were adjusted to raise their muzzles to aim for the masts and rigging. Thorton crouched behind a gun, checked the numbers on the carriage, then lowered it a notch. He shouted to the others to take their aim based on his gun and they did so. They received the corvette's ragged broadside before they closed the distance. He heard the shot thump against the oaken hull beside him and was glad distance had robbed it of its power.

"Ready, lads, steady! We won't waste our powder on a long shot!"

They crouched over the guns. They sweated and waited. The corvette broke off to run north. A cheer went up from the gun crews on the larboard side.

"Silence!" Thorton roared. He crouched on one bent leg with the other flung out for balance. It allowed him to squint along the barrel to be certain of his aim.

They quieted down. They watched and waited. The *Ajax* pursued. The *Arrow* collected herself and gave chase in their wake. She stowed her sweeps and set her sails. The beam reach suited all the vessels, but gradually the *Ajax* pulled ahead. The corvette ran best of all and she slowly pulled away from them. The fugitive rounded the point. The *Ajax* slowed and waited for the *Arrow* to come up. They knew what was around that point and they came around cautiously.

Thorton laughed. "They don't know about the cave," he said. "Or they're afraid of getting trapped."

The Spaniard was still running north along the coast of Majorca as fast as she could go.

Boys brought around ladles of beer to douse the men's thirst. The carpenter and his mates arrived and began patching the hull. The gunner and his mates began repairing the damaged guns. Boys swept up debris and washed blood from the deck with buckets of seawater hauled up by the men. Perry and Thorton came together.

"You're wounded!" Perry exclaimed.

"Oh, this is nothing. A prick is all."

"See the surgeon. Splinters can kill if they work their way into the body."

"I will."

But he didn't. He went aft, but he went up instead of down. He emerged into the fresh air and sunlight and blinked like a ground hog. The Sallee squadron was far south and traveling towards Africa. He wondered how Tangle felt. How could he hope to make a navy out of corsairs? They wanted prizes, not victory. Then he wondered if Shakil was all right and Miss Tahirah too. Had the child been very frightened? He went below in search of them.

He found them huddled in the midshipman's berth. Shakil heard footsteps in the gunroom and poked his head out. He saw the bloodstains on Thorton's chest and sleeve. He spoke softly to Tahirah. "Stay here, I am going to find out if it is safe to come out," he told her.

He stepped into the gunroom and shut the door. The two were alone. "Peter Rais, you're hurt," he said very softly.

Thorton pulled a splinter out of his sleeve and showed it to him. "This is all. Scratches, nothing more."

Shakil grabbed his face and kissed him hard. "I was worried for you!"

Thorton grinned giddily. "It was fun!"

Shakil gave him an exasperated look. "Damn you, you're just like Isam! You're giving me grey hair!"

Thorton squeezed his hand. "I love you."

Shakil did not say what he was thinking: he did not want to love a warrior. It was too hard on his heart. What he said was, "Go to the cockpit. You're a mess."

CHAPTER 28 : HEART OF OAK

Tangle returned to the *Ajax* in time for supper. He had spent the day supervising the repairs to the *Arrow*, met with the officers, then ordered out the boat. The *Dart* (as the *Arrow's* boat was known) carried him back to the *Ajax*. The *Arrow* and the *Ajax* were now alone because the corsairs had abandoned their erstwhile commander to herd their prizes back to Zokhara.

Thorton looked over the side and saw him with the right sleeve of his purple coat torn away. His right forearm was bandaged.

"Bosun's chair!" Thorton ordered.

"Aye aye, sir," replied McDonald. He passed the word and the seat, which was really little more than a wooden swing supported by a line reeved to the yardarm, was made ready.

Thorton looked down into the *Dart* and called in Arabic, "Are you all right, sir?"

Tangle indicated his arm. "Minor burn. I fell against a hot swivel gun."

The boatswain's chair went over. Tangle took a seat and held on with his good hand. He hooked his other elbow around the line. Thus secured he was raised to the deck. The boatswain's pipe trilled the arrival of a commodore and the marines presented arms.

"Welcome back, Commodore," Thorton greeted him.

"Thank you, Peter. I'm glad to see you in one piece. Is it bad?" He indicated the bloody shirt.

The surgeon's mate had taken the splinters out of Thorton and stitched him up, but he was still wearing the bloody waistcoat and shirt. "Not at all. Just a few scratches. I'm glad to see you well."

They were interrupted by a squeal from Tahirah. She came running down from the quarterdeck with Shakil close behind. After the decks had been washed and the dead buried at sea, she had been allowed out of the middies' berth.

"*Baba!*" she shrieked. She flung herself against her father and wrapped her arms around him.

Tangle hugged her tight against him. He kissed the top of her head and asked her gently, "Were you brave?"

They conversed in low Arabic. Finally he parted from her with a sigh. He kissed Shakil on both cheeks and spoke with him, then the girl and her uncle went into the boat to return to the *Arrow*. Shakil paused in climbing over the rail. He and Thorton exchanged a long gaze. They had not had much time together, but it had done Thorton's heart good to glance up from his work and see Shakil watching him.

"Go with God, Peter Rais," Shakil said with feeling.

"Peace be upon you, Shakil Effendi," Thorton replied with suppressed emotion.

After a last look, Shakil disappeared below the gunwale. A minute later and the *Dart* sailed away towards the *Arrow*.

Tangle ascended to the quarterdeck and received Horner's salute and welcome. If the English captain was surprised the corsair kept his word and returned, he didn't show it. They conversed quietly in Spanish, then Tangle went below. He took his meal in his cabin with Akil to wait on him. The English officers had an animated discussion over supper—the battle in the cave, the near misses they had experienced, the behavior of the rovers—all were topics of interest. Thorton said nothing except, "Please pass the salt," and, "I don't know why Kasim Rais didn't obey his commodore."

After supper Thorton rapped on the doorframe of the first lieutenant's cabin. "Who is it?" Tangle called.

"Peter."

"Come in."

Thorton opened the door and stepped in. Tangle was sitting cross-legged on the bunk dressed in just his pantaloons. It was another hot afternoon but the breeze coming through the open window was cool. The white bandage around his forearm was bright against his dark skin and hair. His earrings gleamed against his neck and a blue-checked cloth was tied over his hair.

"Are you well?" Thorton asked. He tried to not look at the powerful chest. He wished the man would keep himself decently covered. It did not bother him when other men lounged about half-dressed, but the corsair distracted him.

Tangle forced a smile. "Brooding. You can guess why."

"Kasim."

He nodded. "The Sallee navy is intent on harassing the Spanish. They were not much concerned about you, so I raised a force of corsairs. I had to promise them prizes, of course." He sighed. "My father-in-law played peacemaker between Kasim and I. It almost worked." He pulled off the kerchief and ran his good hand through his short black hair. A few strands of grey peppered it. "The damn *ferenghi* are laughing at me, I am sure."

Thorton sat down next to him on the edge of the bunk. "The *Arrow* performed well."

"Yes, yes she did. You have kept up their training and discipline. 'Twas a pleasure to command them."

"The British think well of the *Arrow*. They are impressed with the way you went into the cave and won."

Tangle sighed. "Like shooting fish in a barrel. There was no place for the poor devils to go. I want some wine."

Thorton rose. "I'll ask Akil to bring you a cup." He paused at the door. "Isam, don't drink too much. It won't help matters if the English see you drunk."

Tangle stiffened. For a moment Thorton thought he was angry. Then he nodded. "Very well. One cup of watered wine for medicinal use. It will help me sleep."

Thorton stepped out. He spoke to the eunuch who was sitting on the floor mending Tangle's damaged coat, then he turned into his hammock in the cabin he shared with Forsythe. He slept soundly but had vivid dreams. It was not the slender and honest Shakil that made him sweat that night, but the vision of a bold, black-haired Turk.

The next day dawned bright and clear without any Spanish pursuit. Tangle came out, put on a good face, and broke his fast with the officers of the wardroom. Akil and Ra'uf waited on their gentlemen. Breakfast was oatmeal and stewed apples, but Tangle had cinnamon which he generously shared with the other officers. Cinnamon was a rare and expensive spice for men of their standing. They enjoyed it.

Tangle's mood was subdued during the breakfast, but after prayers he recovered himself. He brought out a small, round, blue-glazed vessel flute with four holes in it. He sat on a gun on the quarterdeck and tooted tunes on the humble instrument. Forsythe was curious and hovered near him.

"What sort of instrument is it?" he asked when Tangle took a pause.

"An ocarina. It means 'little goose' in Italian. From the shape, I guess. Do you play an instrument?"

Forsythe shook his head. "No, but I can sing."

Tangle nodded agreeably. "You'll have to give us a tune. What about you, Peter? Do you know an instrument?"

"My stepfather taught me to play hymns on the spinet and the organ."

Tangle did not know what those were, so Thorton mimed playing a keyboard. "Ah, a clavichord!"

"Um, no, although I suppose I could play one. A spinet is smaller. You put it on the table. An organ is bigger. It fills half a church."

Tangle did not understand the spinet, but he nodded. "I have seen those in Christian churches. They have great tall—" He did not know the word for 'pipes,' but gestured to indicate something tall and cylindrical.

Thorton nodded. "Yes, just so."

"I didn't know you were musical, Peter," Forsythe said.

"I haven't played in years. There are no keyboards on warships."

"Sing for us, Albert—may I call you Albert?" Tangle asked.

"If you wish, sir."

"You may call me Isam Rais."

"Isam Rais? What does it mean?"

The corsair smiled. "It means 'Captain Isam.' It is my name. We call our captains by their personal names." Forsythe looked a little bewildered. "Captain Horner would be 'Ebenezer Rais' in my country."

"I see!"

Tangle smiled and lifted the ocarina encouragingly. "Sing something. I'll try to play it."

Forsythe did not need much encouragement. Serving first under the pompous Bishop and later under the dour Horner had not given him many opportunities to demonstrate his skill. He selected 'Heart of Oak' as likely to win the appreciation of his audience. The song was gaining popularity among naval types.

Come cheer up, my lads! 'tis to glory we steer,
To add something more to this wonderful year;
To honour we call you, not press you like slaves,
For who are so free as the sons of the waves?

Heart of oak are our ships, heart of oak are our men;
We always are ready, steady, boys, steady!
We'll fight and we'll conquer again and again.

Tangle figured out the tune and began to play along on his ocarina. The first lieutenant took off his hat and held it over his heart as he sang. His voice carried well. Even Horner turned to listen.

We ne'er see our foes but we wish them to stay,
They never see us but they wish us away;
If they run, why we follow, and run them ashore,
For if they won't fight us, we cannot do more.

The quartermaster and his mate, the helmsman, the midshipmen, and the messenger boy all joined him in the chorus. Thorton, who had a passable tenor, sang along with them.

Horner joined them in the chorus. He was a tuneless fellow, but his stentorian lungs carried the words the entire length of the ship. Ornamented with the more melodious voices of his officers it didn't sound half bad. The men at their holystones joined in. "Heart of oak are our ships, heart of oak are our men; We always are ready, steady, boys, steady! We'll fight and we'll conquer again and again." With the redoubtable Horner as their captain, they had no doubt that they would indeed conquer again and again. Hadn't their own Lieutenant Thorton whipped a pair of frigates with a galiot? Nothing could stop men like them.

We'll still make them fear, and we'll still make them flee,
And drub 'em on shore, as we've drubb'd 'em at sea;
Then cheer up, my lads! with one heart let us sing:
Our soldiers, our sailors, our statesmen and King.

When the song was done, Tangle decided to make the most of the good humor provided by fair weather and victory. "Gentlemen. I'd appreciate it if you would join me for dinner today."

They looked to Horner, who said, "Of course, sir. We would be delighted."

"If I may, Captain, I'd like to sponsor a fishing contest for the men. I fancy one of those swordfish leaping in the sea would provide a fine supplement to my lamb. I'll buy the biggest one for five pounds cash, if you allow it."

"An excellent entertainment, Commodore. I'm sure the men will enjoy it."

Word was passed and the lower decks buzzed with anticipation. The prize was a handsome one—especially for men who had been servants or apprentices who might have had a whole fifteen pounds a year in wages before they were pressed. As a consequence there was very nearly a riot as each mess competed to catch a swordfish. The winning fish weighed twenty stone and overflowed the officer's mess. She was cut up and fed the warrant officers and the midshipmen as well. Her roe was served as caviar. She was not the only fish caught. Even though the other men didn't get the prize money they were well pleased to have it for dinner.

Along with swordfish steaks the officers dined on lamb and couscous, boiled vegetables, and a watermelon for dessert. Perry was released from confinement. Although sulky at first, the fair weather and good food did much to restore his spirits. The wardroom provided wine and soon they were merry. Inevitably, they danced. As the ranking male Tangle was obliged to serve the role of head man dancer for a Virginia reel. Horner graciously partnered with him in the role of head lady dancer. Tangle caught on quickly to the dance's repetitive movements and conducted himself well. Afterwards he was obliged to minuet, rigadoon, and contradance as well. The English (particularly Perry) seemed determine to dance him into the boards, but his stamina proved equal to the challenge.

Reaching the Road of Mahon in the late afternoon they were obliged to leave off dancing and return to work. Tangle returned to the quarterdeck. Flush with exercise and wine, he opened his shirt and flapped his lapels to cool himself. He was not the least bit concerned about showing his hairy muscular chest. Thorton envied him. He was suffocating in his stock and wool coat under the relentless Mediterranean sun.

Tangle addressed the helm and captain. "Keep left. The right channel leads into a shallow cove, Phillipet Bay. It looks like a good harbor from here, but it isn't unless you're a fishing smack or something small."

The small fort of La Mola looked down on them, but the British flag flew over it and did not challenge them. The west wind blew fitfully and they had to order out the sweeps to crawl up the channel to Mahon. Halfway there they reached Lazarette Island and the health inspector came aboard. He reviewed their papers, inspected the ship, and consulted with the surgeon regarding the sick bay. The doctor examined Thorton's burned neck and eye minutely. Although the neck was healing well (it itched now), his left eye had continued to cloud up until everything was shadowed by a milky white veil.

"Cataract," the physician pronounced. "Too bad for you. It will probably cover the entire eye, although if you're lucky it will stop growing." He had a short white wig with his own hair tied in a black hairbag at the nape in the French fashion. The black solitaire went around his neck and tied. His coat was dark blue and he had a medal of some sort pinned to it. He looked like a respectable doctor.

"Cataract?" Thorton asked. "What's that?"

The physician pointed. "The white cloud in your eye. 'Cataract' is the medical name for it, from the Latin *cataracta*, a waterfall. Presumably for the color."

"Can you cure it?"

The physician shook his head. His breezy professional demeanor sobered. "You're going blind in your left eye, Lieutenant. There is nothing I can do about it. Make your peace with God and maybe He will cure you. 'Tis out of mortal hands."

Cold dread clamped hold of Thorton's heart. "Will it go away by itself?"

"I suppose there is always a chance of spontaneous remission, but it would be folly to bet on it."

"Can't you do anything?" Thorton's voice was rising.

The physician busied himself with his black bag and avoided looking at him. Finally he said, "I'm sorry, Lieutenant. I thought you knew. You aren't the first sailor to develop cataracts. Usually they happen in older men. 'Tis a natural part of the aging process for sailors. In your case, the blast from the powder has brought it on prematurely."

Thorton was growing more afraid. "Will it spread to my other eye?"

The physician tilted Thorton's head up and peered at the eye. He took out a magnifying glass. "I don't see any sign of cloudiness at this time. God willing, you won't develop a cataract in your right eye until the natural age to do so."

"Can it be prevented?"

The doctor sighed portentously. "Retire from the sea. 'Tis less common among gentlemen of leisure."

Thorton swallowed hard. "Maybe in a week it won't matter," he finally said.

The physician asked, "Hm?"

Thorton shook his head. The awareness of his upcoming court martial hung heavily over his head.

The physician snapped his bag shut. "You're quite well, I'm afraid. I was hoping I'd get to inspect a case of breakbone fever or one of the other exotic diseases from the Dark Continent, but you're quite healthy. I would have been satisfied to see a nuchal tubercle. I don't suppose you have an interesting deformity?"

Thorton shook his head. He had no idea what a 'nuchal tubercle' was, but he was certain he didn't have one. The cataract was quite enough.

"You're free to go," the physician said. He picked up his hat and bag and made his way back on deck.

CHAPTER 29: PORT MAHON

They arrived at last in Port Mahon. One of the principle ports of the Mediterranean with a fine, large, deep harbor, it was a prime prize and Admiral Walters was making the most of it. The harbor, the town, the forts, all were in his hands. Many of the residents were happy to have him; it had been a British port for more than fifty years before the French had taken it in 1756. The Spanish, never reconciled to the loss of the islands that were part of the Spanish patrimony long before the Iberian peninsula was unified, had taken it back, tit for tat, when France took Barcelona. Badly strained by the demands of the situation, Spain had lost it again in a sharp action with a fresh British fleet. Walters was a hero.

The *Ajax* was hauled out and inspected. That required her to be emptied of everything that was in her: guns, ballast, food, sails, water, tools, personal effects—everything. Horner took quarters in a modest rooming house near the dockyard and his officers joined him, including Thorton. Tangle did not care for the place and switched his domicile to the galiot. Horner had to let him go; Mahon had ended the charade. It had served its purpose; he had delivered Thorton to the authorities in Port Mahon. The renegade lieutenant had surrendered his sword and was now on parole.

The unhappy lieutenant ambled along the quay. With the *Ajax* hauled out there wasn't much for her commissioned officers to do; she was in the hands of her standing officers, but mostly she was in the hands of the commander of the dockyard, a Scottish captain named Cathcart.

The center of town was built from the native tan stone and fine broad stone steps lead down to the water's edge. Ladies under parasols liked to stroll here, and gentlemen liked to stroll there in hopes of seeing the ladies. There were not very many English ladies in Port Mahon, but Thorton saw Admiral Walters go by with a beautiful blonde on his arm. Her lofty wig and French dress were the height of fashion. The lonely lieutenant stayed away from other people and sat down on a step. He was wearing his homemade coat and worn blue breeches along with the brown shoes he'd bought in Zokhara. His white waistcoat had once been good, but that was before the blood stains were bleached out of it and the holes mended. The shops did not yet carry ready-made British uniforms so he was forced to wait for the tailor to make him a new uniform. With the Admiral's victory ball coming up, all the officers wanted new shirts, new breeches, new stockings, new waistcoats, new gold lace for old coats if they couldn't afford a new coat, new hats—all the peacock finery that made a man look his best. The officers of the *Ajax* had been added to the guest list—even Thorton. He didn't want to go, but he supposed he would look guilty if he didn't.

As he watched, a small lateen-rigged boat departed the *Arrow* and skimmed lightly across the basin toward the steps. He stood up and waved to them. There was only one man in an English coat who would wave at Sallee rovers, so they swerved in his direction. As they came closer he saw the purple coat and white turban of an officer—Tangle—and the brown coats of some marines. The boat came along side the steps and the sailors pulled up. The commodore clambered out first, followed by the purser's mate.

Thorton doffed his hat and put his hand to his forehead to bow deeply in the Muslim fashion. "Peace be upon you, Isam Rais," he greeted the man in Arabic.

"And also upon you." Tangle kissed Thorton lightly on each cheek in the French fashion. It was not a Muslim custom, but he had adopted it because it allowed him to kiss men in public. "What news?"

Thorton hardly heard him because his eyes were going past him to the other purple uniform. Shakil grinned at him and came up. Thorton couldn't speak. Instead he grabbed the smaller man by both shoulders and kissed him on each cheek in a paroxysm of emotion. Shakil blushed.

"Have you had breakfast?" Thorton asked his lover.

Shakil replied, "I have. You?"

"I didn't eat this morning. My stomach is in a knot."

Shakil's expression dampened. "Is the court martial soon?"

"Not until after the ball. I guess they don't want to spoil the festivities by hanging me. 'Twould be a gloomy ornament for the admiral's ballroom."

Shakil made a face. "Don't say such things! If the trial is fair, they will set you free and restore your honor. I am praying to Allah to guide them rightly."

Tangle spoke softly, "You should eat, Peter. You'll be in a better mood after you do. 'Tis hard to face the future on an empty stomach. Come along, my treat."

"If you say so, sir."

They went into a tavern near the rooming house. Servants were sweeping the floor and washing the tables. Chairs were set to rights for them and they settled in. Tangle was never one to pass up a meal when it was available; sailors never knew when their next meal was coming. He ordered merguez sausage, eggs, orange juice, and toast with marmalade. Thorton was not hungry, but once the tasty aroma reached his nostrils, he was suddenly ravenous and dug in.

Just then Horner came in from the street. Thorton and Shakil rose and Tangle turned to look at him. "Captain!"

"As you were, gentlemen."

Thorton sat down, but Tangle caught a glimpse of the hungry look Horner gave their plates. "Would you like to join us for breakfast, Captain?"

Horner demurred. "That's quite all right. I had my breakfast earlier. I've been to see Admiral Walters."

"Didn't he feed you, sir?" Thorton asked.

Horner's lips pursed. "'Twas a business meeting, Mr. Thorton." His stomach betrayed him with a rumble. He schooled himself to a stoic expression.

Tangle said in Spanish, "We have plenty, Captain. Why don't you join us? I have enjoyed your hospitality, now it is your turn to enjoy mine."

"Please do," Thorton urged him. He also spoke Spanish. It was the tongue the four of them had in common.

A spot of color mounted to the captain's cheeks. Horner had not sunk the xebec *San Anthurius;* the *Royal Guardian* had. He had not sunk the felucca *Santa Ana* in the cave, either; the *Arrow* had. There was no prize money for Horner. He was even poorer than the other officers because half of his pay went for the support of his family in England. Still he hesitated as pride warred with need. Finally he caved in and sat.

"Thank you, gentlemen."

Another plate was brought. It was piled with food and was quite delicious, especially to a man accustomed to the fare the king provided his officers. Horner dug in. Realizing that he was wolfing his food down, he forced himself to eat sedately. "Walking sharpens the appetite," he said by way of excuse.

"Indeed it does. How did you find Admiral Walters?" Tangle asked. "I am still waiting for an answer to the note I sent him."

Horner was chewing the lamb sausage and washing it down with tea. He took a while to answer. "He is in good health and much preoccupied with re-establishing British control of the island. Cituadella is still in Spanish hands, and so is most of the island west of Mahon."

"Has he fixed the date for the court martial?" Thorton asked. With the *Ajax* out of the water there was nothing else to occupy his mind.

"Not yet."

Thorton muttered, "Damn him. Why can't we do it and be done?"

"He is reviewing the Admiralty orders and consulting with his officers regarding the proceedings. He is also reading my dispatches. I gave you a favorable mention, Mr. Thorton."

Thorton brightened. "You did? I'm grateful, sir."

"Naturally I was obliged to report the honors which His Grace, the Duke of Coimbra, showered upon us."

"Do you think it will influence him?"

Horner drank orange juice and patted his mouth with the napkin. "No."

Thorton sank. "No?"

"Walters is very strict. Duke Henrique is not yet King of Portugal, so he has no authority to bestow such honors. It remains to be seen what happens, even if he does become king. The 'faith of princes' and all that."

"So we're not really knights?"

Horner shook his head. "I'm afraid not, Mr. Thorton. It was a quaint gesture, but it has nothing to back it up."

"Dash it all."

"Admiral Walters has been having some difficulty believing you captured a pair of frigates with a galiot, even though I assured him that I saw it with my own eyes."

"I don't think I like Admiral Walters," Tangle remarked.

Horner cut a piece of sausage with his knife. "He is an upright and moral man. He is particularly concerned by the charges brought under Articles One and Twenty-Eight. If it were only Fifteen there might be hope, given that there are mitigating circumstances. They don't have to hang a man for desertion anymore."

Tangle did not know the *Articles of War*. Thorton explained, "Article One establishes the Church of England. Twenty-Eight is the prohibition on sodomy and buggery. Fifteen is desertion."

Tangle frowned. "Why would they charge you with such things? You converted to Islam, 'tis true, but the others are unwarranted."

Thorton didn't answer. He played with his fork. Tangle turned to Horner for an explanation. Horner ate more eggs.

Finally Horner said, "You have impressed me as a gallant and capable officer, Mr. Thorton. I shall testify as much at your court martial. Please remember that everything you do and say will be scrutinized while you are here. Do not let the temptations of shore debauch you as they do other officers. Remember they are still searching for evidence."

"Aye aye, sir. Thank you, sir."

Horner eyed Tangle. "The *Articles of War* cover officers ashore as well as at sea, Commodore."

It was a warning, but Tangle ignored it. "Will I be allowed to testify?"

"I imagine so."

A silence fell. They thought Horner wanted to say something else, but it took him a while to come around to it. Finally Horner said, "The *Ajax* has a cracked keel. Admiral Walters has decided to sell her for scrap. As of today we are all furloughed and on half-pay. I would appreciate it if you would not spread the news. I am going to find the officers and tell them all myself."

Thorton's face fell. "Aye aye. I'm sorry, sir."

Horner finished eating. "Thank you, Mr. Thorton. But you should feel sorry for Captain Bishop. I was only a temporary captain. I have known my time was short."

"Do they have another place for you, sir?"

He shook his head and rose. "I'm afraid not. I used up what influence I had to get even a temporary position. By the way, there is a rumor of negotiations between Spain and England. With any luck, the war will be over by Christmas."

"No!" exclaimed Tangle. "You can't make an alliance with the Sallee Republic, then drop it at your convenience!"

"'Tis only a rumor, Commodore."

"You wouldn't have shared it if you didn't think there was something to it."

"I cannot speculate, Commodore." He retrieved his hat. "By your leave, I must go to the dockyard. There are papers to be signed and the final inspection made."

They all rose.

Tangle spoke in Spanish. "The Sallee Republic needs able officers like you, Ebenezer Rais. I can get you post with one of our frigates or xebecs."

"Thank you, no. I am an Englishman." Horner put his hat firmly on his head and gave them a nod. "Good day, gentlemen. It has been a pleasure to serve with you. I wish you luck in your future endeavors."

With that he turned and walked out the door. His back was as stiff and erect as ever.

CHAPTER 30 : THE CARRIAGE WRECK

Tangle pestered Thorton to show him the way to the Admiral's house. Thorton demurred—he had already been there once to surrender his sword and he did not care to go again. But Tangle prevailed, and Thorton agreed to show him as long as he did not have to go in. Tangle took a bodyguard of four marines and a purple banner with a single horsetail to demark his rank—Sallee officers of the highest rank preserved the horsetail insignia of their horse-archer ancestors. Tangle's own great-grandfather had been a sipahi archer before going west and becoming a corsair. The banner carrier was accompanied by a pretty blond eunuch boy banging small cymbals together the way an English lord might be announced by a drummer.

Tangle wore his best turban, a snowy white one wrapped around a black fez, his second best dress uniform with gold buttons, highly polished black boots, his scimitar slung from a plain black baldric on his right hip, and gold rings upon his hands. He had borrowed the rings from his officers because he was not in the habit of wearing such jewelry, but he thought it best to make as imposing a display as he could in order to command the attention of the Admiral. The sight of Turks and Moors boldly marching in their streets sent a frisson of alarm through the Catholic inhabitants. No one alive could remember when Muslims had controlled the Balearic Islands, but they knew the old tales.

The cavalcade turned up a steep thoroughfare. Minorca was hilly, and anything not immediately on the waterfront was uphill to greater or lesser degree. The thoroughfares of Minorca were wide and modern, being at least two and a half lanes wide between solid stone buildings. The streets were paved with rectangular paving stones quarried from the surrounding hills.

They stopped for a traffic jam. A splendid coach and four was stopped before a dress shop. This obliged the traffic to channel around it. A sedan chair carried by four porters was maneuvering around the coach while a chaise squeezed next to the wall and forced its way through, eliciting a string of profanity from those it cut off. Underneath the coach a black and white spotted dog barked furiously and nipped at the porters. One of the porters paused to kick the dog.

Behind the sedan chair several carts and buggies slowed and tried to merge into a single line to pass around the coach. Drivers shouted imprecations and snapped their whips; the horses neighed and shook their heads in annoyance.

A sudden cry up the hill beyond the traffic jam rang out. "Gangway! Lookout!"

Startled people looked around, but it was not immediately obvious to those below the coach and sedan chair what was happening. The sedan chair continued moving and was passing beside the horses in their traces when the alarm sounded loud and clear.

"Runaway!"

The clatter of something large and heavy coming very fast down the hill echoed off the walls. A woman screamed. Thorton and Tangle looked around them, but they were hemmed in by the various wagons and chaises. Pedestrians flattened themselves against the wall, or darted into the doors of shops if they were close enough. At that moment a woman stepped out of the dress shop. She wore a high blonde wig topped with silk butterflies above a pale yellow gown with lace ruffles falling from her forearms. Porters carried her parcels toward the rear of the coach. A servant girl held a parasol to shield her from the sun.

Thorton recognized her. "That's Walters' woman!" he exclaimed.

Tangle shouted at her in Turkish, which caused her to pause and look at him instead of uphill toward the commotion. The wild clatter was rapidly drawing near. In the heat of the moment Tangle could not think of any English words, so he lunged forward, wrapped his arm around the woman's waist, and dragged her into the door of the shop. Her porters, seeing the onrushing wagon, dropped her parcels and fled. One of them jumped up and grabbed a lamppost to escape and the other one ran back toward the shop, colliding with the commodore and his mistress. The trio fell against the door, which opened under the assault, and the three sprawled inside. Thorton caught a flash of petticoats and kicking legs as the lady went down, but he was too busy looking for his own escape to care what happened to her. Being half blind in his left eye, he had to turn around frantically in search of his escape.

The runaway wagon pulled by a team of six horses crashed into the chaises and carts. Horses screamed. The crash of wood and flesh snapping and careening into each other was magnified in the narrow space. The coach lurched forward and the coach horses bolted but could not go far in the crowded street.

Thorton saw a window sill above his head and leaped for it. He hauled himself up into the embrasure, gritting his teeth as his wounded shoulder complained. Local architecture was made of very thick walls to keep out the heat of the Mediterranean summer; he found himself perching in a window embrasure about the size of an armoire. Beneath his feet the coach's horses could not get out of the way of the freight wagon. The heavy wagon smashed through the light vehicles, horses, and pedestrians. It ran over some of its own fallen horses, overturned, and spilled its load everywhere.

The stones were chunks of native limestone cut and rough-dressed into pieces two feet by one foot by one foot. They weighed over a hundred pounds each. They went tumbling and smashing among the victims. Someone was crying hysterically and the wounded horses bellowed their agony. Men groaned. One of the sedan chair's porters had fallen under the coach horses and been trampled. The spotted dog barked so hysterically it made itself hoarse.

Thorton's heart pounded in his chest. He looked down, saw fallen men and bright red blood on the pavement. A downed coach horse was thrashing in its traces and its companion was staggering in the harness. The brown coats and purple pantaloons of the Sallee marines were pressed up against the stone wall. The horsetail banner had fallen on the pavement.

Thorton dropped down into the street, slipped in equine blood, and fell. He scrambled up again with red staining his stockings and knees and hands. His breeches were ruined, so he wiped his hands on them. He shouted at the marines in Arabic, "Casualty report!"

They collected themselves and formed up. Lt. Yazid replied, "One wounded!" He rounded on the banner carrier and chewed him out for dropping the banner. The banner carrier scurried to pick it up again and brush the dust off of it.

"Give aid!" Thorton ordered. He darted forward, judging his leap to pass the anguished writhing of the coach horse, and pushed into the shop.

Tangle was on his feet with the sobbing Englishwoman on his arm. Her dress was covered in dust and her wig had toppled off. Her own hair was naturally blond and cut in a bob to facilitate the wearing of wigs. She was clinging to Tangle's arm. Her porter was trying to dust off her skirts. One of her panniers was broken and hung limply.

"Are you all right?" Thorton asked him. Tangle was besmirched with dust as well.

"I'm fine. My God, you're hurt." He stared at Thorton's legs.

Thorton looked down. "'Tis the horse's blood, not mine."

"Praise Allah. Casualty report?"

"One injury among our people." He didn't notice that in an emergency the Muslims were 'our people.' "I have ordered the marines to render aid."

A pair of English army officers in red coats pushed their horses among the wreckage. They began issuing orders. Men who were unhurt started pulling the wounded out of the wrecks and dragging them to the side. A pistol report cracked loudly in the confined space and the thrashing coach horse lay still. A minute later another pistol cracked and another wounded horse ceased her bellowing. There was a short pause, then a third shot rang out. All the horses were quiet. The weeping of servant girls and the oaths of men could be heard more clearly. Inside the English lady was supine on a chaise lounge. The shopkeeper and her girls fluttered around their wealthy patroness to attend her every need. Tangle fled the feminine territory immediately.

Outside Thorton found the yapping dog, picked it up, was bitten for his trouble, closed its muzzle with his hand, and carried it into the shop. He put the dog on the floor and the beast ran to his mistress and began licking her dangling hand. That stopped the yapping to Thorton's great relief. He went outside again.

Tangle and Thorton moved the wreckage of a chaise and lifted an elderly gentleman out of it. Using Tangle's purple coat as a stretcher, they carried him into a bank where several other casualties were stretched out on the floor. Next they found a little girl crying in the street. She was crying too hard to get any sense out of her, so Tangle picked her up in his arms and carried her to the women in the dress shop.

Once the wounded were picked out of the wreckage, the rescuers cut the traces to release the horses. Some of the animals were injured and all of them shied at the sight and smell of dead horses in the street. The Sallee marines lead them up the street and tied them in a small yard in front of someone's house. The inhabitants of the house were gawking at the spectacle but accepted charge of the animals.

The citizens of Minorca were not accustomed to dealing with disasters, but sailors were used to clearing wreckage, transporting the wounded, and making repairs. They soon had a lane opened up. Traffic began to flow slowly. The mayor arrived with his guards and took charge.

"Come, Peter. There's nothing more for us to do here. The mayor will finish it," Tangle said. He pulled his bloody and dusty coat on.

Thorton nodded. "As you wish, sir." Turning to the street, he barked, "*Arrow*, assemble!" in Arabic. They were his marines, after all. He was still the captain of the *Arrow*, in spite of his English coat and pending court martial. He brooded about it.

CHAPTER 31 : ENTRAPMENT

Parting from the Muslims, Thorton passed a pawnshop on his way back to the boarding house. It had a pair of tables outside with various items on display: a lady's hat, a clockenhen, a silver tea service, an embroidered waistcoat, and other items. Thorton merely glanced at them as he walked by. Suddenly he stopped and turned. There on the table was a good mahogany and brass barometer-thermometer. Horner had one just like it. Peering closely at it he realized it *was* Horner's. The captain was on half-pay and likely to be stranded in Minorca for a considerable length of time. Thorton's hand stroked the satiny finish of the wood. Making up his mind, he picked it up and carried it inside. He paid the pawn and had it wrapped in muslin cloth. He carried it back to the rooming house.

Stepping through the door he found Perry in the common room brooding over a pint of beer. In the middle of the afternoon the locals were taking a siesta, but the English were all awake when they ought to have had the sense to sleep through the heat of the day. Perry had unhooked his coat and removed his stock. The ragged tear across his face had closed up and was nearly healed. He had not said much to Thorton over the past week, but there had been no further hazing incidents. Thorton remembered a day long ago on which they had been friends. Perry had tried to teach him how to make small talk and ingratiate himself with others. By a strange quirk of fate, that was the start of all that had lead to this point.

Thorton walked over to the table. Perry raised dark eyes. Thorton smiled a little. "How are you, Roger?" He gestured toward the arm.

"Recovering, but 'tis infected."

"I'm sorry to hear that. I hope you feel better soon." That was what Perry had advised him to say to Forsythe and Chambers when they were seasick.

"Thank you."

"Do you mind if I sit down?"

"Suit yourself."

Thorton pulled out the chair next to him and settled in it, flipping the tails of his coat aside to avoid sitting on them. He put the mysterious cloth-wrapped bundle on the table, but Perry paid it no attention. "You gave me advice once."

"More than once."

The blond lieutenant smiled crookedly. "I know. I was thinking about when you tried to teach me about small talk."

"Is that what this is?"

Thorton wilted. He wasn't sure how to answer the other lieutenant's unpleasant mood. He lowered his eyes. "I just wanted to tell you that I'm sorry for everything."

Perry put the mug down and wiped his mouth on his sleeve. "The coat was a good trick. You've certainly won Horner over. You're his favorite."

"I'm not his favorite!"

"He doesn't like me, and you're a better officer than Forsythe. Who else would be his favorite? Chambers? Jones? Blakesley? Pennybrigg?"

"Forsythe's a good fellow."

"I told you he was."

"We were friends once, Roger. Why aren't we friends anymore?"

Perry rubbed his face. Then he scratched the bridge of his nose because the wound itched. "I don't know. Maybe because you've gotten me into a lot of trouble with your hare-brained adventures. Did you ever think of that? Did you ever think about anyone but yourself and your darling Captain Tangle? My seniority got docked. Because I 'handled the matter improperly.' Because I tried to protect you. Did you even know or care?"

Thorton was horrified. "Roger, I'm sorry! I never thought they would do anything to you! You didn't do anything wrong!"

Losing his seniority had sent Roger Perry to the bottom of the lieutenant's list. The very bottom. No new lieutenants had been made this year because the Admiralty was chock full of junior officers without sufficient berths for them.

"You're senior to me, Peter. Until the court martial gets done with you. If they don't hang you, I think I might do it myself."

Thorton covered Perry's good hand with his own and squeezed it. The look he gave Perry was so earnest that Perry's conscience hurt. He didn't look at Thorton, but he let the other man turn his hand over and hold it tightly in both of his.

"Is there anything I can do to make it up to you? They shouldn't blame you for what I did. I'll tell them it was all my fault. Maybe they'll reinstate your seniority. They could do that."

Perry looked at him. His brown eyes were troubled. "You can get out of hanging if you blame me, you know. Say I made you resign. That's what I got in trouble for, demanding your resignation and letting you go. I was 'overstepping my authority.' You could tell them that you believed I had the proper authority to discharge you, so you didn't desert at all."

"Well, that is what I thought."

Perry jerked his hand away. "I hated Bishop. I opened his secret orders. Forsythe was in jail, too. I didn't bail them out. I didn't have the money, but I probably could have borrowed it. Forsythe would have paid me back. But I knew he wouldn't have the balls to open the secret orders. He would have sat there rotting until somebody from on high told him what to do. I wanted to win glory. I thought I could take some prizes, or maybe even Eel Buff, and come back covered in glory so they'd promote me and dump that toad, Bishop. Well, Eel Buff was in French hands and I didn't take any prizes. I got a court martial though. They commended my zeal and docked my seniority."

"If you'd taken prizes they would have forgiven you."

"I know. I was counting on it." He ran his finger over Thorton's hand.

"You took an awful risk, Perry." Thorton felt a frisson of pleasure slide along his spine as Perry touched him. Perry was sunk in his own thoughts and hardly seemed aware of what he did.

"I envied you. You turned corsair and were snapping up prizes like a madman. Four galleys! I was almost tempted to desert myself."

"I didn't take them, Tangle did. I was down below, refusing to participate in an attack on neutral vessels. That was before we got the news that England was at war with Spain."

Perry took Thorton's hand between his two and gazed into his eyes. "You were his lover."

Thorton blushed. "Briefly. Before I came to my senses. He's married, you know."

Perry smiled crookedly. "You told me. And you promised not to criticize my affairs after that!"

"I haven't, have I?"

Perry caught his breath. "No. You haven't. But Peter . . ."

Thorton's heart was beating faster. "Yes?"

Perry had trouble framing his question. He avoided looking at Thorton by staring at his hand. "You kissed him."

Thorton blushed. "Yes."

"Did you like it? He's so dark and ugly. Not at all like a girl."

Thorton's face was coloring. He cleared his throat, "He's a man. And, um, very manly. I don't like girls. You know that."

"Is that why you kissed me? Because you think I'm manly?" He was holding Thorton's hand tightly as he gazed into his eyes.

"You're a handsome man, but I think it was because you were my friend. Other people don't warm to me."

Perry snorted. "Horner has."

Thorton shook his head. "Ridiculous. He doesn't pay any more attention to me than duty requires."

"You have to read between the lines. Another captain would have clapped you in irons. He didn't."

"Well, that's because he's decent. He's a gentleman."

"I'm a gentleman, but I was mad at you. I wanted to get back at you. That's why I put Chambers up to the trick with your coat. I'm sorry."

Thorton thought he ought to be angry with Perry about that, but he wasn't. Perry was staring earnestly into his eyes. Thorton was mesmerized. "I forgive you."

"Peter . . . Once you asked me to kiss you."

Thorton blushed again. "Well I, ah, um. Yes, I did. Sorry about that." He looked contrite.

"I've been thinking about it."

"Yes?"

Perry screwed his courage to the sticking point. "Could we try again?"

Thorton nearly swooned. It felt like the floor went right out from under his feet. "Do—do you really want to?"

Perry didn't trust himself to speak, so he just nodded. "Not here," he added quickly. "Somebody might see."

Thorton rose. "We can go to my room."

The two rose and went upstairs. Thorton's thoughts were whirling. This was the Perry he remembered, the Perry he'd been infatuated with when he was young and impressionable. A whole four months ago. He wanted very badly to kiss and make up. The loss of his friend had hurt. He let Perry into his room and shut the door. His heart was hammering as he turned to face him.

Perry was nervous. "I want you to kiss me like . . . you know."

"Like a lover?"

Perry nodded. He squeezed his eyes shut. Long black lashes lay against his cheeks and Thorton was hooked.

"I won't do anything else, just a kiss," Thorton assured him.

Perry opened his eyes and nodded again. Thorton stepped up to him. Perry trembled. He looked young and vulnerable. The scar did not diminish his masculine beauty. Not in Thorton's eyes. The wayward lieutenant bent his neck to bring his mouth lightly against the other man's. Perry startled and his lips bumped Thorton's. He licked his lips nervously and his tongue accidentally flicked Thorton's lips. The blond lieutenant groaned and caught Perry in his arms and pressed a warm kiss against his mouth. Perry's back stiffened with resistance, but his mouth answered.

The kiss lengthened until they were both panting. There was nothing chaste about it. Thorton tightened his grip on the brunet man until Perry gasped in pain. Thorton swiftly let go. He had forgotten about Perry's wounded arm. "I'm sorry!"

Perry's face crumpled. "'Tis a Judas kiss, Peter. Admiral Walters told me he'd restore my seniority if I entrapped you."

All color drained from Thorton's face. He staggered back as if he'd been hit. He fumbled for the armchair and fell into it. "Roger."

"I'm sorry, Peter. But it is your fault! You should never have kissed me the first time! None of this would have happened! You're to blame!" He whirled and ran out of the room.

Thorton stared at the door in horror. He swallowed hard. What had Horner told Walters? Did the Admiral know about Shakil? He cast his mind back to breakfast with the captain. Horner had tried to warn him, but he didn't realize how invidious the trap would be.

What about Perry? How much of this last conversation did he mean? How much of it was a lie to beguile the renegade? Truth and half-truth mingled so thoroughly in his words that Thorton could not begin to sort them out. Tears came to his eyes. He scrubbed them with his knuckles but he couldn't make them stop. Perry would testify against him and Article Twenty-Eight would hang him. Yet sharper than fear was the grief of friendship betrayed.

Chapter 32 : Victory Ball

Admiral Walters had taken a fine mansion for his own use. It had been constructed by an English gentleman thirty years earlier when Minorca was a British possession. The Palladian house was tan brick with a tile roof, white columns, and a sweeping arch of a driveway to deliver guests to the front door. Formally shaped shrubbery decorated the lawn. Wings of the house spread out and were connected to the main house by means of columned and roofed breezeways. A long line of carriages arrived promptly at seven of the clock; naval officers were scrupulously punctual when answering the invitation of their Admiral. All gentlemen officers were invited (commissioned officers, senior warrant officers, and midshipmen, leaving out gunners, boatswains, and mates). The invitation was extended to local dignitaries, the captain and first lieutenant of a French corvette, and the captains of several captive Spanish vessels. The guest list numbered more a hundred persons, and it included the former officers of the *Ajax*.

Thorton was extremely glad he'd had a new uniform made. Horner was resplendent in his rarely worn but carefully preserved dress uniform, and all the other officers had spruced themselves up as much as possible. With only a week's warning before the ball, the shops had been overrun by officers improving their appearance.

The majordomo announced the guests. "Captain Ebenezer Horner, formerly of His Britannic Majesty's frigate, *Ajax*. Lieutenants Albert Forsythe, Roger Perry, and Peter Thorton. Midshipmen Nelson Chambers, Niall Jones and Thomas Pettigrew. Reverend Amos Pennybrigg and Doctor Joshua Ferncastle, all formerly of the *Ajax*."

The word 'formerly' hung heavily in their ears; they were a glum spot in an otherwise festive event. They were not alone; Horner was recognized and greeted. Word had gotten around about their adventures. Thorton was pointed out and whispered about by those who knew who he was. He set his jaw and held his head up. Perry made straight for the punch. His arm was out of the sling and the redness of his facial wound was starting to fade, but he had more than one reason to drown his pains. Fortified, he turned his eye to the ladies. There weren't many. Even the homeliest among them had several beaux to dance attendance on her. Thorton got a glass of punch, found it to be well-spiked with rum, and sipped it. He settled between a potted miniature orange tree and a pilaster to watch other people enjoying themselves.

The majordomo announced, "Commodore Isam Rais Tangueli of the Sallee Republic and Miss Tangueli. Lieutenants Nazim and Yazid, Midshipman Kaashifa, Doctor Nadeem, and purser's mate Shakil bin Nakih, of the Sallee galiot *Arrow*."

Thorton nearly dropped his cup. Heads turned to look and a stir went through the room. It had been more than two hundred years since a Muslim of Tangle's rank had visited Minorca. He was splendid in his purple coat, white turban and shiny black boots. Generous amounts of gold lace decorated his chest, sleeves, skirts, and pockets. Gold hoops were in his ears and gold rings were on his fingers.

What made all the ladies murmur "How adorable!" was the little girl on his arm. Miss Tahirah Tangueli was nine at the most. A thin gauzy veil of lavender covered but did not conceal long ringlets of brown hair with a hint of auburn. A cap of golden coins and trinkets held the veil on her head. She was dressed in a lavender gown with long loose sleeves and a bell-shaped skirt. The bodice was decorated with gold braid and buttons in imitation of her father's uniform. The sleeves and skirts were embroidered with stylized trees and leopards in gold. The skirt split to show a lace petticoat, and beneath that, pantaloons for the sake of modesty. She wore lavender slippers on her feet and the slippers were embroidered with golden leopards. Gold earrings hung from her ears—they were the kind that hooked over the top of the ear because they were much too heavy to be suspended by a piercing. Gold bracelets jangled on her wrists. When she saw everyone looking at her she buried her face in her father's arm. He smiled fondly and spoke gently to her until she looked up. She held tight to his arm with both her hands as they entered the room.

Tangle searched among the guests to find Admiral Walters and his hostess. Coming face to face with them, he stopped short. "My lady!" he exclaimed. It was the woman he had saved from the carriage wreck.

"Commodore Tangle!" she replied in equal astonishment. She immediately put her hands out to him and he took them. "I am grateful for the opportunity to thank you for rescuing me. I would have been killed had not been for you! I am sorry I swooned and was unable to thank you properly at the time."

"You have the advantage of me, madame. You know me but I do not know you, but I am glad I was able to help."

Admiral Walters was displeased to discover that the Turk was somehow already acquainted with his woman. "Mistress Anne

FitzGerald is a widow. She keeps house for me. I see you have already met Captain Tangle, Annie." His voice was disapproving.

She smiled warmly at Tangle. "We were not introduced. But he was the one who swept me into his arms and saved me from the runaway wagon. I owe him my life." She continued holding his hands.

Mrs. Fitzgerald was a young widow—young compared to Walters, who was at least fifty. She was a handsome blonde woman of thirty or more. She wore a light blue split skirt gown over a white petticoat. Her white wig with decked with blue flowers and a bluebird. Her gown was low cut and displayed her fine bosom. A small black mole was on the left breast. Her corset cinched her waist tight and lifted her bosom to great advantage. She was average height for a woman, but shorter than her escort, who was not especially tall himself.

Tangle bowed over her hand since she wouldn't let go. "*Salaam.* Peace be upon you and all within this house. I am Commodore Isam bin Hamet al-Tangueli. May I present my daughter, Tahirah Tangueli?"

The little girl curtsied and said in a piping voice, "Peace be upon you." She had practiced her English diligently.

"What a charming child!" Mrs. FitzGerald exclaimed. "How old are you, poppet?"

Tahirah looked to her father for guidance. He translated into Arabic for her. "Nine," she said, holding up the requisite number of fingers.

"I am Mistress Anne FitzGerald. We must become good friends! Do you speak French, darling?"

Tangle shook his head. "She has a little Spanish and more Turkish, plus some Greek. We are both learning English."

"You must let me teach you. Do you know what 'punch' is, Miss Tahirah?"

She didn't and neither did Tangle, or he wouldn't have let Mrs. FitzGerald take his daughter away and get her a drink.

Walters watched them go with a dour expression. Tangle smiled amiably. "I thank you for your invitation, Admiral. I am looking forward to planning joint maneuvers between England and the Sallee Republic."

"Quite," Walters replied sourly.

The admiral was a thick in the waist, not anywhere near as tall as Tangle, and starting a pair of jowls. His wig concealed the fact that he had gone bald. His eyes were green, his face well tanned, his hands gnarled by the start of arthritis. His uniform coat was blue velvet with white reverses, a great deal of gold braid, and solid gold buttons with the Tudor rose design required by the navy. His waistcoat was luxuriously embroidered and a heavy gold watch chain ran across the front of his vest. He wore his waistcoat long in allegiance to the older fashion that was slowly dying out. His blue velvet breeches were perfect, and he wore his stockings pulled up over the hems of his breeches. They were fastened with leather garters. In short, he was the very picture of a conservative, well-heeled gentleman.

Tangle attempted to ingratiate himself with the man even though he knew it was a doomed effort. He knew he was being watched—and judged—by every eye in the place. "Allow me to congratulate you on your victory at Mahon. You have dealt a decisive blow to Spain. I salute you." He had consulted his English-speaking officers to learn how to say what he wanted to say.

"Thank you." Walters could not be an obvious boor in front of his guests, so he said. "I heard about your successes as well."

It was not exactly a compliment, but it was close enough Tangle could pretend it was. He gave a slight bow. "You are kind to notice."

Another guest arrived to pay his compliments, and the Admiral gave his attention to the newcomer. Tangle thought he had done about as much as he could and faded away gracefully.

Shakil intercepted him and they spoke to each other in Arabic. Not a soul around them understood them, which was one of the great benefits of speaking a foreign language. Several other purple coats wandered the grand room with its high ceiling and massive crystal chandeliers. The Muslim purple clashed furiously with the scarlet of the British marines, but both marines and Sallee men were greatly outnumbered by naval officers. The Sallee lieutenant of marines, Yazid, was odd man out in his brown coat and purple pantaloons. He consoled himself by imbibing heavily of the punch. Later he would claim he didn't know it was spiked.

Tangle and Shakil sought out Miss Tahirah and Mistress FitzGerald. The ladies were deeply engaged on the subject of brothers and sisters. Tahirah was regaling the woman with stories about the triplets. She was speaking in a mix of Arabic, Spanish, and Greek. Mrs. FitzGerald had a very slight command of Greek which she was mixing with French. When Tangle stepped up, she smiled warmly up at him.

"May I present my brother-in-law and Tahirah's uncle, Shakil Effendi Nakih?" he asked with a slight bow.

She gave Shakil her hand and he took it and bowed politely over it. "I'm pleased to meet you," he replied. He had acquired the basic necessities of English.

"This is Mistress Anne FitzGerald, our hostess," Tangle explained in Arabic. "Walters' mistress, if I'm not mistaken."

Mrs. FitzGerald gave Shakil a welcoming smile but turned her attention back to Tangle. "Tahirah and I have been having a marvelous conversation, but I don't think I understood her correctly. Is it true you have triplets?"

Tangle smiled and nodded. "Yes. Allah has been generous."

"Your poor wife!" She hesitated. "Is she well?" It was unusual for mother and all the babies to survive a multiple birth.

"Yes, very well. She hit me with a pillow, but she forgave me and we had one more."

"How fortunate for you! I have only one myself. Is Tahirah your oldest?" She seemed disappointed Tangle was not a widower.

Tangle twined his fingers in his daughter's curls and gazed fondly down at her. "Yes, she is. The oldest of six. I know I should not have brought her, but I missed my family. We came up the outside of the Balearic Islands and it was safe enough. Your friend Admiral Walters dealt a hard blow to the Spanish."

"Your wife let you? I am surprised. If it was me—" She grew wistful and her eyes moistened, "I should never let her out of my sight. Excuse me." She turned away and dipped in her reticule for a handkerchief.

"I am sorry, Mistress FitzGerald. I did not mean to make you sad." His baritone was kind.

She gave him a tremulous smile and delicately daubed her eyes. "I have a little girl. I let her go riding—" She had to compose herself. "I used to be very fond of riding myself, Commodore, so I indulged her too much. Now I have nearly met with a terrible accident myself—the world is full of perils we never imagine. I envy men who go into battle. It is better to expect disaster than to be surprised." She patted Tahirah on the shoulder. "You must watch over her very carefully."

"I am sorry for your daughter, Mistress FitzGerald. Did she—?" He did not know how to say it gently in English.

She shook her head. "She's paralyzed from the waist down. She's twelve now."

Tahirah was tugging her father's sleeve and whispering to be told why the pretty lady was crying. Tangle spoke softly to her in Arabic. Tahirah's eyes went big when she heard about the other little girl. Shakil also listened, then composed his face in lines of sympathy since he had no English to express his condolences.

"Where is she? May I play with her?" Tahirah started looking around the room. Tangle had to catch her by the arm to keep her from darting off in search of the other girl.

"She's upstairs," Mrs. FitzGerald explained when Tangle translated.

"May I visit her, please-please-please?" Tahirah asked her father.

Tangle wasn't sure. He asked tentatively. "There are not many little girls here. May they visit?"

Mrs. FitzGerald smiled a lovely sad smile at Tahirah. "You must promise to be very kind and gentle. It hurts her if anyone is rough."

Tahirah gave her solemn promise to be gentle. Tangle let her go, so Mrs. FitzGerald took her by the hand and lead her out of the ballroom. When Tangle turned around, he saw Walters glaring at him.

Tangle murmured to Shakil, "Let's mingle with the guests. I don't want to antagonize Walters any further."

The Sallee commodore chatted with officers who were keen to see the notorious corsair for themselves. Tangle was pleased to extract whatever information he could without arousing their suspicions. He was a man who believed in the value of intelligence. Curious officers wound up talking to him quite a bit. Tangle had an easy way with men and they were soon giving him a full account of their various actions. Eventually the wave of curiosity subsided and somehow, completely by accident, Thorton found Tangle leaning against the pilaster next to him.

"So, Peter. Are you going to spend all night hiding behind the potted tree, or are you going to come out?"

Thorton continued watching a few bright ball gowns swirl among the dark blue coats of naval officers. The chamber orchestra was playing a minuet. "Admiral Walters wants to hang me. He's trying to get evidence by underhanded means. I thought my court martial would be based on the facts, but it won't. If you'll excuse me." He gave Tangle a bitter look and shoved off.

Tangle's eyes narrowed. He did not like the way Thorton had been acting since they reached Minorca. He felt snubbed. Out of the corner of his eye he saw Walters watching them. His temper flared. He did not like to be treated so, but guile restrained his anger. The wily corsair only lost his temper when it served his purpose.

CHAPTER 33 : MISTRESS ANNE'S HONOR

Tangle was not in the mood to strain his limited command of English any further. He walked the garden as a brilliant red sunset cast long shadows across the lawn. The heat of an August day lingered as the breeze died with the sun. He unbuttoned his purple coat and flapped his lapels to get some air. He found a peach tree heavy with fruit and plucked one of the red and gold orbs, took a juicy bite of it, and settled on the grass in the shade of the tree. It was a very pleasant garden with hedges that screened it from the lawn and a bit of half-naked statuary in the middle—perfect for sparking. He wished Thorton were there.

Somewhere a door opened and shut and a dog barked. A little later Mistress Anne FitzGerald turned the corner of the hedge and came into view. He sat up with his legs crossed, stolen peach in hand. He looked supremely guilty. She knelt on the grass in front of him and her eyes ran down the front of his shirt. She smiled warmly at him.

"The girls are getting along very well, in spite of the language problem. Tahirah is really very sweet! Gertrude asked if she was a princess."

Tangle smiled in spite of himself. "I'm glad. The world is much bigger than it looks from the farm. She should see some of it."

"I agree. Girls benefit from education as much as boys. Perhaps more. Boys go on to have careers as officers or doctors or something, but girls become wives and are stuck at home. How much richer their lives will be if they can read and think! Their children will be clever if they have an educated mother."

It was a novel perspective and Tangle had to think about it. He had a half eaten peach in his hand but he could not take a bite in front of her. "Would you like a peach, Mistress FitzGerald?"

"Please, call me Anne. I would love a peach."

So he got up, plucked another perfect fruit, and kneeling on one knee, offered it to her. She smiled up at him and her fingers brushed his lightly as she took it. He settled down on the grass again and took another bite, but she merely held her peach in her lap and watched him. The flesh of the fruit crunched between his sharp white teeth. He felt her scrutiny on him but remained tranquil beneath her gaze.

"Yes?" he asked at last.

She tapped the bridge of her nose. "What happened?"

Tangle had a small hump at the bridge of his nose. "Oh, it was broken a few times. When I was young I fought many times."

"You must have been a veritable gladiator!"

Tangle could not help being flattered. He was not accustomed to women's wiles. He was sitting alone in a garden, eating stolen fruit with a beautiful woman. He took another bite of the peach to avoid speaking. She saw him realize his situation and smiled prettily at him. She scooted a little closer to him.

"You are a very handsome man, you know. You are the most splendid man at the ball."

No man dislikes being told he is 'splendid' and Tangle was vainer than most. He smiled and bantered with her. "I don't believe you. I was told I am dark and ugly."

She shook her head. White ringlets of hair brushed across her bare shoulders and dangled around her neck. Her eyes were blue and her complexion was very fair. The bosom revealed by the cut of her gown was soft and white. "You are tan like mariners always are. It suits you."

Tangle tossed away the rest of the peach uneaten. He pulled out a blue and white checked handkerchief to wipe his fingers and his mouth. "You're right, I'm tan. Tan like a piece of leather! Every inch of me."

"*Every* inch?" she asked with arched eyebrows. "Now I don't believe *you*. You must prove it!"

Tangle was taken aback. Usually he was the one that flirted and provoked with outrageous statements. It was unusual to be on the receiving end. He did not know what to say, but if the truth be told, he liked it. Still, she was a woman and he was married. "Are all Christian ladies so bold?" he finally asked.

She drew her finger down the front of his shirt and over his breastbone. "Do I make you nervous?" she asked in a teasing purr.

"No," he replied instantly. He would never admit to being nervous, not for any reason. Not the mighty corsair!

Her fingertips pressed against him and he leaned back until he dropped back onto his elbows. He watched her in surprise. He wore no waistcoat or cravat so it was very easy for her to get at the buttons of his shirt. She toyed with one of the buttons and watched him through her lowered lashes. Then she unbuttoned the button. He caught his breath and watched her fingers slide to the next button.

"I am married," he told her.

"So is Jonathan. But that doesn't matter to Minorca, does it?"

Another button opened. Tangle was getting worried. He didn't want to offend her, but he didn't want to go any further. "Mistress Anne, you must stop."

She pouted prettily at him, but her eyes were amused. She undid another button. "Do I frighten the bold corsair?" she asked. She bent and pressed her lips to his breastbone.

His heart thudded. "The only woman I have ever lain with is my wife. I don't intend to change!"

She was not willing to admit defeat. "Am I not beautiful?"

"Yes."

"Young?"

"My wife is younger."

Her blue eyes flashed at him. That glimpse of temper let him sit up —and meet Admiral Walters' gaze. Another British officer was with him.

"Anne FitzGerald!" Walters cried.

She whirled around in horror. "Jonathan!"

"You disgraceful whore!"

He flew at her and slapped her across the face. She cried and toppled sideways. He kicked her and began to beat her with his gloves. Tangle leaped up and grappled him. He was bigger, stronger, more fit, and easily knocked Walters on the grass.

The other officer cried, "Gentlemen! Stop!"

Anne got up and ran crying into the house. Walters tried to knee Tangle in the balls, but that only made the corsair mad. He punched Walters in the nose and made it bleed. The other Englishman tried to pull him off. "Enough! Commodore! Admiral! Restrain yourselves!"

Tangle let himself be dragged off. Walters got up and glared at him. "How dare you! You filthy black beast! You Othello! You lecherous Moor!" He pressed his handkerchief to his face.

Tangle had no idea what an 'Othello' was, but the way Walters said it he was sure it was something bad. "I will meet you on the field of honor!"

The commotion attracted attention. Several other officers hurried into the garden. Some of them were Walters' own officers, but one of them was Peter Thorton. He had recognized the Turk's voice.

"'Twill be a pleasure to put a ball through your balls, you vile seducer!" Walters retorted.

Mrs. FitzGerald had been doing the seducing, but it would be unchivalrous to say so. Not to mention, it would wound the admiral's pride to admit his lover had abandoned him for a swarthy foreigner. Tangle laughed. His mirth only made the admiral puff up and rage more. Blood from his nose spattered the front of his white waistcoat and his lace cravat as he hurled insults and invective.

Tangle regarded him coolly. "There is no time like the present. Shall it be swords or pistols?"

"Pistols! Marcus, you'll be my second."

"Of course, sir," his companion replied.

Tangle used his checked handkerchief to wipe Walters' blood from his knuckles. He looked around the small group of officers and noticed Thorton. Thorton noticed he was being stared at, so he stepped forward.

"Sirs?" the blond lieutenant asked.

Tangle spoke. "Lieutenant Thorton. Will you be my second?"

"Aye, sir. I will."

Walters was getting control of himself. "You have ruined my ball with your lascivious antics. I'll not have you ruin my breakfast as well. You'll be dead before the sun sets. Marcus, you'll find a brace of pistols in the drawer of my desk. We'll settle this now."

Some of the other officers attempted to soothe the matter. "Gentlemen, please reconsider!"

Inside the house some of the ladies had found Mistress FitzGerald crying in her room. They opened a window and peered into the garden to see what was happening. When the man returned with the pistols, Mistress FitzGerald gave a shriek and fell back in a faint.

Tangle and Walters walked down to the lawn below the garden. It was a green sward along the edge of a wood. There was pasture at one end and a coach house at other. Everyone came out of the ballroom to watch. Thorton and Marcus Wolfe examined the pistols, loaded them, and since they both belonged to Walters, let Tangle have first choice. The pistols were very handsome with ebony handles and gold tracery. Walters shed his coat and took the other pistol. Thorton held the second pistol while Tangle removed his coat. He draped it over Thorton's arm and took the pistol. The two duelists stepped away from the crowd.

Tangle was dressed in a square tailed tunic that buttoned over the chest and was still half unbuttoned. His tall and rangy figure was obvious without his coat. Walters was much shorter and portly. He could not be called fat, but he was a dumpy man, especially compared to the cat-like grace of the corsair. They stood back to back with their pistols in their hands. Wolfe began to count. They stepped off the paces, then turned and faced each other.

Thorton called out, "Gentlemen! For one last time, I beg you! Abjure this violence!"

Tangle shook his head. "No."

"Never!" spat Walters.

In a window overlooking the garden, Mistress FitzGerald and her lady friends watched the proceedings. They covered their mouths with horror. Yet the lady who was the cause of the proceeding was not entirely displeased that two such important men were going to kill each other for her sake.

"Are you ready?" Each duelist assented. Wolfe continued, "On the count of three, you may fire." He paused. "One . . . Two . . . Three . . ."

The duelists raised their pistols and pulled the triggers. Walters staggered and fell. Wolfe ran to him. Thorton trembled as he looked at Tangle. Tangle was a left-handed man, he had turned his back to the crowd as he raised his pistol. They could not see if he was hurt. When the blond lieutenant ran up to him Tangle turned. Red stained his right arm. Thorton tossed the purple coat on the ground and tore Tangle's sleeve to see better. "Just a crease, thank Allah."

"It stings a little," Tangle replied. "Is Walters dead?"

"I don't think so, but he's badly hurt." He turned to watch other officers use a coat as a stretcher to carry Walters into the house. Mistress FitzGerald had disappeared, but some of the women hung over the window. Thorton used his own handkerchief to bind up Tangle's wound. Tangle's kerchief was used to make a sling to support the wounded arm. Thorton draped the purple coat over his shoulders like a cloak.

Some of the onlookers were bewildered. "What was the cause of the duel?" they asked.

Tangle replied, "A woman's honor. Say no more of it. To discuss it can only do harm to the lady." He spoke Spanish in a low voice to Thorton, "My daughter is in the house, Peter. Can you get her and bring her out? Make certain she does not see what has happened here. I will meet you out front."

"I will."

Thorton handed over the pistol to one of the English officers, then he found his way in through the kitchen and accosted a female servant. The woman brought Tahirah to the front hall and let the two out the front door.

"What has happened, Peter Rais?" Tahirah demanded.

"There was a fight. Your father and another man. They had an argument. Now we must leave." He escorted her down to the driveway.

"Why is Mistress Anne crying?"

"Because she was frightened by the men fighting."

"I don't cry when Zaafir fights."

"That's because you're a very brave girl."

Tangle and Shakil came walking around the side of the house. The Sallee marines were waiting at the foot of the driveway, saw him in his sling, and ran up. Tahirah saw her father and ran to him also. He wrapped his good arm around his daughter, kissed her brow, and whispered reassuring words to her. The marines in their brown coats and purple pantaloons formed up around them and escorted them back to the ship. Thorton watched them go.

Horner came up next to Thorton. "What was that all about?"

"Apparently Admiral Walters is a jealous man. He saw Mistress FitzGerald talking with Captain Tangle in the garden."

Horner raised his bushy eyebrows. "Your commodore is an amorous man. Does he often get into these kinds of scrapes?"

"He dueled Bishop for calling him a pirate. He's sensitive about his honor."

"He may have done you a favor."

"What do you mean?"

"The enmity between them will make the proceedings against you suspect. You can demand the court martial be moved to another location. If they don't move it, you can demand officers to sit on it that are impartial. That rules out Walters and Wolfe." Horner watched the purple and brown cavalcade disappearing down the street. "I suspect the Turk knew that."

"What? You think he picked a fight on purpose because of me? That's preposterous!"

"Is it? You know the man better than I."

Thorton muttered to himself, "I wouldn't put it past him."

"I beg your pardon?"

Thorton shook his head. "By your leave, sir. I would like to go back to the boarding house."

"As you wish."

Chapter 34 : Fire Ships

Thorton's heart thudded in his chest as he walked along the dark quay. The *Arrow* had moved off; Tangle was taking no chances that Walters would order his arrest and send marines to storm the galiot. Her lanterns were lit and marked her location well up the Road of Mahon. He stared at the golden lights and yearned for freedom. His head was a tumult; had Tangle set up the duel on purpose? Everybody was talking about how the lustful corsair had made a bid for Mistress Anne FitzGerald. Those who hadn't known she was Walters' mistress knew it now. Knowing Tangle's proclivities Thorton could hardly credit it, but the corsair was not a chaste man, either.

Had Tangle really tried this desperate ploy to save him, even after he had been so cold to him at the ball? Thorton had turned his back on the man who had been his lover, his friend, his host, his superior officer, his mentor, his every good thing. Only a week ago he had told Horner how much he liked and admired him. Why then had he been so cold to him?

He was afraid of Walters, that was why. It bothered him greatly. The man held his life in his hands, so to curry favor with him, Thorton had cut a friend. He owed Tangle an apology and the sooner the better. He walked along the dock looking for a waterman with no luck. At this hour of the night they were home in bed or wrapped around a pint in tavern. He finally found a boat that he could borrow without the owner's knowledge. He left a few pennies on the dock underneath the mooring line in recompense, then cast off.

He soon coasted up to the galiot.

"What boat?" the lookout hailed him in Arabic.

"*Arrow!*" he replied. A captain was invariably known by the name of his vessel.

"Peter Rais?"

"Himself. Permission to come aboard?"

"Of course, rais!"

The pipes trilled and the marines lined up. Four muskets were presented to the renegade Englishman as he came over the side. He smiled warmly at them as he returned their salutes. They were his men; she was his ship. They were doing him the honors he deserved as their commanding officer. He had missed it.

"Thank you, boys."

Wafor the African boatswain saluted him. "Welcome back, rais. Are you here to stay?"

Thorton shook his head. "No, I gave my parole. I must attend the court martial. However, I need to attend to a personal matter. Is the commodore still awake?"

"I am." Tangle had seen the boat coming and came silently down the steps from the poop deck. His right arm was still in the checked sling.

Thorton felt a rush of emotion as he stepped forward. "I came to apologize. I was rude to you this evening. It was wrong of me. You have been a good and loyal friend to me. I know it and appreciate it."

Tangle watched him warily, then stepped down from the last step. "Walters was watching. I knew you could not be too friendly."

"I know. But he thinks what he thinks. Giving you the cold shoulder would not make him like me better. Isam, I'm sorry."

Tangle shook his head. "'Tis nothing. I thought you were playacting for their benefit. Horner was watching, too." He smiled warmly at the Englishman. Thorton realized he had hurt him, although he would never admit it.

Thorton took his good hand and grasped it. "I know. I told Horner that my feelings for you were the love that a man rightly gives someone he admires and respects. I told him you were my friend and superior officer. He must have thought me a liar."

"Peter, don't be so hard on yourself. It all worked out in the end."

"'Tis not over yet. There is still the court martial. Tomorrow I am going to ask them to move it to Gibraltar on the grounds I cannot get a fair trial here."

Tangle nodded his agreement.

A silence fell. Thorton stared up at him. He was feeling rather warm in his dress uniform. The stock was too tight. The evening had cooled, but still, he was much too warm. It had something to do with those brown eyes staring into his. He flushed and said, "We need to talk."

"Yes, we do. Let's use the chartroom. Shakil and Tahirah are sleeping in the great cabin."

They stepped into the small room. It had once been Thorton's berth, back when Tangle had carried him off and told him that he would work whether he wanted to or not. Thorton had sat at that desk memorizing the Spanish signal book. The corsair captain had stooped beneath the deckhead, bracing his arm against the beam. Just like he was doing now. Thorton had been attracted to him and frightened at the same time. Just like now.

Except now he knew what he feared and desired. He stepped up to Tangle, put his hands up to pull the corsair's mouth down, and kissed him. It was a long slow kiss and it made Tangle groan. He opened his lips and let Thorton's tongue explore his mouth. The renegade pressed up against the corsair's body and embraced him.

He was being unfaithful to Shakil. He knew that. He was being reckless to tempt his lust with the court martial so uncertain. He knew that, too. But he wanted Tangle. He had made himself leave the man for good reasons, reasons that were still good. All of that was in his mind, but his body was in the corsair's embrace. His blood was hot. Lust, only lust, he told himself. He didn't love the man. Not like that. He lusted for him. That was wrong of him, but he lusted anyhow. He was frightened by the intensity of his feelings but couldn't stop. He was devouring Tangle's mouth and Tangle was grinding against him and kissing him back.

He had given his parole. He must go back. He must stop before he hanged himself with his foolishness. He didn't want to go back. He wanted to stay. He wanted to be the captain of his own ship, to worship according to his own faith, to sleep with his own lover. He wanted to be the ruler of his own destiny.

"Shakil." Thorton broke the kiss.

Tangle's eyes flashed. "What about him?"

Thorton wrapped his arms around the corsair's neck. "I've made promises to a lot of people. I have to keep them."

Tangle took a deep breath, straightened as much as the low deckhead would permit, and nodded warily.

"Would it be terribly wrong of me to tup you just once?" Thorton whispered.

Tangle gave him a broad grin. "I think I could find it in my heart to forgive you."

Thorton unbuttoned the purple coat. "I have made up my mind. I have been divided too long. I know who I am and what I want."

Tangle's eyes darkened with lust. He bent his mouth to give the renegade a hard and demanding kiss. Thorton's hands went around his waist beneath the coat. He gripped the muscular buttocks and pulled himself firmly against that warm male body. His own heart was hammering as he lifted his mouth up and let the corsair kiss him as hard as he liked.

Suddenly there was a shout from up above. "FIRE!"

They froze.

"Captains!" Someone was banging on the door.

Tangle stepped out without bothering to button his coat. "What is it?"

"Fire ship!"

Tangle vaulted up the steps to the poop deck. Thorton ran up after him. They stared into the night. One by one five hulks were drifting on the evening breeze into the basin of Mahon. As they watched fires ran up the rigging and into the sails. Fire spread across their decks and climbed their forecastles and sterncastles. Because she was anchored across from the Levantine mole east of town, the *Arrow* was first to see them. The flaming hulks could not help but be swept down upon the docks of Mahon—the *Arrow* with them.

"By Allah," Tangle swore. "The Spanish have caught us napping!"

Thorton was back on his own poop deck and did what any captain would do. He gave orders. "Beat to quarters! Fire warning shots! We must rouse the town! Let slip the anchor!" he bellowed.

Tangle gave him an amused look. "You get so excited, Peter. Lt. Nazim is right here. He can hear you perfectly well."

Thorton glared at him. "Thank you for your comment, Commodore. If you don't mind, I will command my ship the way I am accustomed!"

Tangle stepped aside with a grin and a gesture. "You have the conn, rais."

"Thank you, *kapitan pasha.*"

The fire ships were drifting slowly toward the city. Thorton considered his options. With very little breeze the other ships were not going to be able to get out of the way. The frigates could row, but the *Ajax* was helpless in the dockyard. The battleships could try their boats to tow them, but they would be extremely slow. Three Spanish ships were held prisoner with their crews locked below. Of course the prisoners would try to break out. All of that was true and didn't matter. He had to look to his own ship before he could aid anyone else.

Another warning gun boomed out.

"Out sweeps. Course three points to larboard."

His commands were repeated and the ship bustled. He plotted his course, looked up the masts, and called, "Do you see anything beyond the fireships?"

The lookout was watching the eastern approach intently. "Row galleys. Three at least."

Spanish xebecs could sweep along behind the fire ships and catch anything that escaped. There would be more than three.

"We are going to sink as many of the fire ships as we can, lads. Aim for the hull. 'Twon't do any good to dismast them."

Aruj was at his post on the foredeck. He pointed the guns himself. "Fire at will, Mr. Aruj."

There wasn't much time or space. Aruj took his aim and fired his two small guns. One pocked into the water just before the bow and sent up a white spray that glimmered briefly in the fire light. The other disappeared. Thorton reached into his pocket for his spyglass but didn't have it. He'd been to a ball that evening and left his instruments behind. "Damn. Isam, have you got a glass?"

"In my cabin. I'll get it." He hurried below. He also sent his daughter down to the wardroom and put the nanny and eunuch with her for safekeeping. She would have been safer in the cockpit, but he did not care to expose her to the sights and sounds that were likely to occur there. He returned and handed his spyglass to Thorton. "Peter, please remember my daughter is on board."

Thorton gave him a look. "What possessed you to bring your daughter with you anyhow?"

"I missed her. But never mind that. What do you see?"

"Bow damage. A tiny bit lower. Lt. Aruj, if you please," he murmured.

Aruj couldn't hear him, but he had his own glass and already knew. The big and medium guns roared. The shock went through the *Arrow's* hull, but she was built to take it. Her guns recoiled on either side of the foremast. They were reloaded, then the tackle worked to haul them forward.

"Taking water!" Thorton exulted as he viewed the fire ship in Tangle's glass. "Bow's dropping! Do it again, Aruj! Hard to starboard." The last he directed to the helm.

They circled around the sinking ship. Thorton kept a wary eye on the hulk. It would not do to be caught by the thing before it had completely gone under. They moved on the second fire ship. The bow guns boomed out. They holed her amidships. Twice more they battered her and she too began taking water. She began a slow, graceful heel to starboard that continued at the pace of a minuet. Thorton glanced at the other fire ship. Good, he had enough room, but he wanted more.

"Back oars."

They pulled back and watched the second fire ship complete her roll. Spars and masts disappeared under water. Flames continued shooting from the deck, then she capsized. The flames were extinguished and she floated bottom up before disappearing completely.

"Four row galleys!" bawled the lookout.

Thorton swung his glass. He could see the white splash of oars sweeping—they were rowing without lights. They could see him, too.

Tongues of flame six feet long leaped at him. The balls sent up fountains of water a few rods short.

"Douse lights! Silent running!"

The lights were extinguished and the oarlocks swiftly muffled with shirts.

"Hard a-starboard." Because they were still backing water the maneuver brought their bow around to face the enemy. "Fire as she bears!"

Aruj was sighting in the new target. The two big thirty-two pounders roared and leaped back. The enemy broadside came whistling in a little high. They had overcompensated for the first shot.

"Row, damn you!" Thorton hissed. "Get us out of here!" He kept a wary eye on the slowly sinking wreck off his larboard beam. "Helm a point to larboard." That would send him behind it. The brilliance of its flames would baffle the eyes of men trying to sight on them.

More gunnery sounded. The British ships had cut their anchors and were rowing and towing away from their anchorage. They were firing their guns at long range. Their shot was now added to the dangers the *Arrow* faced. Lights lit along the waterfront, church bells rang, dogs barked, and shadows rushed along the shore.

Thorton tried to peer through the flames of the slowly sinking first fire ship. Her head was well down and her stern was starting to rise. She wouldn't last much longer. The flames that screened him from the enemy also served to screen the enemy from him. The *Arrow* kept backing. He glanced back. The road of Mahon was three miles long, but he was near the end of it. He would run out of room very quickly. He scanned the night. The other xebec-frigates—he knew they were frigates by their square-rigged main and foremasts, dimly seen through the flames and night—were rowing to meet the British. The enemy was prowling without lights—the defenders could not know the size or position of the force coming against them.

His bow guns fired again. He blinked at the darkness, saw the answering spikes of flame as the small bowchasers on the xebec's forecastle spat back at him. Aruj was young; he had good eyes. As soon as he spotted the enemy coming around the fireship, he fired. The crash of wood and the screams of the wounded told the hit. Tangle was tense and silent beside him. As commodore it was his job to coordinate the fleet, but he had no fleet.

"Two points to larboard," Thorton snapped. The galiot circled slowly behind the fireship again. The fire ship's stern was rising higher and higher. She eclipsed the xebec as the enemy vessel brought her broadside to bear. The guns roared and the fire ship shattered. Debris was flung halfway across the distance between the fire ship and the galiot. A few embers flew further and drifted onto the galiot. Crews with sand and wet blankets rushed to douse them. Since the fire ship now had no chance of reaching the city, it was simply an impediment to the attackers and they had removed it.

"Isam, I think you had better take your daughter and launch the boat."

Tangle bolted from the poop.

The galiot was outclassed by the xebec: the xebec was larger, better manned, and better gunned. It was one thing to surprise a wounded and damaged frigate and take her, but quite another thing to be surprised by a strong and fully equipped xebec. Thorton worried about their prospects. Especially since she had consorts and he didn't. The British were too busy with their own plight to render any aid to him, even if they were inclined.

Captain Thorton kept watching the night. He tapped his fingers against his thighs as he counted. He needed to know how fast she reloaded to gage his maneuvers. Aruj could load and fire the bow battery in less than three minutes. If only they could do it in two! They needed more practice. The wreckage of the fire ship was still burning and floating on the surface. It made a slowly dying amber glow between the xebec and the galiot. He watched carefully and saw the dark shadow of the vessel. She wasn't turning, she was drifting slowly and reloading her larboard battery. His finger tapping continued.

"Hard a-starboard! Row, damn you! Reverse charge!"

The men threw themselves on the oars and the *Arrow* gained headway. Or sternway in this case. The xebec let loose her broadside and ten tongues of flame leaped at them. The balls splashed into the water they had been occupying a moment before. One of the shots tore through the fore rigging and parted the jib stay. They weren't using the sails so it didn't matter. There was scant breeze and the waters of the harbor were smooth as glass—except where battle disturbed them.

"Mr. Foster, are the preventers set?"

"Aye, sir."

"Very good. Rig the catch nets."

Foster passed the order. Nets were strung over the waist and quarterdeck to catch debris falling from above.

He heard a splash on the other side of the galiot and looked over. The boat was launched and Tangle was helping his daughter and servants into the boat. Shakil was with him. They spoke quietly, then Tangle went over the side. He wasn't needed on board; he would take care of his daughter. The crew in the boat put their backs to the oars and pulled away. They tried to keep out of the galiot's way, but at the same time used her for a shield so that the xebec would not see them.

Shakil remained behind. He watched them pull away, then mounted to the quarterdeck. He looked into the night but could not penetrate the darkness of war that Thorton knew well. The *Arrow's* captain spared him a glance and a smile. He held out his hand and Shakil squeezed it.

"I am glad you are here, *habibi,*" Thorton said in Arabic.

"I will be in the cockpit," Shakil replied. "I hope I will not see you until the battle is over."

Thorton let go of his hand and nodded. He hoped he would not be among the wounded carried to the lower deck.

A monstrous thunder rumbled up and down the bay, echoing and reechoing from the hills. The Spanish battleships had opened fire.

Chapter 35 : The Inferno

A pair of British battleships collided as they tried to dodge a fireship. Their spars tangled together and their crews cut at them while the fire ship bore down on them. They plied their guns, but she sank too slowly. She listed to starboard in a slow motion, laying down her masts until they came to rest in the rigging of one of the entangled battleships. The fire instantly leaped into the tarred ropes and sails of the British ship. Men hacked at the wreckage and shoved the burning debris overboard; they plied wet blankets and buckets of water; they ran the pumps to spray water on the fire, but the sparks were everywhere. They could not save her and abandoned ship. The tangle of burning battleships drifted against the quay. The docks caught and the fire spread to the shore.

Further up the *Arrow's* bow guns roared. The crash of wood told Thorton that Aruj had hit, but what damage the enemy suffered he didn't know. His hand tapped out the time on his thigh: thirty-eight, thirty-nine, forty, forty-one . . . At one hundred he called, "Reverse charge!"

The men threw themselves onto the oars and backed frantically. They used their entire bodies to make the sweeps move and drag the ship across the placid waters.

The xebec's broadside roared again. This time she overshot their position, but a mighty crack overhead shattered the main antenna. The broken pieces hung suspended by their preventer chains.

"Helm hard a-larboard! Sweeps, slow time!"

The xebec expected her to back to the starboard and rapidly this time. Her next broadside passed high and wide. Thorton continued the zigzagging action. It was the best he could do to baffle the xebec's gunners. She would be catching on, though.

"Hard a-starboard! Reverse charge!" The men sweated and panted. The short charges were exhausting. Although she could row nearly as well to the rear as the front, it was demanding work. There was only so long they could maintain the dash speed—about twenty minutes. He was breaking it into short little spurts. How many times could he do this? Five? Ten? Fifteen? How soon would he run out of room and be caught against the shore with no escape?

The xebec slowly swung her other side to face them. She was listing a little. She pulled towards the southern shore, but she was not abandoning them. She was trying to get clear of the wreckage. The flames were nearly out but burning debris still floated on the water.

Thorton spun around. The north shore was looming near. Thank God the galiot had a shallow draft. It gave him inches more room, and inches might be the difference between life and death. The Spanish xebecs had a deeper draft than the galiot.

"Get the lead out," he barked. The carpenter's mates leaped to obey.

Where was the *Dart?* He scanned dark waters. There, off his stern. She was rowing towards the north shore. If the xebec didn't see her, she would make it. The bow guns roared and leaped. Aruj scored a hit on the bow of the xebec. The xebec answered with her broadside. This time the galiot felt the pain of a well-placed shot. Wood shattered and men screamed. The crew of the xebec cheered. The *Arrow* had many casualties amid the rowers.

"Forward charge! Keep the helm hard over!"

They dashed forward. As they rushed the xebec's stern, the Spanish captain spun in place to bring his broadside into play. "Back larboard! Pull starboard!"

The galiot slowly brought her bow around to face the bow of the xebec. Thorton had only been feinting for her stern. The galiot's bow guns spoke again and smashed the xebec's starboard bow. Spanish screams erupted as one of the guns dismounted and discharged through the gunwale. The other guns traversed as far as they could and fired, but they were too early. The shots went whistling over the poop and abaft the transom. Most of them passed harmlessly into the water, but shattered wood flew across the deck when the rail splintered. The two vessels were closing. Thorton looked into his waist. The *Arrow* had not hired mercenaries this time—the galiot had her own crew, nothing more. The crew of the xebec might outnumber them two to one. He could not win by boarding.

Suddenly he remembered Tangle charging the Spanish galleys and sheering off their oars. He judged his distance. The xebec's sides were higher than his own. If he was wrong she would blow the galiot to pieces. Did he dare it? She was sweeping around. Pretty soon he was going to take her broadside without being able to answer it in any meaningful way.

"Reverse charge!"

He backed away. The galiot circled slowly but faster than the xebec. He had done damage to her larboard; she must have lost sweeps on that side. The enemy could no longer turn fast enough to keep up with him.

"Swivels double grapeshot! Forward charge! Everything you've got, boys!"

They raced toward the xebec. She labored to bring her starboard broadside to bear. Inch by inch they raced. With a groan Thorton saw that she would beat them. There was no backing out. He was committed. "Faster!" he roared.

The broadside roared at point blank range. Shot smashed through the gunwales and left a bloody carnage in the waist—she was striking deliberately for the rowers. Other shot passed just a little overhead. A pair of shots smacked into the starboard quarter. Praise Allah Miss Tahirah was off the ship. That was her sleeping chamber. The guns could not depress enough to hull the galiot below the waterline. They would not sink. The *Arrow* lost some of her own sweeps as she swept along the xebec's side, but the rest were jerked inside and saved. The xebec's sweeps snapped and swatted the men on the other end and sent them tumbling amid the fiery guns. Sweeps and guns were both worked from the weather deck of a xebec—the gunwales of a xebec were truly 'gun' wales. His swivels banged out as they passed, adding carnage to the confusion.

They cleared the xebec and Thorton bellowed, "Out sweeps! Lively, damn you! She'll have our stern!"

The xebec's stern guns fired and Thorton felt the thumps in the *Arrow's* stern below his feet. Shattering wood was making a mess of the captain's cabin. His rowers were now pulling forward and she gained speed. They'd suffered casualties, but marines filled in the bloody places and rowed. They sped away and skimmed along the north shore. To his great relief, the helm answered. The rudder was still working. Behind them the battered xebec did not pursue.

The night was utterly dark under a layer of low clouds, but the glow of the burning dockyard and ships lit up parts of it with a hellish light. A confused line of British defense was firing back at the Spanish. Spanish battleships were bombarding the town from long range behind their screen of xebecs. If they saw the galiot they would blow her to pieces. Thorton did not know Port Mahon. He stumbled across a cove and ordered the galiot to back into it. The water was shallow and she touched mud before she was very far in, but she was hidden from anything not in the immediate vicinity. Her bow guns were loaded and pointed out. She was like a hedgehog that presents her thorny spines to a predator. The men heaved sighs of relief and chatter began.

"Silence! Lt. Nazim, keep those men quiet! Damage report!"

The information began to flow. She had taken twenty-seven shots above the waterline—her starboard side resembled a cutwork tablecloth it had so many holes. Her ribs and knees were damaged too. Her main antenna was wrecked. She had eleven dead and fifty-one wounded, two seriously enough they were not expected to live. Thorton had feared worse.

While they made repairs he went ashore. He climbed one of the hills beside the cove and trained his spyglass on the opposite shore. All of the fire ships had disappeared. The waterfront was burning. Church bells were ringing—he could hear them now that his ears weren't deadened by the firing of his own guns. From his right the British ships were roaring their resistance to the invaders, but they were trapped in the narrow bottom of the basin with little room to maneuver.

As he watched a British frigate broke through the Spanish line of battle and got behind them. She wasn't big enough to do much damage to the battleships themselves, but she blew some of their boats out of the water. The Spaniards blasted the frigate to pieces, but it was too late. Without her boats to tow her, a Spanish battleship was adrift. She threw out her anchor. It dragged and they frantically set another anchor, but the anchored vessel was an easy target and came under heavy fire from the British. With slow majesty she went down under the onslaught.

Ashore, the English battleship trapped against the wharf was a flaming skeleton. Her guns popped and roared as heat set them off. Small arms fire sounded as her muskets and pistols discharged from the heat. The scene was scarlet and orange with tongues of flame shooting hundreds of feet into the air; it seemed as if the ship had sailed into the mouth of Hell itself. Then the powder magazine blew. It was even more spectacular than the explosion of the *San Anthurius*. The *Ant* had been a smaller vessel and daylight had robbed the scene of its brilliance. The battleship was well loaded and they had not been able to drown her magazine—the fire came on too furiously.

An immense orange fireball erupted and the thunderous roar sent a shower of burning debris all around—including into the nearest Spanish xebec and the various small craft tied to the docks of Mahon. Burning brands were flung into the town and spread the fire. The wall of sound flattened the harbor—even though they were half a mile away, Thorton could feel the hot wind of the blast blowing over him. The shock wave sent a circular wave across the basin to lap the hill at Thorton's feet.

Desperate efforts could not save the Spanish xebec. Her sails and rigging were full of embers that readily caught and burned in the still air. They cut her lines and toppled her antennas into the sea in a desperate bid to save her. It was not enough. The order was given:

abandon ship. The nearest Spanish escort did not send boats to pick up — she was fleeing the fiery wreck herself. The same fate could overtake her if she did not put enough distance between them.

The Spanish sailors in the water either drowned or swam to shore, each according to his skills. Slowly the xebec sank into the water: the captain had scuttled her and water flooded her magazine and lower parts. Thus she did not blow but slowly descended to the bottom. The harbor was nine or ten fathoms deep there. Her mast tops remained burning like torches above the surface.

The remainder of the Spanish force withdrew. They had rescued two of the captive vessels, destroyed several British battleships and frigates, burned the docks and dockyards with all their supplies, and damaged at least half the surviving vessels. They had accomplished what they set out to do. Their boats towed them away and their xebecs formed a screen to chase away the frigates and small boats that harassed their retreat. A little while later, a distant roar sounded and a flash of light on Cape Mola showed that the Spanish had blown the fortress' powder magazine. The shock made the earth tremble and sent small waves down the length of the bay. The Spanish victory was complete. The British were in shambles.

The *Arrow* made repairs. She had spare spars, so re-rigged her main antenna. She reinforced her knees and ribs, patched her gunwales and replaced shattered gun port lids. When the Spanish were gone she eased out of hiding and began nosing along the bay. She lit her lanterns and flew the British ensign. She did not want to be taken for a Spanish row galley by trigger-happy Englishmen. They had been searching for about half an hour and had pulled three men aboard when they saw a frigate ahead of them. Thorton recognized her immediately.

He approached and cupped his hands. "Ahoy the *Ajax!*"

"What ship?" Horner shouted back.

Thorton shouted, "Sallee *Arrow!*"

The two vessels grappled with their quarters side by side. The *Ajax* was a little taller so Thorton had to look up at Horner. "What happened?" he asked.

"We launched her. She was on the ways. Nothing had been done to her, so we set her afloat. We didn't have enough crew to fight, but we saved her. The dockyards are burning." The *Ajax* had maybe fifty hands in her.

From the top of the *Arrow's* mast a voice cried out in Arabic, "A boat! Broad on the starboard beam!"

She came up on them and Thorton saw with great relief that it was the *Dart.* He hurried down into the waist and checked the deck. The wounded were below and the dead were being sewn into their hammocks by the sailmaker and his mates. Blood was in the scuppers. He looked over the side and Tangle looked up at him.

"Permission to come aboard?" the commodore asked him.

"Not yet," Thorton told him. He ran over to the larboard side and called up. "Captain Horner, may I ask a favor of you? Commodore Tangle and his daughter are in the boat and we are not in a fit condition to receive a little girl. Can you bring them on board until we are ready?"

"With pleasure."

Thorton ran back to the starboard. "Go 'round and board the *Ajax*. She has no casualties or damage." He spoke English so that the little girl would not understand.

Tangle nodded. "Understood. Thank you, Captain."

Miss Tahirah was impatient and wanted to go back to her cabin, but her father shushed her. "They were in a fight and some things got broken. We are going to visit Captain Horner while they fix it."

She wrapped her arms around her father and buried her face in his neck. She was tired and cranky. "No!"

He held her in his arms and spoke over her head to the cockswain. The boat pulled around the sterns and came up on the frigate's other side. Tangle could see the damage the *Arrow* had taken and knew he had been right to take his daughter away. Father and daughter climbed aboard the *Ajax*.

Thorton spoke to Horner. "I'll return to the *Ajax* as soon as the *Arrow* has been taken care of, sir."

"That will be fine, Mr. Thorton. Perhaps you can join us for breakfast."

"Thank you, sir. 'Twill be my pleasure."

That done he went below and visited the cockpit.

Shakil looked up. "Are you hurt, rais?"

"Praise Allah, no. I'm fine. Are you?"

"No, this is not my blood." He was stripped down to his shirt with a leather apron over his clothes. His shirtsleeves and the apron were stained with red. His hands and arms were red to the elbow. He looked like a butcher.

Thorton spoke quietly to each of wounded. One was out of his senses and did not know him, another wept and called for his mother. Thorton stopped by each hammock and looked the men in the eyes and thanked them for their work. They wanted to know how it turned out, of course. He told them the truth, but not all of it.

"The Spanish were forced to retreat. They did not take the town." He didn't mention that the town was burning and refugees were fleeing.

Thorton watched Shakil supporting a man's head as he gave him water. There was a quiet strength in the man. Here, in the most hellish place on earth, he moved with a quiet dignity. He comforted the dying and tended the wounded. It was a filthy job with no glory in it, yet he did it with a gentle calm that soothed the men. Loblolly boys were men unfit for any other sort of work. Nobody accepted the job if he could do anything else, yet Shakil had volunteered for it. Thorton's good eye misted over. He knuckled his eyes and found his hands covered in the grit left behind by gunsmoke and adrenalin.

He leaned in close and whispered in his ear, "I love you, *habibi*."

Shakil smiled up at him. He spoke very softly. "Thank you, Peter Rais. I love you, too."

CHAPTER 36 : COURTS MARTIAL

Burying the dead took days. Naval officers, ordinary seamen, marines, townsfolk, prisoners, slaves, each were buried in churchyards and group funerals held. More than three hundred were dead. Everyone knew one or more who had been killed, two or more who were wounded or homeless. Men, women, and children fled the town with whatever they could carry and were camped in the hills around it.

Then came the grim business of the courts martial. Four British ships had been lost, two were aground, and five damaged, out of a fleet of fifteen. A variety of merchant vessels and small craft had also been lost or damaged. The dockyard was in utter ruins. British power in the western Mediterranean had been broken. Somebody had to be to blame. Once the immediate repairs, funerals, and reorganizations had been accomplished, the courts martial were held aboard the flagship.

At eight of the clock in the morning a gun was fired to announce the solemn assembly. The flagship, *Terror*, was in pristine condition— her crew had labored feverishly to not only repair her damage, but to holystone her decks to whiteness and polish her brass until it shown. Her rigging was taut, the hammocks stowed with care, all her guns run out, and the crew at attention in their places, as if the Admiral wished to present an example of what a British ship should be and how it should be manned. Anything was possible for a flagship with first claim to all supplies, even after a violent defeat. Rear Admiral Wolfe stood on the quarterdeck, but Vice Admiral Walters, incapacitated as he was, remained abed.

Tangle came from the *Arrow*, dressed in his purple uniform and blue-checked sling. Horner and Thorton came from the *Ajax*. Other officers joined them, each awaiting their turn to testify. It was a subdued group. Some were wounded and all were exhausted after five days of frantic recovery work. The captains who had lost their ships were wan and their eyes were hollow. They had already surrendered their swords.

The president of the court martial was Captain Cathcart from the naval yard. He had a shaggy blond mane of hair and bushy whiskers. Bright blue eyes peered from a fleshy face. His voice carried a trace of Scots in it. He was flanked by three captains on each side, making a total of seven captains. A long table covered with a green baize cloth ran from starboard to larboard and the captains sat behind it with their backs to the stern windows and gallery. Copies of the *Articles of War* were at hand, along with ink wells and prayer books, quills and paper. A judge-advocate at a small desk to the side took notes and the sergeant-at-arms in his red coat and gorget stood on the other side.

It was Tangle's turn to testify.

Cathcart asked, "Did you fire the first shot at the Spanish?"

Horner translated into Spanish because the Turk's English was not good enough to answer legal proceedings with confidence. Horner was one of the few officers fluent in Spanish.

"No, it was Peter Rais Thorton, captain of the *Arrow*." Thanks to the roominess of a second-rate battleship, Tangle was able to stand up straight while giving his answer. Even so, his turban brushed the beams over head.

There was a certain amount of consternation at that answer. "Do you mean Lt. Peter Thorton of the *Ajax*?"

"I do."

"How came he to be on the *Arrow*?"

"He came to pay a social call on me following my duel with Admiral Walters. I was wounded in the arm and he wanted to see how I was. We saw the fire ships and he did what any captain would do when standing on his own quarterdeck: he fought. I and my daughter and servants left in the ship's boat. We took refuge on the north shore. He sank two fire ships and wounded a xebec."

"You saw this with your own eyes?"

"I did."

"Where was the *Arrow* at the start of the action?"

"At anchor off the Levantine mole. After my duel with the admiral I felt safer there."

"Why do you call Thorton captain of the *Arrow*?"

"After he resigned his British commission he accepted a Sallee commission. The *Arrow* is his ship."

The captains conferred. After a moment of hushed conversation, Cathcart said, "We will defer questions on that matter until Thorton receives his court martial."

"I await your pleasure."

"Thank you. No further questions."

Tangle bowed and exited the cabin. The sun was rising and the day was getting hot. He unbuttoned his coat, then unbuttoned his shirt half way to the waist in a vain attempt to cool off. The careless indifference with which Tangle opened his clothes made Thorton a little jealous. He was buttoned up tight in his uniform. The wool coat was open over the waistcoat but the stock was suffocating him. He took off his cocked hat and fanned himself with it.

A moment later Thorton was called. After the swearing in and routine questions, Cathcart asked him, "Where were you at the commencement of the Spanish action?"

Thorton stood straight and stiff with his hat tucked under his arm. "I was aboard the *Arrow*. I was calling on Commodore Tangueli."

"Who fired the first shot?"

Thorton hesitated. He was never one to boast. "I had the honor of firing a warning shot. I am uncertain who fired the first shot that actually engaged the enemy."

"Did you hear any shots before the one you fired?"

"No, sir."

"Describe your action with the enemy."

"We perceived a line of five fire ships being set alight, so we fired on the nearest. She began to sink, so we fired on the next. The second went down quickly. We discovered a line of Spanish xebecs advancing under oars and engaged one. We dueled with her for about an hour before breaking off. We took twenty-seven shot betwixt wind and water. Twelve dead, fifty wounded. We took shelter in a cove on the north bank to make repairs and saw a ship explode. We could not tell which one it was from our position. We came out and searched for survivors. We picked up our boat and met the *Ajax*."

There were some other questions, then they dismissed him. He went back out on deck. Other officers were pacing as they waited their turns to testify. Some stared into space. It was not their fault they were taken by surprise—everybody had been surprised. The Mola fort had been taken with ease. With most of the officers ashore for the ball, it was the perfect time for the Spanish to strike. Tangle's duel with Walters had been a lucky stroke: by cutting the affair short it had caused many of them to return to their ships early and sober.

After a pause for lunch the courts were reconvened. Thorton's court martial was last of all. The sun was westering by the time he was finally called. No one was left but Tangle and the officers of the *Ajax*. They were hot and tired of standing and waiting all day, but finally it was coming to an end.

None of the captains that made up the board particularly liked sitting in judgment on Thorton—not with it fresh in their minds that his warning had given them a chance against the Spanish. It had gone badly enough, but if he had not sunk two of the fireships, Horner would have not had time to get the *Ajax* off the stocks, and several other vessels would not have been able to come out and challenge the Spanish. Mahon might have fallen.

Thorton remained standing stiffly at attention. He stared at the beam over Cathcart's head. The president spoke in his light brogue. The sergeant-at-arms stood guard over him with his naked sword upright in his hands.

"The Admiralty directs that you be charged under Articles One, Two, Fifteen, Twenty-Eight, Thirty-Two, and Thirty-Five. After due examination of the matter before us, this court finds no evidence to support prosecution under Article Twenty-Eight and dismisses the charge."

Thorton swayed and sucked in a deep breath. That one had carried the death penalty. After what he and Shakil had done that night after the attack, he was guilty. Battle does things to a man, things that only a lover can soothe. They could still hang him for desertion if they wanted, but they could choose to inflict some other punishment as well. He might escape the noose.

"What answer do you make to the remaining charges?"

"I plead guilty under Article One. I converted to Islam. I plead not guilty to Article Fifteen. I am uncertain what specific actions are covered by the others. I would be grateful if the court would enlighten me so that I may answer properly."

"Article Two relates to Article One. We shall examine you to see if you have committed blasphemy or tempted others into apostasy or other sins against the Church of England."

Thorton brightened. "I plead not guilty, sir."

"Thirty-Two shall apply if you are found guilty of behaving in a fraudulent or deceitful manner, or otherwise engaged in conduct unbecoming an officer."

"I plead not guilty to that charge also, sir."

"Article Thirty-Five applies to any other defect of your conduct not covered by the other charges."

"Not guilty, sir."

"The court acknowledges your guilty plea under Article One and enters pleas of not guilty to Two, Fifteen, Thirty-Two, and Thirty-Five." The neatly powdered and bewigged secretary wrote it down. "What evidence do you offer on your own behalf?"

"May I ask on what date I am supposed to have deserted, sir?"

"Eh, when last you were with your ship?"

"I was with my ship this morning until called to this court, sir."

"Hm?" Cathcart consulted his fellow captains. They whispered together. He leaned his head to hear them, then addressed him. "You are charged with leaving the *Ajax* last spring and going off with the Sallee rovers until arrested last . . ." He had to pause and look up the date.

"May I ask if the court is prepared to accept the judgment of the French prize court?"

"Eh? What has that to do with it?"

"I went aboard the *San Bartolomeo* when she foundered as ordered by Captain Bishop of the *Ajax*. Captain Tangle took the *Bart* as a prize. I was with them until Correaux. Does my alleged desertion begin when I was sent onto the *San Bartolomeo,* or when Captain Tangle carried me off from Correaux?"

"We have no way of knowing the business of the French prize court. Begin at the beginning."

Thorton reached into the satchel hanging from his shoulder. "I have the judgment of the French prize court. I submit that I was not a deserter at that time."

The secretary came out from behind his desk and carried the papers to the table. Some of the officers could read French and translated for the others. They considered the matter.

"Did you return to the *Ajax* after the prize court?" Cathcart asked.

"I did, sir. The *Ajax* came in that morning right after court let out. I attended a banquet with Captain Bishop the following evening."

"Will other witnesses be able to corroborate this testimony?"

"Aye, sir. Forsythe was at the banquet and so was Captain Tangle. Lt. Perry had charge of the ship while we were ashore."

The captains huddled again. After a bit of discussion, Cathcart said, "We will accept the ruling of the French prize court regarding matters within its purview."

"Thank you, sirs." That was a relief. It established Tangle to have been lawfully acting as a privateer. A charge of piracy could not be laid against him now.

Thorton collected himself and continued. "During the dinner aforementioned, Captain Tangle quarreled with Captain Bishop and challenged him to a duel. Bishop selected Forsythe as his second and Tangle selected me. He asked me in front of the other guests, so I felt I could not refuse, but I advised them both to reconcile and not take such desperate action. Sadly, they refused. Forsythe and Bishop left, then Tangle and I left. Captain Tangle was very drunk, and I'm sorry to say, disorderly. He wanted to take some target practice that night which I thought unwise. I escorted him to his ship and put him aboard. I slept on the floor by his cot to prevent him from doing any mischief.

"The next morning we proceeded to the designated place where the affair of honor was conducted. The French police came and attempted to arrest us. I am told they caught Forsythe and Bishop. Tangle and I fled and made it back to the galiot, *Santa Teresa,* now named the *Arrow.* He persuaded me to come aboard by telling me that it was very likely that the French were coming after us, but if we were aboard the ship they could not arrest us. So I went aboard and he launched. I asked him to deliver me to the *Ajax,* and I thought he would do so because he drew along side. Unfortunately, he informed Lt. Perry that he would not deliver me but was carrying me off. We had a heated discussion in which some unfortunate remarks were made on all sides. Tangle told Perry to send my dunnage over and he did. He threatened to make use of his pistol if disobeyed."

"Did Lt. Perry attempt to rescue you?"

Thorton didn't want to make Perry look bad, but he didn't want to share the details of the discussion, either. He tried his best to cover them both. "No. I don't think he could have done anything. Tangle made it clear he was kidnapping me. Short of engaging in a ship to ship action, there was nothing he could do."

"Do you really think Captain Tangle would have fired on the *Ajax?*"

"Aye, sir. He never bluffs."

"Did you try to escape?"

Thorton was crestfallen. "No, sir. I was in shock."

Cathcart gave him a long look. "Was your dunnage delivered?"

"Yes, sir."

Cathcart's look grew more severe.

Thorton said hastily, "Captain Tangle was standing over me. He wouldn't let me leave." It wasn't much of an excuse. He felt a trickle of sweat run down his spine.

"How and when did you return to the *Ajax?*"

Thorton said cautiously, "That was later. First I ran into the *Ajax* at Eel Buff."

"What happened then?"

"I told Acting Captain Perry that I had converted to Islam. He told me I couldn't hold a commission if I was a Muslim and asked for my resignation, so I gave it to him. He wrote me a receipt. I thought I had done all that was necessary to depart His Majesty's service in honor. I thought it was sufficient to follow Acting Captain Perry's orders, sirs."

"Do you have a copy of the letter of resignation and receipt?"

He opened his satchel again. "I do."

He produced his copybook and the original receipt. They were taken over to the table and examined. Cathcart shuffled through the other papers on the table before him and produced one which he reviewed. He passed it among the other captains.

"According to this, Mr. Perry overstepped the bounds of his authority and was docked his seniority in punishment. He had no right to accept your resignation."

"I didn't know that. He was my superior officer so I obeyed him, sir."

A fly buzzed through the stuffy room and Cathcart waved it away. "Why did you convert to Islam? Did the rovers threaten or torture you?"

"No, sir. I converted of my own free will. The First Commandment is 'Thou shalt have no other God before Me.' Ergo, there cannot be such a thing as a 'three-personed God.' Islam corrects the error of the Trinity."

"Sacrilege!" growled a small dark captain.

"I have already pleaded guilty under Article One, sir," Thorton answered mildly.

"Thank you, Captain Johnson," Cathcart said. Returning to Thorton he asked, "How came you to this extraordinary conclusion?"

"The rovers set a good example. They prayed the most sincere prayers I had ever heard, so I asked them for an explanation. Captain Tangle and I debated religion and morality several times. But there is no way to argue with the First Commandment. There is one God and only one God worthy of worship, and Mohammed correctly communicated this commandment."

"You err," snapped Captain Johnson.

Captain Cathcart was secretly in sympathy with the unitarian view, but he couldn't say so. "Enough! Lt. Thorton has already pleaded guilty under Article One. Go on to the other charges, Lieutenant."

"I don't know what to say about them, since I don't know exactly what I am supposed to have done."

They asked questions about the time and place of his Sallee commission, conditions on the Sallee ships, and other matters. Finally they dismissed him and called for Horner.

The opening questions established that he had been made temporary captain of the *Ajax* during Bishop's convalescence after the duel.

"How long have you known Lt. Thorton?"

"A little more than a fortnight now."

"How came you to meet him?"

"I witnessed his defeat of two Spanish frigates in the Bay of Algeciras. He then came aboard my vessel."

"Tell us about that."

Horner gave a brief and unembellished account of the event.

"You witnessed this yourself?"

"I did."

"Did Thorton come aboard the *Ajax* of his own free will?"

"He did."

"What happened then?"

"Lt. Perry arrested him in accordance with our instructions from the Admiralty."

"How did Thorton behave aboard the *Ajax* after his arrest?"

"He gave me his parole, so I assigned him duties as a supernumerary lieutenant. He had rescued the pretender to the throne of Portugal, Duke Henrique. Commodore Whittingdon put His Grace aboard the *Ajax* disguised as a midshipman to bring here, so I assigned Thorton to instruct him and watch over him. After Lt. Wright was killed at Alborán and Duke Henrique transferred to a Portuguese warship, Mr. Thorton served as third lieutenant. He is an efficient officer."

"How was his speech? Did he castigate or harangue his fellows? Did he promulgate Islam or insult the Church of England?"

"He is a taciturn man, generally confining himself to the giving and following orders and answering questions put to him. The only time I ever heard him talk about Islam was when I asked him about it. He never performed Muslim prayers or spoke about it to any member of the crew as far as I am aware."

"Did he participate in the Divine Service?"

"He attended the same as all my officers."

"Did he take communion?"

"We did not observe communion."

"Do you think his conversion to Islam to be voluntary and sincere?"

"I do."

"Why do you think he converted? Was he displeased with his former captain? Was he dissatisfied with the British service?"

Horner said, "All I know is that he told me he believed the doctrine of the Trinity to be in error."

"Did you attempt to correct his error?"

"I am not a minister. I left it in the hands of our chaplain, Reverend Pennybrigg. He was zealous in his duty but ultimately unsuccessful."

"If you were given a choice, would you want Thorton to return to the *Ajax*?"

"If given a choice, I would take Lt. Thorton with me wherever I am assigned."

"You find him trustworthy and honest?"

"I do. He has kept his word in all things, including difficult things. He does not snivel or equivocate. In short, if he says he will do a thing, he does it. He is an obedient and capable officer."

Horner was dismissed from testimony but required to stay to translate for Tangle again. The Turk was sworn in again.

"Tell us how you came to know Peter Thorton."

So Tangle recited the story of how Captain Bishop of the *Ajax* had sent Peter Thorton and several men on board to succor the *San Bartolomeo* when she was in danger of sinking, but the Spaniards panicked and abandoned ship, then Bishop panicked and cut the grapples before recalling his men.

That point caused considerable consternation. "Wait, you say he ordered the grapples cut, then called the men back?"

"He did indeed. Lt. Perry was at the rail and protested. Two of the men made it back, but one fell and was killed between the ships. Thorton, Maynard, and MacDonald were stranded. Speaking of which, are you going to court martial Maynard and MacDonald? Because if Thorton deserted, so did they. If they aren't charged, Thorton shouldn't be charged. It isn't fair to blame one man but excuse the others."

"That is irrelevant to the question of whether you carried Lt. Thorton away from Correaux against his will."

"Oh, is that what you want to know? Yes, I did. I kidnapped him plain and simple."

"Why did you do that?"

Tangle did not know that charges under Article Twenty-Eight had been dropped. He watched the captains warily. "He is a highly capable officer and I needed competent officers. Most of the men in the galley have never been leaders. Thorton is an extremely good officer."

"How did you know that?"

"When the *Bart* was in danger of sinking he served as her first lieutenant. He told me it was his duty to see the ship safely to rendezvous with the *Ajax* at Correaux. He was willing to do anything consonant with that obligation, but he was strict about refusing to do anything contrary to his English duty. For example, when I ordered him to make false signals to deceive the *Ajax*, he refused. I confined him to his cabin and another man made the signals. Mr. Thorton also advised

Maynard and MacDonald regarding their duties. In short, he exasperated me repeatedly."

Cathcart suppressed a smile. "How did he exasperate you?"

"I offered him a Sallee commission, but he refused it. I made it as tempting as I possibly could. I spoke to him about wealth, glory, promotion, rank, fame, sex, freedom—everything a man craves I offered him. He turned it all down. I berated him and even threatened him, but he still refused."

"When did he accept a Sallee commission?"

"After he converted to Islam and tendered his resignation to your navy. We knew that England was at war with Spain then, so he acted as my first lieutenant when we raided the Spanish. He did not care for the life of a corsair, though. He often praised the English way of doing things and recommended that I adopt them. He even attempted to persuade me that I should join the French or British navy, but I am a patriot. I fight for my own country, not yours."

"I ask you again: when did Lt. Thorton accept a Sallee commission?"

"In Tanguel. Lord Zahid recruited us to participate in the reform of the Sallee naval forces. We were pleased to join. Thorton has influenced me—" He suddenly stopped. "More than I had realized." He tugged the white streak in his beard.

"I was born a corsair. My father was a corsair and his father before him. I was raised to the trade. But Peter Thorton looks beyond what is right in front of his nose. He made me see longer and farther. He made me realize that nothing would ever come of being a corsair. I could be rich and famous, but in the end, what matters? Wars must win something worth winning. They must win territory and dignity. Later, in Zokhara, he spoke to the Dey and the Vizier and said the same thing. The Dey listened.

"My reasons for taking him were selfish, but it was the best thing I have ever done for my country. If it weren't for Peter Thorton, I would be laying waste the Spanish coast in a fit of rage. Have you any idea how filthy and vicious a galley is? I wanted to tear the Spanish limb from limb and stuff their mouths with their own excrement. But I couldn't do it. I was trying to prove to Peter Thorton that I was a better man than that."

Horner had a hard time keeping up with the translation. A silence grew after he had finished speaking.

Cathcart coughed to break the spell. "An extraordinary account, Commodore. You do realize that by freely admitting you kidnapped an officer of the British navy you are opening yourself to having charges brought against you?"

Tangle shrugged. "I did what I did. I won't do a thing then deny it. But if you do lay charges against me, the gloves are off. I will fight and die rather than submit to captivity. That will be the end of the alliance between England and the Sallee Republic."

"Captain Horner. Have you considered charges?"

Horner had kept himself impartial during the translation. "I don't see the need. It happened before the alliance. Since then Commodore Tangueli has been cooperative, sirs."

Cathcart steepled his fingers together and looked at his fellow captains. They conferred quietly and shook their heads. "No further questions."

CHAPTER 37 : JUDGMENT

Thorton was waiting on deck when Tangle and Horner came out. Perry was there as well, but the two of them were ignoring each other.

Tangle crossed to the blond lieutenant with a frown. "They didn't ask me about Article Twenty-Eight. They only wanted to know about me carrying you off. They threatened to arrest me for it, so I think they believe you didn't desert."

"Oh, they dropped the charges under Twenty-Eight. Didn't they tell you?"

"No." Tangle thought how close he had come to saying something that would have ruined that.

Perry was listening. "What? They dropped Twenty-Eight?"

Thorton nodded.

"Walters lied to me! Damn him! The hell he put me through, for nothing! That son of a bitch!" He whirled away. No one but Thorton knew what he was talking about. They left him alone to brood in bitter silence.

The minutes ticked by. Thorton consulted his watch. Five minutes later he checked it again. Tangle massaged his injured arm. Perry paced in agitation. Horner clasped his hands behind his back and waited. He was very good at waiting—the service often required it.

"Lt. Perry," the sergeant-at-arms in his red coat called him. Perry whirled around, took a deep breath to compose himself, and entered the stateroom.

Perry was in there a long time. Thorton bit his lips. Tangle cradled his wounded arm against his chest. Horner watched Thorton and Tangle. Time dragged. At last Perry emerged. The corners of his mouth turned down and his eyes flashed resentment at Thorton. He went to stand by himself. No one spoke to him.

"Lt. Thorton," the marine sergeant-at-arms called.

Thorton trembled and swallowed. He gave Tangle a beseeching look. Tangle replied softly, "Go with God, Peter Rais."

Thorton took a deep breath, squared his shoulders, and walked into the great cabin. His legs were wooden and he could hardly make them move. There on the table was his sword. If he were convicted, the point would face the door. If exonerated, the hilt would face him. It lay sideways. His heart thundered in his ribs. He stood and waited with his eyes on the sword. He was more terrified than he had ever been in his life. No enemy had frightened him half as much. All they could do was kill him. The court martial could disgrace him.

"Peter Thorton. This court martial finds you guilty under Article One of the *Articles of War*. It finds you not guilty under Article Two. It finds you not guilty under Article Fifteen. It finds you not guilty under Article Thirty-Two. It finds you guilty under Article Thirty-Five. Specifically it finds you guilty of being absent without leave and improperly accepting a commission from a foreign power.

"The court imposes the following penalties: that you be stripped of your commission and disrated to the rank of midshipman, that you forfeit all pay for the period in which you were absent without leave, and that you pay a fine of twenty-five pounds sterling to be stopped from your pay until the sum is made up in full. It remands you to the *Ajax* to serve out the remainder of your time as a midshipman, or whatever position the captain shall deem fit."

Thorton's heart leaped and fell as the judgment was pronounced. When they announced his disrating and return to the *Ajax*, he stared at them with stricken eyes. "Thank you, sirs," he said in a ghastly voice.

The marine sergeant approached him. He cut away the gold braid from his collar with his dirk. Cathcart rose and returned his sword to him. Thorton blinked back tears.

"Dismissed."

Thorton took the sword, saluted and walked out. He couldn't see where he was going and knocked his head on the lintel. The blow nearly knocked him down. He didn't feel it. He ducked under and stepped out onto the deck.

Tangle, and if the truth be told, Horner, cheered to see him walking out sword in hand, but from the expression on his face they feared the worst. They all saw his torn collar. Tangle approached him quickly.

"What is the decision?"

"Guilty on One and Thirty-five. Not guilty on Two, Fifteen, and Thirty-Two."

"That's good! They won't hang you!"

Thorton shook his head. "They've stripped me of my rank. I'm a midshipman again. Or whatever position my captain chooses for me. I must serve out the remainder of my time on the *Ajax*."

Tangle touched the torn collar. "They didn't have to do that. Why not dismiss you from the service?"

"I've been fined twenty-five pounds to be stopped from my pay, too."

"Oh, that's nothing. I'll pay it." It was more than a quarter of a lieutenant's annual salary. The corsair dipped into his pocket and pulled out a handful of coins. "Will they take Spanish *reales* or Sallee sequins? I have very little British money."

Thorton was staring blankly into space and didn't answer. He was still in shock.

Horner said, "I'll take care of it."

Tangle let him have the money. Horner pocketed it and went inside. While he was gone, Perry stared bitterly at Thorton. "They let you off easy."

"I can never get a commission, Roger. I'm stuck at midshipman for life."

"'Tis your own damn fault, but they blame me. 'Did you try to rescue Lt. Thorton?'" he said in a mocking voice. "'Was he coerced into converting?' I told them you did it of your own free will." He spat the last words at him.

Tangle gave him a baleful eye. "You did your part. You were never Peter's friend."

"How would you know? I practically supported him when he was a furloughed midshipman with no pay!"

Thorton put his tricorn back on his head with a heavy sigh. He hardly seemed to hear the two men who professed to be his friends quarreling with each other. "To serve out my time. Allah defend me if Bishop returns!"

Tangle objected. "You're not staying. I'll buy you out. I'll take care of it."

Perry glared at Tangle in fury. "Of course you will, you god damn sodomite! Do you think I believe that scene you staged at the Admiral's ball? I know you better than that!"

Thorton tried to pull himself together. "Roger, you don't know anything about it."

"I know you like kissing men," he hissed. "I know exactly how much you like it." He rounded on Tangle. "Did he tell you how he kissed me earlier this week, how badly he wanted me? You won't fool people much longer, Peter. They'll find out you're nothing but a whore!"

Thorton's teeth gnashed together and he clenched his fists in rage. "That is an insult that can only be wiped out in blood!"

"I told you I'd kill you if they didn't hang you, Peter Thorton, and by God I'll do it!"

"Name the time and place. Bring your pistol."

"Pistols suit me perfectly. I am fully recovered from my wound."

"I'll be your second, Peter," Tangle said quietly.

"Who is your second, Roger?" Thorton asked through clenched teeth.

"I don't give a damn."

Horner came out and said, "Your fine is paid, Lieutenant Thorton. Your receipt." He stopped and looked at the three of them staring at each other with angry expressions. "How now, gentlemen, what's this?"

Perry spoke. "Thorton has challenged me to a duel and I have accepted. Tomorrow morning at dawn, on the quay, with pistols."

Thorton nodded abruptly. "I'll be there."

"Gentlemen! This is a bad end to the business. You must let the judgment of the court stand. Whatever was between you is over now."

"'Tis not," Perry hissed.

Horner shook his head. "Dueling is a filthy habit that has been the waste of too many lives."

"Go to Hell," Perry replied.

"You are insubordinate, Mr. Perry!"

"He's not in his right mind," Thorton excused him. "Will you be his second, sir? He hasn't named one. Maybe you can bring him to his senses."

Perry swore a vile oath then and whirled away.

Horner said, "You may have twenty-four hours leave to arrange your affairs, Mr. Thorton. Return to the *Ajax* after this is settled."

"Thank you, sir."

Thorton sat in the bow of the *Dart*. What if Perry was right? He had violated Article Twenty-Eight the night of the fire ships in spite of the impending court martial. He couldn't help it. Before that he had professed his love to Shakil but pressed himself hot and hard against Tangle. And yes, he had liked kissing Roger Perry. Color slowly mounted in his face as he remembered it. Embarrassment overrode shock. His eyes came into focus. He turned his head a little to the side so that he could see Tangle clearly without the cloud in his left eye obscuring his view.

Tangle was watching him with a worried look. The rover sat in the sternsheets of the boat and never complained, not even when his wounded arm was bumped by the cockswain adjusting the sail. Those brown eyes broke from his to glance at the man, then came back to him. Thorton thought him handsome. He had gotten used to the dark skin and the hump in the bridge of his nose. Those small defects did not detract from the coffee-colored eyes and the high cheek bones, the long hooked nose or strong jaw with the short neat beard. The white streak in the beard bothered him though. Tangle was ten or fifteen years older than him, older even than Ebenezer Horner who seemed positively ancient. Horner had the dignity a man his age ought to have—he would never go chasing after a junior officer. In short, Tangle did not behave like a British captain. Even so, he liked him for it. He closed his eyes and tried to sort himself out.

Did he want to stay with the *Ajax*? What sort of career would he have as a midshipman for life? He could become a master's mate. Master was a perfectly respectable job that paid almost as well as captain. It didn't carry the same glamor as the commissioned ranks did, but he could have a successful career. He looked down at his coat and pulled the torn collar out where he could see it.

The loss of his rank burned him more than anything they could have done to him. He had thought he would hang as a lieutenant. How hard he had worked for his promotion! How well he had studied! He wanted his insignia back. He wanted to prove to them that they could not keep Peter Thorton down. He had what it took to be a captain and a good one. Had he not defeated two frigates with a galiot? What about sinking two fire ships and warning the port? Did those things mean nothing? He remembered the incredible rush of battle. Fear, yes, but the exhilaration of pitting everything he had against the enemy overrode it. He had the killer instinct. Horner had it, Tangle had it. Such men would never be content with a plain coat, forever bowing and scraping before a captain of inferior abilities.

He thought he understood Horner a little better. How it must have rankled him to be a mere substitute, not truly the master of the vessel he commanded! Yet to be a substitute captain was infinitely preferably to being forever stuck as a warrant officer. He realized he had missed Tangle speaking to him.

Thorton cleared his throat. "I was distracted in my mind. What did you say?"

"From this I presume the *Ajax* is still in commission and Horner is her captain?"

"I don't know. They didn't say."

Tangle sighed. "'Twas a bad business, but not as bad as it could have been."

"If you say so, sir."

"You are alive and free, Peter. You cannot wish for more."

Thorton sighed and lapsed into silence.

CHAPTER 38 : DUEL AMID THE RUINS

Shakil looked up in surprise and pleasure when Thorton let himself into the great cabin aboard the *Arrow*. He was giving Tahirah a lesson in mathematics. They had only told the girl that Thorton must go and give a report to the other captains; they did not tell her about the court martial. She tossed her slate down and jumped up to see him.

"Peter Rais!" She ran over and hugged him.

He smiled and patted her hair. "Good morning, Miss Tahirah. Are you bored? Maybe your Baba will take you ashore today."

Tahirah instantly zoomed out of the cabin to carom into her father and demand to go ashore. She was terribly bored being cooped up on the ship.

Shakil rose and waited quietly. He noticed the torn collar. "What happened?"

"I am disgraced, but alive. A midshipman again." They sat down on the locker with its velvet cushions and Thorton leaned his head on the other man's shoulder. "I must serve out the remainder of my commission aboard the *Ajax*. As long as the *Ajax* is afloat, I belong to her. Please Allah, don't let Bishop come back! If Horner is my captain I can bear it."

Shakil stroked his brow and kissed his forehead. "How long?"

"I don't know. Her keel is cracked. If they scrap her, days. If they repair her, months or years."

Shakil winced. "I will wait for you."

Thorton sat up. "Tomorrow I duel Perry."

Shakil tensed. "What happened?"

So Thorton told him. Shakil listened in silence. "He's angry at you. He resents your successes. He wants to punish you as they have punished him."

"They are being unfair to him."

"Yes. And he is taking it out on you, which is unfair of him."

"I wish it was over. I don't want to spend another winter in England."

"I'm sure Isam will find a way to obtain your freedom. If money is what it takes, I will buy you from them."

"You would do that for me?"

"Yes. I love you."

Thorton slipped to his knees and embraced his waist. "I love you, too. When I am with you I am tranquil. You give me peace and make me happy. No one else has ever made me feel that way."

Shakil stroked his hair and kissed his brow. He smiled softly, but didn't tell him how much of a trial it was to love and worry about him. Loving Peter Thorton made his life anything but peaceful. Thorton lay his head on Shakil's breast and listening to the soothing sound of the man's heartbeat. Finally he rose with a sigh.

"I must mend my coat." He took it off, and Shakil brought a sewing kit. He did not have any buckram so could not make a new collar; instead he stitched two large white patches onto the collar in token of his lowly rank. It would have to do. Maybe seeing them would satisfy Perry that he really had been punished. Thorton sat with the coat in his lap for a long time and just stared at the midshipman's patches. To disrate him was the second worse thing they could have done to him.

Shakil watched him quietly. "Lieutenant to captain to midshipman must be hard for you."

Thorton nodded. "Thank God for Horner. Without him it would be Hell. If it were Bishop I would desert in a moment."

"Come to bed. I'll make you forget all that."

Dawn broke rosy pink and cool. Tendrils of fog drifted across the placid waters of the basin. Thorton joined the crew in their morning prayers. He was right between Shakil and Tangle. How he enjoyed worshipping in congregation with his brothers in Islam! Shakil lead the prayers. For his verse he selected, "Behold! It is surely Allah Who is the Most Forgiving, the Merciful." They broke their fast with a piece of fruit and biscuit, then rowed toward the dark shore.

The *Dart* nosed among burned timbers of the wharf and tied up to a charred stump of a piling. They climbed up onto the quay. The neighborhood was a low black smear. The fire had burned the dockyard and now it lay in rubble. There were no streets, just a snow of black ash that was gritty and sticky on account of the heavy fall of dew. A trail one cart wide had been tramped down the main street that ran along the waterfront. Other trails lead down side streets. Here and there were parts of stone or brick walls still standing but few of them were more than waist high. Close at hand was a wall two stories high with empty windows and door. The rest of the house had fallen. No bird sang, no cricket chirped. No squirrel ran—and no rat, either. Nothing lived under that great black pall.

Perry was standing with his back to the water. He was staring at the burned naval yard, or perhaps just staring. There was no sign of Horner.

Thorton walked up to him with his shoes crunching on cinders. Perry was up to his ankles in ash. His white stockings were ruined.

"Roger."

Perry turned around and looked at him. "Captain Horner sends his apologies. He is delayed. The flagship called him over."

"They'd better reinstate him as captain. It wouldn't be fair, not after he saved the *Ajax*."

Perry nodded abruptly. "Not fair to any of us."

Thorton nodded his agreement. A silence fell. "How is your arm?" he ventured.

"Well enough. A little stiff, but I can shoot fine."

"I'm glad to hear that. What about—" He gestured a little towards Perry's face. It was an effort to speak as if it were a normal conversation. He sounded stiff and stilted.

"It still itches." He put his hand to his face and rubbed. The mark ran from his left brow across the eyebrow and nose and onto the right cheek.

"You're lucky you didn't lose your eye."

"Very lucky," he agreed. "You're lucky they didn't stretch your neck."

"Very lucky." Thorton nodded.

Another awkward silence.

"Roger, I don't want to duel you. Let's apologize and put it behind us. Please?"

"I hate your guts. Do you have any idea what you did to me?"

"I didn't anything to you!"

Perry gave him a contemptuous look. "You're such a child. You have never understood other people's feelings, least of all mine. You're older than me, but act like my baby brother! You really don't know, do you?"

Thorton shook his head.

Perry glanced past him to where Tangle and Shakil were standing on the scorched stones of the quay. "Walk with me."

So they walked along the narrow trail. Perry turned down a side street. They disappeared behind the single standing wall. Out of sight of the Muslims, he turned to face Thorton. The heaps of rubble were were all around. The sun sent golden rays but revealed only ruins. Here was an iron post that had been a hitching rail, over there a set of cracked marble steps leading to nothing.

"You left me, Peter! You said you loved me, and then you left me for that damn Turk! You confessed your love for me in front of everyone, and I believed you! A week later I find you with a turban and

Tangle as your lover! What am I to think of that, Peter? You are either a liar or a whore. The Peter Thorton I knew would have never done such a thing. But you turned out to be somebody different! You have dukes and commodores for friends now! Horner fawns on you! And what happened to me? I was reprimanded and docked my seniority for being your friend." His voice was bitter.

"Well, ah, you turned me down. You didn't want me. Not . . . like that." His face was getting red. "I was lonely. He was persuasive."

"Damn it! You put such thoughts into my head!" Perry nearly shouted. He struggled to control himself. "And Walters, with his dirty nasty mind, asking me questions, insinuating that I was that sort of man, telling me that if I didn't seduce you, he'd have me up on the same charges! I don't deserve to be treated like that."

Thorton felt ill. His mind attempted to grapple with the enormous pettiness of it all. He shook his head. "I'm sorry, Roger. Walters shouldn't have done that."

"I kept wondering . . . after you said that you had kissed him. That it was 'enough.'" He jerked his head toward the wall beyond which the Muslims were standing. "I couldn't figure out what you were talking about. Admiral Walters made the details very clear. I knew you couldn't be doing the filthy things he thought you were doing. But he wouldn't listen. He thinks what he thinks."

Thorton was pink in the face. He cleared his throat. "I don't think it is filthy the way we did it. It was just . . . ardent. But I suppose everyone else would think it was, because we are men. But I don't see why it can be all right for you to do it with a woman, but if I do it with a man, 'tis hideous."

"I don't know. I mean, if you'd committed the sin of Sodom, that would be dirty, but it would be dirty if you did it with a woman, too. Why is it so much worse with a man than a woman? I never thought about it before. I don't want to think about it now! But I can't stop thinking about it. I can't get it out of my head." He shook his head as if to dislodge the pernicious thoughts.

Thorton watched Perry carefully. He was afraid to say something that might interrupt the other man's meandering progress towards a change in attitude. He patted Perry's good arm in an attempt at a reassuring gesture.

Perry's brown eyes were troubled. "Do you know what really bothers me?"

Thorton shook his head.

"Do you remember when we'd sleep together, and that was all, just sleep? Sometimes I'd crawl into bed with you and we'd snuggle to

keep warm. Sometimes I would lie there wishing you were a woman."
He was getting pink on his own account.

Nothing could have astonished Thorton more. "You did? Why?"

"Because I was lonely and cold, and you were my best friend.
Sometimes I wished you were more than a best friend, except that I
didn't. I mean, I wished I had a woman who was a friend like you."

Thorton tried to follow the convoluted logic in that statement.
Before he could work it out, Perry muttered, "Damn it," grabbed his
face and kissed his mouth hard.

Thorton simply stood there for a moment, but then his eyes closed
and he kissed him back. He couldn't help himself. So many times he
had longed to be in Perry's arms! He had kept it to himself until that
fateful spring day aboard the *Ajax*. None of this would have happened
if he had kept silent forever. The real reason he had not tried to escape
when Tangle carried him off was because he could not stand to face
Perry after admitting he loved him.

Did he love him still? He felt like he did. His mouth was acting like
he did. His blood was surging through his veins and his arms were
around the other man. Perry wrapped his arms around him kissed him
wildly. He was dizzy and his lips parted. Perry took advantage of that
small surrender and thrust his tongue into Thorton's mouth. He
groaned. The two clenched tightly together.

Thorton loved Shakil. He had sworn it only this morning. Yet he
did not feel the world whirling around him when he kissed Shakil. Why
was he so fickle? Had he convinced himself that he loved Shakil
because he couldn't have Perry? What if he could have Perry? His
fingers clawed the wool on the English lieutenant's back. He pressed
himself hard against the other man and felt his flesh answering the heat.

Perry suddenly broke the kiss. He was panting and flushed. "Do
you have any idea how jealous I was when you ran off with that
hideous Turk? You said you loved me, but you went with him."

Thorton was completely bewildered. "But you didn't want me."

"What does that have to do with anything?" Perry replied in
exasperation. "Don't you know men want what they can't have?"

"I have no idea," Thorton replied with complete honestly.

"You offered yourself to me and then you gave yourself to him
instead. He doesn't deserve it! A stranger! And a ribald seducer to
boot!"

"You're jealous of Tangle?" Thorton thought he'd been as
astonished as possible when Perry kissed him, but he was even more
astonished by this admission.

"Furious. I'd challenge him, but I think he'd plug me. I don't want to die at his hands. When he challenged Walters over that woman, I wanted to strangle him. He's been playing games with all of us."

"Is that why you called me names? Because you're angry with him?"

Perry looked sheepish. "I shouldn't have done that. I'm sorry."

"He isn't my lover anymore. He was for a little while, but I came to my senses. I met his wife. She's very nice and probably beautiful. I jilted him months ago."

Perry brightened. "Good for you. Men like that are not to be trusted. He was taking advantage of you. Lord knows you are a simpleton when it comes to love or anything else. I didn't know how to make you see sense. I thought maybe, if you were still sweet on me, I could distract you."

Thorton's face fell. "That's all this was? A distraction?"

Perry looked down and shuffled his feet. He cleared his throat. "Not entirely." He looked sidewise at Thorton. "You're a surprisingly good kisser. Believe me, I know."

Thorton fidgeted and looked away. "Ah, yes. I do believe you're qualified to make judgments on that account." He was supremely flattered to be called a good kisser. He had been celibate for twenty-nine years and now in the course of one week he had kissed three different men. It chagrined him and made him fear he was becoming the sort of flirtatious beau he had condemned other men for being. He asked cautiously. "Did you like kissing me?"

Perry hesitated, then admitted, "Yes."

"I like kissing you, too, but I don't think we should."

Perry was silent for a long time. "Perhaps not. But I was wondering . . ."

Thorton was feeling giddy. "Don't you have sweetheart?"

Perry shook his head. "The butcher's wife was my last mistress. I don't miss her, although I do miss her muttonchops."

"Surely there's a local girl?"

"I don't speak Spanish. And we of the *Ajax* are hardly the most desirable suitors. Even a chambermaid expects more than we can offer."

"I can't be your sweetheart. I wish you'd said something before."

"I couldn't say anything. It was only last night when I was staring into the dark and thinking about killing you that I understood myself. My thinking finally boiled down to, 'If I can't have him, nobody can!' He took off his hat and worried the brim. "I am fond of you, you know."

Thorton was mesmerized by those big brown eyes looking so earnestly at him. His conscience pained him as he thought about Shakil waiting for him. But at the same time, he was shamelessly delighted to be pursued by three handsome men. It almost made up for a lifetime of celibacy. "We should kiss and make up."

Perry caught his hand and kissed it. "And more than kissing."

Thorton shook his head violently. "Article Twenty-Eight."

"We won't violate it. You'll show me."

Thorton was longing to violate it fully and at great length. He rubbed his free hand over his face. "Um, I already have."

Perry's grew wroth. "But you just said you and the Turk—" He was nearly choking with fury.

"'Twas not Tangle. He's rather disappointed, too."

"What? If not him, who?"

"Shakil bin Nakih. I met him in Zokhara. Recently our feelings reached the point where . . ." He struggled to put it delicately, "They needed stronger expression."

Perry's jaw dropped. "That pretty little . . . what is he, a purser's mate?"

Thorton nodded.

"A purser's mate, of all things!"

"He's a very good purser's mate. Pursers have much better reputations in Sallee because they don't cheat the men. Shakil is very honest and highly respected for it. That's why they call him 'Effendi.' 'Tis a term of respect."

"You didn't waste much time once you got started, did you?"

Thorton gave him a level look. "You have no right to pass judgment. Not when I've seen you running after four different women at the same time!"

"I didn't manage to catch them all."

"Neither did I!"

Perry turned the hat in his hands. He smiled ruefully. "We've made an awful hash of it, haven't we, Peter? But you, you've had grand adventures! Two frigates with a galiot! How the deuce did you manage it? That's another reason I'm jealous of you, you know."

"You can come with us if you like. The Sallee rovers always have a place for good officers. Your skills matter more than political influence or favoritism. You wouldn't have to worry about Walters any more."

"Are you enticing me to desert?"

Thorton shook his head. "Not at all. If you're thinking of leaving the service, you must submit your letter of resignation and wait for the Admiralty to respond. I've learnt that lesson quite well."

Just then they heard Tangle's voice calling out loud and strong, "Boat coming!"

They hurried back to the shore to see Horner's gig stroking over the placid waters of the bay. The cockswain moored the boat and Horner climbed up. His carriage was more erect and his face more animated than they had seen. There was even a spring in his step.

He returned their salutes crisply. "I have news, gentlemen. The *Ajax* is back in commission. She will be repaired and resupplied. With our losses in the recent battle, the navy needs her. She'll be serving as a dispatch runner. I will continue as her captain until Bishop recovers."

"Congratulations, sir!" Thorton replied. The others chorussed their felicitations as well. They were all happy for Horner, although three of them were not happy about Thorton back on the *Ajax* as a midshipman.

Horner smiled. It was hard for him to turn from that good news to the dreadful business that had brought them all to the quay this foggy morning, but he was a man with an iron will. He gave the duelists a stern look. "As for the two of you, I will take it amiss if you deprive me of an able officer just when I need him."

Thorton and Perry looked at each other. Perry spoke. "We have made up our quarrel, sir."

Horner brightened. "I'm glad to hear it. Hence forward we will have no more bad blood on the *Ajax*. Is that understood?"

"Aye aye, sir," Thorton replied.

"Aye aye, sir. Let's be done with it and get the *Ajax* ready for sea," Perry agreed.

Tangle was displeased. He turned and walked away a few steps. Shakil hovered between his lover and his brother-in-law. Tangle stared out at the water for a moment while he mastered his temper.

He turned around and said coolly, "I bid you good day. I am going to call on Admiral Wolfe, so don't get too fond of your new midshipman. Shakil." He jerked his chin toward the *Dart*.

Shakil hesitated, then turned and hurried after him. He kept glancing back over his shoulder at Thorton as he climbed in.

Horner watched the little lateener catch the west wind and pull away. He said nothing.

Perry asked, "How much trouble do you think he'll cause?"

Thorton replied, "A lot. He's angry now."

CHAPTER 39 : THE FORTUNES OF WAR

The *Ajax* lay careened in Phillipet Bay. The officers and men were living ashore in tents made of old sails. Thorton was the only one among the officers who was adequately equipped; the rooming house near the dockyard had burned. Thanks to his Sallee prize money, he could draw supplies out of the *Arrow* to meet his own needs. As captain of the *Arrow*, he also directed that a bolt of linen and a bolt of tan duck be donated to the officers of the *Arrow*. The officers' stewards were able to make each of them a new linen shirt and a pair of breeches. There was no blue wool or anything else necessary to complete a British uniform on the *Arrow*, so the Ajax's officers had working clothes and the dress uniforms they were wearing the night of the battle. Half the fleet was in similar straits. Given the circumstances, Horner was quite surprised to find his barometer-thermometer hanging on his tent pole. No one could tell him how it got there. The pawnshop had burned along with everything else.

Midshipman Thorton was supervising men as they ran supplies over the mudflat on a sledge to be hauled aboard. The *Ajax* was careened on the mudflats. The crack of a musket shot came from the British bivouac on Cape Mola. Further along the shore the crew of an advice boat leaped into action. They launched the boat and were ready to go when the courier came running down the hill.

"The French fleet!" he gasped in answer to the queries. He jumped into the advice boat and they shoved off. They rowed like mad and flew up the road to Mahon.

Horner snapped, "Keep those men working!"

Thorton's hand went to his pocket and hauled out his tawse. The men snapped back to work. The other officers shouted to their men with a renewed sense of urgency. To be caught careened on the beach with the enemy coming up was a horrible thing. It required effort to remind themselves that they were no longer at war with France. All the same, they did not want to be caught helpless on the beach. It would take two days to fill the *Ajax* with all her supplies, even supposing the improvised dockyard would be able to supply them, but every sailor would much rather be afloat than afoot. They strained mightily at their lines.

"Mr. Thorton!" Horner summoned him.

Thorton ran over and presented himself. Like every officer he was in his shirtsleeves and breeches. He had tied a blue-checked cloth over his head to save it from the sun.

"Go up there and see what you can see."

"Aye aye, sir."

Thorton ran up the hill to the fort. The sentries would not let him pass—they were jumpy after the Spanish attack. He had to go around the bivouac to get up high enough to see. The French fleet was streaming out of the north in a long line. He counted seven line-of-battleships, five frigates, and their victualers. They were about fifteen miles northeast of Minorca and on course for the island. He ran down and reported.

Horner said, "Hm." He put his hands behind his back and began to pace. Thorton waited further instructions. Horner was lost in thought and turned back towards him before he realized he'd left the demoted midshipman standing there. He glanced at the *Ajax* which had reached the water and was starting to right herself. "Thank you, Mr. Thorton. Return to duty."

Slowly, majestically, the *Ajax* rose up like a proper ship. With nothing in her she was extremely high in the water. All her ballast had to be stowed, not to mention, water, food, firewood, sails, and everything else. All of that had burned in the destruction of the dockyard. They didn't even have hammocks. She did have guns. Perry's job, in concert with the gunner, had been to fetch the long barrels out of the debris, clean them, test them for trueness, and if fit, bring them back to the *Ajax*. They had abandoned several of the guns but most of them were thought to be serviceable. They were stored under canvas while new carriages were built for them. A pressed man who had been a blacksmith worked to make the iron fittings they'd need. Thorton had charge of rigging a whip to lift the ballast into the hold. Forsythe was down inside supervising the placement.

With a fair breeze the French would reach the harbor entrance by sunset. Would they risk entering a strange harbor in the failing light and dying breeze? Could the *Ajax* mount her guns by then? Why was Thorton afraid of the French? Was it just an old habit left over from the previous war? Or was it because Minorca had been French until Spain took it in retaliation for losing Barcelona, and the English had taken it from the Spanish? The French would want it back. Of that Thorton was certain.

The *Arrow* went skimming by. She had been caught in port by a Spanish fleet only a few days ago; she did not intend to let herself be bottled up by a French fleet even if the Sallee Republic and France were old allies. Thorton watched her put to sea with yearning in his heart. She had been his ship. He paused to wipe his face on his sleeve. Closing his right eye, he could see nothing but a haze covering his left eye. Shapes were dark and blurry. He was a half-blind, disgraced midshipman with no future. Despair welled up in him.

Near sunset Horner sent Thorton up the hill again. The French fleet was heaving to just off the northeast flank of Minorca. They would not make a night entrance. They fired a salute to the British flag flying on the hilltop and the small battery returned it. The rolling thunder of the salute echoed from the hills. The *Arrow* lay hove to south of the harbor entrance. The purple flag of Sallee was flying from her stern and the broad pennant of a commodore was at her masthead. Thorton ran down the hill and made his report to Horner. A French cutter passed unmolested on her way to town.

"Thank you, Mr. Thorton. Send the hands to dinner. We'll work through the night."

Fitting her out properly would have taken days; they didn't have that much in supplies or time. Horner had already bought some gunpowder off the *Arrow*; he had enough for a few broadsides and nothing more. He had a week of water and wine, and a few days of salt pork, raisins, olive oil, bread, and local vegetables. Finally, near dawn, the hands were able to tumble into their blankets on the hard planks of the gundeck. They slept between the guns, heaped in corners, and crammed next to each other. Midshipman Thorton, acting third lieutenant of the *Arrow*, had a straw pallet made by his steward to cushion the ropes of his bunk. He toppled into it and slept the sleep of the dead.

After an hour's nap Thorton joined the other exhausted officers to break their fasts and go on deck. A boat was coming along side.

"Dispatches, sir."

Horner opened them immediately. His face grew grim. He nodded to the lieutenant. "Thank you, Lieutenant. I regret that I am unable to offer you any hospitality. We must hurry to complete our repairs."

The lieutenant saluted and departed.

"Gentlemen. I will see all commissioned and warrant officers in my cabin immediately."

It was a solemn crowd that gathered. No curtain screened the great cabin's windows; not even a curtain between sleeping chamber and saloon. Horner had a hammock like an ordinary sailor and not much else. His officers were as poor and barren as his cabin. They were dressed in makeshift clothes, rumpled, dirty, and tired.

"We have orders. We are to proceed with what supplies we have on hand to carry dispatches to Gibraltar. We leave immediately. If we are successful in running the blockade, we will take on whatever supplies we can get at Gibraltar, and place ourselves at the disposal of Commodore Whittingdon. Admiral Walters is ordered to relieve the siege of Gibraltar. Due to his incapacity, Rear Admiral Marcus Wolfe is in command."

He paused as he looked around the group. "Admiral Wolfe has decided to abandon Minorca. The British fleet will leave at noon today."

The officers stood in silence as they absorbed the news. The battered fleet would have no base of operations unless they made Gibraltar. The Spanish fleet at Algeciras was much larger and ought to be done with its repairs. It was a gloomy prospect.

"Food is half rations immediately. We should have just enough to make Gibraltar that way. You may permit the men to fish as much as is consistent with their other duties. We should have enough water and wine, but I caution you to impress upon the men that we must not waste a drop. There is no grog. Wine will be served instead, watered four to one. We set sail immediately. The old sails we used as tents may be cut up into hammocks. That will keep the men occupied and make them more comfortable."

It was a glum bunch that made their way out of the wardroom and started working. The anchor was raised to a cheer from the crew; they were happy to be going to sea and getting away from the black shroud of Mahon. They hadn't heard about half rations yet. As the *Ajax* came out and saw the French fleet waiting they fell silent. Even the densest among them knew it boded ill for Mahon.

The wind was fair and pleasant out of the northeast, blowing strong and cool. It broke the August heat and suited their course well. Horner ordered out all sails—he had one good suit and a few old sails that had been scavenged from other vessels. The sailmaker and his mates were at work altering and mending the old things to fit the *Ajax*. Canvas swamped the deck where they worked.

The *Arrow* saw them coming out the Road of Mahon and swooped over to join them.

Thorton reported, "*Arrow* to *Ajax*, 'Query?'"

"Acknowledge. Send, 'Invite commodore to visit.'" Horner stared silently across at the *Arrow*. The Salletine had gorged herself on supplies—she had cash money and had bought up whatever she needed to fill her hold. Food was cheap on Minorca and she had stuffed herself with the knowledge that she could sell the excess in Zokhara. By the rules of hospitality he ought to be offering the commodore dinner, but that was something he could not bring himself to do. It would hurt morale if the officers dined while the hands were on half rations.

The *Dart* came skimming over the waves with Tangle in the sternsheets. He came over the side with the ceremony due his rank and met Horner on the quarterdeck. He had brought Shakil with him, but Thorton had no chance to speak to him. Horner, Tangle, and Shakil spoke Spanish for a while, then the Muslims went back to their ship. Shortly thereafter the two vessels hove along side and grappled. Seven cargo nets full of barrels and crates were swayed up out of the *Arrow* and into the *Ajax*. The *Arrow* had accepted a British letter of credit for seven tons of foodstuffs. Managed carefully, they could eke out the trip to Gibraltar at normal rations now. The pursers and their mates met and signed the necessary papers.

The two vessels ran south together. The *Ajax* let the *Arrow* take the lead out of deference for Tangle's rank. "Toss the log, please," Horner said.

"Five knots," came the answer. The *Ajax* could have made excellent speed if she were by herself; the wind was on her best point of sail.

"Mr. Thorton. Make a signal, 'Submit, more speed.'"

The *Arrow* replied, "Am making best speed with load and wind." The *Arrow* was deep in the water—her lading marks had vanished.

Horner sighed and resigned himself to a slow passage. "Acknowledge. No further signals."

Still, there was activity on the *Arrow*. Thorton reported, "She's lacing on her bonnets, sir."

Once the *Arrow* had her bonnets on she gained speed.

"Toss the log."

"Six and a quarter knots, sir," Thorton reported.

Horner grunted, "Better." The *Ajax* could have made eight knots in those conditions.

A little later the lookout hailed the deck, "British ship coming out of Mahon!"

The men all went to the gunwale to watch, then climbed in the rigging to get a better view. At first they cheered the sight of the British flagship, *Terror*, but she turned south, following in their wake. She did not go to meet the French. Another battleship came out, then another. A battle ship came towing a hulk, then another battleship came towing another hulk. A tartan and a schooner came along in their wake; they were the victualers. The crew grew silent. There was only one reason why the British would tow their hulks out of Port Mahon: they were abandoning it.

The French fired their salutes, but as soon as the last British ship cleared the entrance, they glided gracefully in to take possession. Half an hour later and the French flag rose over the ruins of Fort Mola. Port Mahon was lost without a shot being fired.

Thorton took off his kerchief and held it over his heart. The other officers did the same. It was like attending a funeral. They were glad they were far enough away they did not need to render honors to the French flag now flying over Minorca.

CHAPTER 40 : THE RESOLUTE

Early that evening the wind backed to the northwest. Perry had the watch. Thorton and everyone else not needed on deck were below trying to catch up on sleep after their long night. Change woke Midshipman Thorton. He lay blinking in his bunk and wondered what was different. Gradually he realized different parts of his anatomy were being jostled against different parts of the bunk. The ship was coming about. Why? He listened, but there were no piped calls. He rolled himself out of the bunk, landed on wobbly legs, fell to his knees, yawned, knuckled his eyes, and got up.

The stewards were setting the table for supper. They had Thorton's food ready so that he could eat before going up on deck. "What news?" he asked Ra'uf in Arabic.

"We've wearing back north," he replied. "Lt. Perry thinks he heard guns and Isam Rais signaled us to go back."

Thorton was fully awake now. He ate his couscous and beans quickly—loyal Ra'uf knew Thorton didn't care for the weevil infested hardtack the ship provided. He drank hot coffee (Ra'uf knew he would need a jolt of the bitter herb, too). The other bleary officers tumbled out of their cots to stumble to the table.

"What news?" they asked.

Thorton told them. They woke instantly at the word 'gunfire.' Down in the wardroom they couldn't hear it, but they knew Horner wouldn't go chasing after a chimera. Something was out there. Something bad.

Thorton presented himself on the quarterdeck with a salute. Horner was already on deck. He'd brought a cup of tea with him and was sipping it as he stood at the windward rail. The captain had slept even less than his officers. He kept an ear cocked to the north.

Thorton strained his ears and could hear the faint rumble of gunnery carried by the wind.

"A sail!" the masthead lookout sang out.

Every man grew tense and alert. Horner handed his cup and saucer to the air. The quartermaster leaped to take it. He held it awkwardly and wondered if he should pass the word for the steward. Horner pulled his spyglass out of his pocket and studied the horizon. He turned and started to hand it to Thorton.

"Mr. Thorton, you have the best—" He started to say out of habit, paused as he saw Thorton's milk-glass eye and said, "I beg your pardon. Mr. Pettigrew, to the masthead with a glass, if you please," he corrected himself.

Pettigrew accepted the use of Horner's glass and hurried up. A little heavier than he should have been, he had to pause a moment in the top to catch his breath. He trained Horner's spyglass on the horizon.

When he was gone, Thorton said, "I can see well enough with one eye, sir."

"Very good, Mr. Thorton," Horner replied.

Thorton was annoyed he was not the one sent running to the masthead anymore. He had to wait like everyone else to find out what could be seen.

"Ship, hull down, course northeast," Pettigrew called down.

Her course said she had come out of Majorca, but there were no ships in Portocristo when they had passed by a week before, only frigates and smaller craft.

"Is she firing?"

"No, sir. No gunsmoke. Wait, another sail!" A pause. "Course northwest, converging with the first!"

Horner took his tea back. He said conversationally, "Clear for action." He finished his tea placidly as all around him men leaped to make ready for battle.

The few sea chests on board were stowed well down in the hold, hammocks were put into the netting—Horner had overlooked men stringing hammocks during the day to get some sleep after working all night. Kits and furniture were cleared away to let the gundeck be worked without interference. With so little aboard the *Ajax* she cleared right quick. The men stood waiting. Nothing could be seen from the gunwales. They climbed into the rigging to get a better look.

"Another sail! That's three now! One running south, two on either side coursing to intercept!"

It could only be Spaniards running to intercept a British ship. Somewhere over the horizon a desperate battle was being fought and this was the lead ship of the convoy. It would be two hours before they met. The sun was starting to slant down the western sky.

"Send the hands to supper, then douse the galley fires." Horner made sure his men went to battle with their bellies full.

"Make a signal, 'Ship on south course. Two ships on course to intercept." The *Arrow* was not so tall as the *Ajax* and wouldn't be able to see as much of the horizon as they did.

The *Arrow* acknowledged, then sent, "Clear for action."

Half an hour later the hands had all eaten and were taking naps. The galley fires were doused. There was nothing to do but wait. Most of the officers slept while they had the chance. Even Horner settled into a hammock chair on the quarterdeck and napped. Forsythe and Perry were off watch. Instead of going below they tucked themselves into the corner of the quarterdeck, leaned on each other, and slept. Thorton stood his watch tensely.

Gunnery grew louder and more sails came into sight over the horizon.

"Deck! Gunsmoke!"

Horner opened his eyes and unfolded his sleeping body as if he hadn't slept at all. Stepping over to Thorton, he handed his glass to him. "Mr. Thorton, go up, if you would."

Perry's head snapped up, but Forsythe continued sleeping.

Thorton mounted the rigging at a brisk but steady pace. He climbed the futtock shrouds to go around the top and settled in next to the lookout.

"I can't make out their colors yet, but my guess is a pair of Spaniards pouncing on an English ship, begging your pardon, sir," the lookout said.

He moved to the leeward side to let Thorton have the windward. It was not a post for a man afraid of heights. Thorton studiously avoided looking down.

Thorton fished the spyglass out of his pocket, put it to his good eye, and studied the scene. He could make out a bit of red and yellow at the stern of the western ship. "That's a Spaniard on the larboard all right." A puff of smoke appeared from her bow guns. Fifteen seconds later the report came to him.

"Deck! British ship under attack by two Spanish!" Thorton bellowed.

The British fugitive was bowling along at great speed. She had every scrap of canvas set and was running on her best point of sail, due south before the northwest wind. The sun was sinking into the west. The easternmost of the two Spaniards was several miles off and out range, but she fired a gun. Thorton didn't see the splash and had no idea how near she came. It would be a random shot at that range, but she was doing her best to menace the British. If they succeeded in doubling her, she was done for.

The closer Spaniard tacked and presented her larboard broadside. The pall of smoke blew from her and later the rumble of her guns came to Thorton. He fancied he could smell gunsmoke but perhaps it was only his imagination. Down below Horner had already given the order,

"Beat to quarters." The snares rattled their urgent tattoo. Ahead of them the *Arrow* could not see as much as they saw, but she heard the drums on the *Ajax* and beat to quarters herself.

Thorton came down to make his report, but was interrupted.

"Signal from *Arrow*, sir," said Chambers. "Arabic. I can't make it out."

Thorton scanned it. "Prepare to tack," he translated. Spanish was the common language of the Sallee and English allies, but it would not do to broadcast their moves to the enemy. Tangle resorted to Arabic and hoped Thorton was equal to the task.

There was no way to help the British battleship by getting caught between two fires—not when a single broadside of the Spanish battleship carried more weight of metal than the entirety of the two smaller vessels. Instead Tangle would try to cross her wake and pester her enough that the British ship could get past her. It was a dangerous business, like a pair of terriers snapping at the heels of a bear. Suddenly a splash erupted in the water beside the galiot.

Horner grabbed the glass back from Thorton and looked. "Are they shooting at her?" The sternchasers on the ship would be at awfully long range.

"She's jettisoning cargo, sir."

Heavy as she was, it was a wise move. Cargo nets worked the forward and aft hatches and provisions went over the side. The *Ajax* fended off one of the tuns of provisions that passed too close as she followed in the *Arrow's* wake. The minutes ticked past and the gap between the forces narrowed.

The Spaniard saw them coming up. She presented her starboard battery and fired at them, but it was extreme long shot. A few of her balls fountained in the sea in the general vicinity of the *Arrow*. She might get a lucky shot on them. Yawing like that delayed the Spaniard's approach to the British battleship a trifle; slow her enough and the British ship might shoot by and leave her behind.

"Why does she not attack?" Perry asked. The *Articles of War* required British captains to be as aggressive as possible in engaging the enemy. Charging the Spaniard would inflict real damage on her while putting more distance between her and the second Spaniard.

"Mr. Thorton, go up, and have a look."

So Thorton scrambled back up. They were close enough now to see the tattered sails and jury-rigged topmasts on the fore- and mainmasts. Her bowsprit was half shot away and with it her watersail, forestay, and one of her headsails. Her sides were pocked full of holes. In places the planking between the gun ports was smashed so that she grinned an ugly, gap-toothed grin. He could make out her lion figurehead in red paint. "The *Resolute,*" he identified her.

On the far horizon a column of smoke rose from a burning ship. There were more sails, some bright and sharp, others ragged and drifting. He could not make out the flags. One was sinking, two were adrift, one was on fire. A pair of battleships doubled another and he could guess at the fierce hand to hand fighting on her deck. Scanning her carefully he saw the admiral's long pennant tangled in the tops. The *Terror* was being boarded.

The *Arrow* opened fire. It was long range, but he saw the shots plunk into the sea a cable's length from the stern of the Spanish battleship. "Take her rudder, Archie!" he yelled, followed by, "Damn," as the Spaniard kept her course. The lookout gave him a look, but didn't say anything.

He ran back down to the deck to report. He was tired but adrenalin kept him going. Horner's naturally grim face grew even grimmer. "'Tis the Spanish fleet out of Palma, I'd wager. There would have been just enough time for a spy to fly to Majorca and bring the fleet out."

More Arabic signals. "*Arrow* to *Ajax,* 'Fire as she bears. Dismast her,'" Thorton translated. Vessels as small as the *Ajax* and *Arrow* had little chance of hulling her. Inconveniencing her long enough to help the British battleship escape was all they could do.

"Acknowledge."

The Spaniard yawed again and presented her starboard battery. She must consider the frigate more dangerous than the galiot because she sent her balls screaming at them. The range was long and the shots dropped into the water in a ragged line short of their position. Thorton's heart was pounding, but Horner issued another conversational order. He might as well have been playing whist.

"Chain shot, Mr. Thorton. Aim for the masts. Wait for my command."

The Spaniard yawed back again to menace the British ship. Her larboard battery spoke and she heeled to starboard in reaction. The *Arrow* took advantage of her maneuver to go about and present her stern guns. The two barked out. They were not nearly as heavy as her bowguns. It was like shooting corks at a bull.

"Stand by to tack," Horner said.

"Stand by to tack!" The order was passed and the hands made ready.

"Helm a point to larboard, please." She answered and the Spaniard was in their sights. "Fire."

"Fire!" screamed Forsythe and Perry to their crews. By tacit agreement Thorton with his ability to read Arabic signals was the executive officer. Forsythe had taken his place on the larboard gun deck.

Holes appeared in the Spanish sails very high up. The Spaniard yawed again and the *Ajax* received her broadside. Shot whistled over head and timbers crashed down. She was aiming for their rigging to disable them.

"Helm hard over!" Horner raised his voice to be heard over the noise.

The *Ajax* swung around and for a heart-stopping moment it seemed she might miss stays, but she came around and presented her other side to the Spaniard.

"Fire!"

The thunder of the guns and cloud of smoke obscured the action, but the lookout above the fray shouted, "A hit! Main topmast!"

The men cheered. Meanwhile the *Arrow* had brought her bow to bear and was thumping the Spaniard's stern. Whether she hit the rudder Thorton didn't know. Clouds of gunsmoke obscured the scene and made his eyes water. He rubbed his sleeve across his face to clear his vision.

"*Arrow* to *Ajax*, 'Break off!'" Thorton translated signals.

The Spaniard was continuing to close with them. They could not withstand her broadsides if she got into effective range. On the other side the *Resolute* continued to gain headway, but her escape was by no means certain.

"Do not acknowledge, Mr. Thorton. Maintain course. Load and hold your fire until my signal. Aim for the foremast."

Now they were in a race. The allies had to escape or the Spaniard would fall on the smaller craft with vengeful fury. Belatedly Thorton remembered that Tahirah and Shakil were on board the *Arrow*. A cold hand tightened around his heart. If captured they would probably be held for ransom, but Tangle would hang. The thought of the Turk dangling with a hood over his head and his hands bound behind his back made him ill.

The *Arrow* was running on a broad reach. It was her best point of sail, but her guns could not answer the Spaniard in that position. More cargo went over her sides.

The distance closed. Thorton looked quickly to Horner, but the captain stood resolutely on his quarterdeck. The Spaniard yawed to bring her larboard to bear upon the British battleship. More smoke wreathed her as her broadside thundered out. The *Resolute's* guns worked in a ragged rhythm; she did not have the full power of her broadside left. Still, even a shot up battleship posed more danger to the Spaniard than the two smaller craft together.

"Prepare to come about. Our course will be due south. Fire on my signal. You may acknowledge now."

The orders were passed. The distance closed. Horner stood at the windward rail with his watch in hand. "Fire!"

The starboard guns belched smoke and fire. Her shot peppered the forward rigging and sails of the Spanish battleship.

The larboard guns ran out on the Spaniard. They were no longer in cadence; some ran out faster than others. Horner shouted, "Helm hard over!"

The *Ajax* swept through her turn as two decks of the Spanish battleship opened fire. Some of the shots dropped into the water where she would have been had she held her course, but most of them tore through the sails and rigging, doing unto the *Ajax* as the *Ajax* had done unto her. Timber and sail came crashing down to be caught in the debris netting.

Thorton shouted, "Clear that wreckage!"

Injured men cried and others leaped to hack at the debris and shove it over the side.

As she turned, the *Ajax's* larboard battery delivered a rolling broadside as one by one the guns came to bear. All her fire was poured into the forward portion of the Spaniard's rigging. Her forestay parted and her jib went flying. A cloud of gunsmoke blew across and wreathed the quarterdeck in the smell of brimstone and blood.

"Well done, Forsythe," Thorton whispered.

Horner snapped, "Damage report!"

"Fore topmast is cracked, sir!" came the reply.

"Fish that topmast immediately," Horner replied. "Ease the weather tack and lee sheet." He had to relieve the strain before the mast snapped entirely and carried away the topsail and several sailors. The *Ajax* slowed perceptibly with her foresail out of action.

"Ease weather tack and lee sheet, aye!" Thorton's voice carried and MacDonald acknowledged.

"Set the fore course," Horner added.

The fore course was set while timber was hauled out of the hold and raised up. The carpenter and his mates splinted the topmast with the timber and rope. The *Ajax* was not adequately equipped; hurt her too badly and she would not recover.

The galiot pulled ahead. Her sternchasers sent their small balls popping against the foremast of the Spaniard without discernible damage.

Meanwhile, on the other side, the *Resolute* was abreast the Spaniard and they traded broadsides again. The heavy thunder rolled across the sea in a relentless storm of iron hail. The sun sank onto the western horizon in a bloody embrace. The embattled ships sent long shadows across the waves. The wind backed further to the west and grew fitful.

The lookout shouted, "Spanish battleship, two points off the stern, range mile and a half!"

The second Spanish battleship was at extreme long range. To bring her broadside into play would require turning, which would cost her time, which wasn't worth it. Better to save her shot for a more certain blow at closer range.

Both broadsides of the nearer Spaniard were firing at will. Thorton's glass, which was Horner's glass, finally revealed her name to him: *San Felipe*. She was a handsome third rate battleship mounting sixty-four guns. Thirty-two of them faced him from her double row of ports. Orange fire spit at him and a cloud of smoke bloomed around the vessel. She was gaining on the frigate. The *Ajax* yawed left to fire, then right to run away. Her zigzagging path complicated the aiming of the Spanish guns. The *San Felipe's* gunners were neither good nor bad, and more balls came whistling over head. Something parted and a line went whipping past Thorton's ear with a buzz like a giant hornet. He put his hand to his ear and it came away bloody.

The creak of timbers and rush of falling canvas made them all look up and flinch. The debris caught in the netting, but one of the ribands that supported it parted. Net and sail came down in a white cascade and swamped the starboard guns. The gunners fought their way out from under the canvas.

Thirteen year old Jones shouted, "Clear the guns, you sons of b—"

"Mr. Jones! Profanity is not required," Horner corrected him. "I do hope you were going to say 'bachelors' just now."

"Uh . . . Yes, sir."

"Carry on, Mr. Jones."

"Aye aye, sir. Clear those guns, you sons of bachelors!"

"'Tis unbecoming for a lad of tender years to use such language. We must set him a good example, Mr. Thorton."

"Aye aye, sir," Thorton replied. There was nothing else he could say. Fortunately, the Spaniard pounded them again and put an end to the discussion.

Splinters flew and Thorton was spattered in someone else's blood. He had to swing his head around to bring his good eye to bear; the helmsman had been cut in two. Another man was straddling the body to seize the wheel. He wanted to order someone to move the dead man out of the helm's way, but everyone was busy. He bent down, seized the dead man's ankles, and pulled. The lower half of the body separated from the upper and entrails and blood smeared across the deck. He dragged the legs aside then went back and grabbed the upper part of the torso. He tried not to look at what he was moving.

Jones was white under the black grit of gunpowder. Thorton gave him a smile and a Roman thumbs up. He did not realize he had gore all over himself from dragging the dead man.

The quarterdeck guns banged out. They hit and Thorton was pleased to see a breach in the side the *San Felipe*. Now only thirty-one guns were slamming them. Eighteen-pounders, given the way the ball had destroyed the helmsman's midsection. The quarterdeck guns were roaring all around him—the well disciplined broadsides had disintegrated into opportunistic firing. Each gun on each ship was loading and firing as fast as possible. The din was continuous. Horner had lost his hat and his grey-blond hair was blowing in the breeze. His thin form was perfectly erect in spite of the bloodstain ruining his left stocking. It was silk, Thorton noted. All the officers who could afford it wore silk stockings in battle. It was easier for the surgeon to cut silk if he had to operate on them. The *Arrow* fired on the Spaniard—she had not abandoned her consort. Thorton was profoundly grateful. The *Arrow* could stand the pounding even less than the *Ajax*, but Tangle would not abandon his ally.

More holes appeared in the *Ajax's* sails but the topmast was fished and the topsail was going up. With the sail set she began to gain way, but she was still in range and the *San Felipe* mauled her again. Meanwhile, the galiot had drawn well ahead. She had transferred her big guns aft and the thirty-two pounders boomed out together. The foremast on the Spanish battleship cracked and leaned, but did not come down. The *Arrow* was within range and the Spaniards hacked away debris and yawed to bring her bow guns to bear.

Balls passed through the galiot's sails and her main antenna was struck. It cracked and the tack drooped, but thanks to her preventers, did not fall. She hauled her antenna nearly to an upright position and proceeded to fish the shattered pieces together, but she had lost most of her speed. With the Spaniard running down on her, the *Arrow* put out her sweeps and rowed dead to windward. It was her only chance at escape.

The *Arrow* went scampering across right under the *Ajax's* bows. Men shouted, "Fend off! Fend off!"

The lateener cleared their bows, but not without stopping a few hearts.

The *Ajax* let loose her larboard broadside at short range. Forsythe was trying for the Spaniard's fore quarter and he got it. One of her headsails went flying. Thorton hoped the foremast would fall without the support of her stays, but alas, it didn't.

Now the *Ajax* was a shield for the galiot. There was no point in dying to protect the galiot; Horner gave no order to slow. The *Ajax* was desperately trying to outrun the battleship herself. The Spaniard seemed intent on running them down. In a collision between the battleship and the little frigate, the frigate would do nothing more than scrape the paint on the battleship as she went under.

"Brace those yards sharp!" Horner said crisply.

"Brace sharp, you rotten whoresons!" Thorton shouted.

"Mr. Thorton. What did I just say about setting a good example for the boys?"

Thorton goggled at him. Several more pieces of choice invective strangled in his throat as he replied, "Aye aye, sir. Good example it is. Brace sharp, lads. Brace sharp!"

If they could sail even one point closer to the wind than the Spaniard they could escape. The galiot had her antenna mended and was running close-hauled on a diverging course.

Meanwhile the British battleship running on the *San Felipe's* other side suddenly backed wind and stalled. The *San Felipe* overshot her. The British ship crossed her stern at extremely short range and poured her entire larboard broadside into the tail of the Spaniard. The Spanish battleship yawed and a cheer went up aboard the battered British ship: they had taken her rudder. An answering shout went up on the *Ajax*.

The *San Felipe* was forced to run away to leeward while she repaired her rudder and fought to get the ship back under control. Her broadside kept firing and more splinters and sailcloth were flying about the deck of the *Ajax*. Jones screamed and went down as the binnacle shattered. Thorton stooped and checked him; he was alive. He had long knife-like pieces of wood piercing his cheek, throat and arm.

"Stretcher!" Thorton roared. He broke off the splinter that split Jones' cheek and carefully extracted the piece from his mouth. The boy had broken teeth and his tongue was torn. He was making a high keening noise. Thorton rolled him onto his side so the blood drained out of his mouth.

Jones thrashed on the deck, "Hurts!"

"If you stay on your back you'll drown in your own blood!" Thorton snapped at him.

Jones whimpered and curled into the fetal position. Thorton broke off the splinter in his throat but didn't extract it. That would take a surgeon's hand. Two men came up, picked up the boy between them, and carried him below. Thorton stood up.

Horner spared him a glance. "Are you hurt, Mr. Thorton?"

Thorton inspected himself. He had a splinter about six inches long embedded in his thigh. He hadn't noticed. He plucked it out. "No, sir," he replied with perfect honesty. In his mind, 'hurt' was screaming on the deck like Jones.

The allies ran west until the coast of Majorca forced them to tack. Little by little the distance widened between them and their pursuers. At sunset, the Spaniards broke off the chase. Night fell, and with it, the wind.

CHAPTER 41 : THE FOURTH LIEUTENANT

Dawn found the three vessels fifty miles away and alone in a vermilion sea. There was no sign of any Spanish; no, nor any British, either. They feared the *Resolute* was the only survivor of the debacle of the day before.

When Thorton dragged himself onto the quarterdeck, Horner was already on deck. He looked unperturbed even as he favored his wounded leg. The three vessels were hove to in a line abreast. The *Resolute* was sending her casualty list. "Forty-seven dead, two hundred and eleven wounded. Captain dead, first lieutenant dead, second lieutenant dead, two midshipmen dead, sailing master dead, quartermaster dead, two lieutenants wounded . . ." The list went on. She carried a little over five hundred officers and men and a contingent of a hundred marines. Her casualties exceeded forty percent. The *Resolute* had run for her life. Her carpenter and his mates were at work patching her upperworks, her sailmaker and his mates were at work on the sails. The dismal clank of pumps drifted across the water. They had worked through the night and were working still.

The *Resolute* finished with, "Need officers."

Horner stared at his three lieutenants. Forsythe cringed and hoped he would not be sent over. Perry was keyed up and alert but refused to even hope he would be picked. Slowly it seeped into Thorton's awareness that he might be the prime candidate.

Horner spoke. "Acting Lieutenant Thorton. Take MacDonald, Ferncastle, and Chambers with you to the *Resolute*. Signal whatever help is needed."

"Aye aye, sir." He bawled for Ra'uf, the boatswain, doctor, midshipman, the boat, and hands to man it. A quarter of an hour later and they were hooking onto the *Resolute's* chains and Thorton went up the side. It was a long climb up the much taller vessel. He came in through the entry port to the sound of pipes.

"Acting Lieutenant Peter Thorton of the *Ajax*, at your service, sir." He saluted.

The other man returned his salute. He was a middle-aged lieutenant with bandages around his thigh. He was unshaved and blood had dried on the sleeve of his uniform. "Third lieutenant James Powell, acting captain of His Britannic Majesty's battleship *Resolute*."

"How can I aid you, sir?"

Powell gestured helplessly. "Everything. We're overwhelmed with casualties. I've had no sleep. Midshipman Mortimer is the ranking midshipman but I can't leave the ship in his hands."

"Is he very young?"

Powell bit his lip. "No, sir." He hesitated. "He's just not . . . a suitable leader, sir. I didn't dare sleep."

Thorton's eyes narrowed. "Speak plainly, man."

"I hate to speak ill of a fellow officer, but he's a cruel and petty. If I leave him alone, I'm afraid he'll use his position to bad advantage. Please don't repeat that!"

"Of course not." Thorton digested the import of the message. "How are your marines?"

"Shot up, like the rest of us. Major Throgmorton is dead. Lieutenant Button is in command. He's wounded, but he's on his feet. He's got a guard on everything—there was an attempt to break into the rum last night."

"All right. I suggest you invite Commodore Tangle and Captain Horner to breakfast. Midshipman Mortimer can't get up to mischief with superior officers on board."

Powell hesitated. "The great cabin is shot to pieces. I really can't offer them hospitality."

"Good God, man! They know what shape you're in. They don't expect lace doilies!"

Powell wavered. "If you think so."

"Get Horner and Tangle over here. You won't have any more trouble from insubordinate underlings."

"Very well."

They went up to the quarterdeck. Mortimer was on watch. He was a tall, thin fellow with black hair and a scar across his forehead. He was at least thirty-five. He noted the white patches on Thorton's collar. Presuming himself to be senior (he was senior to almost every midshipman in the navy), he did not salute. He loitered casually by the taffrail.

Powell said, "This is Midshipman Francis Mortimer."

Mortimer sauntered up. "Hullo," he said.

Thorton's carriage was erect and his one good eye was sharp and clear. He looked Mortimer up and down. His voice was crisp. "I am Acting Lieutenant Peter Thorton. You salute me and call me 'sir.'"

Mortimer gave him a supercilious examination. He had two decades of experience in bullying midshipmen. "I have more seniority than you, midshipman."

"But considerably less command experience," Thorton snapped back. "You will make your salute or be confined to quarters until you learn your place."

"Aye aye, sir," Mortimer said in an insulting tone. He touched his hand to his hat.

"Are you the signal midshipman?" Thorton asked in the same crisp voice.

"I am the only midshipman on deck."

"Excellent. Acting Captain Powell has a message for you."

Powell said, "I want you to signal the Sallee commodore . . ." He broke off as he realized that Mortimer wasn't listening to him.

Mortimer kept staring at Thorton. "You're Thorton, the turncoat."

"I'm Acting Lieutenant Thorton, your superior officer. Make the signal."

Mortimer tucked his hands in the pockets of his breeches. "You're not in charge here."

Thorton's eyes narrowed. "I distinctly heard Acting Captain Powell give you an order, mister."

"Or what?"

Several things immediately shot through Thorton's mind, one of which was 'midshipmen are not exempt from corporal punishment.' He turned to Powell, "Permission to administer discipline, sir?"

"Go ahead. I've never had any luck with him myself," Powell replied.

"Thank you, sir."

He met Mortimer's insolent eyes as he stepped forward. He kneed the older midshipman in the balls as hard as he could. Mortimer doubled over and Thorton put his hand on the back of his head and shoved. Mortimer sprawled on the deck.

"Marines! Arrest this man. Confine him to quarters until further notice."

Taken completely by surprise, Mortimer writhed on the deck. Startled marines came running to collect him. "You traitorous son of a bitch! I'll get you!" he shouted as he was dragged away.

"I doubt it," Thorton replied.

Powell was pale. "He's one of the few able-bodied officers left," he explained apologetically.

"You're better off without him," Thorton replied. He went to the signal box and made the signal himself.

"'Submit, captains to *Resolute*.'"

Tangle knew that Thorton would not call him over without good reason. The *Arrow* acknowledged and a moment later the signal went up, "All captains to *Resolute*."

The *Ajax* acknowledged.

Thorton told Powell, "You receive the officers. I'll make a tour of inspection. Give me someone who knows his way around."

Thorton started at the top and went down level by level. He asked questions, poked his nose in places he never would have dared if the captain were alive and Powell wasn't a ninny. He learned a great deal about the ship from the sullen attitude of her men. Captain Oberon had not been a popular man.

Eventually Thorton found his way to the cockpit. The entire orlop deck had been turned into a hospital. The wounded were everywhere. In hammocks, on the deck, curled up in corners, jammed next to men who had died and not been noticed. The stink was horrible—blood and puke and gunpowder and shit and sweat. The heat was stifling.

"Cut some scuttles in the deck! Get some air down here!" Thorton told the doctor.

"I've been busy." The man was soaked in blood to his armpits. Tubs full of amputated limbs leftover from the day before were nearby. He was stitching up a man with a torn chest.

"Never mind. I'll see to it."

The doctor ignored him and kept on stitching.

Thorton stumbled over a man in a lieutenant's uniform lying on the deck. His eyes and ribs were both bound by reasonably clean bandages. His coat was rolled up for a pillow and his shirt was open. His pigtail was half unraveled so that his hair stuck out in all directions. He appeared asleep or unconscious.

"Who is it?" Thorton asked.

"Lieuthenanth Abby. He'sh fourth on the Athamanth. We fished him outh of the thrink when the Athamanth wenth nown. Lieutenant Lanley noth hish heath blown off, sho Abby thook hish plashe and worshed hish nuns." The informant was missing both front teeth. The bloodstains in his beard said that it was a recent loss.

"*Aramanth?*" Thorton asked. He could not make sense of the man's words.

"*Adamant,*" somebody else explained. It was difficult to tell where the voice was coming from with all the men packed so close together.

"Abbewhynshethal," the gap-toothed sailor replied.

"No, 'tis Abblesynthawick," the man in the hammock above contradicted him. "He's Welsh."

"Abbiwinthamsaw," said a midshipman with his arm in a sling. "I served with him on the *Adamant*."

"Blown to hell, poor sods," the anonymous voice concurred.

"Who's there?" the blinded lieutenant asked in a slurred voice. He was not well enough to explicate the matter of his name and ship, but he knew they were talking about him.

"Acting Lieutenant Peter Thorton of the *Ajax*. I have been sent to render aid. How are you?" He knelt on one knee beside the man.

"I can't see."

"Your eyes are bandaged."

"Damme, I finally meet Peter Thorton and I can't see!" He was a freckle-faced young man of about five-and-twenty years. He had a slender build and fair hair. His nose was small and turned up at the end. He had a mischievous, elfin look, or would have, if he were not so pale.

"There's nothing to see," Thorton assured him.

"I heard all about you," the wounded lieutenant whispered. "I asked for every story I could get about you and Tangle." He had to pause for breath after such a lengthy speech.

Thorton blushed. "Oh, most of them aren't true. Not about me, anyhow."

Abby groped for his hand. Thorton caught it and gave it a gentle squeeze. "I was hoping they were all true," the wounded lieutenant whispered.

That startled Thorton quite a bit. He thought about the different rumors that must have been going around. Stories about his desertion or kidnapping, his affair with Tangle, the battles with the Spanish . . . He was uncomfortable with the younger man's admiration. He cast around for a safer topic. "Do you have family?"

"Yes, I'm the bastard son of the Earl of Falmouth. He gives me two hundred pounds a year. In exchange, I stay away and don't embarrass him." He said it flatly.

A lieutenant earned a seventy-five pounds a year. Abby was comfortably well off with his allowance. Thorton said, "You're lucky. I'm half an orphan. My father died when I was ten."

"Thorton, there's something I want to ask you," the wounded lieutenant whispered. He held tight to Thorton's hand.

"Yes?"

"Is it true about you and Tangle?" He kept his voice low.

Thorton stiffened. "That is an impertinent question." He looked around frantically to see if anyone was listening.

"I know, and I'm sorry. If-if Perry was just talking—I'm sorry." His voice trailed off. "Please . . . I won't tell anyone. But I need to know."

"Why?"

The lieutenant couldn't see. He groped Thorton's arm up to his face and his fingers spidered over his expression to try and read it. "Because I need to know if I am the only one . . ."

Thorton froze. Finally he bent over the man and whispered in his ear, "You're not the only one."

Abby's fingers traced the line of his jaw. He sighed deeply. "I'm glad."

Thorton took hold of the wandering hand. "I'm sorry."

The lieutenant's hand loosened in his. "That's all . . . I wanted . . ." He fell back into a half-swoon. His bandaged chest rose and fell in shallow susurrations.

Thorton stared at him for a long time. He remembered how hard it had been to keep the secret locked up inside himself; how hard he had tried to be the ideal officer as insurance against discovery; how the strategy had failed; how he longed for someone to unburden himself to. If he had met someone like himself, someone he could respect, would it have made a difference? Surely it must. He understood part of why he was drawn to Tangle now; Tangle was a successful captain whose abilities outweighed his proclivities in the minds of his countrymen. Somehow he had risen above it, and in Thorton's imagination, so great was his personal magnetism that he would be able to shield other men in his service. Men like Peter Thorton.

He laid the lieutenant's hand on his stomach and lightly brushed his hair back from his face. Then he went on deck to meet the captains.

CHAPTER 42 : THE ROCK OF GIBRALTAR

Horner took command of the *Resolute*. Forsythe and Perry went with him to supplement her surviving officers. Powell was exhausted and his wound infected. He was glad to surrender command to Horner. He fell into his cot and sank into a deep and dreamless sleep. Forsythe and Perry began to work. Perry stood watch while Forsythe made the quarter-bill and received all the reports. Forsythe could calculate how many men were needed for each task, how many pieces of wood, how much cloth, what tools, how much laudanum, when the funerals would be held—he excelled at administrative details. Perry's strength was in the commanding of men. He could make decisions and give orders without agonizing over them. He had the charisma that could cajole or coerce a man into doing what needed to be done, even when the man in question was exhausted. The men did not resent it because he worked just as hard. He put his back to the capstan more than once and climbed into the rigging to help replace a shattered block.

Horner supervised it all, examining reports, interviewing officers both warrant and commissioned, and giving orders. Mortimer behaved himself to Horner; Horner was a post-captain and one of the most promising men in the bottom half of the Admiralty's captains list. Horner was qualified to command a line of battleship, and if he had been a wealthy man, he would have held out for a position worthy of his seniority and rank. However, Horner was a poor widower with children to support, and the pay he received as a substitute for Captain Bishop aboard the *Ajax* was more than the half pay of a post-captain on furlough. On the other hand, Horner also carried with him the knowledge that his command would be minutely examined by his superiors. He attended meticulously to every obligation aboard the *Resolute*. He was soon as exhausted as Powell, but he kept going through sheer force of will.

The wounded who were not from the *Resolute* were transferred to the *Ajax*, including Lt. Abby and Midshipman Jackson. They crammed the *Ajax's* cockpit. The *Arrow* offered to take casualties as well, but Horner thought it best if British casualties were cared for in British hulls. The *Ajax* received seventy-five casualties: all the survivors from the *Adamant* and other rescued sailors, plus some of the moderate cases from *Resolute*. The worst cases were too unwell to move and the best cases didn't need to move.

Horner wrote up a warrant making Thorton the acting first lieutenant of the *Ajax*, which meant that in the absence of Horner, Forsythe, and Perry, he was the frigate's de facto captain. He had had experience commanding a hospital ship, which was effectively what the *Ajax* had become. Abby, in spite of his blindness, became Thorton's acting first lieutenant. Chambers became the acting second lieutenant, and midshipman Jackson of the *Adamant,* who had a broken arm, became the acting third lieutenant. One of the master's mates and the captain of the foretop became acting midshipmen. Jones was on the casualty list.

Abby was given Forsythe's cabin. He needed to totter only a few feet to the private roundhouse to relieve himself. He was too badly hurt to be able to stand his watches, so he lay in Horner's hammock chair on deck with the bandage over his eyes. He could sense when people were moving about him and had an uncanny way of reading their emotions even when they didn't speak. He had a keen ear for the ship and could judge by the feel of the wind and sun how she was. He asked for and received reports from the binnacle, the sky, the lookouts, the helm— whatever he needed. He gave commands easily and the men obeyed. When he was off duty he was glad to have Thorton as a visitor in his cabin. He knew how to ask questions that would get the taciturn officer talking, and he never tired of hearing Thorton's adventures. Thorton grew very fond of him.

Six days after they left Minorca they sighted the Rock of Gibraltar. As they beat slowly westward against the prevailing wind, the sound of gunnery came to their ears.

"Deck! A fleet!" the lookout sang out as they rounded the Rock at a goodly distance.

"What flag?" Thorton shouted back.

"Red! Not British!" the lookout replied.

Thorton pondered. "What else?" he called up.

"Just red."

"Mr. Chambers, go up with a glass. See what you can see."

Chambers ran up the shrouds with the only spyglass in the ship. He turned the glass on the strange ships. They were very strange indeed. Battleships and frigates of ancient line complete with sprit topsails and water sails, xebecs, feluccas, and caicqs, as well as more familiar vessels such as brigantines, ship-sloops, and luggers. Their ensigns were red as blood and sported three white crescents, each with a star in its arms.

"The Turks, sir!"

"What are they doing?" Thorton called back.

"Encircling Sebta. There's smoke over Fort Hacho!"

The word ran swiftly through the ship: the Turkish navy was investing Sebta. They gazed at the sight in awe and wonder. The Turkish navy had not participated in any major naval action in over two decades. Its craft were a mixture of old Levanters and new construction.

Chambers returned to his post on the quarterdeck. "Signal from the *Arrow*, sir. I can't make it out. 'Tis Arabic."

Thorton took the glass back and studied it. "'With the help of Allah comes victory.' 'Tis from the Qu'ran."

Abby continued reclining in the hammock chair. "Apt," he commented.

An answer went up on a small vessel that was gliding between the fleet and the approaching squadron of allies. Thorton studied it a while. "I can't make out the vessel's name, but they are signaling the *Arrow*, 'Thou seest men entering the religion of Allah in troops.' 'Tis the following verse."

"What a strange little bugger that boat is," Jackson said as he watched the Turkish patrol boat approaching.

"What does she look like?" Abby asked.

Jackson explained, "A sort of hermaphrodite ketch with a very tall mainmast for her size. She carries a square course and topsail. She has a water sail beneath her bowsprit and a small mizzenmast carrying a lateen sail."

"How many guns?"

"Looks like six. I see three on this side."

"She's a caicq," Thorton explained. "I saw a few in Zokhara. They're a sort of cutter."

She moved smartly over the water in spite of her strange rig. The caicq came within hailing distance of the *Arrow*, then her officer went on board. After a brief conference the *Arrow* made English signals.

Chambers spoke, "*Arrow* to all ships, 'Continue to Gibraltar. Spanish blockaded by Turks.' *Resolute* take position two cables off my stern. *Ajax* take position two cables off *Resolute's* stern."

"Acknowledge."

The Turks let them through, thanks to the Sallee commodore's flag and a flurry of Arabic signals, only some of which Thorton could read. The three sailed unmolested into Algeciras Bay. The *Ajax* and *Resolute* made the British private signal by dipping their jacks twice and booming one gun. The *Arrow* made signals that acquainted the British fleet defending Gibraltar with her identity. Immediately a signal was hoisted,

"Sallee commodore invited to flagship. All captains report to flagship immediately," Chambers informed Thorton.

The three vessels dropped anchor and their boats went over the side. Horner took Powell with him. Thorton took Abby with him because he was the senior surviving officer of the *Adamant*. It was a dismal gathering that clambered through the entry port of the *Pegasus*. Abby had to be hauled up in a bosun's chair. Last time Thorton had come aboard in good health fresh from a smashing victory against two Spanish frigates. Now the right side of his chest ached, he was blind in one eye, and he had a hole in his thigh. He was not nearly as full of vim as he had been the last time.

Commodore Whittingdon was seated behind his desk, but he rose and came out to receive their salutes. They doffed their hats, except for Tangle, who kept his turban where it was. He was wearing a practical turban made of cloth wrapped around his head like a desert nomad—he had anticipated difficulty with the British deckhead and opted for the smallest turban consonant with his dignity. As it was, he still had to crouch a little.

Whittingdon greeted Horner in a friendly voice. "Horny! Good to see you again. Given the circumstances I fear you have bad news for me."

Horner asked, "I have news, sir. But may I beg leave to present Commodore Isam al-Tangueli of the Sallee navy first?" Turning to Tangle he said, "This is Commodore Gabriel Whittingdon."

"Peace be upon you, Commodore," Tangle replied in a pleasant baritone.

"Thank you. Welcome aboard, Commodore. I am delighted to make your acquaintance at last. I have heard a great deal about you," Whittingdon replied.

Tangle smiled faintly. "Some of it may even be true."

"Come, come! You are too modest! Quite the celebrated character! I had Captain Estrada for dinner the other night—we're being quite civilized about besieging each other—and he was voluble regarding your exploits. The Spanish are positively afflicted with woe at your escape. Sherry?"

Tangle smiled crookedly. "Who?"

Whittingdon was already pouring wine into a cut crystal goblet. "Wine," he replied. He held the glass out to Tangle.

"Thank you."

Whittingdon poured one for himself but not the officers. Tangle settled onto the plushly upholstered cushions on the locker top and folded his legs up like the Turk he was. Whittingdon gave him a short look for sitting without permission, then concluded that it was a cultural difference which he must tolerate in the name of diplomacy. He turned back to the British officers. "Who is this?"

"Lieutenant Powell, third lieutenant of the *Resolute*," the man replied.

"And you?"

"Alan Abby, fourth lieutenant of the *Adamant*," the blind lieutenant replied.

Whittingdon gave them distasteful looks. The presence of lieutenants when he had called for captains boded ill. "I'll need a full report, gentlemen."

Horner briefed him regarding the loss of the British fleet. Whittingdon's demeanor grew grimmer. His chin sank into his ruffles and he listened without looking at Horner. When it was done, he fixed his eye on Powell.

"You ran?" He tried to restrain himself, but his scorn was plain to hear.

Powell blanched. "We had forty percent casualties, sir. Captain Oberon ordered it before the sharpshooters felled him."

Whittingdon gave him a long searching look. The stricken expression on the lieutenant's face confessed his shame. None of them had to say what they all thought about a captain taking flight while British ships were fighting and dying. "There will have to be a court martial, of course."

"I know, sir." Powell's voice was sickly.

Whittingdon transferred a distasteful look to Abby. "And you. You were the highest ranking officer aboard the *Adamant* and you abandoned it?"

Blind Abby could not see the look he was being given, but unlike Powell, he was confident that he had done what the navy and his captain required. Calmly he replied, "Captain Jewell gave the order to abandon ship. We were on fire and sinking. He stood his quarterdeck to the last, sir."

Whittingdon grunted. "How many survived?"

"Sixty-three were picked up by the *Resolute*. I presume the rest dead or captured, sir."

Whittingdon sipped his sherry and made a face as if the flavor displeased him. "My God. What a loss. What about the rest of the fleet?"

"The *Resolute* picked up a few men from the *Lyon* and the *Earl of Exeter*. The *Lyon* was captured and the *Earl of Exeter* sunk. We did not find any other survivors, sir," Horner replied. "Possibly some will make it into Gibraltar, but we have been alone all the way through the Sea of Alborán."

Whittingdon dropped into his desk chair. "A complete debacle—absolute disaster—Mahon lost!—just like that. I suppose the Spanish will send me their demands within the week. Walters is an idiot." He sighed portentously.

He fixed his gaze on Thorton next. His eyes came to rest on the white patches on his collar. "What's this?" he barked.

Thorton replied, "The court martial in Port Mahon found me guilty of violating Articles One and Thirty-Five. They disrated me and fined me twenty-five pounds. I apologize that I was unable to make a white collar, sir. I had to improvise." His voice was crisp. Standing next to Abby and Powell had put his own misfortune into perspective. He was neither blind nor a coward and had lost neither ship nor fleet. He had merely embarrassed himself by converting to Islam and being absent without leave.

Whittingdon grunted. He went back to Horner. "So you made a disgraced midshipman acting captain of His Majesty's frigate, did you?"

"Aye, sir." Horner's face was immobile.

"What on earth possessed you to do that?"

"He was the best qualified for the job, sir."

"Was he?"

"Aye, sir."

Whittingdon leaned back in his chair. He gestured to Tangle. "Commodore, I wonder if you can add anything to this tale of woe."

Tangle had remained silent as he listened to the entire exchange. Although his English was imperfect he understood the situation well enough. "Admiral Walters is to blame. He was too busy celebrating his victory to secure Minorca."

"A harsh assessment. Not one that I can include in an official report." Whittingdon drank more sherry, then refilled his glass. "More wine, Commodore?"

"Thank you, no."

"What is your opinion on the conduct of these officers? I'm sure you have one."

Tangle replied carefully, "Captain Horner has earned my respect. Thorton I have had a high opinion of ever since I met him. I am not acquainted with either Powell or Abby. However, I visited the *Resolute* after the action. She was shattered. Lt. Powell deserves a measure of respect for salvaging the ship instead of losing her to the Spanish."

Powell's throat muscles twitched, but he made no sound. No one else said anything.

Tangle did not view the matter from the same perspective as the British. He continued speaking, "If it was a Sallee battleship we could ill afford to lose her and would be pleased to have her back. However, I understand that Britain has over a hundred battleships, so perhaps losing a ship and all the lives in her means little to your king."

A piquant silence fell. Whittingdon avoided looking directly at Tangle. Tangle remained bland as he sipped his sherry.

Horner broke the silence by reaching into his pocket and pulling out a white envelope. "Dispatches, sir."

"Very well, let's have them."

The British officers handed them over. Everyone of them, with the exception of Tangle, had to submit a written report to the Admiralty. Whittingdon opened them and read them through one by one. The British continued standing at attention while Tangle continued lounging at his ease and sipping sherry. Eventually Whittingdon finished reading their reports. He fanned himself with the last one.

"Very well, Ebenezer. I'll warrant you as acting captain of the *Resolute* until the pleasure of the Admiralty be known. I'll warrant Forsythe for the *Resolute* on the same terms, but Perry has to go back to the *Ajax*. You can't have nothing but midshipmen commanding a frigate. It simply won't do. Now that the Turks have come up we can get supplies. You'll repair the *Resolute* and disembark your casualties. We'll pull some hands from other vessels to make up your needs."

"Thank you, sir."

He rifled through his desk drawer and pulled out a form. "Thorton, I'm issuing you a lieutenant's commission. I'll have to commit some folderol to make it legal and I can't restore your seniority, but you're a lieutenant again." The quill scratched on the commission as he filled in Thorton's name and pertinent details.

"Thank you, sir." Thorton was stunned that the man could rewrite his fate like that, but Commodore Whittingdon was now the senior officer in command of what little remained of British power in the Mediterranean.

"We can't have blind lieutenants standing watch, either. 'Tis the hospital for you, Mr. Abby."

"Sir!" Abby protested. "If I am to be furloughed, may I choose my own location? I do not require a hospital, sir."

Whittingdon paused with the quill in his hand. "Very well. But keep yourself handy for the court martial. I require your parole."

Abby drew himself up straight. "Of course, sir." He unbuckled his sword-belt and held it out. Horner laid it on the commodore's desk.

Whittingdon eyed it. Then he said, "Powell."

Powell swiftly removed his own sword and laid it on the desk next to Abby's. "You have my parole, sir."

"You'll continue aboard the *Resolute* until the court martial."

"Aye aye, sir."

Another form came out of the desk and he filled it in. "Jackson is now a midshipman on the *Ajax*. He'll need to testify at the court martial, too. Make certain he shows up." Whittingdon kept writing. "Pass the word for my clerk."

Powell was enervated and Abby was blind. Horner and Tangle were of sufficient rank not to play messenger boy. Newly commissioned Lieutenant Thorton went to the door, stuck his head out, and told the marine sentry, "Pass the word for the captain's clerk."

Whittingdon sanded the papers lightly and cleaned his quill. The silence grew heavy as no one spoke. "I have further news, and I regret to say it will not please you." He avoided looking at them.

"Sir?" Horner asked, bracing for the worst.

The clerk arrived. The commodore handed papers to him. "Copy these. Get Smythe and Williamson to sign off on that one—immediately." The clerk saluted and took the papers and went out. Whittingdon looked up at them.

"Horace Bishop has recovered. He's here, waiting for the *Ajax* to come in. I'll send him over as soon as the paperwork is done."

Thorton's heart fell. Powell had no idea what that announcement portended and was too sunk in his own misery to care. Abby, who had heard most of Thorton's story, tensed. Horner remained bland. He was glad to have a position, however precarious it might be, as the temporary captain of a battleship. If he was lucky they would decide to make him the permanent captain of the *Resolute*.

"Aye aye, sir," Horner replied. "I'll move my things immediately."

"Aye aye, sir," Thorton said dispiritedly. He was glad to be a lieutenant again, but he doubted it would protect him from Bishop's spite. The man had caned him before and he expected to be caned again.

"You're short a few lieutenants on the *Resolute*. I'll give you my fourth, Jonathan Smiley. He's a damn good officer. He's also the nephew of the Earl of Leicester—influential man, very influential. Takes an active interest in his nephew's career. Pass the word for Smiley." He was filling out yet another form. "That will be all, gentlemen. Dismissed."

The British officers shuffled to the door.

"Commodore Tangueli, I wonder if you would be good enough to sup with me today?" Whittingdon asked.

"With pleasure," the Turk replied.

"Until then."

Tangle set down his wine glass and ambled out.

CHAPTER 43 : CAPTAIN BISHOP

A hat appeared in the companionway. It was followed by a fleshy pale face above a cloud of lace, which was followed in turn by golden epaulettes on each shoulder in the Continental fashion. Then the captain set foot on the deck and surveyed the knot of officers on the weather deck of the *Pegasus* coolly.

"Ah, Thorton. I see the renegade has returned. We have unfinished business."

"Who's that?" blind Abby asked. He didn't like the tone and couldn't see the gold lace.

"Captain Horace Bishop, captain of His Britannic Majesty's frigate *Ajax*," the newcomer replied ponderously. "And who are you, sirrah?"

The blind lieutenant drew himself up straight and saluted. "Lieutenant Alan Abby, formerly fourth lieutenant of the *Adamant*, and natural son of the Earl of Falmouth," he replied haughtily.

"I'm glad to see you have recovered your health, Captain Bishop," Horner interjected politely.

"I doubt it," Bishop snapped in reply. "I'll trouble you to move your things immediately. I am resuming command of the *Ajax* this instant."

"Of course. I'll attend to it immediately. Thorton, Abby, come." They went over the side and returned to the *Ajax* in the *Ajax's* boat, which left Bishop stranded on the deck of the *Pegasus*. Before he could realize that they had deliberately left him behind, Tangle stepped forward.

"Bishop Rais," he said in Arabic. He folded his arms over his chest. "We meet again. I'm happy to say that I too have recovered my health."

Bishop's head snapped around. "What the Devil are you doing here?"

"I have accepted an invitation to sup with the commodore."

Bishop sneered at him. "Are you sure you're not supposed to be waiting table for him?"

Tangle stared coolly back at him. "We're meeting commodore to commodore to plan joint action with the English, Sallee, and Turkish navies. May I remind you that you are merely a frigate captain representing the weakest naval power in the Mediterranean?"

"I should have killed you when I had the chance!"

Tangle snorted. "You tried and failed. Unless you have been practicing your marksmanship, which I doubt, I have nothing to fear from you." He turned his back on the man. He went over the side into the *Dart* and was rowed back to the *Arrow*.

"Get me a boat!" Bishop snarled. The ill-tempered captain was no better liked aboard the flagship than the *Ajax*, so the cockswain took his time about it.

Horner had all his things loaded in a boat for the *Resolute* by the time Bishop finally arrived on board the *Ajax*. MacDonald the boatswain trilled his pipe and four marines lined up to present arms. The drum and fife ruffled, and Bishop swung over the gunwale and advanced between the line of marines to meet the knot of officers at the end. Horner saluted him.

"I relieve you, Captain," Bishop said coldly.

"Aye aye, Captain. The ship is yours," Horner replied.

"All hands on deck."

"All hands on deck!" the boatswain bawled. The officers and midshipmen passed the word. The cry was carried down the hatches and into the bowels of the vessel. Men boiled up on deck and lined up. The officers went and stood by their divisions.

Bishop pulled his orders from his breast pocket and read them in a stentorian voice. He followed it with a homily. "And if any of you has grown soft and slack in my absence, you will discover what it is like to work for a true taskmaster. You will do your duty or be punished to the fullest extent of the law."

After that Bishop disappeared into his cabin to terrorize the seamen bringing his dunnage. Perry, Abby, Thorton, Jackson, Ferncastle, Pennybrigg, Blakesley, and the master's mates gathered on the quarterdeck. They were all in the gloomiest possible spirits as they discussed the return of the *Ajax's* rightful captain.

Abby spoke to Thorton. "Do you think Tangle will take me aboard the *Arrow* as a gentleman volunteer?"

Thorton glanced around to make certain no one was listening, then dropped his voice. "He might. I'll recommend you. Just stay out of reach. He's randy!"

Abby leaned close to Thorton and whispered, "I wouldn't mind. He's handsome!"

"How would you know? You're blind!"

"I saw him at the victory ball, but I never got the chance to speak to him."

A string of oaths erupted from the great cabin below their feet. The noise came clearly through the skylight. They all quieted and listened. One word was very clear as the captain howled, "Thorton!"

A white-faced Thorton ran hastily down the steps and presented himself to the sentry at the door. The sentry knocked.

"Come in!" snarled Bishop.

Thorton took a deep breath, then with a trembling hand, opened the door, and entered.

Bishop held a piece of paper in his hand. "What's this?" he demanded as soon as he saw Thorton.

"I don't know, sir," Thorton replied with perfect honesty.

"This is more of your treacherous lies, that's what it is! Your filthy, conniving, desperate, despicable plots and defamation!"

"I protest, sir. I know nothing about that paper!"

Bishop crumpled it up and threw it at him. "Liar!"

Thorton caught it and unfolded it. He kept one eye on the fuming Bishop. The man was so red in the face he might burst. He paced violently up and down the cabin. "You've had it in for me ever since you first laid eyes on me. You've been scheming and plotting my downfall all along!"

Thorton looked at the paper. It was a section of instructions given to the captain by Whittingdon regarding personnel aboard the *Ajax*, including Thorton's promotion to lieutenant. He heaved a sigh of relief —he hadn't done anything wrong. "'Tis just the dispatch, sir."

"I'll have you caned, mister! Caned, for the lying, deceitful traitor you are!"

Thorton replied levelly, "I am a commissioned officer not subject to corporal punishment. If you have a complaint about me, sir, I demand a court martial."

"You are insubordinate, mister!"

"You are deranged, sir!"

"Insults! Insubordination! Treachery!" Bishop's hand flew and slapped Thorton hard across the face.

"I demand satisfaction on the field of honor. You had no right to strike me."

"You cannot challenge your superior officer!"

"You cannot strike a subordinate officer!"

Bishop slapped him again so hard Thorton's head snapped around.

Thorton ground his teeth together. "That is an insult that can only be wiped out in blood. Choose your second. I will wait for you on the beach." He turned his back on the enraged captain and stalked out of the cabin. He slammed the door for good measure.

The knot of off-duty officers hurried down the steps to meet him on the deck. Thorton said, "Roger and Alan, will you be my seconds? I have challenged Bishop to a duel. I will meet him on the beach immediately."

Bishop's stentorian voice came clearly to them as he stalked through the coach. "THORTON! YOU WILL STAND AND FACE ME!"

"Of course, sir. On the beach. I await your pleasure. Cockswain!" He went over the side and into the *Ajax's* boat. He had not been the acting captain long, but the men were in the habit of obeying him. Most of them preferred him over Bishop, too. They carried him and his seconds ashore willingly.

Thorton strode across the wet, hard packed sand of the lower beach. Perry helped Abby out of the boat. Abby was carrying a box he had hastily fetched. Back at the *Ajax* another boat was launched. Sunlight glinted on Bishop's epaulette. Thorton detested his French airs all out of proportion to the offense at that moment. No other British captain with whom he was acquainted had adopted the French fashion of wearing epaulettes. The hypocrisy of it made his teeth grind. He couldn't wear his turban, symbol of England's ally, but Bishop could call him traitor while wearing a French officer's insignia, the symbol of England's long term and much-hated enemy.

"I'm going to kill the son of a bitch," he announced. He watched Bishop's boat drawing nearer with every stroke of the oar.

"Your pistol, rais," Abby said quietly. He opened the box. Inside lay a matched set of pistols with mother of pearl handles. The flintlocks were trimmed with silver inlay.

"They're beautiful," Thorton breathed. He lifted one reverently.

Perry came over and took the other one. He studied it carefully, nodded, and began to load it. "A fine weapon."

"A gift from my father," Abby replied off-handedly. "He's generous with gifts. You could even say they're bribes."

"Bribes for what?" Perry asked.

Neither Abby nor Thorton answered him.

The crunch of sand announced the arrival of Bishop's boat. The captain swore, "Get it up on the beach, you lazy sons of bitches."

They jumped out and hauled the boat up on the sand—which they had planned to do anyhow. To be sworn at and ordered to do it made them set their jaws and glance at each other with angry looks, but they didn't talk back.

Bishop climbed onto the sand without getting his feet wet and walked up the beach. The sound of a pistol shot was loud in the afternoon air.

Bishop grew pale in the face and said, "Murderer." He dropped senseless on the sand.

Everyone stared—Perry most of all. "I didn't fire!"

Thorton and Abby had been standing next to him. They'd heard a shot—but not from Perry.

"What happened?" Abby asked anxiously.

"I didn't shoot him!" Perry's voice was rising frantically.

Thorton took the gun from him and found it cold and still loaded. "If not you, then who?"

Reverend Pennybrigg and Doctor Ferncastle knelt over the fallen captain. They opened his clothes and examined him thoroughly. "Where are you hurt?" they asked.

Bishop didn't answer. They rolled him over, but there was no wound that they could find on his front or back.

Ferncastle opened his black bag and pulled out smelling salts. He waved them under the prostrate captain's nose. Bishop jumped and sat up immediately. "What?"

"Where are you hurt, sir?" Ferncastle asked.

Bishop patted himself down but could not find any wound. "That foul fiend tried to kill me!" He pointed at Perry.

"I didn't!" Perry protested. "The gun has not been fired!"

The chaplain and doctor frowned at him.

"'Tis true," Thorton said. "The gun is still loaded and the barrel is cold. See for yourself." He extended the weapon hilt first.

Ferncastle got up and examined the gun. He cocked it, pointed it at the ground, and pulled the trigger. The gun barked and jumped in his hand. The ball buried itself in the sand. "This gun didn't fire, but somebody did. Was it the Spanish?"

The possibility that they might be ambushed by the Spanish at the foot of Gibraltar filled them with alarm. They looked around in sudden concern, but there was nothing to be seen.

"If nobody shot him, why is he on the ground?" Thorton asked in annoyance.

Bishop picked himself up off the ground and started dusting himself off. "I thought I was shot," he huffed.

Perry started laughing. Abby snickered, but that made his injured ribs hurt and he had to hold them. Thorton laughed in spite of himself. Ferncastle was feeling rather aggrieved and turned on Bishop. "You sheep-hearted oaf! You fainted at the sound of a shot!"

"I didn't!" Bishop protested.

" You were quite insensible," Reverend Pennybrigg told him.

" But who fired the shot?" Abby asked again.

Thorton stared past them and said, "I know."

They turned and read the signals flags flying on the wounded battleship, "*Resolute* to *Pegasus*, 'Powell is dead.'"

The disgraced Powell had returned to the *Resolute*, put a pistol to his head, and pulled the trigger.

Bishop lay prostrate in his cabin for the rest of the day. Perry, as the senior lieutenant, dutifully informed the flagship that Bishop had suffered a relapse of his heart condition. That was the official diagnosis, but everyone on board the *Ajax* knew the real reason. Bishop would not emerge from his cabin. Ferncastle went in, found him drunk, and sent a request for a medical consultation. A little while later and the commodore's own doctor studied Bishop, discussed his case at length with Ferncastle, questioned the witnesses to his collapse, and came to the conclusion that the heart condition had so weakened Bishop's nerves he was likely to collapse at any loud sound. That barred him from combat.

Whittingdon furloughed him. He would go back to England. At home the Admiralty would be in no mood to humor a captain who fainted at the sound of a shot when they had lost their Mediterranean fleet. Bishop's career was finished.

The following morning Thorton received a dispatch. It was a warrant making him the acting captain of the *Ajax* "until the pleasure of the Admiralty be known." The wardroom cheered him, then he walked upstairs and entered the great cabin. Bishop and his property were gone —the rug, the bed curtains, the desk, the dishes, the chandelier—all gone. Thorton was captain of four painted walls and a varnished floor.

He dropped down on his knees and prostrated himself. He prayed a prayer of thanksgiving to the almighty Allah. He didn't know how long his warrant would last. Not more than a few weeks—just long enough for the dispatches to arrive in England, a new captain to be picked, and orders to be sent back along with the new captain. It didn't matter. He had been given the honor because of his abilities, in spite of everything.

"*Allahu Akbar,*" he ended his prayer. "God is great."

THE END

www.ingramcontent.com/pod-product-compliance
Lightning Source LLC
Chambersburg PA
CBHW062135170626
46813CB00002B/708